Longarm hauled out his .44 and slid over to the doorway, standing well to one side as he asked softly, "Who's there?"

"It's me, Mabel Hanks! I've been so worried! I heard there was a shooting, and—"

"Nobody hurt, ma'am . . . but having folks shooting at me goes with the job."

"May I come in for a moment?"

"Ma'am, I ain't decent. I just took off my britches."

She laughed softly and asked coyly, "Not even a shimmy shirt? I can't sleep and, well . . ."

Longarm considered, then . . . what the hell . . . and unlocked the door.

Mabel Hanks slipped in and shut the door behind her . . . as she murmured, "You must think me shameless."

He did, but he said, "I'll snuff the candle so's we can talk without fluster. You must have something pretty important on your mind . . ."

Longarm's gorge was rising. Morton was almost unconscious now, hanging limply by his bound wrists. In spite of his resolution not to interfere, Longarm had had a bellyful of the spectacle.

He elbowed through the packed crowd until he stood in the front rank of spectators. Spud was raising the whip for another cut at Morton's bloodstained back when, without seeming to aim, Longarm fired. The heavy rifle slug ripped into the ground between Spud's feet. Spud leaped back, letting the whip drop from his hand.

"That's enough," Longarm announced. His voice was flat; he did not need to raise it to be heard in the stillness that hung like a shroud over the plaza. "The show's over."

TABOR EVANS

LONGARM

DOUBLE #1

DEPUTY U.S. MARSHAL

JOVE BOOKS, NEW YORK

THE BERKLEY PUBLISHING GROUP
Published by the Penguin Group
Penguin Group (USA) Inc.
375 Hudson Street, New York, New York 10014, USA
Penguin Group (Canada), 90 Eglinton Avenue East, Suite 700, Toronto, Ontario M4P 2Y3, Canada
(a division of Pearson Penguin Canada Inc.)
Penguin Books Ltd., 80 Strand, London WC2R 0RL, England
Penguin Group Ireland, 25 St. Stephen's Green, Dublin 2, Ireland (a division of Penguin Books Ltd.)
Penguin Group (Australia), 250 Camberwell Road, Camberwell, Victoria 3124, Australia
(a division of Pearson Australia Group Pty. Ltd.)
Penguin Books India Pvt. Ltd., 11 Community Centre, Panchsheel Park, New Delhi—110 017, India
Penguin Group (NZ), 67 Apollo Drive, Rosedale, North Shore 0632, New Zealand
(a division of Pearson New Zealand Ltd.)
Penguin Books (South Africa) (Pty.) Ltd., 24 Sturdee Avenue, Rosebank, Johannesburg 2196,
South Africa

Penguin Books Ltd., Registered Offices: 80 Strand, London WC2R 0RL, England

This is a work of fiction. Names, characters, places, and incidents either are the product of the author's imagination or are used fictitiously, and any resemblance to actual persons, living or dead, business establishments, events, or locales is entirely coincidental.

LONGARM DOUBLE #1: DEPUTY U.S. MARSHAL

A Jove Book / published by arrangement with the author

PRINTING HISTORY
Jove edition / August 2008

ISBN: 978-0-515-14508-3

JOVE®
Jove Books are published by The Berkley Publishing Group,
a division of Penguin Group (USA) Inc.,
375 Hudson Street, New York, New York 10014.
JOVE is a registered trademark of Penguin Group (USA) Inc.
The "J" design is a trademark belonging to Penguin Group (USA) Inc.

PRINTED IN THE UNITED STATES OF AMERICA

10 9 8 7 6 5 4 3 2 1

NOVEL 1

———◆———

Longarm

Chapter 1

One gray Monday morning it was trying to rain in Denver. A herd of warm, wet Texas clouds had followed the Goodnight Trail north, tripped on the Arkansas Divide, and settled down to sweat itself away in the thin atmosphere of the mile-high capital of Colorado.

In the Union Yards a Burlington locomotive sobbed a long, lonesome whistle as Longarm awoke in his furnished room a quarter of a mile away.

For perhaps a full minute, Longarm stared up from the sagging brass bedstead at the smoke-begrimed plaster ceiling. Then he threw the covers off and swung his bare feet to the threadbare gray carpet and rose, or, rather, *loomed* in the semidarkness of the little corner room. Longarm knew he was tall. He knew he moved well. He didn't understand the effect his catlike motions had on others. His friends joshed about a man his size "spooking livestock and making most men thoughtful, with them sudden moves of his." But Longarm only thought it natural to get from where he'd been to where he was going by the most direct route. He was not a man who did things by halves. A man was either sleeping or a man was up, and right now he was up.

Longarm slid over to the dressing table and stared soberly at his reflection in the tarnished mirror. The naked figure staring back was that of a lean, muscular giant with the body of a young athlete and a lived-in face. Longarm was still on the comfortable side of forty, but the raw sun and cutting winds he'd ridden through since coming west as a boy from West-by-God-Virginia had cured his rawboned features as saddle-leather brown as an Indian's. Only the gunmetal blue of his wide-set eyes, and the tobacco-leaf color of his close-cropped hair and longhorn moustache gave evidence of Anglo-Saxon birth. The stubble on his lantern jaw was too heavy for an Indian, too. Longarm ran a thumbnail along the angle of his jaw and decided he had time to stop for a professional shave on his way to the office. He was an early riser and the Federal Courthouse wouldn't open until eight.

He rummaged through the clutter atop the dresser and swore when he remembered he was out of soap. Longarm was a reasonably clean guy who took a bath once a week whether he needed it or not, but the sociable weekend activities along Larimer Street's Saloon Row had left him feeling filthy and his mouth tasted like the bottom of a birdcage. He picked up a half-filled bottle of Maryland rye and pulled the cork with his big ivory-colored teeth. Then he took a healthy slug, swished it around and between his fuzzy teeth and cotton tongue, and let it go down. That took care of dental hygiene this morning.

He poured tepid water from a pitcher into a cracked china basin on a nearby stand. Then he spiked the water with some more rye. He dipped a stringy washrag in the mixture and rubbed himself down from hairline to shins, hoping the alcohol would cut the grease enough to matter. The cold whore-bath stung the last cobwebs from his sleep-drugged mind and he felt ready to face another week working for Uncle Sam.

That is, he was ready, but willing was another matter. The new regulations of President Hayes's Reform Administration were getting tedious as hell, and lately, Longarm had been thinking about turning in his badge.

He scowled at himself in the mirror as he put on a fresh flannel shirt of gunmetal gray and fumbled with the foolish-looking shoestring tie they had said he had to wear these days. Back when U.S. Grant had been in the catbird seat, the Justice Department had been so surprised to find a reasonably honest lawman that they'd been content to let him dress any old way he pleased. Now the department was filled with prissy pink dudes who looked like they sat down to piss, and they said a deputy U.S. marshal had to look "dignified."

Longarm decided that the tie was as pretty as it was likely to get and sat his naked rump on the rumpled bed to wrestle on his britches. He pulled on a pair of tight, knit cotton longjohns before working his long legs into the brown tweed pants he'd bought one size too small. Like most experienced horsemen, Longarm wore neither belt nor suspenders to hold his pants up. He knew the dangers of a sweat-soaked fold of cloth or leather between a rider and his mount moving far or sudden. By the time he'd cursed the fly shut, the pants fit tight as a second skin around his upper thighs and lean hips.

He bent double and hauled on a pair of woolen socks before grunting and swearing his feet into his low-heeled cavalry stovepipes. Like the pants, the boots had been bought a size too small. Longarm had soaked them overnight and put them on wet to dry as they'd broken in, molding themselves to his feet. Like much of Longarm's working gear, the low-heeled boots were a compromise. A lawman spent as much time afoot as he did in the saddle and he could run with surprising speed for a man his size in those too-tight boots.

In boots, pants, and shirt he rose once again to lift the gunbelt from the bedpost above his pillow. He slipped the supple cordovan leather belt around his waist, adjusting it to ride just above his hip bones. Like most men who might be called upon to draw either afoot or mounted with his legs apart, Longarm favored a cross-draw rig, worn high.

It hardly seemed likely that his gun had taken it upon itself to run low on ammunition overnight, but Longarm had attended too many funerals of careless men to take such things for granted. He reached across his buckle for the polished walnut grip and drew, hardly aware of the way his smooth, swift draw threw down, instinctively, on the blurred image in the mirror across the room.

He wasn't aiming to shoot himself in the mirror. He wanted to inspect one of the tools of his trade. Longarm's revolver was a double-action Colt Model T .44-40. The barrel was cut to five inches and the front sight had been filed off as useless scrap iron that could hang up in the open-toed holster of waxed and heat-hardened leather.

Swinging the gun over the rumpled bed, Longarm emptied the cylinder on the sheets, dry-fired a few times to test the action, and reloaded, holding each cartridge up to the gray window-light before thumbing it home. Naturally, he only carried five rounds in the six chambers, allowing the firing pin to ride safely on an empty chamber. More than one old boy had been known to shoot his fool self in the foot jumping down off a bronc with a double-action gun packing one round too many.

Satisfied, Longarm put his sixgun to rest on his left hip and finished getting dressed. He put on a vest that matched his pants.

Those few who knew of his personal habits thought Longarm methodical to the point of fussiness. He considered it common sense to tally up each morning just what he was facing the day with. Before bedding down he'd spread the contents of his pockets across the top of the dresser. He made a mental note of each item as he started stuffing his pockets with a calculated place on his person for each and every one of them.

He counted out the loose change left from the night before, noting he'd spent damned near two whole dollars on dinner and drinks the night before. The depression of the '70s had bottomed out and business was starting to boom again. He was overdue for a raise and prices were getting outrageous. A full-course meal could run a man as much as seventy-five cents these days and some of the fancier saloons were charging as much as a nickel a shot for red-eye!

He dropped the change in his pants pocket and picked up his wallet. He had two twenty-dollar silver certificates to last him till payday unless he ran into someone awfully pretty. His silver federal badge was pinned inside the wallet. Longarm rubbed it once on his woolen vest and folded the wallet. Then he slipped on his brown frock coat and tucked the wallet away in an inside pocket. He wasn't given to flashing his badge or his gun unless he was serious.

He dropped a handful of extra cartridges into the right side pocket of his coat. The matching left hand pocket took a bundle of waterproof kitchen matches and a pair of handcuffs. The key to the cuffs and his room went in his left pants pocket along with a jackknife.

The last item was the Ingersoll watch on a long, gold-washed chain. The other end of the chain was soldered to the brass butt of a double-barreled .44 derringer. The watch rode in the left breast pocket of the vest. The derringer occupied the matching pocket on the right, with the chain draped across the front of the vest between them.

Longarm tucked a clean linen handkerchief into the breast pocket of his frock coat and took his snuff-brown Stetson from its nail on the wall. He positioned it carefully on his head, dead center and tilted slightly forward, cavalry style. The hat's crown was telescoped in the Colorado rider's fashion, but the way he wore it was a legacy from his youth when he'd run away to ride in the war. Longarm "disremembered" whether he'd ridden for the blue or the gray, for the great Civil War lay less than a generation in the past and memories of it were still bitter, even this far west. It didn't pay a man to talk too much about things past, out Colorado way.

Ready to face the morning, Longarm let himself out silently, slipping a short length of wooden matchstick between the door and the jamb as he locked up. His landlady was supposed to watch his digs, but the almost invisible sliver would warn him if anyone was waiting for him inside whenever he returned.

Longarm moved through the dark rooming house on silent, booted feet, aware that others might still be sleeping. Outside, he filled his lungs with the clean, but oddly scented air of Denver, ignoring the slight drizzle that he knew would blow over by noon.

His furnished digs lay in the no-longer-fashionable quarter on the wrong side of Cherry Creek, so Longarm crunched along the damp cinder path to the Colfax Avenue Bridge. He noticed as he crossed it that Cherry Creek still ran low and peaceable within its adobe banks. He hadn't thought the unusual summer rain was worth his yellow oilcloth slicker. It figured to last just long enough to lay the dust and maybe do something about that funny smell.

Longarm prided himself on his senses and liked to *know* what he was smelling. He could sniff a Blue Norther fixing to sweep down across the prairie long before the clouds shifted. He could tell an Indian from a white man in the dark, and once he'd smelled lightning in the high country just before it hit the ridge he'd just vacated. But he'd never figured out why, in winter, spring, summer, or fall, the town of Denver always smelled like someone was burning autumn leaves over on the next street. He'd seldom *seen* anyone burning leaves in Denver. Aside from a few planted cottonwoods in the more fashionable neighborhoods there were hardly enough trees in the whole damned town to matter. Yet there it was, even now, in the soft summer rain. That mysterious smell was sort of spooky when a man studied on it.

On the eastern side of Cherry Creek the cinder pathways gave way to the new red sandstone sidewalks they were putting down along all the main streets these days. Colfax Avenue had gas illumination, too. The town was getting downright civilized, considering it had been just another placer camp in the rush, less than twenty years before.

Longarm came to an open barbershop on a corner and went in for a shave and maybe some stink-pretty. His superiors had taken to commenting on a deputy who reported to work smelling like Maryland rye, and the bay rum that George Masters, the barber, splashed over a paying customer didn't cost extra.

He saw that the barber already had a customer in the chair and sat down to wait his turn. A stack of magazines was piled next to him and, deciding against Frank Lesley's *Illustrated Weekly,* he picked up a copy of Ned Buntline's *Wild West* magazine. Longarm didn't know what the people who put it out had in mind, but he considered it a humorous publication.

He saw that there was another yarn in this month's issue about poor old Jim Hickock. Old Jim had died in Deadwood damned near five years ago, but they still had him tearassing around after folks with a sixgun in each hand. For some reason they kept calling Old Jim "Wild Bill."

There was a comical article about crazy Jane Canary, too. The writers called her "Calamity Jane" and had her down as Jim Hickock's lady love. Longarm chuckled aloud and wet his thumb to turn the page. The last time he'd seen Hickock alive he'd been a happily married man, and the last gal on earth Jim or any other sane man would mess with was Jane Canary. If anyone really called her "Calamity," it was probably because they knew she'd been tossed out of Madame Moustache's parlor house in Dodge for dosing at least a dozen paying customers with the clap!

Longarm saw that the barber was about finished with the first customer and he put the magazine aside. As the other man rose from the chair, George whipped the barber's cloth aside and Longarm saw that the customer's right hand was on the butt of the Colt Walker riding his right hip!

Longarm crabbed to one side. His own gun appeared in front

of him as if by magic, trained on the stranger's bellybutton. Longarm said, "Freeze!" in a soft, no-nonsense tone.

George was already well to one side with a swiftness gained from cutting hair this close to the Larimer Street deadline. The man half out of the barber's chair snatched his hand from the butt of his holstered revolver as if it had suddenly stung him and his face was chalky as he gasped, "Mister, I don't even *know* you!"

"I ain't sure as I've seen you before, either, old son. You got a *reason* for coming up out of that chair grabbing iron, or were you just born foolish?"

"I don't know what you're talking about! I was just shifting Captain Walker, here, to ride more comfortable-like!"

"Well, that old hog leg's a heavy gun and what you say's almost reasonable, but hardly common sense. If you aim to wander through life with that oversized sixgun dragging alongside, you'd best learn not to make sudden moves toward it around grown men!"

The other, perhaps ten years younger than the deputy, licked his lips and said, "Mister, I have purely learnt it! I swear I never saw a gunslick draw so fast before! I don't know who you are, but you must surely have one dangerous job!"

"The name is Custis Long—Deputy U.S. Marshal Custis Long—which I'll allow can leave a man thoughtful. Where've I seen *you* before, friend?"

The youth moved clear of the barber chair, keeping his hands well out to both sides as he smiled and answered, "I doubt as you've seen me at all, Marshal. My handle is Jack Robinson and I just came up from Texas. I'm riding for the Diamond K, just outside of town, these days. And that sixgun trained on my middle is making me a mite skittish, dang it!"

Longarm nodded thoughtfully. Then he lowered the muzzle to his side as he asked the barber the price of the cheroots in the open cigar box on the marble counter. George said they were a nickel each, so Longarm said, "Have a smoke on me, then, Tex. I'll allow we was both still half asleep, so let's part friendly and forget it, hear?"

The cowhand clumped over to the counter and helped himself to a cheroot, saying, "That's right neighborly of you, Marshal. Am I free to mosey on?"

"Sure. You don't aim to give me a shave, do you?"

They both laughed, and as Longarm took his place in the chair, the younger man left. Longarm stared after him thoughtfully until his booted footfalls faded up the walk outside. The barber brought a hot towel, but Longarm motioned it away and said, "Ain't got much time, George. Just run your blade through this stubble and I'll be on my way. Don't want to report in late again and I ain't had breakfast yet."

The barber nodded and started to swivel the chair around to face the mirror. Longarm shook his head and said, "Leave her facing the doorway, George."

"You still edgy about that young cowboy, Mister Long? He looked harmless enough to me."

"Yeah. He said he was from Texas, too. I'll take this shave sitting tall, if it's all the same to you."

The barber shrugged and went to work. He knew the deputy wasn't a man for small talk in the morning, so he lathered Longarm silently, wondering what he'd missed in the exchange just now. The barber was still stropping his razor when the open doorway suddenly darkened. The youth who'd apparently left for good was back, with the Colt Walker gripped in both hands and his red face twisted with hate.

Longarm fired three times as he rose, pumping lead through the barber's cloth from the short muzzle of the .44 he'd been holding in his lap, as the barber dove for cover.

When George Masters raised his head, Longarm was standing in the doorway, the cloth still hanging from his neck and the smoking .44 in his big right fist as he stared morosely down at the figure sprawled on the wet sandstone paving in the soft summer rain. Masters joined the lawman to stare down in wonder at the death-glazed eyes of the stranger who'd left his Colt Walker inside on the tiles as he fell. Masters gasped, "How did you *know,* Mister Long?"

Longarm shrugged and said, "Didn't, for certain. He's changed a mite since I arrested him down in the Indian Nation four or five summers back. He shouldn't have said he was from Texas. It came to me who he was as he was walking away. He was wearing high-plains spurs. That's how he come back so quiet. Most Texans favor spurs that *jingle* when they walk. His hat was wrong for Texas, too."

"My God, then you was ready for him all the time!"

"Nope. Just careful. Like I said, it was a good five years back and I could have been wrong. A man in my line arrests a lot of folks in five years."

Their discussion was broken off by the arrival of a uniformed roundsman of the Denver Police Department. He elbowed through the crowd of passersby now gathering around the body on the walk and sighed, "I hope somebody here has an explanation for all this."

Longarm identified himself and explained what had happened, adding, "This here's what's left of one Robert Jackson. He'd changed his name bass-ackward to Jack Robinson but he hadn't learned much since I beat him to the draw a few years back. He'd gunned a Seminole down in the Indian Nation and was supposed to be doing twenty years at hard labor in Leavenworth. I don't know what he was doing in Denver, but, as you see, he don't figure to cause nobody much bother."

"You're going to have to come down to the station house and help us make out a report, Deputy Long. I hope you don't take it personal. I'm just doing my job."

"I know. I got a job to do myself, so let's get cracking. The boss is going to cloud up and rain all over me if I come in late again this morning."

The sky had cleared by the time Longarm left the police station and resumed his walk up Colfax Avenue. Up on Capitol Hill the gilded dome of the Colorado State House glinted in the rain-washed sunlight, but the civic center, like the rest of Denver's business district, nestled in the hollow between Capitol Hill to the east and the Front Range of the Rockies, fifteen miles to the west.

Longarm came to the U.S. Mint at Cherokee and Colfax and swung around the corner to walk to the federal courthouse. He saw he was late as he elbowed his way through the halls filled with officious-looking dudes waving legal briefs and smelling of macassar hair oil. He climbed a marble staircase and made his way to a big oak door whose gold leaf lettering read: *UNITED STATES MARSHAL, FIRST DISTRICT COURT OF COLORADO.*

Longarm went inside, where he found a new face seated at a rolltop desk, pounding at the keys of a newfangled engine they called a typewriter. Longarm nodded down at the pink-faced young man and said, "You play that thing pretty good. Is the chief in the back?"

"Marshal Vail is in his office, sir. Whom shall I say is calling?"

"Hell, he knows who I am. I only asked was he *in.*"

Longarm moved over to an inner doorway, ignoring the clerk as he bleated, "You can't go in *unannounced,* sir!"

Longarm opened the door without knocking and went in. He found his superior, Marshal Vail, seated behind a pile of papers on a flat-topped mahogany desk.

Vail looked up with a harassed expression and growled, "You're late. Be with you in a minute. They've got me buried under a blizzard that just blowed in from Washington!"

Longarm sat on the arm of a morocco leather chair across the desk from his superior and chewed his unlit cheroot to wait him out. It seemed that all he ever did these days was wait. A banjo clock on the oak-paneled wall ticked away at his life while Longarm counted the stars in the flag pinned flat on the wall over Vail's balding head. Longarm knew there were thirty-eight states in the Union these days, but his eyes liked to keep busy and the marshal wasn't much to look at.

In his day, Marshal Billy Vail had shot it out with Comanche, owlhoots, and, to hear him tell it, half of Mexico. Right now he was running to lard and getting that baby-pink political look Longarm associated with the Courthouse Gang. There was something to be said for working in the field, after all. Vail wasn't more than ten or fifteen years older than Longarm. It was sobering for Longarm to think that *he* might start looking like that by the turn of the century if he wasn't careful about his personal habits.

Vail found the papers he was looking for and frowned up at Longarm, saying, "You've missed the morning train to Cheyenne, god damn your eyes! What's your tall tale this time, or did you think this office opened at noon?"

"You know a feller called Bob Jackson, supposed to be doing time in Leavenworth?"

"Oh, you heard about his escape, eh? He's been reported as far west as here and I've got Collins and Bryan looking for him on the street."

"You can tell 'em to quit looking. He's bedded down peaceable in the Denver morgue. I shot him on the way to work."

"You *what*? What happened? Where did you spot him?"

"I reckon it's fair to say he spotted me. He must have taken it personal when I arrested him that time, but I can't say his brains or gun hand had improved worth mentioning. The Denver P.D.'s doing the paperwork for us. What's this about a train to Cheyenne?"

"Slow down. Before you leave town you're going to have to file a full report on the escaped prisoner you just caught up with."

"All right, I'll jaw with that jasper you have playing the typewriter out front before I leave. Who are we after in Wyoming Territory?"

Vail sighed and said, "I'm sending you to a place called Crooked Lance. Ever hear of it?"

"Cow town, a day's ride north of the Union Pacific stop at Bitter Creek. I've seen it on the map. I worked out of Bitter Creek during the Shoshone uprising a few years back, remember?"

"That's the place. Crooked Lance is an unincorporated township on federally owned range in West Wyoming Territory. They're holding a man with a federal want on him. His name's Cotton Younger. Here's his arrest record."

Longarm took the sheet of yellow foolscap and scannned it, musing aloud, "Ornery pissant, ain't he? Says here Queen Victoria has a claim on him for raping and killing a Red River breed. What are *we* after him for, the postal clerk he gunned in Nebraska or this thing about deserting the Seventh Cav during Terry's Rosebud Campaign against the Dakotas?"

"Both. More important, Cotton Younger is reputed to be related to Cole Younger, of the James-Younger Gang. Cole Younger's salted away for life after the gang made a mess of that bank holdup in Minnesota a couple of years back. Frank and Jesse James are still at large, and wanted for everything but leprosy."

Longarm hesitated before he nodded and said, "I can see why you'd like to have a talk with this Cotton Younger, Chief, but does picking up and transporting a prisoner rate a deputy with my seniority?"

"I didn't think so, either, at first. You know Deputy Kincaid, used to work out of the Missouri office?"

"Know him to say howdy. He working this case with me?"

"Not exactly. Like you said, it seemed a simple enough chore for a new hand. So I sent Kincaid up there two weeks ago."

"And?"

"That's what I want you to find out. I can't get through to Crooked Lance by wire. Western Union says the line is down in the mountains and both Kincaid and his prisoner are long overdue."

Longarm consulted his watch and said, "I can catch the

afternoon Burlington to Cheyenne, transfer to the transcontinental Union Pacific, and maybe pick up a mount before I get off at Bitter Creek. Who do I report to in Crooked Lance?"

"Wyoming Territory was sort of vague about that. Like I said, the settlement's in unincorporated territory. Apparently a local vigilance committee caught Cotton Younger riding through with a running iron in his saddlebags and ran him in as a cow thief. They were holding him in some sort of improvised jail when they asked the territorial government for a hanging permit. Wyoming wired us, and from there on you know as much as I do."

"Vigilantes picked him up, you say? He's lucky if he's still breathing regular. I don't care all that much for vigilantes. Not many left, these days."

"I gathered the folks in Crooked Lance are leery of lynch law, too. I'd say their so-called committee is just an ad hoc bunch of local cowmen. The town itself is a handful of shacks around a post office and general store. I don't know how in the hell Kincaid could have got lost up there."

Longarm got to his feet and said, "Only one way to find out. If the wire's up when I get there, I'll let you know what happened. If it ain't, I won't. Figure on me being back in about a week. I'll need some expense vouchers and a railroad pass, too."

"My secretary will take care of that before you leave. Would you like to take a couple of extra hands with you?"

"I work as well alone, Chief. No sense getting spooked till we find out what happened. Kincaid and his prisoner might well be on their way this very minute and I'd play the fool tearassing in at the head of a posse for no good reason."

"You handle it as you've a mind to, but for God's sake, be careful. I don't aim to lose *two* deputies to . . . to whatever!"

As Longarm was leaving, Marshal Vail called after him, "Damn it, son, you might have offered me an educated guess to chew on while I'm waiting here!"

Longarm turned in the doorway to say, "If I knew any more than you I'd likely be able to save myself the trip, Chief. You ain't paying me to guess. As I see it, I'm to go and fetch them two old boys."

"I'm going to be sweating bullets anyway, until you come back with some reasonable explanation. You said a week, right? What am I to do if you *don't* come back in a week?"

Longarm considered before he shrugged and said, "Don't know, but it won't be my problem, will it?"

"What do you mean, it won't be your problem? Are you saying you'll be back in a week unless you're no longer alive?"

Longarm didn't answer. That was the trouble with men who worked behind an office desk. Instead of thinking, they got into the habit of asking all sorts of foolish questions.

Chapter 2

Longarm sat alone on a green plush seat near the rear of the passenger car of the U.P. local-combine. Somewhere up ahead the Wyoming sun was going down. He smoked a cheroot and stared out the dirty window with one booted foot braced against the cast-iron frame of the empty seat facing him. The train was climbing the Rocky Mountains, but you couldn't tell. The sunset-tinted scene outside seemed gently rolling prairie, for the snow-clad spine of the Continental Divide dipped under a vast mountain meadow near South Pass. Some accident of geology had left an annex of the high plains cattle country stranded in the sky.

The Indians had found this easy way through the Shining Mountains long before they'd shown it to the mountain men, who'd mapped it for the covered wagon trains and, twenty years later, the transcontinental railroad.

Longarm wasn't crossing the continent. He was about an hour and a half from the jerkwater stop at Bitter Creek, at the rate they were moving. He hoped there'd be a tolerable hotel in Bitter Creek; he planned on a good night's sleep between clean sheets and, if possible, a bath, before he spurred a horse for Crooked Lance. He was hoping someone there might know where the fool town was; Longarm had a War Department survey map saying it was one place, while the map he'd asked the land office for had it in another. Either way, it was a good distance to ride on a fool's errand.

A voice pitched high, with a slight lisp, asked, "Are you a cowboy, mister?" and Longarm swung his eyes from the window to stare morosely at what had climbed up on the seat facing him. It had long blond curls, but was wearing a velvet Little Lord Fauntleroy suit, so it was probably a boy. Longarm remembered seeing the child get on with a not-bad-looking gal in a feathered hat at Medicine Bow, so the sissy-looking kid was liable to be hers. Longarm decided the father had to be damned ugly, if that pretty little thing down at the other end of the car had given birth to anything so tedious to look at.

The prissy little boy repeated his question and Longarm, remembering his manners, smiled crookedly and answered, "I'm sorry, sonny. But I ain't a cowboy. Ain't no Injun, either."

"You look like a cowboy. We saw some cowboys riding horses back near that last town. My name is Cedric and I'm almost seven and when I grow up I'm going to be a cowboy!"

Longarm's face softened, for he'd been seven once, so he nodded soberly and said, "You look like you have the makings of a top hand, Cedric. You ever ride a bronc?"

"Well, I used to have a pony, before my daddy had to go away with the angels of the Lord."

"Oh? Well, I'm purely sorry about that, sonny. It's been nice meeting up with you, but don't you think you'd better go back and keep your mother company?"

Cedric pulled his tiny feet up on the green plush, stood on the seat, and shouted down the length of the car, "Mommy! Mommy! Can I stay here and talk to this cowboy?"

Heads turned and a rustling of soft laughter filled the car as Longarm wondered if crawling under the seat might seem too obvious a way to vanish. Only half the seats were filled, this far out on the local run, but everyone on earth seemed to be looking his way.

Before the brat could yell again, the woman seated near the front of the car got up and moved their way, her pretty face mortified under the bouncing feathers of her black-veiled hat. Longarm now noticed that she was wearing black widow's weeds and that she moved nicely, edging around the potbellied stove in the center of the car. As she came nearer, the deputy rose from his seat, took the cheroot from his mouth, and tipped his Stetson, murmuring, "Your servant, ma'am."

"I'm terribly sorry, sir," she replied, as Longarm tried to decide if she was blushing or just glowing prettily in the red light of evening.

She took Cedric by the shoulder and shook him gently as she warned him in a low tone, "I've told you a hundred times it's not *refined* to *shout* like that, darling!"

"Aw, hell, Mom, I was just talking to the cowboy!"

A few seats away a man tried not to laugh out loud and failed, and this time the woman seemed really flustered. Longarm pointed at the seat across from his and muttered, "Why don't we all set? We'll be stopping soon and your Cedric ain't fretting me all that much."

The woman hesitated, then took a seat by her noisy darling, not looking at Longarm as she murmured, "I'm not in the habit of speaking to strangers, sir, but . . . oh, Cedric, what am I to *do* with you?"

Privately, Longarm had considered a good sound birching as good a way to start as any. Aloud, he said, "I know I'm a stranger, ma'am, but if it's any help to you, I'm a deputy United States marshal, so it ain't like you've fallen in with thieves, should anyone ask."

Cedric chortled, "Oh, boy, a *sheriff!*"

More to shut him up than with any idea that it might be of interest, Longarm corrected, "No, sonny, a marshal ain't no sheriff. You'll understand it better when you grow up." He didn't add, "*if*." The poor young widow woman had enough on her plate as it was.

The lady pursed her lips as if coming to a brave decision before she said, "Allow me to introduce myself to you, Marshal. I am Mabel Hanks, widow to the late Ruben Hanks of Saint Louis. You've met my son, Cedric, to my considerable mortification."

"Well, I'm Custis Long and pleased to meet you both and he'll likely outgrow it, ma'am. Are you getting off at Bitter Creek?"

"Yes, my late husband has a sister there. Or, rather, she and her husband live just north of there, at a place called Crooked Lance."

"Do tell? I hope somebody's meeting you, then. Crooked Lance is more than a day's ride from where we're all getting off."

Mabel Hanks looked stricken as she flustered, "Oh, dear, I had no idea! How on earth will we ever get there? You don't suppose I'll be able to hire a hansom cab in Bitter Creek, do you, Mister Long?"

"Not hardly. Don't your kinfolks know you're coming?"

"I'm not sure. My sister-in-law was very gracious to invite us to come and live with her, and frankly, we have little other choice right now. We, ummm, were not left in very gentle circumstances by my late husband's unexpected passing."

"My daddy made beer in Saint Louis," Cedric offered in a piping voice, adding for the whole car to hear, "The angels of the Lord took him when a streetcar ran over him one morning."

"Cedric, dear heart, will you please be still?" the mother gasped. She looked as if she were about to cry. Longarm quickly cut in with, "You say you're coming out invited, ma'am. Can I take it you wrote your kin what train they could expect you to arrive on?"

"Of course. The railroad was a bit hazy on just when, but I sent them a telegram by Western Union when we boarded at Omaha."

"You sent the wire to Crooked Lance, ma'am?"

"Of course. Western Union says there's an office there. Is something wrong? Forgive me for presuming, but I seem to detect an odd look in your eye, sir."

Longarm shrugged and said, "May as well come right out and say it, then. The telegraph line's been down for some time, ma'am."

"You mean they couldn't have gotten my message? They won't be waiting for us? Oh, dear! Oh, what are we to do? What's to become of us?"

Longarm could see more heads turning as the widow matched her infernal brat's damned noise with considerable attention-getting near-hysterics of her own. He quickly soothed, "Now simmer down, ma'am. It's not all that big a shucks! Your kin will be there. Crooked Lance is only out of touch, not swallowed up by wolves!"

"Yes, but they won't be waiting for us at the station in Bitter Creek, and you say there are no cabs, and . . . oh, Lord, I don't know what we're to *do*!"

"Well, now, let's just eat the apple a bite at a time, ma'am. I'll help you get your things from the station to the hotel once we arrive, which shouldn't be all that long now. Once you've et, and bedded down Cedric here, we can ask about Bitter Creek for friends of your kin or something. Shucks, there's a chance someone from Crooked Lance will be there."

"But what if—"

"Don't cross your bridges before you come to 'em, ma'am. At the very worst, you'll arrive in Bitter Creek unexpected and have to spend a day or so at the hotel till your kinfolks know you're there and send a buckboard to fetch you. As to *how* they'll know, I'll tell 'em. I'll be riding to Crooked Lance come sunup, and if you give me a message for anyone in Crooked Lance, I'll likely deliver it within a day or so."

Cedric grinned and asked, "Can't we go to see Aunt Polly with *you*, mister?"

It was a fool question, but Longarm saw that the widow seemed to think the kid's question made sense, so he shook his head and said, "Not hardly. The army mount I borrowed from Fort Laramie is alone with my saddle and trail gear in the freight section behind us. Don't seem likely the three of us would fit comfortably in a McClellan saddle, and if we could, the old army bay couldn't carry us far enough to matter." To the widow he added, "I've already thought of a hired buckboard, ma'am, and I'd be proud to give you a lift, if I had any idea where the town was and how much trouble I'd have getting there."

He saw the hope in her eyes as she insisted, "Forgive my boldness, but, as you see, I'm desperate. We'd be willing to take our possible discomforts with good grace, if only—"

"*You* might be, but I wouldn't, ma'am," Longarm cut in explaining, "You see, I'm not paying a social call in Crooked Lance. I'm on U.S. Government business and, while I'll be pleased to tell your kin where to find you, there's no way I could see fit to expose you and the boy here to possible danger."

"Danger?" she gasped, "I had no idea! Are you going to Crooked Lance to *arrest* someone?"

"Let's say I'm just having a look-see, ma'am. I don't mind talking about myself, but Uncle Sam's business is sort of private. No offense intended, but we do have these fool regulations."

"Oh, I understand, sir. Forgive my stupidity! I never meant to pry!"

The conductor saved Longarm from having to think up a gracious answer as he came through the car, calling out, "Next stop Bitter Creek, folks! We'll be pulling in about ten minutes from now. Please have yourselves ready to detrain sudden, as we ain't stopping to jerk water on the downgrade!"

"We'd better go back to our seats," the widow said, but she didn't seem to be moving. She licked her lips and, not looking at him, asked, "Is, uh, this hotel in Bitter Creek liable to be expensive, sir?"

"Don't know. Never stayed there before."

"You don't suppose they'd charge more than a dollar a night, do you?"

"Dollar a night's pretty steep for a trail town hotel. Might be less. Can't hardly be much more, ma'am."

"Oh. You're sure you'll be able to reach Crooked Lance within two days at the most?"

"No, ma'am, I said I aimed to try."

"Oh, dear."

If she'd been leading up to it, she was pretty slick. He stared at her for a long hard minute, then he shrugged and said, "If you need a loan, just till I can get word to your kinfolks . . ."

"Sir!" she gasped. "Whatever are you suggesting?"

"Ain't suggesting. Offering. Seems to me you and the boy, here, are in a pickle. I won't insult no lady with numbers, but if you'll let me put a few day's room and board on my own tab . . ."

"That's out of the question, sir! I can see you are a gentleman and I understand your offer was meant in kind innocence, but *really* . . . !"

"Let's say no more, then, ma'am. It was a fool thing to say to a lady."

For the first time she smiled at Longarm, lighting up the dusk-filled space between them a bit as she said, "On the contrary, it was . . . well, I'd hardly call it gallant, but I understand, and I think you're a very sweet person, Mister Long."

Longarm looked out the window, red-faced, and said, "I see some lights up ahead. We're pulling in to Bitter Creek. Would you be likely to cloud up and rain all over me if I helped you with your things?"

This time she laughed, a pretty skylark laugh, and said, "I'd be honored if you escorted us to the hotel, Mister Long."

Longarm got to his feet to follow as she rose and moved back to her own seat for their luggage, with little Cedric in her wake between them. Longarm noticed that she had a nice, trim waistline, too. If only she didn't have that ugly little kid with her . . .

Under his breath, he muttered to himself, "Now just you back off, old son! They didn't send us up here to spark a widow woman, ugly kid or no! How are you going to get them, their luggage, and your own mount and gear unloaded without losing more'n half of it? Damn that prissy kid. What's he gotten you into, anyway? Don't you know better than to talk to strangers on a train?"

Chapter 3

The hotel in Bitter Creek wasn't much, but it was the only one they had. After checking the widow and her son into one room and himself into another, and ignoring the leer in the old desk clerk's eye, Longarm went out, leaving her and the boy at the hotel and his army bay in the livery stable next door. It was still early evening and the streets of Bitter Creek were crowded, not because there were a lot of people in town but because the town was so small.

Nobody around the hotel had ever heard of the Widow Hanks or her in-laws at Crooked Lance. It was hard enough to find someone who'd admit there might *be* a place called Crooked Lance, "a day or so up yonder."

That wasn't much help.

Longarm strode down the plank walks until he came to the town marshal's office and went in. The deputy he found seated at a packing-case desk seemed impressed by his federal badge and willing to help. So Longarm hooked his rump over the corner of the improvised desk and asked where in thunder Crooked Lance might be, adding, "This place I'm looking for is downright spooky, Deputy! If you tell me it's been shifted again . . ."

"Hell, we got it on a map over on the wall, Deputy Long. You wouldn't be the one they call Longarm, would you?"

"You can call me that. You can call me anything but late for breakfast if you'll answer some questions."

"I figured you was Longarm. That jasper they're holding up in Crooked Lance must be somebody important, huh?"

"You know about Cotton Younger up in the Crooked Lance jail?"

"Sure. All sorts of people have been coming through here looking for him. I've been showing 'em the same map you see on yonder wall. Seems like a lot of fuss and feathers over a cow thief, if you ask me!"

"Did another deputy U.S. marshal pass this way, asking for directions to wherever?"

"Sure, couple of weeks back. You looking for *him,* too?"

"Maybe. Was his name Kincaid?"

"Yep, now that you mention it, that's who I think he said he was."

"All right. We know Kincaid got as far as here and was last seen headed up to Crooked Lance. Who were these others you say were interested in that old boy they have up there?"

The deputy considered before he replied, "Don't remember the names. There was a feller from the Provost Marshal's Office, War Department, I think he said he rode for. Then there was this lawman from Missouri, county sheriff I think. Oh, yeah, and there was one real funny-lookin' jasper in the damndest-looking outfit you ever saw. Had on a red jacket. I mean *blinding* red! Ain't that a bitch?"

"Northwest Mounted Police?"

"Don't think so. He said he was from Canada. What in hell did that poor cow thief up there *do?*"

"Enough to get a lot of folks riled at him. Funny nobody seems to have gotten to him, though! Tell me what you know about Crooked Lance."

The other lawman shrugged and said, "Ain't much to tell. Just a two-bit crossroads. Ain't hardly a proper town, like Bitter Creek."

"It's my understanding this Cotton Younger's being held by a vigilance committee. How does your boss feel about vigilantes operating in his neck of the woods?"

"Don't make no nevermind to us. Crooked Lance is a long,

hard ride from here. Besides, they ain't what you'd call *mean* vigilantes. Just some old boys who keep an eye out for road agents, cow thieves, and such. They've never given folks hereabouts no trouble."

"Do you know who runs things up there?"

"Hell, nobody runs Crooked Lance. It's just a wide spot in the road. There's a post office and the storekeeper tends the wire for Westen Union, when the line's up. There's no schoolhouse, no city hall or nothing. It's just sort of where the stockmen shop a mite and get together to spit and whittle of a quiet afternoon."

"How come it rates a telegraph office, then?"

"That's easy. The stockmen have to keep in touch about the price of beef. They ship beef here at Bitter Creek, but they have to know when to herd it down out of the high country."

"Makes sense. Got any ideas on why that wire's down?"

"Ain't got idea one. Some fellers from Western Union rode out a few days ago to fix it. Next night it went out again. Likely high winds. This whole country's halfway to heaven, you know. Hardly a month goes by without at least some snow in the high passes, hereabouts."

"Been having summer blizzards this year?"

"No, not real blizzards. But as you'll likely see when you study yonder map, there's some rough country between here and Crooked Lance. Wire could get blowed out a dozen ways in as many stretches of the trail. The valley Crooked Lance sets in is lower and warmer, half the year. But it's sort of cut off when the weather turns ornery."

"Telegraph office open here in Bitter Creek?"

"Should be. Doubt you'll get through to Crooked Lance, though. Feller I know with Western Union says they've given up for now. Said they'd wait till the company decides on a full reconstruction job. Figures they're wasting money fixing a line strung on old poles through such wild country. Said they'd likely get around to it next year or so."

"I'll get Western Union's story later. You know any names to go with the folks up in Crooked Lance?"

"Let's see, there's the Lazy K, the Rocking H, the Seven Bar Seven . . ."

"Damn it, I ain't goin' up there to talk to *cows*! Who in thunder owns them spreads up there?"

"Folks back East, mostly. The town's hardly there to mention,

but the outfits are big whopping spreads, mostly owned by cattle
syndicates from Chicago, Omaha, New York City, and such. I understand the Lazy K belongs to some fellers in Scotland. Ain't
that a bitch?"

"I know about the cattle boom. Let's try it another way. You
say they ship the beef from here. Don't somebody *drive* them
herds to Bitter Creek?"

"Well, sure. Once, twice a year they run a consolidated herd
over the passes to our railroad yards. The buyers from the Eastern
meatpackers bid on 'em as they're sorted and tallied in the yards.
Easier to cut a herd amongst corrals and loading shunts, so . . ."

"I know how to tally cows, damn it. Don't any of the Crooked
Lance riders have names?"

"Reckon so. Most folks do. Only one springs to mind is the
one they call Timberline. He's the tally boss. I disremember what
the others are called. They mostly go by Billy, Jim, Tex, and such."

"Tally boss is usually a pretty big man in the neighborhood,
since the others have to elect him. You know this Timberline's
last name?"

"Nope. But you're right about him being *big*. Old Timberline's
nigh seven feet tall in his Justins. Seems to be a good-natured
cuss, though. The others hoorah him about having snow on his
peak, ask him how the weather is up yonder around his nose, and
stuff like that, but Timberline never gets testy."

"But he's in charge when the Crooked Lance hands are in
town?"

"If anybody is, it's him. He's the ramrod of the Rocking H,
now that I think on it. I think it was Rocking H hands who caught
that cow thief of yours." He paused to think, then nodded, and
added, "Yep, it's comin' back to me now. They found him holed
up in the timber with a running iron on him. Dragged him into
town for a necktie party, only some of the folks up there said it
wasn't right to hang a stranger without a trial. From there on you
know as much as myself."

Longarm saw that they were tracking over the same ground
again, so he got to his feet and said, "I'll just have a look at your
survey and be on my way, then."

He strode over to the large, yellowed map nailed to the wall
and studied it until he found a dot lettered "Crooked Lance." It
was nowhere near the locations given by the conflicting government surveys, but Longarm opined that the folks here in Bitter

Creek had the best chance of being right. He ran a finger along the paper from Bitter Creek to Crooked Lance, noting forks in the trail and at least three mountain passes he'd have to remember. Then he stepped back for an overall view.

The sudden movement saved his life.

The window to his right exploded in a cloud of broken glass as what sounded like an angry hornet hummed through the space he'd just occupied to slam into the far wall!

As Longarm dropped to the floor, the deputy marshal rolled backward, bentwood chair and all, and from where he lay on his back, shot out the overhead light as another bullet from outside buzzed in through the broken window. Meanwhile, Longarm had crabbed sideways across the floor to another window, gun in hand.

As he risked a cautious peek over the windowsill, the other lawman crawled over to join him, whispering, "See anything?"

"Nope. Everyone outside's dove for cover. There's light in the saloon across the street, so they ain't in there. You move pretty good, Deputy."

"I've been shot at before. You reckon they're after you or me?"

"I'd say it's on me, this time. How do you feel about that narrow slit between the east end of the saloon and the blank wall over there?"

"That's where I'd be, if I was shooting at folks hereabouts. I'll scoot out the back way and circle in while you mind the store, savvy?"

Longarm considered it before he answered. He was the senior officer and it was his play. On the other hand the local lawman knew the lay of the land and it was pretty dark out there. Longarm said, "Go ahead. I'll try to make up something interesting to keep 'em looking this way."

As the deputy crawled away in the dark and Longarm heard the creak of an invisible door hinge, he moved to one side and gingerly raised the sash of the other, unbroken window. Nothing happened, so he risked another peek.

Then he swore.

The street was filled with people now, and a burly figure with a tin star pinned to his chest was clumping right toward him, gun in hand, and shouting, "Hey, Morg! You all right in there, son?"

Longarm got to his feet and stood in a shaft of light from outside, holstering his own gun as the door burst open. What was obviously the missing deputy's superior officer froze in the doorway, his gun pointed at Longarm, and asked, "You have a tale to tell me, mister?"

"Deputy Morgan and me are friends, Marshal. He's out trying to get behind somebody who just busted your window. He should be back directly."

"I heard shots and come running. What's it all about?"

"Don't know. Them who did the shooting never said. By the way, your young sidekick's pretty good. He had the light out before they'd fired twice. Sounded like they was after us with a .30-30."

"Old Morg's good enough, I reckon. How'd you get so good at reading gunshots, mister? I disremember who you said you was."

Longarm introduced himself and brought the town marshal up to date. By the time he'd finished, the marshal had put his gun away and Deputy Morgan had crossed the street to rejoin them.

Morgan nodded to his boss and said to Longarm, "Long gone, but you figured right about that alleyway. Way I read the signs, it was one feller with a rifle. Had on high-heel, maybe Mexican, boots."

The deputy held out a palm with two spent cartridges as he added, "Looks like he packs a bolt-action .30-30. Funny thing to use in a gunfight, ain't it?"

Longarm shrugged and said, "I'd say he was out for sniping, not fighting. The heel marks over there say much about the size and weight of anybody?"

"Wasn't anybody very big or very small. I'd say, aside from the fancy boots and deer rifle, most any hand for miles around could be made to fit. Dirt in the alleyway was packed hard. Feller in army boots like yours wouldn't have left any sign at all."

The older Bitter Creek lawman said, "Whoever it was has likely packed it in for now. The whole town's looking for him. Morg, you'd best start cleaning up this mess in here. I'll mosey around town and see if anybody spied the cuss. They'd remember a stranger in Mexican heels."

Longarm asked, "What if one of your local townsmen walked past in three-inch heels, maybe with a rifle in hand?"

"Don't think so. Folks don't take much notice of folks they know."

"I'd say you're right. How many men in town would you say could fit the bill?"

"Hell, at least a baker's dozen. Lots of riders wear Mexican heels and half the men in town own deer rifles. But I'll ask around, anyway. There's always a chance, ain't there?"

Longarm nodded, but he didn't think the chances were good. By now, if anyone in Bitter Creek had any suspicion of who'd shot out their own town marshal's window, they'd have come forward.

Unless, of course, they knew, but didn't aim to say.

Chapter 4

The clerk at the Western Union office gave Longarm much the same tale about the line to Crooked Lance as the deputy had. Longarm took advantage of the visit to wire a terse report to Marshal Vail in Denver. He brought his superior up to date and added that the big frog in the Crooked Lance puddle seemed to be a very tall rider called Timberline. It was the only information Vail might not have about the murky situation. They knew in Denver that Kincaid had gotten this far. At a nickel a word it was pointless to verify it.

Leaving the Western Union office, Longarm headed for the hotel the hard way. The sniper with the .30-30 *could* have been after the local law, but he doubted it. If someone was trying to keep him from getting to Crooked Lance, it meant they knew who he was. If they knew who he was, they might know he was staying at the hotel.

So Longarm followed the cinder path between the railroad tracks and the dark, deserted cattle pens until he was beyond the hotel entrance on Main Street. He found a dark side street aimed the right way and followed it, crossing Main Street beyond the last lamppost's feeble puddle of kerosene light. He explored his way to the alley he remembered as running through the hotel's block, then, gun drawn, moved along it to the hotel's rear entrance.

The alley door was unlocked. Longarm took a deep breath and opened it, stepping in swiftly and sliding his back along the wall to avoid being outlined against the feeble skyglow of the alley. He eased the door shut and moved along the pantryway to the foot of the stairs. Beyond, the shabby lobby was deserted, bathed in the flickering orange glow of a night lamp. The room clerk was likely in his quarters, since there'd be little point in tending the desk before the next train stopped a few blocks away.

Longarm climbed the stairs silently on the balls of his feet and let himself into his rented room with the hotel key he'd insisted on holding on to. He struck a match with his thumbnail and lit the candle stub on the dressing table. There was no need to fret about the window shade. He'd chosen a side room facing the blank wall of the building next door and had pulled the shade before going out. But a man in his line of work had to consider everything, so he picked up the candlestick and placed it on the floor below the window. There was no chance, now, of its dim light casting his shadow on the shade, no matter how he moved about the room.

The room was tiny, even for a frontier hotel. The bed was one of those funny contraptions that folded up into the wall. Longarm opened the swinging doors and pulled the bed down, sitting on it to consider his next move.

His keen ears picked up the sound of voices from the head of the fold-down bed. The widow and little Cedric were in the next room and the partition between the folding beds was a single sheet of plywood. Be interesting, Longarm thought, to stay in this hotel when honeymooners were bedded down next door. The widow was talking low to her son, likely telling him a bedtime story. When one of them moved he could hear their bedsprings creak.

He remembered saying something about having a bite with the woman and her child. But it was later than he'd figured on and it didn't make much sense to take a lady to dinner with a rifleman skulking around out there. It sounded like they were in bed, anyway. He had the names of her Crooked Lance kin written down on an envelope she'd given him, so there was no sense pestering her further.

Longarm looked at his pocket watch. It was getting on toward nine o'clock. He put himself in the boots of the rifleman and studied hard. If the sniper still meant business, he'd be likely to wait around until . . . midnight? Yeah, midnight was a long, lone-some stretch and it would be cold as hell out there by then, at this altitude. Sensible move for the sniper would be to hole up for a while and make another try at sunup. He'd told lots of folks he was riding out at dawn. The livery stable? It would make more sense for him to be waiting up the trail to Crooked Lance, where nobody in town would hear a gunshot. The sniper would want to be there first, so . . . yes, he knew what to do, now.

Longarm stood up and got undressed, spreading his clothes and belongings with care, to be ready to move out suddenly after a few hours of rest. He was down to nothing but his flannel shirt when someone rapped softly on his door.

Longarm hauled out his .44 and slid over to the doorway, standing well to one side as he asked softly, "Who's there?"

"It's me, Mabel Hanks! I've been so worried! I heard there was a shooting, and—"

"Nobody hurt, ma'am. I'm purely sorry we couldn't have din-ner and all, but having folks shooting at me goes with the job."

"May I come in for a moment?"

"Ma'am, I ain't decent. I just took off my britches."

She laughed softly and asked coyly, "Not even a shimmy shirt? I can't sleep and, well . . ."

Longarm considered, then he decided, what the hell, he'd *told* her, hadn't he, and unlocked the door.

Mabel Hanks slipped in and shut the door behind her, turning her eyes away from his long, naked legs as she murmured, "You must think me shameless."

He did, since she'd let her long, brown hair down and was wearing a long pink cotton nightgown and fluffy bedroom slip-pers, but he said, "I'll snuff the candle so's we can talk without fluster. You must have something pretty important on your mind."

As he crossed the room to drop gingerly to one naked knee and pinch out the candle with his fingertips, he noticed that she'd taken a seat on the foot of his bed. It was getting pretty difficult to take this situation in any way but a pretty earthy one, but in country matters, as in all others, Longarm moved cautiously. There was always that one chance in a hundred that a gal was sim-ply stupid about menfolks. She didn't *look* like a loose woman.

He stood over her in the almost total darkness, putting his gun away as he asked, "What's little Cedric up to at the moment, ma'am?"

"He's fast asleep, the poor darling. I'm afraid the long trip tired him."

"*You* ain't tired all that much, eh?"

"I'm afraid I'm not. It's difficult to fall asleep in a strange place . . . alone." Then she blurted out, "Heavens, what am I saying? I didn't mean that the way it sounded!"

Longarm moved over to the door and locked it.

She gasped, "What are you doing, sir?"

"Just making sure we don't get shot. The key's in the lock, when you're ready to leave, ma'am."

"Oh, I thought . . ."

"What can I do for you, ma'am? You're purely beating about the bush like you thought a wounded grizzly was holed up in it."

"I've been thinking about your offer of . . . well, help. This is terribly embarrassing, but I just counted out our remaining funds and, and, oh, Lord, this is all so sordid!"

Longarm fumbled for his pants and fished out a pair of ten-dollar eagles. He handed them to her in the dark, noticing how smooth her fingers were, as she suddenly took his hand in both of hers and pressed a cheek to it, sobbing, "Oh, *bless* you! I simply didn't know what we were going to do!"

"Heck, it ain't like I'm sending little Cedric through college, ma'am. You can pay me back whenever you've a mind to. I don't reckon there's anything else you need, huh?"

Her voice was blushful in the dark as she said, "There *is* one thing more, but I just can't bring myself to ask it—Custis."

"You just ask away—Mabel. It pleasures most gents to be of service to a pretty gal."

"Well, you know I'm a recent widow and . . . this is just terribly embarrassing, but my late husband used to help me out of my, um, corset."

"Oh? Didn't know you had one on. Not that I looked too close before I snuffed the candle."

She got to her feet, her scented hair near Longarm's nostrils as she murmured, "I can't get at the laces without help. It's a new model with steel stays instead of whalebone and it's cutting me in two! Would you think me shameless if I asked you to unlace me from the back?"

"I could give it a try, but I ain't had much experience with such things. I've never worn one, myself." He hesitated, wondering why his mouth felt so dry as he added, "Uh, how do I git at it?"

Mabel Hanks slipped the nightgown off over her head and dropped it on the bed, saying, "Don't worry, I'm wearing a shift under the corset so it's not as if . . . isn't this silly? We've hardly met and here you are undressing me! Whatever must you be thinking?"

Longarm didn't think it would be polite to say, so he kept his mouth shut as he ran his suddenly too-thick fingers along her spine, feeling for the knot of her corset laces. He noticed that her breathing had become rapid and shallow. He found the slip knot and untied it. She reached behind herself to guide his wrists as he unlaced her. The tight corset suddenly snapped free and fell to the floor. She took a deep breath and gasped, "Oh, that feels so *good!*" A woman really needs a man if she intends to dress fashionably, don't you think?"

Longarm ran his hands up to her bare shoulders, turned her around, and hauled her in for a blindly aimed kiss. He missed her mouth on the first try, but she swung her moist lips to his, and for a long moment they just stood there, trying to melt into one another in the dark.

Then he picked her up and put her gently across the mattress, dropping himself alongside her as, still kissing, he ran his free hand down the front of her thin silk shift to the warm moisture between her trembling thighs. She tried to mutter something between their pressed-together lips as Longarm parted her knees with his own. And then he was in her, his bare feet on the rug and her hips almost hanging over the edge of the mattress as he drove hard and deep. She gasped and moved her face to one side, sobbing, "Whatever are you *doing* to me?" as her legs belied her protest by rising to lock firmly around the big man's bouncing buttocks.

He came fast, stayed inside her, and moved them both farther onto the bed for a more comfortable second encounter, taking his time now, as their heaving flesh got better acquainted. She suddenly moaned and raked her nails along his back, almost tearing his shirt as she sobbed, "Oh, God! Oh, Jesus Christ! It's been so *long!*"

She'd dropped her expected modesty completely now and was responding like a she-cougar in heat, digging her nails in and raising her knees until her heels were crossed behind Longarm's neck. He was hitting bottom with every stroke, and eased off a bit, aware that he could be hurting her, but she pumped hard to meet his thrusts and growled, "All of it! I want it all inside me! Oh, Jesus, it's coming again!"

He didn't know which of them she meant, but it didn't seem important as, this time, they had a long, shuddering mutual orgasm and she suddenly went limp. Longarm knew he was heavy, so after lying there long enough to catch his breath, he shifted his weight to his elbows and eased off a trifle.

She sighed, "Don't move. Just let it soak inside me till we can do it some more. You're still nice and hard. My, there certainly is a *lot* of you, isn't there?"

"It's been a while for me, too, Mabel."

"I'm so happy, darling. I know you think I'm an absolute hussy, but I don't care. I don't care if you think this is what I had in mind all the time!"

"Didn't you?"

She hesitated, then answered roguishly, "You know damned well I did, dear heart. Women may not be supposed to want such things, but I was married for nearly eight years and, well, I don't care if you think I'm bawdy!"

"Hell, gal, what's sauce for the goose is sauce for the gander. There's nothing to be ashamed of. We just done what's natural."

"Can we do it again? This time I want to do it naked, with me on top!"

Longarm rolled off her, slipped out of his shirt, and lay back, spreadeagled, as she tore off her last shreds of silk, and giggling like a naughty schoolgirl, climbed above him, with a knee by each of Longarm's hip bones. She toyed with his moist erection, guiding herself onto it with her hands. He sighed with pleasure as she suddenly dropped her pelvis hard, taking it deep with a breathless hiss of her own.

And then she was moving. Moving up and down with amazing vigor as she leaned forward, swinging her nipples across Longarm's face as she almost shouted, "Suck me! Suck my titties!"

He did, but not before he softly warned, "Take it easy! You'll wake the kid! That partition between our rooms is paper-thin!"

"I don't care. He's too young to know what we're doing and he's a sound sleeper anyway. Oh, dear God, isn't this *lovely*?"

Longarm allowed that it was, but as he lay there, holding a nipple between his lips as she went wild, he heard a soft plop above the louder creaking of the bed springs. Longarm's keen ears were educated. So he knew what it was. The key he'd left in the door had just fallen on to a sheet of paper!

Longarm ran a big hand under each of Mabel's thighs and

heaved, catapulting her up over him to crash, screaming, against the plywood partition at the head of the fold-down bed. At the same time, Longarm rolled off the mattress, grabbed the bed frame, and lifted hard, folding the bed, with Mabel in it, up into the wall.

Stark naked, he moved toward the door, snatching his .44 as he passed his gunbelt hooked over a chair. He heard running footsteps from the other side of the door, so he opened it and leaped sideways into the hallway, facing the stairwell in a low crouch for a split second to see nothing there, then pivoting fast to train his gun down the other end of the hallway. He saw that the door to Mabel Hanks's room was ajar, spilling candlelight across the shabby carpeting. Longarm made the door in two bounds, hit it with a free elbow, and landed in the center of the room, back to the wall and facing the other fold-down bed.

The bed was empty. It figured. Longarm grabbed the metal footrail of the bed and slammed it up into the wall. Then he covered the small, froglike figure who'd been hiding under it with the muzzle of his sixgun and said, "All right, you little son of a bitch, on your feet and grab some sky!"

Little Cedric without his blond wig was even uglier, and his voice was deeper as he got to his little feet, saying, "Take it easy, Longarm. I'm a lawman, too!"

"Let's talk about it in my room. Your . . . mama is standing on her head against the wall. *She's* likely got something to tell me, too!"

He frog-marched the midget out to the hall as the hotel's desk clerk appeared at the far end, asking, "What in hell's going on up here?"

Then he saw a full-grown naked man holding a .44 on what looked like a little boy in a velvet suit and decided to go away.

Longarm herded the creature called Cedric inside and slammed the door. Covering his odd captive as he bent to retrieve the doorkey from where it had landed on a sheet of newspaper, he shook his head and said, "Serves me right. I should have known better. Anybody can fox a key out of the inside keyhole to land on a paper shoved under the door. What were you fixing to do once you pulled it through on the paper, Cedric? You don't look big enough to whup me with your fists. No offense, of course."

"How'd you get on to us, Longarm?"

"Let's see what you're packing in that sissy little suit before we talk. Unless that's a cow I hear bellowing inside the wall, your partner's likely anxious to rejoin us."

He frisked the midget, relieving him of a man-sized S&W Detective Special .38 and saying, "Shame on you, sonny!" before he motioned the dwarf to a seat in a far corner and, still covering him, relit the room's candle. Then he went over to where Mabel Hanks was yelling curses through the mattress and pulled down the folding bed.

The naked woman rolled out of the wall and sat up, staring wildly around through the hair hanging over her face as she gasped, "What in the hell's *happening*?"

The she spotted the midget in the corner and sighed, "Oh, shit!"

"Let's talk about it," Longarm suggested. He saw the girl moving as if to get to her discarded nightgown and said flatly, "You just stay put, honey. It ain't like we're strangers and have to be formally dressed. Either one of you can tell me who the hell you are, as long as *somebody* says something sudden."

The one called Cedric said, "We're private detectives. Our badges are in the other room. You want to see 'em?"

"I'll take your word for it. Why were you detecting *me*? I don't remember being wanted anywhere. Last time I looked, I was toting my own badge for Uncle Sam."

Cedric said, "Hell, we know that. We're out here after the reward."

"What reward would that be, friend?"

"The one on Frank and Jesse James, of course. Our agency works for the railroad and the James-Younger Gang has been playing hell with their timetables. We was on our way to Crooked Lance, same as you, to fetch that Cotton Younger back to Missouri."

"Don't you mean to make a deal with him? Maybe a deal to spring him loose in exchange for Jesse James's new address?"

The midget detective shot a weary glance at his naked female partner and sighed, "I *told* you they said he was a smart one, Mabel. Look what your hungry old snatch has gotten us into, *this* time!"

"Oh shut up, you little pissant! It's not *my* fault! I told you you were overplaying your part!" She smiled timidly at Longarm and added, "You might as well know the truth. I'll admit I did try to find out what you might know about Cotton Younger and the odd situation up in Crooked Lance. You see, one of our agents came out here a week ago and—"

"Spare me the details. I know something in Crooked Lance seems to eat lawmen fer breakfast. As to overplaying parts, I'm sort of interested in why Cedric, here, was trying to creep in on us just now."

"I done no such thing!" the midget protested, adding, "I had my ear against the plywood when all hell busted loose out there! I can see someone was using the old paper trick, but, honest Injun, you are barking up the wrong tree."

"Why were you hiding under the bed, then?"

"Hell, I was scared! I heard running in the hall, cracked open the door, and saw you bounce out stark naked with a full-grown gun in your fist! Before you could turn and blow my fool face off I dove for cover. You know the rest!"

"You're likely full of shit, but saying you ain't, did you get a look at anyone attached to them running footsteps?"

"No. Whoever it was made the stairwell before I got to the door. Ain't you aiming to put that gun away?"

"Maybe. Tell me something a man with his head against that plywood might have heard."

"What are you talking about? All I heard was you an' Mabel— you know."

"I don't know. I know what she was saying as I heard the key hit paper. If your ear was next to that plywood, you must have heard it, too."

The woman blushed, for real this time, and stammered, "Longarm, you're being nasty!"

But Longarm insisted, "Cedric?" and with a malicious grin at the naked woman on the bed, the midget said, "She said what you were doing to her was just lovely."

Longarm lowered the muzzle of his .44, nodded at the woman on the bed, and said, "You can get dressed now."

Mabel Hanks leaned over, grabbed up her nightgown, and put it on, gathering the other things in one hand. He saw she was looking at the two gold eagles lying on the rug near the foot of the bed and said, "Leave 'em be, honey. I don't know what I owe you, but twenty dollars seems a mite steep, considering."

"You—you son of a bitch!"

"Will you settle for two bucks? I understand it's the going price these days. I don't hold it against you that we never finished the last time."

She swept grandly out, too mortified to answer. The midget

dropped off the chair with a smirk and edged his way for the door, saying, "I'd be willing to split that reward, if you want to talk things over."

"You talked just enough to save your ass, old son. And by the way, you need a shave. You and Mama hit Crooked Lance with that stubble on your pretty little chin and there might be some who haven't my refined sense of humor!"

Cedric hesitated in the doorway with a sly smile on his ugly little face as he asked, "You don't aim to give our show away, Longarm?"

The big lawman laughed good-naturedly and asked, "Why should I? I've enjoyed the show immensely!"

Chapter 5

The sky was a starry black curtain fading to gray in the east as Longarm reined in on the Crooked Lance Trail and sat his mount for a time, considering the ink blots all around them. He'd slipped out of the hotel a little after three in the morning, gotten his borrowed army bay from the livery without being seen, and was now a distance from the town that he judged about right for a bushwhacking.

In the very dim light of the false dawn he could just make out a granite outcropping, covering the trail. Longarm clucked to the bay, eased him around to the far side, and tethered him to one of the aspens growing there. He slid the Winchester .44-40 from its boot under the saddle's right fender and dismounted. He soothed the bay with a pat and left it to browse on aspen leaves as he climbed the far side of the outcropping. He knew the treetops behind him would hide his outline against the sky as the light improved. He lay atop the rock, levered a round into the Winchester's chamber, and settled down to wait. If he'd timed it right, the sniper with that .30-30 deer rifle would be getting up here just about now, and if the rifleman knew the lay of the land along this trail he'd have a hard time picking a better place to set his own ambush.

A million years went by, and the sky was only a little lighter.

Longarm was used to waiting, but he'd never liked it much. The
stars were going out one by one from east to west, but the sniper
seemed to be taking his own good time. What was the matter with
the fool? He wasn't dumb enough to stake out the front of the
damned hotel, was he?

He wondered if Kincaid or any of the other missing lawmen
had run into this situation. It made more sense than a town where
they shot strangers on sight. Kincaid or any of the other missing
men could be buried anywhere for a full day's ride or so. The
folks in Crooked Lance, for all he knew, could be just as puzzled
as everyone else. With the wire down, they were cut off, so nobody there would know who was coming or when.

He took a cheroot from his vest pocket and put it between his
teeth, not lighting it, as he studied what he knew for sure.

It wasn't much, but he could assume the hands who'd captured
Cotton Younger and locked him up were acting in good faith. If
they'd been on the outlaw's side, they wouldn't have captured him.
If they hadn't wanted the law to know they had him, they'd have
just killed him and kept still about it. Could it be an escape plot?

Maybe, but not on the part of the folks in Crooked Lance, for
obvious reasons. The most likely candidates to plot an escape
would be friends of Cotton Younger, and if it was true he was tied
in with Frank and Jesse James . . . possible, but wild. None of the
James-Younger Gang had ever operated this far west, and if it
was them, they were acting differently than they'd ever acted before. He'd studied the working habits of the James-Younger
Gang. They were given to moving in fast, hitting hard, and moving out even faster. Cotton Younger was being held in a log jail,
probably loosely guarded by simple cowhands. If the James-
Younger Gang had ridden out here to spring him, he'd have been
long gone by now and there'd be no need for all this skulldug-
gery.

On the other hand, the gang had been badly shot up in Minnesota and were scattered from hell to breakfast. If a lone member of the old clan was trying to help his kinsman . . . that might
fit.

Behind him in the fluttering aspen leaves a redwing awoke to
announce its undisputed ownership of the grove. It sounded more
like a wagon wheel in need of grease than a bird, and it meant the
sun was getting ready to roll up the eastern side of the pearling
sky. Longarm could see the trail he was covering more clearly

now. In less than an hour things would have color as well as form down there. His sniper was either a late riser or stupid. Or he'd given up for now.

Longarm decided to wait it out till full light. Half the secret of staking-out lay in waiting out that last five minutes. It was tedious as hell, but he'd made some good arrests by simply staying put a little longer than common sense seemed to call for. It was a trick he'd learned as a boy from a friendly Pawnee.

Another bird woke up to curse back at the redwing and a distant peak to the west was pink-tipped against the dark blue western horizon as it caught the sunrise from its greater altitude. Innocent travelers would be taking to the trail soon. Where in thunder was his sniper?

Longarm's eyes suddenly narrowed and he stopped breathing as his ears picked up the distant scrape of steel on rock. He saw two blurs moving into view up the trail. What he'd heard was a horseshoe on a lump of gravel.

He could see who it was now. A lone rider on a big black plowhorse, with a teammate tagging along behind like an oversized hound. As the odd group came nearer, Longarm saw that the man on the lead mount was carrying a rifle across his knees. He was riding bareback, his long legs hanging down to the end in big bare feet. The top of him was clad in patched, old-fashioned buckskins, a fur hat made of skunk skin with two feathers cocked out of one side, and a long, gray beard covering the upper third of his burly chest.

He was peculiar-looking, but Longarm decided he was likely not his man as he studied the weapon the rider was packing. It was an old Sharps .50. Single-shot and wrong caliber. The lack of high heels, or even boots, was comforting, too. Longarm flattened himself lower against the granite to let the stranger pass without needless conversation. The odd old man and his pets passed by the lawman's hiding place without looking up and vanished on up the trail. Longarm stretched to ease his cramped muscles, then settled down to wait some more.

It was perhaps five minutes before he noticed something else, or, rather, noticed something missing.

The birds had stopped singing.

Longarm rolled over and up to a sitting position, his rifle across his knees, as he faced away from the trail into the aspen grove his mount was tethered in. The old man in the feathered fur hat was stepping out from between two pale green aspen trunks, the battered Sharps pointing up the slope at Longarm.

Longarm nodded and said, " 'Morning."

The other called out, "By gar, m'sieu, she must think she's vairie clevaire, him! Myself, Chambrun du Val, she has the eyes of the eagle!"

"I wasn't laying for *you,* Mister du Val. My handle's Long. I'm a deputy U.S. marshal on government business and I'd take it kindly if you'd point that thing someplace else."

"Mais non! You will throw down your weapon at once! Chambrun du Val she's demand it, him!"

"Sorry, I don't see things quite that way. You got the drop on me and I got the drop on you. If there's any edge, it's on my side. You got one round in that thing. I got fifteen in this Winchester."

"Bah, if Chambrun du Val she shoot, it is all ovaire!"

"You fire, old son, and you'd best do me good with your one and only try, for I can get testy as all hell with a buffalo round in or about my person! But I don't see this as a killing situation. I'd say our best play would be to talk things over before this gets any uglier."

"What is m'sieu's explanation for making the ambush, eh?"

"I told you, I'm a lawman. I was staked out here for a bush-whacker who took a shot at me in Bitter Creek last night. What's your tale?"

"Chambrun du Val she is going to Crooked Lance to kill a beast, he."

"Feller named Cotton Younger?"

"Exactement! How does m'sieu know this thing?"

"Cotton Younger's wanted in Canada, and if you ain't a French Canuck you sure talk funny for Wyoming. Are you a law-man or is your business with Cotton Younger more personal?"

"The animal, she is murdaire mon petite Marie Claire! Chambrun du Val she swear on the grave revenge!"

"Well, you can stop aiming at *me,* then. We're on the same side. My boss sent me up here to carry Cotton Younger in for a hanging. Along with what he did up Canada way, he's killed a few of our folks, too."

"Bah! Hanging, she is too good for this Cotton Younger! It is the intention of Chambrun du Val to kill him in the manner of les Cree!"

"You'll likely have to settle for a hanging. One of your own

Northwest Mounties is up in Crooked Lance ahead of us both.
There's a sheriff from Missouri and at least a brace of private detectives working for the railroads, too. At the rate it's going, he'll
be long hung before either of us gets there, so do you reckon we
should shoot each other or get on up to Crooked Lance some time
soon?"

"M'sieu knows the way?"

"More or less, don't you?"

"Mais non, Chambrun du Val, she is, how you say, looking for
Crooked Lance."

"Well, I see the man I was laying for up here on these rocks
don't seem anxious to show his face, so I'll be neighborly and
carry you there if you'll promise not to shoot me."

The old *voyageur* lowered the muzzle of his buffalo gun, so
Longarm swung his own muzzle politely to port arms and slid
down the granite to join him. As they walked together to where
all three horses were munching aspen leaves, Longarm asked,
"How well do you know Cotton Younger, Mister du Val?"

"Chambrun du Val, she's nevaire see the beast, but she will
know him. It is said the animal is big and very blond. They call
him Cotton because his hair, she is almost white. Also, she is now
in the jail at Crooked Lance, and, merde alors, how many such
createures like this can there be in any one jail, ah?"

"They say he's related to some who rode with the James-
Younger Gang a few years back. You hear anything about that up
Canada way?"

"Mais non, this createure rode alone through the Red River du
Nord Countrie. Chambrun du Val was off on the traplines when
he murdaire mon petite Marie Claire. Mon merde on what he do
down here in les States. He shall die, most slowly, for what he do
to Marie Claire!"

Longarm untethered his bay and swung up in the saddle, slipping the Winchester into its boot as he led off without comment.
Behind him, the old man leaped as lightly as a young Indian
aboard the broad back of his huge black gelding, calling its mate
to heel with a low whistle.

The French Canadian waited until they were free of the trees
and out on the trail before he called out cheerfully, "M'sieu has
not considered Chambrun du Val just had the opportunity to
shoot him in the back?"

Not turning his head, Longarm called back, "You don't look

stupid. You've got enough on your plate without gunning a U.S. lawman for no reason this far south of the border."

"M'sieu is a man who misses little, ah?"

Longarm didn't answer. What the man had said was the simple truth. The old-timer's eyes were sharp as hell and, together, they stood a better chance of riding into Crooked Lance alive.

Once they got there, Chambrun du Val would be one more headache. He'd want to kill the prisoner. The other lawmen ahead of Longarm would doubtless argue over who had first claim on Cotton Younger, too. In fact, by now, it was a pure mystery what the owlhoot was *doing* in that jail up ahead. The Mountie, the Missouri sheriff, or *some* damned lawman must have gotten through by now. Anyone riding in would be packing extradition papers, so why wasn't anyone riding *out* with Cotton Younger?

Longarm leaned forward and started to urge his mount to a faster pace. Then he eased off and shook his head, muttering, "Let's not get lathered up, old son. We've a long ride ahead and farther along we'll know more about it. Riding ourselves into the ground ain't going to get us there, so easy does it. Whatever in thunder is going on has been going on for weeks. It'll keep a few more hours."

Chapter 6

The Crooked Lance Trail was longer and rougher than Longarm had anticipated. He and his fellow traveler rode through old burns where charred lodgepole trunks and fetlock-deep ashes obscured the trail. They crossed rolling meadowlands frosted with sweet-smelling columbine and climbed through steep passes where patches of dusty snow still lay unmelted and the air was thin, cold stuff that tasted like stardust. They forded whitewater streams and rode gingerly over vast stretches of frost-polished granite, keeping to the trail by reading sign. The seldom-used trail vanished for miles at a time under new growth or windblown forest duff, but a mummified cow pat or the bleached, silvery pole of the telegraph line led them to the next stretch of visible trail. Longarm noticed that the single line of copper wire was down in more than one place as they passed a telegraph pole rotted away at its base. He couldn't really tell whether the line had been torn up by the harsh winds of the high country or by someone intent on silencing it. You could read it either way.

The journey ended when they rode down into a flat-bottomed valley cradled among high, jagged peaks. Longarm reined in, and as the Canadian paused beside him, he studied the cluster of log buildings down the slope. He counted a dozen or so buildings

surrounded by corrals, near an elbow of the sluggish stream drain-
ing the valley bottom. It looked peaceful. He saw some ponies
hitched in front of some buildings and figures moving quietly along
one unpaved street. Two of them appeared to be women in gathered
print skirts and sunbonnets. A cluster of men were sitting on the
boardwalk in front of a larger building, their boots stretched before
them in the street, as they talked quietly or just sat there waiting for
something to happen, as men tend to do in small towns.

Longarm said, "Let's ride in," and ticked the bay gently with
a heel, loping slowly down the slope with du Val following.

He made for the building with the most people around it and
reined in again. Nodding down at the quartet of cowhands in front
of what he now saw was the general store, he said, "Howdy."

Nobody answered, so Longarm said, "Name's Long. Deputy
U.S. Marshal Long. This other gent's called du Val."

One of the men looked up and stared soberly for a time before
he asked, "Is that a McClellan saddle?"

"Yep. They tell me there's a federal prisoner being held here
in Crooked Lance."

"Maybe. How do you keep from bustin' your balls on that fool
saddle? You couldn't *give* me one of them durned fool rigs to
ride!"

There was a low snickering from the others as Longarm stared
at the one who'd voiced the comment. Longarm said, "I ride a
government saddle because I ride on government business and
because a McClellan's easy on a horse's back. So, now that I've
answered your question, friend, suppose you answer mine?"

The village jester turned to one of his cronies and asked, inno-
cently, "Did you hear him ask a question, Jimbo?"

"Can't say. He talks sort of funny. Likely on account of that
ribbon-bow 'round his neck, don't you reckon?"

The French Canadian swore, swinging his Sharps around as he
roared, "Sacre God damn! You make the jest at Chambrun du Val?"

The one called Jimbo snickered and said, "Hell no, Pilgrim,
we're making fun of your funny-looking sidekick, here. Where'd
you ever find him? He looks like a whisky drummer. Hey, do you
sell whisky, boy?"

"What did you say?"

"I asked if you sold whisky, boy."

Longarm dismounted ominously and strode over to the one
called Jimbo as the latter got to his feet with a smirk. Longarm

said, "Asking a man what he does for a living is reasonable. Calling him a boy can get him testy."

"Do tell? What do you do when you gets *testy,* boy?"

Longarm's sixgun appeared in his right hand as he kicked Jimbo in the kneecap, covering him and anyone else who wanted a piece of the action as Jimbo went down, howling in agony.

The first lout who'd spoken leaped to his own feet, gasping, "Are you *crazy,* mister?"

"I could be. But now that we've changed *boy* to *mister,* let's see what else we can work out. As I remember, I was asking some fool question or other, wasn't I?"

Jimbo rolled to a sitting position, grasping his injured knee as he moaned, "God damn it, fellers, *take* him! He's busted my fucking leg!"

One of the cooler heads among the Crooked Lance crowd sighed, "*You* take him, if you've a mind to. This is gettin' too serious for funning. The man you want is across the way in yonder log house, lawman."

"Now that's more neighborly. Who do I see about taking him off your hands?"

There was a moment of silence. Then the informative one shrugged and said, "You'd have to clear it with Timberline, I reckon. He ain't here."

"He's the ramrod of the Rocking H, right?"

The other nodded and Longarm asked, "Who's guarding the prisoner over there, right now?"

"I reckon it's Pop Wade. Yeah, it's Pop's turn over to the jail. Pop won't give him to you, though. Nobody does anything hereabouts 'less Timberline says they can."

Longarm saw that the Canadian had swung his big gelding around and was heading for the jailhouse. He trotted after du Val and called out, "Slow down, old son. I know what you're thinking, but don't try it."

Du Val ignored him. The Canadian crossed the open stretch just ahead of Longarm and pounded on the plank door, shouting curses in French. Longarm took him by the elbow and swung him around, trying to disarm him as gently as possible. But gentleness wasn't effective. The old man was red-faced with rage and Longarm's English wasn't making any impression on his hate-filled mind. So as the others ran across the street toward the jail, he tapped du Val with the barrel of his .44, hitting him just below the ear.

Du Val collapsed in the dust like a rag doll as the jailhouse door flew open and a worried, middle-aged man peered out. One of the hands from the general store looked soberly down at the unconscious man and opined, "You *do* be inclined to testiness, by God! Was you birthed this ornery, mister? Or is it something you et?"

Longarm handed the unconscious Canadian's weapon to the jailer, saying, "You'd best put this away. This old boy rode all the way from the Red River of the North to gun your prisoner. I'd like a look at him myself."

The jailer hesitated. One of the town loafers suggested, "You'd best let him, Pop. This one's a purely ornery cuss!"

"Timberline ain't going to like it," the jailer said as he stood aside to let Longarm enter.

The interior was divided into two rooms. The rearmost room was closed off by a door of latticed aspen poles and barbed-wire mesh. As Longarm's eyes adjusted to the gloom, he saw a tall, blond man standing just inside the improvised cell, staring at him with a mixture of hope and utter misery. As the jailer followed him across the room, Longarm nodded to the prisoner and said, "I'm from the Justice Department, Mister Younger."

The prisoner shook his head and said, "That well may be, but I ain't Cotton Younger! I keep telling everyone I ain't, but will they listen?"

Pop Wade snorted, "Listen to the jaybird, will you? The son of a bitch was catched fair and square stealing Lazy K cows and he matches them reward posters to the T!"

"I never stole cow one! Where in hell would I *go* with a stolen cow?"

"You saying you never had that running iron in your possibles, son?"

"All right, I did have a length of bar-iron I sort of picked up along the way. That don't prove all that much!"

"It proves you had the tools of the cow thief's trade, God damn your eyes!"

Longarm had heard this same discussion almost every time he'd talked to a man in jail and it was tedious every time. He said, "What you done hereabouts ain't the question, Mister Younger. I'll be taking you to Denver to talk to the judge about some other matters."

"God damn it, I ain't Cotton Younger! My name is Jones. Billy Jones from Cripple Creek!"

"Jesus H. Christ, son, can't you do better than Jones?"

"Hell, *somebody* has to be named Jones, don't they?"

"How about James? Ain't the Younger and the James boys kin?"

"How should I know? I ain't kin to nobody named James *or* Younger. I'm jest Billy Jones, from Cripple Creek, and ever'body hereabouts is crazy!"

"Well, then, you got nothing to worry about when I carry you back to Denver, have you?"

"Why in hell do I want to go to Denver? I was on my way to Oregon when these crazy folks hereabouts damn near killed me and started callin' me an outlaw! I don't want to go to Denver!"

"'Fraid you're bound there, just the same. You answer the description and I'm just the errand boy, not the judge." He turned to the jailer and said, "I got his papers right here. You want me to sign for him, Mister Wade?"

Pop Wade said, "Can't let you have him. It ain't my say who goes in or out of here, mister."

"What are you talking about, you can't let me have him? I'm a deputy U.S. marshal with a federal warrant on this cuss, God damn it!"

"I don't doubt that for a minute, mister. There's a Canadian Mountie, a Missouri sheriff, and a whole posse of other lawmen over at the hotel who say the same thing. The committee says it ain't made up its mind yet."

"What committee, what mind, and about what?"

"Vigilance Committee of Crooked Lance. This here Cotton Younger is their prisoner until they says different. Ain't nobody taking him nowhere till Timberline and the others say it's fitting."

Longarm considered.

He could take Younger away from the elderly jailer easily enough, and the hands out front would likely crawfish back long enough for the two of them to ride out. On the other hand, it was a long ride to the nearest place he'd be able to hold him safely.

Longarm shrugged and said, "I'd better have a talk with those other lawmen and this big hoorah called Timberline."

Chapter 7

The hotel in Crooked Lance wasn't as fancy as the one in Bitter Creek. It wasn't a hotel, in fact. The family who owned the general store and ran the post office and telegraph outlet had a livery shed and an extra lean-to partitioned into tiny, dirt-floored cubicles they rented to those few riders staying overnight in town. The family's name was Stover and they were inclined to take a profit wherever one could be found. The so-called hotel had a sort of veranda facing the muddy banks of the valley stream, on the far side from the one street. There, Longarm found another quartet of moody men, seated on barrels, or in one case, pacing up and down. The man on his feet wore the scarlet tunic of the Northwest Mounted Police, trail-dusty and worn through at one elbow. The other three wore civilian clothes, but one had a tin star pinned to his lapel. As the storekeeper introduced Longarm to his fellow lawmen, the Mountie asked, "Are you the person who just beat up a Canadian citizen?"

"'Fraid so. Where'd they put old du Val? By the time I came out of the jailhouse they'd carried him off."

"He's inside, with a concussion. They told us you'd beaten him unconscious. I'd say you owe me an explanation, since I'm here on Her Majesty's business and . . ."

One of the others said, "Oh, shut up and set down, dammit. You know he's a U.S. marshal!" To Longarm he added, "I'm Silas Weed, from Clay County, Missouri. This here's Captain Walthers from the U.S. Army Provost Marshal's office, and the gent with the big cigar is a railroad dick called Ryan."

Longarm nodded and hooked a boot over the edge of the veranda as he said, "My outfit's missing a deputy called Kincaid. Any of you met up with him?"

There was a general shaking of heads, which didn't surprise Longarm. He turned to the one called Ryan and asked, "Are you from the same detective agency as a funny couple called Hanks, Mister Ryan? They said one of their agents was missing, too."

Ryan grimaced around the stub of his cigar and growled, "Jesus. Are you talking about a female traveling with a dwarf?"

"Sounds like the same folks. You with their outfit or not?"

"God, no! Cedric Hanks and his wife work alone! They're bounty hunters, not detectives! Where'd you run into them?"

"Bitter Creek, headed this way. You say the gal's his *wife*?"

"Yeah, when he ain't pretending to be her little kid. Ain't that a bitch? They run con games when they're not hunting down men with papers on 'em. If you met up with that pair you're lucky to have the fillings in your teeth!"

"They were likely lying about having a partner up here, too, then. What's the story on that prisoner over yonder, gents? I take it all of us rode up here on the same errand."

The man from the provost office snapped, "The army has first claim on him. He's not only wanted on a hanging military offense, but I was here first!"

Sheriff Weed said, "The hell you say, Captain! Clay County's papers on him have seniority. We've been after him a good six years!"

The Mountie wheeled around and challenged, "Not so fast! Your own State Department has honored Her Majesty's warrant for the murder of a British subject!"

Longarm smiled crookedly at the railroad detective, who smiled back and said, "That's half of the problem. The other half is the Crooked Lance Vigilance Committee. They say they're holding Cotton Younger for the highest bidder."

"The *what*? These cowpokes hereabouts are holding a man for ransom with four—make that *five*—lawmen in town?"

"They don't see it as ransom. It's all the damn paper Cotton

Younger and his kin have out on 'em. He's worth five hundred to the railroad I work for. Clay County, there, says he's worth about the same to Missouri. Queen Victoria ain't been heard from, but she'd likely pay some damn thing, and Army, here, says the standing offer for deserters runs three to five hundred, depending. I'd say Army was low bidder, up to now. How much is he worth to the Justice Department?"

"Don't know. My boss never mentioned a reward."

"There you go, old son. You just made last in line!"

Longarm stuck a cheroot between his teeth and thumbnailed a match as he gathered his thoughts. Then he shook his head and said, "I don't see it that way, gents. Justice Department outranks all others."

"All but Her Majesty's Government!" the Mountie amended.

"No offense to your Queen, but her writ doesn't carry much weight in U.S. federal territory, which Wyoming happens to be. Before we fuss about it further amongst ourselves, what's keeping the five of us from at least getting back to the rails and telegraph with the prisoner? Seems to me it'd make more sense to let our superiors fight it out, once we had him locked in a civilized jail."

The Missouri sheriff asked, "The jail in Bitter Creek?"

"Why not? It's got bars and a telegraph office we can get to."

"Town marshal down there's sure to want a split on the reward."

Longarm snorted, "Oh, for God's sake, this is the dumbest situation I've ever been in, and I've been in some pissers! We're talking about a shiftless thief with a lousy five hundred on him, and—"

"No, we ain't," the railroad dick cut in, "We're talking about *ten thousand* dollars, no questions, cash on the barrelhead!"

Longarm frowned and snapped, "Ten thousand dollars on that tall drink of water over yonder?"

"Hell, no, on his kinfolks, Frank and Jesse James! Between the state of Missouri, the Pinkertons, and a dozen small banks and such, either one of the James boys is worth at least that, dead or alive. Should any man nail both, he'd collect more like twenty!" He shrugged and added, "I ain't that greedy, myself. I'd settle for either."

"Yeah, but the prisoner here ain't Frank or Jesse James. When I just talked to him, he denied even being Cotton Younger."

"What else did you expect, Longarm? Once he's getting fitted for that hemp necktie, he'll talk, all right."

Sheriff Weed chimed in, "That's for damn sure. Our only problem seems to be just who gits him, and how to convince the locals who caught him that they'll have a share in the reward."

"Ain't everyone counting unhatched chickens, gents?"

Weed nodded and said, "Sure they are. That's what's holding up the parade. Nobody here can promise a reward for a James boy still at large. Getting some of these dumb cowboys to see it that way can be a chore. All of us have tried, one time or another."

Longarm muttered, "I don't believe this! There's five of us, damn it! If any *two* of you would back me, I'd be riding out of here with Cotton Younger within the hour!"

He waited to see if there were any volunteers. Then he asked Weed, "How about it, Sheriff?"

"Would you turn him over to me as soon as we rode free?"

"God damn it, you're obstructing justice!"

"No, I ain't. I came all the way out here from the County of Clay to arrest that boy and that's my aim. That's my only aim. I don't pull chestnuts out of the fire for other lawmen."

Longarm looked at the army agent, who shrugged and said, "I have my orders."

"How about you, Mountie? You up to backing my play?"

"On the condition I take him back to Canada? Of course."

Longarm knew better than to ask the railroad dick. He took a drag on his cheroot and said, "Somebody, here, has to start thinking instead of being greedy! How long do you all figure we can just sit here, stalemated, like big-ass birds?"

The railroad dick said, "I got time. I'll allow it's a Mexican standoff now, but sooner or later somebody has to cave in. I don't mean for it to be me!"

Captain Walthers said, "I sent a telegram to the War Department. I'm waiting for further instructions."

Sheriff Weed said, "I got some old Missouri boys riding out to back my play."

The Mountie said nothing. His service was only a few years old, but Longarm had heard about their motto.

Turning to Weed, he said, "You've come from the owlhoot's old stamping grounds, Sheriff. Before we get ourselves in any deeper, is there a chance that pissant over at the jail could be telling the truth? We're gonna look silly as all hell if it turns out he's *not* the Cotton Younger all of us are fighting over."

Weed said, "It's him, all right. How many tall, skinny owl-hoots with a wispy white thatch like his can there be?"

The railroad dick nodded and said, "I've seen photographs of the kid sitting next to his cousin Cole Younger, and Frank James. He's older now, and his hair's gone from almost white to pale yellow, but it's him."

The army man smiled a bit smugly and said, "At the risk of finding something to agree on with the rest of you, I have his army records and they fit him like a glove. He deserted from Terry's column as a teenaged recruit. He's no more than twenty-five now. He's a few pounds heavier, but the height is right on the button. They let me measure him. It would be possible to make an error of half an inch, but his records don't. He's exactly six-foot, six and three-quarter inches. He tried to tell me he'd never been in the army, too."

Longarm nodded, satisfied at least with the identification of the prisoner, if nothing else. Before he could go into it further, the door to the hotel banged open and Chambrun du Val came out loaded for bear. He scowled at Longarm and roared, "Salud! Porquoi you hit Chambrun du Val? Where is mon rifle? Sacre! I think she will kill you, me!"

As the burly older man lurched across the veranda at Longarm, the railroad dick put out a boot and tripped him, sending du Val sprawling on his hands and knees as Longarm stepped clear with a nod of thanks. Before du Val could rise, Longarm snapped, "Now listen, old son, and listen sharp! Your war is over. You ain't going to harm a hair on Cotton Younger's head. I ain't asking you, I'm telling you."

"I kill him, but first, by gar, I kill you!"

"Oh, shut up, I ain't finished. You ain't going to kill me because I don't aim to let you. On the other hand, I can't watch you around the clock and still get anything done, so I'm counting on your good sense about the prisoner over at the jailhouse. You gun that old boy and you can say good-bye to breathing. Forgetting me and these four other lawmen, he's worth God knows what to a whole valleyful of vigilantes, and if they decide to string you up for murdering their prisoner, I for one wouldn't stop 'em!"

"Chambrun du Val, she fears nothing, him!"

"Maybe, but you think on it before you make any more sudden moves." The Mountie came over to help the old man to his feet, saying, "I'll take over, Longarm."

He took the old man by the arm and walked him off for a fatherly talk. Longarm noticed the Mountie was speaking French, but a few paces off the old trapper laughed and swore, "Merde alors! M'sieu speaks like a Paris pimp! The English of Chambrun du Val, she is more betaire than these strange noises m'sieu regards as French!"

The laugh was a good sign. Longarm decided the old man would be all right for now and turned back to the other three on the veranda, saying, "It's early yet. I'm going to have a talk with this Timberline everyone in Crooked Lance looks up to. Any of you know how I can find him?"

Sheriff Weed said, "He'll likely be riding in later. He's the foreman of the Rocking H, about six miles down the valley."

"He comes to town every night? Don't they have a bunkhouse at his spread?"

"Sure, but he's interested in our stalemate here."

The railroad dick added, "Interested in Kim Stover, too. Her spread's just outside of town, behind them trees to the north."

"I'll bite. Who's Kim Stover? Any kin to the rascal who owns this hotel and everything else in town worth mention?"

"Old Stover's her father-in-law. Miss Kim's the widow of his late son, Ben. They tell us he was run over by the trail herd, summer before last. Matter of fact, she don't seem to get along good with her in-laws."

Captain Walthers sniffed and chimed in, "Who could blame the poor woman? You saw the unwashed lout who's taking advantage of us at two bits a night. The Stovers are white trash!"

Longarm didn't ask if the widow was good-looking. She had the la-di-da young officer defending her and the big froggy of the valley courting her. He blew a thoughtful smoke ring. "Like I said, it's still early. I'll just mosey out to the Rocking H this afternoon and see what this Timberline gent has to say about the burr he's put under my saddle."

Longarm walked around the building to where he'd left his bay in the livery shed. As he was saddling up, the others drifted in and started untethering their own mounts.

The railroad dick said, "The boys and me will just tag along to sort of keep you company, all right?"

"You trust each other as much as you trust me?"

Sheriff Weed grinned and said, "Not hardly," as the Mountie and du Val came in from their stroll. The older man's two big black geldings were the only ones not in the livery shed. Du Val let them run free like old hounds, but Longarm knew they'd come when he whistled. He led his own mount out from under the low overhang and waited politely as the others saddled up. There was no sense trying to get a lead on them. Wherever he went, it seemed likely he'd have company.

Chapter 8

As it turned out, it wasn't a long ride. The railroad dick had fallen in beside Longarm's bay as the federal man led off. They were passing a windbreak of lodgepole pine and the detective had just said, "That cabin over there's the Lazy K, Kim Stover's place," when they both spied two riders swinging out to the main trail from the modest spread.

One was a hatless woman with a halo of sunset-colored hair and buckskin riding togs. She rode astride, like a man. She sat her mount well, though.

The rider to her left was a man in a mustard Stetson and faded blue denim, on a gray gelding almost as big as one of du Val's plowhorses. The man needed a big mount. He was at least a head taller than any human being should have been. Longarm didn't ask if he was Timberline. It would have been a foolish question.

The two parties slowed as they met on the trail.

Since all of them except Longarm had been introduced, the railroad dick did the honors. Timberline smiled, friendly enough, and said, "Glad to know you, Deputy. Like I always say, the more the merrier!"

The girl was less enthusiastic. She nodded politely at Longarm, but sighed, "Oh, Lord, another lawman is all we need!"

The others had told him the big ramrod was sparking the widow, so Longarm swung in beside Timberline as the entire group headed back to Crooked Lance. He explained his mission as Timberline listened politely but stubborn-jawed. The leader of the local vigilantes was maybe thirty, with coal-black sideburns, and clean-shaven. He sat his gray with the relaxed strength of a man used to having horses, and men, do just about anything he wanted them to.

He heard Longarm out before he shook his head and said, "If it was up to me you could have the rascal, Deputy. Hell, I was for just stringing him up the afternoon we caught him skulking about this little lady's spread."

"Yeah, I heard you found him with a running iron on him."

"Well, to tell the truth, I can't take all the credit. Miss Kim, here, spied him hunkered down near the creek in some brush as me and a couple of my hands rode up to her front porch. Had not ladies been present, that would have likely been the end of it. The skunk lit out when he saw us coming. Windy Dawson, one of my hands, made as nice an overhand community-loop as you've ever seen and hauled the thief off his pony at a dead run. Miss Kim, here, said not to kill him right off, so Windy dragged him into the settlement and we threw him in the jailhouse."

He swung around in his saddle to say to the girl on his far side, "You see why we shoulda strung him up that first day, honey? I *told* you he was a mean-looking cuss, and now we even have a *federal* lawman up here pestering us for him!"

The widow said, "Nobody's getting him until they do right by the folks up here!" and Longarm saw he'd been barking up the wrong tree. The lady might not be related by blood to the money-hungry Stover family, but she'd surely picked up some bad habits from her in-laws!

Speaking across Timberline, Longarm said, "What you're doing here ain't legal, ma'am."

Behind him, Sheriff Weed called out, "Save your breath, Longarm. I've laid down the law till I'm blue in the face and nobody hereabouts seems to know what law *is*!"

Longarm ignored him and explained to the determined-looking redhead, "You're holding that Cotton Younger on a citizen's arrest, which is only good till a legally appointed peace officer can take him off your hands."

Kim Stover's voice was sweetly firm as, not looking his way, she said, "The Crooked Lance Committee of Vigilance was elected fair and square, mister."

"I hate to correct a lady, but, no, ma'am, it wasn't. Crooked Lance ain't an incorporated township. The open range hereabouts ain't constituted as a county by Wyoming Territory. So any elections you may have held are unofficial as well as unrecorded. I understand the position you folks are taking, but it's likely to get you all in trouble."

For the first time she swung her eyes to Longarm, and they were bitter as well as green when she snapped, "We're already in trouble, mister! You see a schoolhouse hereabouts? You see a town hall or even a signpost telling folks we're *here*? Folks in Crooked Lance are *poor*, mister! Poor hard-scrabble homesteaders and overworked, underpaid cowhands without two coins to rub together, let alone a real store to shop in!"

"I can see you're sort of back in the nothing-much, ma'am, but I fail to see why you're holding it against me and these other gents."

"I never said it was your fault, mister. We know who's fault it is that Crooked Lance gets the short end every time! It's them durned big shots out in the country you all rode in from. The cattle buyers who shortchange us when we drive our herds in to Bitter Creek. The politicians in Cheyenne, Washington, and such! They've been grinding us under since I was birthed in these mountains, and now we mean to have our own back!"

Timberline noted the puzzled look in Longarm's eyes and cut in to explain, "When Miss Kim's husband, Ben, was killed, them buyers over to the railroad tried to get her cows for next to nothin'! Luckily, me and some of her and Ben's other friends made sure they didn't rob her before Ben was in the ground. We drove her herd in with our others and all of us stuck together on the price of beef."

Kim Stover added bitterly, "A little enough herd it was, and a low enough price, after all the hard work my man put into them durned cows!"

Longarm nodded and said, "I used to ride for the Jingle Bob and a couple of smaller outfits, ma'am. So I know how them Eastern packers can squeeze folks, dead or alive. But Uncle Sam never sent me here to bid on beef. I'm packing a federal warrant on that owlhoot you folks caught, and I mean to ride out with him, one way or another."

"Not before we settle on the price," Kim Stover snapped.

Timberline added, still smiling, "Or whup damn near every rider in this valley, fair and square!"

"There's five of us, Timberline."

"I know. I can likely scare up thirty or forty men if push comes to shove. But I don't reckon it will. These other four gents and me have had more or less this same conversation before you got here. And, by the way, in case you ain't asked, the five of you ain't together. We figure you'll be bidding against one another before Cotton Younger leaves this valley."

Sheriff Weed called out, "I've told you I'll split the reward with you all, Timberline. This federal man aims to carry him to Denver, where they'll likely hang him without even asking about Frank and Jesse James!"

There was an angry muttering from the other lawmen and du Val spat, disgusted. The railroad dick laughed and told Longarm, "Ain't this a caution? We get into this fix every time we talk to these folks. My own bid's highest of all, but nobody listens. If you ask me, they're just funning us. I'm getting to where I wouldn't be surprised if that jaybird in the hoosegow wasn't in on it with these valley folks!"

Longarm considered the idea seriously for a moment. It made as much sense as anything else he'd heard that afternoon. He asked Timberline and the girl, "Have you folks thought about the *who* as much as the how much?"

Kim Stover asked what he meant. Longarm said, "The reward might have greeded you past clear thinking. I, for one, could promise all the tea in China, were I a promising sort. But, on the hoof, your prisoner's worth two hundred and fifty to you, period, and assuming you can take the word of whoever among us you turn him over to."

Timberline began, "The reward on the James boys—"

Longarm cut in to insist, "Cotton Younger ain't no James. He's small fry. So the most he's worth in *any* place is maybe five hundred, split with the arresting officer. That is, with *some* arresting officers."

Sheriff Weed said, "Damn it, Longarm!"

But Longarm ignored him to go on, "County officers are allowed to accept rewards. Federal officers ain't. If either of you can count, you'll see I've just eliminated one temptation."

The army man, Captain Walthers, cried out, "Hold on there! I'm a federal officer, too!"

Longarm nodded and said, "I'll get to you in a minute, Captain. I'm trying to cut the sheriff out of the tally at the moment!"

Weed yelled, "I told 'em I'd let 'em have the whole reward, God damn your eyes!"

"Well, sure, you *told* 'em, Sheriff. Likely, if you was to double-cross these folks out here in Wyoming, the folks in Missouri would vote against you next election, too."

He saw the widow Stover's eyes were going *tick-tick-tick* in her pretty but bitter-lipped face, so he dropped the attack on the sheriff to say, "The railroad dick, here, is a civilian who's working for the reward and nothing else. If he double-crossed you . . . well, being in the cattle business, you must know how fair a shake you'll get from the courts against the railroads and such."

The railroad dick sighed and said, "Next time that French Canuck tries for you . . ."

"It was ornery, but you just tried to outbid the rest of us. Like I was saying, a deputy U.S. marshal ain't allowed to accept rewards. So if I agreed to forward such rewards as was due . . ."

"I can see what you're trying to pull," snapped Kim Stover. "It won't work. We know better than to trust any of you to send us the money!"

Timberline laughed and said, "I keep telling you we've been over this same ground, Longarm. You'd best see if Uncle Sam's ready to pay that ten thousand. We ain't piggy. We'll sell the owl-hoot to you for half what both James boys is worth, and if anybody gets the other ten—"

"Back up, Timberline. You're starting to talk about the national debt again. Number one, we don't know whether Cotton Younger knows where either Frank or Jesse James is hiding out. Number two, we don't know whether he'll be willing to tell us, if he does."

Timberline shrugged and said, "I could get it out of him in five minutes if the little lady here would let me talk to him my own way!"

Kim Stover shook her head and insisted, "I said there'd be no hanging and no torture and I meant it. We're poor but decent folks in Crooked Lance." Then she spoiled it all by adding, "Besides, they'll have ways of getting him to talk, once they pay us for him. I reckon once they've paid us the ten thousand, they'll get him to say whether he knows or not!"

By now they were moving down the main street of the settlement and further argument was broken off as the railroad dick groaned, "Oh, no, that's all we need!"

A buckboard was parked in front of the general store. A woman in a canvas dust smock and feathered hat was being helped down from her seat by a midget dressed in dusty black. Little Cedric had abandoned his disguise and was puffing a two-bit cigar under his black porkpie hat.

Timberline choked and asked, "Jesus! What is it?"

Longarm said, "Meet Mister and Mrs. Hanks, but don't play cards with them."

As Mabel looked up at the party reining in around them, Longarm touched the brim of his Stetson and said, "Evening, ma'am. I see you got here after all. I asked around for your kin, but nobody here seems to know 'em."

Cedric Hanks said, "Oh, stuff a sock in it, Longarm. We're here fair and square with an honest business proposition."

Before they could go further into it, the Northwest Mountie moved up beside Longarm and asked, "Did you see where du Val was heading, Deputy?"

Longarm twisted around in his saddle to count heads as he frowned and replied, "Never saw him drop out. Not that I was watching."

The army agent said, "I was, but I didn't think it was important when he dropped back. Who cares about the old drifter, anyway?"

"I do!" snapped Longarm, kicking his bay into a sudden lope as he tore over to the jail and slid from the saddle, drawing as he kicked in the door. The startled jailer, Wade, jumped up from his seat with a gasp, even as Longarm saw the jail was empty except for Pop Wade and the prisoner.

Longarm put his sidearm away with a puzzled frown, explaining, "That old Canuck is up to something. I thought he was heading for here."

He stepped back to the doorway as the Mountie and Sheriff Weed came in, guns drawn. Longarm shook his head and said, "Nope. We were wrong. You think he's in the hotel?"

Weed said, "Not hardly. His two geldings ain't in sight, neither. You reckon he's lit out?"

Longarm said, "Maybe. But why?"

"He was a funny old cuss. Said he'd come to gun this jasper, here. Likely he saw there was no way he could, and—"

"After riding all the way from Canada, without even saying adios? I rode in with him. Du Val didn't strike me as a man who makes sudden moves without a reason."

The prisoner bleated, "You fellers got to protect me! I don't like all this talk about my getting gunned!"

Ignoring him, the Mountie said, "The reason I was keeping an eye on him is that there's something very odd about that man. For one thing, I don't think he's a Red River breed."

"You waited till now to tell us? *I* took him for a Canuck."

"No doubt, but then, you don't speak Quebecois."

"You mean when you and him were talking French and he said yours was sissy?"

"Yes, he said I spoke with a Parisian accent. My mother was named DeVerrier. My Quebecois is perfectly good."

"Why in thunder didn't you say so?"

"Like you others, I've been playing my own hand for Her Majesty. I knew he was an imposter, but I didn't know why. I still don't know why, but, under the circumstances—"

The railroad dick came over to join them, saying, "He ain't anywhere near the general store or hotel, gents. What do you reckon his play might be?"

Longarm said, "He's either lit out for good, or he wants us to think he's lit out for good."

"Meaning another play for our prisoner, come dark?"

Longarm moved over to the cage and asked the prisoner, "You have a friend with a long gray beard and a passable Canuck accent?"

"I never saw the varmint! Pop, there, told me about him trying to bust in, but—"

"Or bust you out," Longarm cut in, turning away. He didn't expect the prisoner to confirm his suspicion, but it was worth thinking about.

Sheriff Weed said, "We'll have to take turns tonight, keeping an eye peeled for the hombre."

Longarm stared morosely at him for a moment before he shook his head and said, "That's doing it the hard way. Why sweat him out when I can *ask* him what he's up to?"

"Ask him? How do you figure to ask that old boy word one, Longarm? None of us knows where he *is*!"

"Not right now, we don't. But there's a good hour's daylight left and I know where he turned off the trail."

"Hot damn! You reckon you can track him down before sunset?"

"I aim to give it one good try."

Chapter 9

Longarm rode his bay slowly through the crack-willow on the wrong side of the creek, snorting in annoyance as he spotted another big hoofprint in a patch of moist earth. The man calling himself du Val was wasting their time and getting himself brush-cut for nothing. There was little use taking to the tall timber to hide your trail when you traveled with two big geldings wearing oversized draft shoes. The sun was low and he was well clear of the settlement now. The evening light made the occasional hoofprint easy to read in the orange, slanting rays. In fact, aside from the way du Val had vanished and the odd tale the Mountie told, the signs read as if the old-timer was simply heading for Bitter Creek without taking too many precautions about his trail. Longarm considered that as he rode on. Was du Val setting him up for a bushwhacking, or had he simply given up?

Longarm ducked his head under a low branch and, as he rode out into a clearing, spied one of du Val's pets, grazing quietly in the gauzy light. The other was outlined against pale aspen trunks across the clearing. Neither mount had a rider.

Longarm reined back into the shadows of the treeline, sweeping the far side cautiously with his eyes. He slid the Winchester from its boot as he dismounted.

He circled the clearing instead of crossing it, clucking to the gelding near the treeline as he approached it. Neither plowhorse paid much attention to him. They were tired and settled in for the evening. They were either stupid, even for farm animals, or nothing very exciting was about to happen.

Longarm saw a human knee sticking up out of the long grass near the grazing animal he was approaching. He froze in place to study it, then moved closer, his Winchester at port-arms. The man lying in the grass on his back groaned. Longarm dropped to one knee, raising the barrel of his rifle and feeling with one hand under the long beard as he said, "Evening, du Val. Where'd they hit you?"

"Lights and liver, I reckon," the old man sighed, his French Canuck accent missing. Longarm's hand came out wet and sticky as the dying man complained, "He didn't have to do it. I'd never have told."

Longarm wiped his fingertips on the matted beard, then lifted it away from the old man's chest, which was tattooed with a panoramic scene of a once-important sea battle. Someone had put a rifle bullet right between the Monitor and the Merrimac. Why he was still breathing was a mystery. He was one tough old man.

Longarm asked, "Who bushwhacked you, Sailor?"

"You figured out who I am, huh? You're pretty sharp, Longarm."

Longarm cursed himself for offering a digression and insisted, "Who did it? It ain't like you owe him loyalty."

"He must have thought I was on your side. We rode in—"

And then the old man was gone. Longarm cursed and got back to his feet, gazing about for sign. It was getting too dark to track, and the two tame geldings told him no strangers were about. They knew him as well as they had known their dead master. He'd noticed they were shy of others.

Longarm circled back to where he'd left his own mount. The body would keep for now in the chill night air and it might be sort of interesting to keep the others in the dark for now. Nobody but the one who'd killed the man who'd called himself du Val knew who he was, or where, right now.

Despite the roundabout path the old man had taken, it was only a short ride back to Crooked Lance. The sun was down by now but the sky was still lavender with one or two bright stars as

Longarm rode in. The settlement was crowded with shadowy figures, mounted or afoot, and as Longarm passed a knot of horsemen he heard a voice mutter, "That's the one who kicked old Jimbo."

Ignoring them, Longarm rode first to the log jail, meaning to have a discussion about the bearded mystery man with the prisoner. But he didn't. A quartet of cowhands stood or squatted by the doorway, and as Longarm dismounted, one of them waved his rifle barrel wildly and said, "No you don't, stranger. Our orders are to hold Cotton Younger tight as a tick and that's what we aim to do."

"Hell, I wasn't fixing to eat him. Just wanted to ask him some more questions."

"You ask your questions of the Vigilance Committee, hear? Go along now, friend. Windy, here, was tellin' us a funny story and you're spoiling the ending."

Longarm led his bay by the reins to the livery, peeled off the McClellan and bridle, and rubbed the horse's brown hide dry with a handful of straw before bedding it for the night in a stall.

He went around to the hotel, where he found the others in the so-called dining room, pinned to the back of the general store. The table was crowded but Sheriff Weed made room for him on one of the bench seats, asking softly, "Find anything?"

"Read some sign. The old man's gone," Longarm replied. He counted noses, saw that the other lawmen and the Hankses were at the table, and asked, "Where's Timberline and the gal?"

"Likely spooning. Saw Kim Stover talking to some hands around the jailhouse just before they rang the dinner bell. I hope you ain't hungry. Considering we're paying two bits a day for room and board, this grub is awful."

Someone dropped a tin plate in front of Longarm. He glanced up and saw it was one of the storekeeper's womenfolk. It was either his wife or his daughter. It hardly mattered. Both were silent little sparrows. The storekeeper himself wasn't at the table. Longarm put a cautious spoonful of beans between his lips and saw why. He helped himself to some coffee from the community pot to wash the beans down. With plenty of sugar and a generous lacing of tinned milk it was just possible to drink the coffee.

The others were hungrier, or maybe didn't have spare food in their bedrolls, so they ate silently, as people who live outdoors a lot tend to do. The only conversationalist at the table was Mabel

Hanks, down at the far end. She was buttering up Captain Walthers. She'd likely sized him up, as Longarm had, as a man with an eye for the ladies. Her midget husband ignored her play, spooning his beans more directly to his mouth, since his head rode lower above the table. A picture of the two of them in bed rose unbidden to Longarm's mind and he looked away, shocked a bit at his own dirty imagination.

One of the sparrowlike Stover women brought an apple pie in from the kitchen next door and when Longarm smiled at her she blushed and scooted out. He decided she was the daughter. They were both ugly, had heads shaped like onions, buck teeth, and mousy brown hair rolled up in tight buns. The best way to tell them apart was by their print dresses. The mother wore white polka dots on blue and her daughter's print was white on green. The older mountain woman had likely given birth at sixteen or so, because there wasn't a great gap in their ages. They both looked forty and driven into the ground.

Longarm gagged down half the beans and helped himself to a slice of pie, which turned out to be another mistake. He was glad he had packed some pemmican and baker's chocolate. Glad he wasn't a big eater, too.

He saw that the railroad dick was getting up from the table, either in disgust or to relieve himself outside. Longarm pushed himself away from the table to follow, catching up with the detective near the outhouse.

"Call of nature?" grinned the railroad dick, holding the door of the four-holer politely. Longarm said, "Social call. Go ahead and do whatsoever. I want to talk to you."

The detective stepped back outside, saying, "It'll keep. What's on your mind, Longarm?"

"Got a deal for you. You got any papers on a Missouri owlhoot called Sailor Brown?"

"Hell yes, I do! He rode with James and Younger when they robbed the Glendale train!"

"Good reward on him?"

"A thousand or more. You know where he is, Longarm?"

"Yep. The reward is dead or alive, ain't it?"

"Of course. What's the play?"

"I'm sending you into Bitter Creek with his body, which I'm giving you as a gift in exchange."

"Exchange for what? You say his . . . body?"

"Yeah. That old man calling himself du Val was really Sailor Brown. He likely heard they had a friend of his here and rode in with that fool tale to see if he could bust the boy out. I got him on ice for you in a place we'll discuss if you're willing."

"Willing to what?"

"Drop out of this game. You must know your chance of taking Cotton Younger away from the vigilantes and us other real lawmen ain't so good. On the other hand, you've come a long way, so you've been waiting, hoping for a break. All right, I'm giving you one. You carry Sailor Brown to the U.P. line and telegraph at Bitter Creek and collect the bounty on him. How does that strike you?"

"Strikes me as damn neighborly. Naturally, you're expecting a cut."

"Nope. Can't take any part of the reward. It's all yours. I'm going to tell you where the body is and then I'll expect you to be long gone."

"Leaving you with one less rival to deal with, eh? All right. I'm a man who knows enough to quit whilst he's ahead. You got a deal. Who killed Sailor, you?"

"Nope. Don't know who bushwhacked him. That's why, if I was you, I'd pick him up tonight and scoot. I'll ride up the mountain with you to help you pack him on a horse, and to make sure you get away safe. The one who shot him might have other ideas on the subject."

"Jesus. You reckon they'll have the body staked out?"

"Doubt it. Looks like somebody just shot him down like a dog and left him for the crows. You'd best take that piss now. I'd like to get the two of you off my hands before bedtime."

The detective laughed and said, "I admire a man who thinks on his feet, and you do think sharp and sudden. How'd you know *I* wasn't the killer?"

"You, Weed, and the Mountie are the only ones who couldn't be."

"And I'm the one without a real badge. All right, you've gotten rid of me. How do you figure to get rid of the others?"

"It ain't your worry, now. I eat the apple one bite at a time. So take your piss and let's get cracking."

Chapter 10

By eight-thirty the railroad dick was packing the dead outlaw over the mountains to the transcontinental railroad and Longarm was getting off his bay in front of Kim Stover's cabin.

Light shone through the drawn curtains and somewhere inside a dog was yapping, so Longarm wasn't surprised when the door opened before he'd had a chance to knock.

Kim Stover peered out at him, the lamplight making a red halo of her hair as Longarm said, "Evening, ma'am. You folks rode off before I could get around to asking one or two more questions."

"Mister Long, if you've come to make your bid for Cotton Younger—"

"Uncle Sam don't work that way, ma'am, but let's leave your odd notions aside for now. You see, there seems to be more'n one outlaw working this neck of the woods. He took a shot at me in Bitter Creek the other night, and tonight I learned he wasn't funning. I thought we might talk about it."

"Are you suggesting one of my friends took a shot at you?"

"No, ma'am. I think you and yours are just being surly. You see, somebody came up here to bust Cotton Younger out of your so-called jail. Somebody else gunned him. But that's all been looked after. What I wanted to ask you about was new faces in the valley."

"You mean since we captured Cotton Younger? You've met them all by now."

"How about before your friends caught the boy skulking 'round? You have any new hands on the spreads, hereabouts?"

She shook her head and said, "No. Everyone I know in Crooked Lance has been here for some time."

"How much time is some, ma'am?"

"Oh, at least five years. Wait a minute. Timberline did hire some new hands when they made him ramrod of the Rocking H. The cattle company that owns it has expanded in the last few years. There's Windy Dawson, came to work two, maybe three years ago—"

"He's that short, fat feller who throws good?"

"Yes, Windy's one of the best ropers in the valley."

"I took him for a top hand. I'd say he was a cowboy, not a train robber. Anyone else you can think of?"

"Not really. Windy's the newest man in the valley. There's Slim Wilson, but he was hired earlier and, like Windy, is considered a hand who knows his way around a cow. I'd be very surprised to learn that Slim wasn't a man who started learning his skills early, and he's no more than twenty-odd, right now."

"What about Timberline?"

"Are you trying to be funny? He's cowboy to the core, and was one of the first men hired by the Rocking H."

"Just asking. A man his size stands out in a crowd, too, and I don't have anything like him on any recent flyers. You mustn't think I'm just prying for fun, ma'am. It's my job to put all the cards out on the table for a look-see. I'd say what we have here is a lone gunman who hides good on the ridgelines, or somebody playing two-faced."

"Your killer has to be one of the men on your side, then. What was that you said about an attempted jailbreak?"

Longarm hesitated. Then he said, "I reckon it's all right to level with you, ma'am. That old French Canuck I rode in with wasn't. He made that fool play at the jailhouse door to get a look at the prisoner and maybe slip him a word or two. But he wasn't out to kill Cotton Younger. He was sent, or came here on his own, to set a kinsman free."

"And you saw through his scheme? You do know your job, don't you?"

"Well, it was the Mountie that made him for a fake Canuck. Who gunned him, or why, is still pure mystery. From the few words I got out of him before he died, he seems to have had a misunderstanding with someone, and I know it wasn't the man you have locked up; they never got to see each other."

"Oh, that must mean there's another member of his gang here in Crooked Lance! But why are you telling me all this? I thought you were cross with me and mine."

"I am, a mite. You see, ma'am, this notion you have of holding our prisoner for some sort of fool auction is getting serious. You folks in Crooked Lance are playing cards for high stakes with professionals, and—no offense intended—some of your cowhands could get hurt."

"You know our stand about the money, durn it."

"Yep, and it's getting tedious. You ain't a stupid woman, Miss Kim. You must know time is running out on you. Any day now, the army will send in a troop of cavalry to back Captain Walthers, or a team of federal officers will be coming to see what's keeping me. If I was you, I'd go with the Justice Department. One feller just made himself a modest bounty tonight, by cooperating with me."

"Could you give me something in writing, saying we were due the reward on Younger and his gang, whenever they're caught?"

"I could, ma'am, but it wouldn't be worth the paper it was written on. You see, Cotton Younger has to stand trial before it's legal to hang him, and there's always that outside chance some fool jury might set him free. The reward's for capture and *conviction*. As to Frank and Jesse James, us federals might make a deal with Younger and we might not. I could put in a good word for you if it was a federal man that caught them rascals, but there's others looking. So the James boys might get caught by other folks. They might get turned in for the reward by anybody. They might never be caught at all, since nobody's seen hide nor hair of either one for a good two years or more. You see how it is?"

She sighed and said, "At least you're likely more honest than some of the others. Sheriff Weed's promised us the moon, but he gets cagey every time I ask him to put it in writing."

"You're not likely to get anything on paper, and if you do, it won't be worth all that much. The position you've taken just won't wash, ma'am. The longer you hold that prisoner, the more riled at you his rightful owners are going to get."

She hesitated. Then, with a firmer tilt to her head, she said, "I have to think about it. You've got me mixed up, as you doubtless intended."

Longarm believed in riding with a gentle hand on the reins, so he tipped his hat and said, "I'll just let you sleep on it, then. Good night, ma'am. It's been nice talking to you."

They were waiting in the shadows as Longarm rode out to the main trail. He saw they weren't skulking, so he didn't draw as Timberline and another tall man fell in on either side of him as he left the redhead's property. Longarm nodded and said, "'Evening, Timberline."

"What was you pestering Miss Kim about, Longarm?"

"Wasn't pestering. Wasn't cutting in on you, either. As she'll likely tell you, it's no secret I was asking questions."

He turned to the other rider and asked, "Would you be Slim Wilson?" The youth didn't answer. Timberline said, "A stranger could get hurt, messing about my intended, mister."

"I gathered as much, but like I said, that ain't my play with the widow. I only want what's mine. That owlhoot you and she are holding in defiance of the law."

"Oh, hell, that pissant's caused more trouble than he's worth! If she'd just let us string the rascal up and have done with him, the valley could get back to its business, raising cows!"

"Why don't you just let me take him off your hands, then? We'd all ride out and you could be free to pick posies for your gal, Timberline."

"It's tempting, but she'd never talk to me again. You may have noticed Kim Stover is a stubborn woman, Longarm."

"I did. You really want to marry up with her?"

"Hell, yes, but she's stubborn about that, too. Says she has to know me better. Hell, I've known her half a dozen years already, but she's skittish as a colt about a second try." Timberline's voice dropped lower as he confided, "That Ben Stover she was married to was a mean-hearted little runt, just like his father over to the general store."

"I noticed his old woman and the gal look tuckered, some. Haven't had more'n two words with the storekeeper. Seems a moody cuss."

"He is. Beats both his wife and the girl. Ben Stover used to

whup Miss Kim when they first married up. That is, he did until me
and him had a friendly discussion on his manners."

"I take it you've always been right fond of Kim Stover."

"You take it right, pilgrim. And don't think I can't see that
you're a good-looking man, neither. You see where this friendly
talk is taking us?"

"Yep. We're almost to the store, too. Look, Timberline, I said
I ain't sparking the widow and I don't lie any more'n most gents.
I got enough on my plate, without fighting over women."

"All right, I'll let you off this time, boy."

Longarm's .44 was suddenly out and almost up Timberline's
nose as he reined in, blocking the bigger man's mount with his
own as he purred, "You did say *mister,* didn't you?" He saw the
one called Slim about to make a foolish move and quickly added,
"Stay out of this, Slim. You make me blow his face off and you
figure to be next, before you can clear leather!"

Timberline kept his free hand well clear of his holstered hog
leg as he gasped, "You hold the cards, Longarm! What in thunder's got into you?"

"I don't take kindly to being bullied and I don't like being
talked down to. You may have taken the simple truth as crawfish-
ing, but let's get one thing straight. I ain't been riding you, so I
don't mean to be rode. You got that loud and clear?"

"Mister, you have made your point, so point that thing somewheres else."

Longarm said, "*Mister* is all I was after," and lowered the Colt,
holding it down at his side as he added, "I reckon this is where we
say good night, don't you?"

Timberline nodded and said, "Yep, and I'll be parting friendly
for now, since I suspicion we understand one another."

Longarm sat his mount quietly as the other two swung around
and rode back toward Kim Stover's spread. He didn't know if
Timberline had been calling or just watching. It wasn't really his
business. The big ramrod and the stubborn redhead were welcome to one another.

But he couldn't help wondering, as he rode to the hotel, what
that sulky little spitfire would be like in bed.

Chapter 11

Longarm awoke in the pitch-black little room, aware that he was not alone. He pretended another snore as his right hand slid under the cornhusk pillow for his derringer. He'd left his room key there, too, this time. Wasn't it safe to sleep *anywhere*?

He flinched as cool fingers brushed his naked shoulder and a soft whisper sighed, "Oh, pretty! So pretty!"

"Mabel?"

"Hush! Oh, do be still! He'll hear us and he can be so cruel!"

Longarm felt the shabby blanket lift as a cool, nude body slid into bed with him. He moved over to make room on the narrow little cot as his mystery guest flattened small, firm breasts and a work-hardened, almost boyish body against his warmer flesh. As she buried his face in loose, fine hair and began to nibble his collarbone, Longarm folded her in his big arms and muttered, "Did you lock the door behind you, ma'am?"

She placed a palm over his mouth and hissed, "Yes! Oh, don't make a sound! His ears are sharp and his temper's not of this world!"

She waited until she saw he wasn't going to say anything, then slid the hand, moist from his lips, down the front of his body. All the way.

Longarm lay there, as puzzled as he was aroused as she took his penis in her hand and began to play with it, whispering, "Oh, so pretty. I want! I need!"

And then she'd forked a thigh over and was on him, riding him as if in the saddle, astride a trotting pony. Longarm tightened his buttocks and drove up to meet her as she ground her pubic bone against his, hissing like a pleasured cat with each movement. He ran his hands up and down her spine, noticing how the bones rode under her tight, smooth skin like those of a half-starved Arapaho camp dog. Then, wider awake and getting more interested, he got a firm grip on each of her small, lean buttocks and started helping her on the downstrokes. She was good, damned good, whoever she was, and she pleasured him the first time fast. As he gasped in enjoyment she kept going, sliding and moaning her own pleasure as the wetness seemed to add to it.

Longarm was still able to serve her, but the first flush had cleared his mind enough to wonder what in hell was going on. This hellcat rutting with him wasn't Mabel; she moved no way at all like this one. It couldn't be Kim Stover, could it? Nope, there was more *to* the redhead than this skinny little bundle of pure lust. That left . . . hell, *that* hardly seemed likely!

And then she shuddered, stiffened, and fell forward, kissing him full on the lips as she ran her tongue between them. It was old Stover's wife or daughter, sure enough. Both of them had buck teeth.

Longarm was a gentleman of the old school, so he didn't laugh. The poor, ugly little brute had done her best to please him, and in the dark, kissing her chinless little face wasn't all that bad. She nestled into him like a lost kitten, kissing him over and over as Longarm felt warm wetness on his cheek and knew she was crying.

He rolled her over to his side and cuddled her, kissing the tears from her eyelids gently as he petted her trembling, nude flanks, as if he were calming a spooked pony or a kicked dog. She buried her face in the hollow of his neck and whispered, "Oh, you're so nice. So very nice. I knowed it when first I seen you!"

Longarm frowned in the darkness, trying to see his way out of this mess. How was a gent supposed to deal with a lovesick critter like this? Good God! How was he going to explain it? He could already see the jeering looks of the others at the breakfast table. Both mother and daughter were ugly as sin, and come to think of it, which of the damn fool Stover women had he just laid?

Longarm started exploring her flesh gently with his free hand, looking for wrinkles, stretch marks, or some such sign. There wasn't a fold of loose skin clinging to her thin, muscular body. Her skin was smooth and nice to feel. He tried to picture the two worn-out looking women who'd served dinner. Both had been skinny and scared-looking. Scared little sparrows that never looked a man in the eye. He was hoping like hell it was the older one. She moved like a gal who knew the facts of life, and Jesus H. Christ, if it was the unwed daughter . . . !

The woman took his explorations to mean desire and responded with caresses of her own. She suddenly slid her hips from the cot and trailed her unbound hair down Longarm's belly, grabbing him again and kissing his semierect penis teasingly. Longarm sighed and let her give him a French lesson, for he was in as much trouble already as he was likely to be.

She got him back in the mood amazingly fast, considering her buck teeth and all, so Longarm pulled her up from where she was kneeling and climbed aboard to do it right. Her legs locked around him and she started wagging her tail like a happy puppy. It was a funny way for a gal to move herself, but it was pure heaven, and in the dark it was easy to forget what she looked like in broad daylight.

They made love, wildly and as silently as church mice, for perhaps a full hour. Then she suddenly leaped up, unlocked the door, and was gone without a word.

Longarm made sure the door was locked again, then sank back on the cot, puzzled. It wasn't as if he'd never had anything as good, but it hadn't been bad, considering. You never could tell, just by looking at a woman, could you?

He stretched out on the moist blanket, suddenly grinning as the old trail song sprang to mind.

> . . . I humped her standin' and humped her lying . . .
> If she'd had wings I'd have humped her flying!
> Come a ti-yi-yippee all the way, all the way,
> Come a ti-yi-yippee all the way!

Then he frowned and muttered, "It ain't funny, you damn fool stud! How in God's name are you ever gonna face that gal at breakfast, and more important, which of them Stover women was it?"

Breakfast came like death and taxes and there was no way to get out of biting the bullet. So, although he took his time getting dressed, Longarm finally went in to join the others around the plank table, braced for damned near anything.

All but the railroad detective were there ahead of him, of course. One of the Stover women came out of the kitchen and put a tin plate of buckwheat cakes in front of him without comment. Longarm watched her back, saw the gray in her tied-up hair, and decided it couldn't have been the mother.

The midget, Cedric Hanks, called down the table, "Where's that dick, working for the railroad? Anybody seen him this morning?"

Longarm broke into the puzzled murmurings to announce, "I sent him to Bitter Creek. Don't seem likely he'll be back."

The Mountie smiled thinly and asked, "So you've eliminated one of us? How do you propose to get rid of me, Longarm?"

"Don't know. Still thinking about it."

Captain Walthers said, "I warn you, Deputy, you'll have the War Department to answer to if you try to . . . whatever you did to that other man!"

"Don't get spooked, Captain. I didn't use nothing but sweet reason on him. It ain't my way to threaten. Ain't my way to brag, neither. Speaking of which, is there any chance some of your friends at the War Department might be sending in a squadron or so of cavalry? I just counted heads across the street. There's a good two dozen cowhands and such loafing around the log jail. Don't know if they're fixing to lynch the prisoner, run us out of town, or both."

Sheriff Weed said, "I moseyed over to jaw with that Timberline just now. They seem more cautious than unruly. Timberline says since you rode in, some of the Vigilance Committee's getting anxious."

"Could be. Timberline tried to crawfish me last night."

"Do tell? What happened?"

"I didn't crawfish worth mention. He's likely surprised to meet up with somebody who ain't afraid of him."

Weed laughed and agreed, "That's the trouble with growing as big as a moose. Most fellers leave their brains behind once they top six feet. Get used to having their own way without the effort the rest of us have to put out. You been following that trouble they've been having down in New Mexico Territory, Longarm?"

"Lincoln County War? Last I heard, it was over. New governor cleaned out both factions' friends in high places and appointed new lawmen. What's Lincoln County to do with hereabouts?"

"Just thinking about a matter of size they got mixed up on down there. You ever hear of Kid Antrim?"

"Billy the Kid? Sure, he's called Kid Antrim, Billy Bonney, Henry McCarthy, and God knows. There's a federal warrant on him for killing an Indian agent, but other deputies are looking for him. I take it you don't know where Kid Antrim's hiding, these days?"

"No, I was talking about his size. Kid Antrim can't be more'n five foot four, and he's killed more men than men like Timberline ever even have to punch. You see my point?"

"Saw it long before you took us all over the Southwest Territories to say it. When folks crowd me, I just crowd back. I didn't have to spin no yarns to Timberline. I suspicion we've got it straight, about now."

The daughter came in from the kitchen with a fresh pot of coffee and placed it on the table, looking neither at Longarm nor at the others as she scooted out again. Weed said, "Ain't they something? Act like they expected one of us to grab 'em and run off to the South Seas or a Turkish harem with 'em."

"Mountain folks are bashful," Longarm said, feeling much better.

The storekeeper, Stover, came in to glare down at everyone and ask, "Is everything to your pleasure, gents? Excuse me— *lady* and gents?"

Mabel Hanks dimpled prettily and said, "My husband and I were just admiring your cutlery. Wherever did you get such a splendid service? It's so—so unusual."

Stover said, "It's odd stock from a bankrupt mail-order house, mostly, ma'am. I reckon some of it's all right. We don't stint on guests in Crooked Lance."

Stover saw there were no complaints forthcoming, so he went back to tend his other enterprises as Captain Walthers smiled at Mabel knowingly. The army man was wrapped about her finger, right enough. But how was a U.S. marshal to use that? Longarm knew the woman could be bought, but the captain didn't look like a man who would desert in the middle of a mission.

After breakfast they all filed out back to walk by the creek or sit on the veranda, waiting for something, anything, to break the deadlock, as what promised to be another tedious day settled in.

Longarm managed to get the army man aside as the latter was checking out his own big walking horse in the livery. Longarm watched Walthers clean the walker's frogs with a pointed stick for a time before he cleared his throat and asked, "Would you be willing to take a federal prisoner back to Bitter Creek for me, seeing as we're both federal officers?"

"You mean Cotton Younger? Of course, but how are we to get him away from those crazy cowboys across the way?"

"Wasn't talking about him. As I see it, we're stuck in this bind with the vigilantes till somebody sends help or they come to their senses. I'd say that could take at least a week. Meanwhile, I'm figuring to make an arrest. I mean, *another* arrest."

"Oh? You mean you've identified someone here in Crooked Lance as a wanted man?"

"Ain't rightly sure just *what* he's up to, but I got a charge that will stick, if I could get him before a judge."

"I see. And you think I'd be fool enough to transport him back to civilization, leaving you with one less of us to contend with?"

"Hell, you're not about to get Cotton Younger. Why not take in at least *some* damn prisoner and let me share the credit with you?"

"Longarm, you really should have gone into the snake-oil business! Are you telling me any truth at all? I'll bite. Who's our suspect, and when are you going to arrest him?"

"Pretty soon. Are you aiming to help?"

"Help you arrest a man on a federal charge, certainly. Transport him out of here for you? Never!"

"Well, it was worth a try. Make sure you get that hind shoe. It looks like your walker's picked up a stone."

As he stepped outside, Walthers followed. "Not so fast. I'd like to know what you're up to."

"Since you ain't helping, it ain't your nevermind, Captain."

"You intend to take him alone?"

"Generally do. We'll talk about it after."

Leaving the army man watching, bemused, Longarm hunted down the Mountie and repeated his request. The Canadian lawman's response wasn't much different. He was willing to back a fellow officer's arrest, but he had no intention of leaving Crooked

Lance without Cotton Younger. Longarm decided he'd never met such stubborn types.

He strolled back to the veranda and hunkered down, sitting on the edge, as he pondered his next move. He knew he didn't intend to ride out with any prisoner but the one they'd sent him for. On the other hand, he couldn't just let his intended victim run free much longer. The man was dangerous, and Longarm had no idea what his play was. You eat an apple a bite at a time, and the prisoner in the jail would likely keep for now.

He saw that the midget detective and his wife were over by the stream. Cedric, for some reason, was skipping rocks across the water. Likely it came from pretending to be a little boy most places they went.

Sheriff Weed was seated in a barrel chair down at the far end, smoking a cigar and digesting his cast-iron buckwheats. Longarm half turned, still seated, and said, "I've been going over what you said about Kid Antrim, Weed."

"Do tell? Thought you said you wasn't after him right now."

"Ain't. I've been counting strikes. I'd say knowing one of Billy the Kid's less written-up handles makes it strike three. You mind telling me who the hell you are?"

Weed suddenly rose from the chair, frowning through a cloud of tobacco smoke as he asked, "Strike *what*? What in tarnation's got into you? I told you I was Sheriff Weed of Clay County, Missouri!"

"That was strike one. I didn't see why a county sheriff would ride all the way out here in person, 'stead of sending a deputy, in an election year. But, like I said, that was just strike one. You coulda been a *dumb* sheriff from Missouri."

"I don't like being called dumb, but have your full say, son."

"All right. Last afternoon, over by the jailhouse, you called Chambrum du Val an *hombre*. That was strike two, Weed. Folks from Missouri don't call men hombres. That's Southwest talk. Maybe Texas or New Mexico. But, what the hell, you could have picked it up from Ned Buntline's magazine or somebody you rode with one time, and anyway, you don't call a man out on two strikes, so I waited till you let that slip about the Lincoln County War, down in the Southwest—"

The man calling himself Sheriff Weed went for the S&W at his side. He didn't make it. Longarm fired, sitting, with the derringer he'd been holding in his lap, then dove headfirst and rolled across the grass, whipping out his sixgun as he bounded to his feet, dancing sideways as he trained it at the end of the veranda.

Then he stopped and lowered the unfired .44, knowing he didn't have to use it now. The man called Weed was spread-eagled in the dust beyond the end of the planks, his heels up on the veranda with his hat between them. As Longarm moved over to stare soberly down at the glazed eyes staring sightlessly up at him, he was joined by the other two lawmen and the odd detective team.

Captain Walthers gasped, "My God! Did you have to kill him?" and the Mountie shouted, "You can't be serious! I know that man! He's the sheriff of Clay County, Missouri!"

Longarm shook his head and said, "Not hardly. Maybe something on him or in his possibles can tell us who he really was."

As Longarm knelt to go through the dead man's pockets, a bunch of local cowhands and Kim Stover ran around the corner of the building. The storekeeper himself came out cursing, but with neither his wife nor his daughter in evidence.

At the same time, Timberline rounded the cluster of buildings on the far side, gun in hand. He slowed down as he took in what had happened and approached the crowd around Longarm saying, "What did he do, Longarm? Call you a *boy*?"

Captain Walthers said, "Longarm, I hope you had a federal charge against that man. As the senior federal officer here—"

"Oh, don't tell us all you're dumb, Captain. Let us figure some things out for ourselves. Of course I had a charge. It's a federal offense to impersonate an elected official, which a sheriff is. This badge he had pinned on his vest says 'Sheriff,' but it don't say what county, Clay or otherwise. Man can pick a toy badge up in most any pawnshop. He's got nothing with a name on it in his wallet. What's this?"

Longarm unfolded a sheet of stiff paper he'd taken from the dead man's breast pocket and spread it on Weed's chest. Kim Stover gasped and said, "Oh, dear, it's got blood on it."

"Yes, ma'am. Bullet went through it. It's a telegram, federal flyer sent to every law office worth mention a week or more ago. This particular one's addressed to the Territory of New Mexico, Santa Fe. Likely where this feller stole it."

Walthers blustered, "Damn it, man, what does it say?"

"What we all know. That Cotton Younger's been picked up as a cow thief, here in Crooked Lance."

"But if he intercepted it in Santa Fe . . . what do you make of Weed, a bounty hunter?"

"That's a likely guess. Since Lew Wallace cleaned up New Mexico, the territory's filled with unemployed guns. From the way he spoke at the breakfast table, I'd say he rode with one side or the other in the Lincoln County War and has been looking for a new job. He heard about the folks here holding Cotton Younger, heard about the herd of rewards it might lead to, and was playing Foxy Grandpa. He did make you the best offer for your prisoner, didn't he, Miss Kim?"

The redhead grimaced, not looking at the body, as she nodded and turned away. Longarm decided to push her further off balance by observing brutally, "Yep, no telling how many bounty hunters we'll have riding up here before long. Might even have the James and Younger Gang paying us a visit, as word of your hospitality gets around. You folks might as well know, one of Cotton Younger's old sidekicks has already come and gone."

Timberline blinked and said, "The hell you say. Who *was* the varmint?"

The midget, Cedric, chortled, "The railroad dick! I knew it!"

Longarm shook his head and continued searching the corpse. "Nope. He's taking Sailor Brown in for me. The Mountie, here, gets credit for unmasking him. He was that old-timer pretending to be a Canuck."

Timberline asked, "Who shot him, you or the feller working for the railroad?"

"Don't know who shot him. I suspicion it was the same one that shot Deputy Kincaid, the man from my outfit who never got here. Kincaid was from Missouri, so he might have known members of the James-Younger Gang on sight. I suspicion that's why he was kept from getting here. Though, now that I think on it, my own reception in Bitter Creek wasn't all that friendly."

Timberline said, "Hot damn! I see it all, now! This feller you just gunned down was pretending to be a Missouri sheriff! Don't that mean—"

"Slow down. It don't mean more than another cud to chew, Timberline. Weed, here, couldn't have shot the old man. Anybody could have done whatever to my partner, Kincaid. This situation's getting more wheels within wheels than an eight-day clock."

He found a pocket watch with an inscription and read, " 'To

'Alexander McSween on his fifth wedding anniversary.' Looks like real silver, too."

"You reckon that was the jasper's real name, Longarm?"

"Not hardly. Alexander McSween was on the losing side of the Lincoln County War. They gunned him down with his wife watching, a couple of summers ago. I'd say this bounty hunter was one of them that did the gunning. No wonder he was so interested in Kid Antrim. The Kid rode for McSween. He made a bad slip by calling Billy the Kid *Antrim* instead of *Bonney*. Nobody aside from a few federal officers knows that name, outside Lincoln County."

Kim Stover's face was pale as she asked, "Do you think there's a chance Billy the Kid could be headed this way, Mister Long?"

Longarm considered nodding, but thought honesty was perhaps the best policy when a lie might sound foolish. He shook his head and said, "Doubt it. Kid Antrim's likely in Mexico, if he's got a lick of sense. He's a gunslick, not a bounty hunter. No way a wanted man could collect a reward. Unless, like this jasper, he figured to dress up like a lawman."

He saw her relieved look and quickly shot it down by repeating, "All we have to worry about is Frank and Jesse James and company."

Someone asked about the disposal of the remains and Stover quickly said, "I'll bury him right decent for ten dollars. I figure there's at least ten dollars on him, ain't there, Deputy Long?"

Longarm made a wry face and got to his feet, brushing off his knee as he said, "You'll likely want two bits from him for breakfast, too."

Stover nodded, pleased to see the big lawman was so agreeable, and oblivious of the disgusted looks others were casting his way.

Longarm said, "I'd best see if he had anything in his room," and walked to the doorway, leaving the others to work out the funeral details as they saw fit. He saw that the Mountie was right behind him, but didn't comment on it until the two of them were alone in the dead man's room. As Longarm spread the contents of "Weed's" saddlebags on the bed, the Mountie said, "That was smoothly done, Longarm."

"Oh, it only made sense to have the drop on him before I told him he was under arrest."

"Come now, I've made a few arrests myself. You know you could have taken him alive."

"You don't say?"

"I do say. You tricked him into slapping leather because you had no intention of having to take him in, without the man you came for."

"I heard you Mounties were tolerable good. You likely know this job calls for considering things from all sides before you move. It didn't pleasure me to trick that fool out there into making things simple, but I couldn't leave him running loose."

"I know what you did and why you did it. I know you got rid of the railroad detective rather neatly, too. I think it's time we got something straight between us, Longarm."

"I'm listening."

"My organization's not as old as your Texas Rangers, but we operate in much the same way."

"I know. You always get your man. I read that somewhere. Don't you reckon that's a mite boastful?"

"No, I don't. I have every intention of taking that prisoner, Cotton Younger, before Her Majesty's Bar of Justice, and I'll kill anyone who tries to stop me!"

"You talking about me or them vigilantes all around outside?"

"Both. I've had just about enough of their nonsense and I'm not too happy about the way you've been trying to whittle your opposition down to size. I warn you, if you make any attempt to run *me* out—"

"Hey, look here, he's got a copy of this month's *Cap'n Billy's Whiz-Bang*. It's pretty humorous. You oughta read it sometime. Do wonders for your disposition. Nobody's aiming to run you out, old son. I didn't run the old man or the railroad dick out of Crooked Lance, and I shot that other feller fair and square. What's eating you? You are a real Mountie, ain't you?"

"You want to see my credentials?"

"Nope. My boss told me to expect a Mountie here, and I doubt anyone else would want to wear that red coat." Longarm's eyes narrowed thoughtfully.

The Mountie asked, "What's wrong? You look like you just thought of something new."

"I did. I'm starting to feel better about that feller I just shot. There *was* somebody from the Clay County sheriff's office coming out here. That bounty hunter must have waylaid him! Somewhere in the mountains there's at least two lawmen buried!"

The Mountie put a hand in his tunic and took out a leather billfold, saying, "I insist you read my Sergeant's Warrant. You'll note it gives my description in addition to my name."

Longarm scanned it and said, "You're likely Sergeant Foster, right enough."

"William DeVerrier Foster of the Royal Canadian Northwest Mounted Police, to be exact. May I see *your* identification?"

Longarm grinned and took out his own billfold, showing his badge and his official papers to the other. The Mountie nodded and asked, "Have you checked Captain Walthers's credentials?"

"Didn't have to. I asked him a few trick questions since we met. Besides, who but an army man would be after a deserter? You got a point. Maybe you *do* get your man, most times."

"Do I have your assurance you'll not try to get rid of me as you did the others?"

Longarm nodded and said, "You got my word I won't shoot you or try to buy you off with reward money."

He'd already decided there had to be some other way.

Chapter 12

Longarm didn't ask Captain Walthers to show his ID. He knew the Mountie would, and it was just as well they didn't get to be friends.

By noon the dead man had been buried, amid considerable whooping and shooting off of cowpokes' guns. One could get the impression that folks in Crooked Lance didn't get many occasions for a celebration. Longarm didn't attend the funeral. He was not a friend of the deceased and it seemed an opportunity to have a word with the prisoner.

It wasn't. A pair of hard-looking men with rifles stood by the log jail and when Longarm said he wanted to talk to Cotton Younger they told him it would be over their dead bodies.

He considered this for a moment, and decided it wasn't his best move.

As he walked over to the general store, Cedric fell in step at his side, taking three strides to each of Longarm's as he puffed his big cigar and piped, "We're gonna have to make our play damned sudden, Longarm. Cotton Younger don't figure to keep much longer."

"How'd it get to be *our* play, and what are you talking about, Cedric?"

"There's advantages to being a detective knee-high-to-a-grasshopper, big man. Us little fellers can get into places most folks don't consider."

"You been listening to folks from under your wet rock?"

"That's close enough. Want to know what the talk in town is, now?"

"Maybe. What's making you so friendly all of a sudden?"

"I don't like you, either. Never have liked you, even before you had your way with my woman, but I don't play this game for likes or don't likes. I'm in it for cash. You want to trade more insults, or do we work together?"

"Depends on what we're talking about, Cedric. Suppose you start with something I don't know."

"They're fixing to lynch Cotton Younger."

"What? That don't make a lick of sense, dammit!"

"You met anybody in this one-horse town with a degree from Harvard yet? I overheard some of Timberline's hands talking about a necktie party. You see, the redhead, Kim Stover, is the brains behind the scheme to build up Crooked Lance with the proceeds of . . . whatever. When I say 'brains,' I ain't saying much, for as me and Mabel see it, the game is as good as up. Ain't nobody here in town fixing to get paid a thing but trouble."

"That's what we've all been telling 'em."

"I know, and everyone but that stubborn widow woman can see it."

"Then why don't Timberline turn the prisoner over and have done with the mess?"

"He can't. He's in love with the redhead and she'd never speak to him again if he double-crossed her like that."

"All right, so how else does he figure to double-cross her?"

"Like I just told you, with a sudden necktie party! He won't be taking part in it, of course. His plan is to be over at the redhead's, trying to steal a kiss or better, when all of a sudden, out of the night—"

"I got you. 'Some of the boys got drunk and riled up about that running iron, Miss Kim, and I'm pure sorry as all hell about the way his neck got all stretched out of shape like that.' "

"That's one thing they're considering. Another is having him get shot trying to escape. Either way, it figures to happen soon."

"They say anything about me and the other lawmen?"

"Sure. They don't figure three big men and a dwarf can stop

'em. I reckon you're the one they're calling a dwarf. Timberline told 'em not to shoot none of us, 'less we try to stop the fun."

Longarm stopped at the storefront and leaned against a post as the midget put a tiny boot up on the planks to wait for his next words.

Longarm mused, half-aloud, "The Mountie would fight for sure and go down shooting. Walthers might try, and get hurt . . ."

"You and me know better, right?"

"Against at least fifty armed drunks? You're sure you got it right, though? Timberline's got the odds right, but there ain't much that can be said about his thinking. Hell, he doesn't have to kill the prisoner. They could just let him go with an hour's head start and you, me, the others would be hightailing it out of the valley after him. They'd never see any of us again and Timberline could go back to courting his widow woman. Maybe consoling her on their mutual misfortune."

"I never said he was bright. I only told you what he planned."

"You reckon he might see it, if it was pointed out to him?"

"He might. Then again, knowing his play was uncovered, he might make his move more sudden. There's over fifty men in and around town this very moment."

"I get the picture. When were they planning to murder the poor jasper?"

"Late tonight. The redhead's gone home in a huff, saying the way ever'body's drinking and carrying on over the funeral is disgusting, which I'll allow it is. Timberline figures to ride over to her spread, maybe playing his guitar or something as stupid, just so he's not there when they string the boy up. Later, of course, nobody will remember just who done the stringing, the rest of us will likely ride off, and . . ."

"All right, what's your plan, Cedric?"

"We in this together? You'll split us in?"

"Cedric, I'm tempted as hell to lie to you, considering the choices I got, but you're too smart to think I can divide a reward I'm not allowed to accept."

"Hell, who cares about the paper on that pissant, Cotton Younger? It's *Jesse James* that me and Mabel's out to collect on! He knows where the James boys are!"

"You figure I'd let you get it out of him, Apache style?"

"Don't have to. Already made the deal. Like I said, us little folks can get into the damndest nooks and crannies."

"You talked to the prisoner in the jail?"

"Sure. Got under the floor last night and we jawed awhile through a knothole. He don't like the idea of getting lynched all that much, so I convinced him his only way out of it was to make a deal. His life in exchange for the present address of Frank or Jesse. He says he don't know where Frank is, but that he knows how to get to Jesse. Half a loaf is better than none, I always say."

"Where'd he say Cousin Jesse was?"

"He didn't. Said he'd tell us once he was clear of Crooked Lance and crazy cowboys with ropes. You think I'd bother to spring the rascal if I knew?"

Longarm took out a cheroot and lit it, running the conversation through his mind again to see where the yarn didn't hold together. He knew the little bounty hunter would lie when it was in his favor, but what he said made sense. Longarm nodded and said, "All right, we get him out right after sundown and make a run for it. You'd better head out early with Mabel and your buckboard. I'll join you at the first pass and we'll hole up somewhere. You'll get your talk with Cotton Younger and then we split up. They'll probably come boiling up out of this valley like hornets when they find him gone, but you and your woman will be riding into Bitter Creek innocent, and I know my way around in the woods at night."

"Was you born that stupid or did a cow step on your head, Longarm?"

"You know a better way?"

"Of course. I got a key to the jailhouse, dammit!"

"You stole Pop Wade's key? How come he ain't missed it yet?"

"Because I never stole it, big brain! I had Mabel jaw with the guards whilst I took a beeswax impression, standing damn near under Pop as he stared down the front of Mabel's dress. I got some tools in my valise, and once I had the impression—"

"I know how you make a duplicate key, dammit. I'll allow it makes it a mite easier, but not much. We still got to get you and your woman out safe while I bang the guards' heads together some."

"Mabel's going to take care of the guards for us."

"Both of 'em at once?"

"Don't be nasty, dammit. Part of *their* play is to keep the drinking and whooping going on all afternoon and long past sundown. Mabel's gonna mosey over, sort of drunklike, with a bottle. If you meet her and she offers you a drink, don't take it. Mabel's still pissed off at you for the way you spoke to her in Bitter Creek."

"So she gives them knockout drops, we unlock the door and slip the prisoner out quiet, leaving the necktie party to discover things ain't as they seem, long after the four of us are gone. Yep, it's a good plan."

"We'd best split up and meet later, then. Part of our plan is that you and me ain't been all that friendly. I'll give you the high sign after supper and we'll move in around . . . when, nine o'clock?"

"Sounds about right. Summer sun'll be down about eight. Gives us an hour of dark to spring the prisoner, maybe two, three 'fore they come for him and all hell breaks loose. I'll see you at supper, Cedric. My regards to the missus."

"You fun like that in front of Mabel and it can cost you, Longarm. I'm used to being hoorahed. Used to having a woman with round heels, too. But she can be a caution when she's riled at you, and you've riled her enough already, hear?"

Longarm looked down at the little man, catching the hurt in his eyes before he hid it behind his big cigar. Longarm said, "What I said was said without thinking and without double-meaning, Mister Hanks. Whatever you and your woman have between you ain't my business and I'd take it neighborly if we could forget what happened the other night in Bitter Creek. What I done, I done because I was a man and a man takes what's offered. Had I known she was your wife, I wouldn't have. Now that I know she is, I never aim to again."

"Jesus, Longarm, are you *apologizing* to me?"

"I am, if you think you got one coming."

The midget suddenly seemed to choke on his cigar, grinned, and held out a little hand, saying, "By God, *pardner*! Put 'er there!"

Chapter 13

Supper took what seemed a million years, complicated by the terrible cooking of the Stover women and the fact that one of them, at least, was probably planning to crawl into bed with him as soon as she dared. Longarm watched both the mother and daughter for some sign, but neither one met his gaze, and he felt less guilty about what had happened. He'd likely never know which of them it had been, but whichever, she was not only a great lay but damned good at her little game. He wondered how many other times it had happened, and how, if it was the daughter, she kept from getting in a family way. He'd decided she must know about such matters. But, try as he would, he couldn't puzzle out her identity. They both had the same lean figures and onion heads. The one he'd been with had been experienced as hell, but that didn't prove it was the mother. The daughter was no spring chicken, either, and if she'd done it before, she'd had more practice than most spinsters who looked like poor plain sparrows. He hoped she'd know how to take care of herself, though, because anything he'd fathered with either one figured to be one ugly little bastard!

There was little table conversation as, outside, from time to time, a gun went off or some cowhands tore by at a dead run, whooping like Indians. Neither the midget nor his wife looked up when Captain Walthers sighed and asked, "How long do you imagine they'll carry on like that? You'd think they'd never had a funeral here before!"

Longarm waited until Cedric excused himself from the table and made as if to go outside to answer a call of nature. Longarm followed at a discreet distance, and on the veranda, Cedric slipped him the key, saying, "Mind you wait for Mabel to get them ass-over-teakettle. I'll move the buckboard out along the trail a mile or so and wait. Mabel gives 'em the bottle and lights out to join me. Give 'em fifteen minutes to pass out before you do anything dumb. You figure on running for it or riding him out?"

"I'll play my tune by ear. Might be riding double, 'less I can steal a mount for Younger."

"All right. You won't see us. We'll be hid. I'll watch the trail and whistle you in. See you . . . when? Nine-fifteen?"

"Give us till nine-thirty before you know I failed. If we don't make it, you and the lady just come back from your ride as if nothing happened. I might need help or I might be dead. I'll expect you to do what you have to, either way."

"I told Mabel you apologized. She says she ain't mad at you no more."

Longarm left the midget and went to his room. He gathered his possessions and threw them out the window to the narrow space between the hotel and the livery shed. Then he locked the door from the inside, climbed out the window, and picked up his belongings before moving quietly to the horses.

His bay nickered a greeting and Longarm put a hand over its muzzle to quiet it. He saddled and bridled the bay and was about to lead it out when something whispering endearments plastered itself against him. He steadied the thin woman in his arms and whispered, "I'm going out for a little ride, honey. Meet me later in my room."

"Just once! Just do it once right now. I want! I need!"

"Honey, the whole damn place is up and about! Have you gone crazy?"

"Yes, crazy for your pretty thing inside me! Please, darling, I have to have it or I'll scream!"

Longarm considered knocking her out, but it didn't seem too gallant and, besides, he couldn't see her tiny jaw to hit it. She was fumbling at his fly, now, whimpering like a bitch in heat. He could feel that she wore nothing under the thin cotton dress. He could tell she was going out of her fool head, too!

Muttering, he led her into a stall and pressed her against the rough boards, letting her fish his half-erect penis from his fly as he loved her up and kissed her to shut her fool mouth. He had to brace his hands against the planks, but she was equal to the occasion, lifting her hem with one hand as she played with him with the other.

He was a tall man and she was short and standing up could be the hard way but she must have done it this way before, too, for she raised one leg, caught him around the waist with amazing skill, and literally lifted herself into position, throwing the other leg around him as he slid into her amazingly positioned hungry moistness.

"Keerist!" He marveled as she settled her lean thighs on his hip bones. She moaned with lust as she gyrated wildly with her tailbone against the rough planks. Longarm moved his feet back, swore when he felt he'd stepped on a horse turd, and started pounding as hard as he dared without knocking down the flimsy stall. He managed to satisfy both of them, for the moment, and as she slid to her knees to talk French, he managed to get her to her unsteady feet and moving in the right direction by soothing, "Later, in my room. We'll do it undressed and I'll lick you to death besides!"

She scampered away in the dark with a knowing chuckle as Longarm got his breath back and wondered how much time he'd lost.

He led the bay out, tethered it at a safe distance, and came back. He worked mostly by feel as he saddled the captain's walking horse with Walthers's own army saddle, bridled it with the first headgear he found, and led it out behind him, soothing the nervous walker with honeyed words. He recovered his own mount and led both over to the creek, where he led them across and tethered them to a willow.

Then he splashed back, crossed the inky darkness of the Stover grounds, and after a long, cautious look-see, scooted across the road. He worked his way through the shadows to the back of the log jail. The chinked corner logs afforded an easy climb to the almost-flat roof. Longarm crept across the roof until he could peer over at the two guards by the front door. Then he settled down to listen.

It took forever before one of the guards asked, "Any sign of him?"

"It's too early, Slim. The gal said he'd be coming about nine."

"We're supposed to be knocked out, ain't we? What say we sort of scootch down?"

"*You* scootch down, dammit. We got more'n an hour to kill 'fore he comes over from the hotel."

"I wish we had a man inside. That big bastard's faster'n spit on a stove with that .44 of his, and I ain't never gunned nobody before."

"Don't worry, I have. He won't have a chance. I'll just blast him with both barrels of number-nine buck as he bends over to see if I'm sleepin' sound."

Longarm decided he'd heard as much as he needed to. So he gathered his legs under him, dropped off the roof, and materialized before their startled eyes, pistol-whipping the one with the shotgun into unconsciousness as he warned the other quietly, "You say *shit*, and you're *dead.*"

The frightened guard didn't do anything but drop his Henry rifle to the earth without a word. Longarm knew that the key the midget had slipped him was probably worthless, so he said, "Open her up."

"I don't have a key, mister."

"Are you funning with me, boy?"

"Honest to Gawd! Pop Wade has the key, not us!"

"Is Younger inside?"

"Yes, but—" And that was all he had to say about it as Longarm knocked him out, slid him down the logs to rest by his partner, and went to work on the door.

One blade of Longarm's jacknife would have gotten him arrested if he'd been searched by a lawman while not carrying a badge. The cheap, rusty lock was no trouble for his pick. He opened the door silently and went in, squinting in the darkness as he called out quietly, "Younger, you just keep still and don't say a word till I tell you to."

"What's going on?"

"That was *three* words, you son of a bitch. Say one more and I'll feed your heart to the hawks!"

There was no further comment from the improvised cell as Longarm picked the lock. He told the prisoner to come out, locked his wrists behind him with handcuffs, and taking the youth by the elbow, said, "You come this way and make sure it's silent as well as sudden." The prisoner tripped over one of the unconscious guards and gasped, "Who done that?"

"I did. Shut up and stand right there while I roll 'em inside and lock the door. All that idle chatter of yours is making me testy as hell!"

It only took half a minute to shove the guards inside and lock the door a second time. He grabbed Younger's elbow again and led him at a trot across the road, through the Stovers' grounds, and across the creek. He boosted the prisoner up into his own saddle, knowing his own bay would be predictable on the lead. Then he climbed aboard Captain Walthers's walker and led out at a brisk pace as the prisoner yelped, "Jesus! I can't ride like this! There's a big slit in this saddle an' my balls is caught in it!"

"You just hush and do the best you can, boy. My orders are to bring you in dead or alive. You yell one more time and I don't have to tell you which it'll be."

The prisoner fell silent, or tried to, as Longarm followed the trail he'd followed du Val—or Brown—along, by memory. He managed to miss riding through a tree, but the branches whipped both of them in the dark as Longarm set as fast a pace as he dared to in the dark. Once the prisoner announced, apologetically, that he was about to fall off.

Longarm said, "You fall and I'll kill you," and the boy's horse-manship seemed to improve miraculously.

Longarm led his charge to the clearing he remembered and beyond, guiding himself by the stars as he glimpsed them through the overhead branches. They weren't on any trail he knew of. The riders from the valley would know every trail for a good two days' ride from Crooked Lance. They rode through timber and they rode through brush. A couple of times they almost rode over cliffs, but Longarm trusted his mount to see by starlight well enough to avoid obvious suicide, given a gentle hand on the reins and not pressed faster than its night vision could cope with. As they topped a rise high above the valley, Longarm reined in and looked back and down. They were too far away to hear more than an occasional rallying shot, but little lights were buzzing back and forth on the valley floor. Longarm chuckled and said, "They've missed us. But there's no way to even try to read our sign before sunup, so we'll rest the critters here for a minute and be on our way."

The prisoner decided it was safe to speak and asked, "What in thunder is going on?"

"I'm not sure. Couple of folks was setting me up to get killed. Before that, they told me plans were afoot to do the same for you. Could have been true. Could have been another lie. As you see, it don't make no nevermind, now."

"You're the federal man called Longarm, ain't you? Jesus, am I ever glad to see you! You see, it's all a misunderstanding, so you can take these irons off me, now."

"That'll be the day, boy. You're wearing them cuffs till I have you safe in federal custody, which just might take a while. I'll help you when you have to eat or take a leak. You ain't the first man I've rode like this with, Younger."

"God damn it, my name is Jones!"

"Whatever. Like I said, that ain't my job. I was sent to transport you back to Denver, and since both of our critters are still breathing, we'd best be on our way. Hold on to the cantle with your fingers if that McClellan's not your style. Didn't you ride a McClellan when you were with Terry on the Rosebud, a few years back?"

"I don't know what you're talking about. I never deserted from no army!"

"Now, did I say anything about desertion? You stick to any yarn you aim to."

"It ain't no yarn, God damn it! You got the wrong man!"

"Well, if I find out I have, once we get you before a judge in Denver, I'll apologize like a gent to you. Meanwhile, Jones, James, Younger, or whomsoever, that's where you and me are headed, come hell, high water, or a full Sioux uprising!"

Chapter 14

Longarm was tough. Ten times tougher than the good Lord made most men, but his prisoner was only human, and the horses were only horses.

By sunup, he could see he was running all three into the ground and reined to a halt in a tangle of bigleaf maple. He helped his prisoner down and Cotton Younger simply fell to the damp leaves and closed his eyes, falling asleep on his side with his raw, chained wrists behind him. Longarm removed the bits from the animals' pink-foamed mouths after hobbling each with a length of latigo leather. He didn't think either one was in condition to walk away, let alone run, but a front hoof lashed to a hind would discourage them from bolting, should they get their wind back before he was ready to move on.

He'd watered both mounts an hour before dawn at a chance rill of snowmelt, so they were happy to drop their heads and graze the hurt from their muzzles in the sweet-scented orchard grass and wild onion growing in the dappled shade. He unsaddled both, spread the saddle blankets over tree limbs for the wind to dry, then found a patch of sunlight where he placed the saddles bottoms-up. Some said it wasn't good for the sweat-soaked leather, but Longarm had heard that those little bugs Professor Pasteur was writing

about over in France weren't partial to sun baths. He'd risk a
cracked saddle skirt against a festered saddle sore any day. He'd
started this play by riding out with the two best mounts he knew of
in Crooked Lance. He was depending on keeping them that way.

Captain Walthers's tall mount, after eating a few bites of
greenery, was already leaning against a tree trunk, head down and
eyes closed. The army man hadn't fed it enough oats for its size,
most likely. The older army bay he'd borrowed from the remount
section he had picked because he looked like a tough one, and he
seemed to be living up to Longarm's hopes. He was nearly worn
out, but still stuffing his gut like the wise old cuss he was. There
was no telling when they'd be taking a break in such good graz-
ery again.

Longarm considered the wild onion and other herbage as he
rubbed both mounts down with Captain Walthers's spare cotton
drawers from the saddlebags the fool had left attached. Here in the
shade it was choice and green, but hardly touched, except for an
occasional rabbit nibble. Longarm saw the healed-over trunk
scars where a long-dead elk had rubbed the velvet from his antlers
on a good day to fight for love. Once, a grizzly had sharpened his
claws on a tree beyond. The sign was fresher. Maybe from early
that spring. Longarm patted his mount's rump and said, "Yep,
we're on virgin range, old-timer. Don't know just where in hell it
is, but nobody's run cows through here in living memory."

Leaving all three of his charges for the moment, Longarm circled through the shapeless mass of timber, fixing its layout in his
mind for possible emergencies. He came to an outcropping of
granite, studied it, and decided it would be a waste of time to climb
up for a look-see. Even if the top rose above the surrounding treetops, which it didn't, there'd be nothing to see worth mentioning.
The land was flattening out as they approached the south-pass
country. If a posse from Crooked Lance had found their trail yet, it
would be too far back to be visible on gently rolling timberland.
Longarm went back to the sleeping prisoner, grabbed him by the
heels, and dragged him over to the outcropping, as he half-awoke,
complaining, "What the hell?"

"Ain't smart to bed down next to the critters," Longarm explained, adding, "Horses nicker to one another at a distance. I figure that if ours get to calling back and forth with others skulking
in on us . . . never mind. If you knew a damn thing about camping

in unfriendly country, you'd have never got caught by folks who weren't even looking for you."

He placed the prisoner on dry forest duff, strode over to the granite outcropping, and hunkered down with his back against its gray wall, bracing the Winchester across his lap with his knees up, folding his arms across them, and lowering his head for forty winks, Mexican style. He'd almost dozed off when the prisoner called out, "I can't sleep with my hands behind me like this, durn it!"

"You can sleep standing on your head if you're really tired, boy. Now put a sock in it and leave me be. I'm a mite tuckered myself, and by the way, I'm a light sleeper. You move from there in the next half hour or so and you'll be buried a yard from wherever I find you."

"Listen, lawman, you're treating an innocent man cruel and unusual!"

"Shut up. I don't aim to say that twice."

Longarm dozed off. He might just have rested his mind a few minutes. It wasn't important, as long as it worked. In about an hour he lifted his head, saw the prisoner was where he'd last seen him, and felt ready to face the world again.

But he was not an unreasonable taskmaster. Longarm knew others might still be tuckered while he was feeling bright-eyed and bushy-tailed, so he let the prisoner snore as he smoked a cheroot all the way down, chewing on his own thoughts. He had no way of knowing some things, but when in doubt, it paid a man to consider the worst, so he tried to decide just how bad things could possibly be. The idea that the others had simply given up never crossed his mind.

The midget and his woman had sold them out. The reason could wait for now. Timberline and the Crooked Lance riders would be following, if only because Kim Stover insisted. Certainly the Mountie, and probably Captain Walthers, would be tracking them, too. Either with the posse or riding alone. Whoever was tracking would have picked up the sign at sunup, not that long ago. At best they'd just be over the first rise outside of Crooked Lance, a good eight to ten hours behind him, even riding at a breakneck pace. They would have to ride more slowly than he had, because they'd have to watch the ground for sign. They'd have to scout each rise before they tore over it, too; they knew he had guns and could have dug in almost anywhere. Yes, he and the prisoner were in fair shape for a cross-country run. Anyone following would have some trouble catching up.

Longarm started field stripping and cleaning the Winchester in his lap as he considered what he'd be doing if he was riding with the vigilantes instead of running from them. He decided to appoint the Mountie, Foster, as the most dangerous head of a combined posse, which was the worst thing he could picture tracking him. An experienced lawman wouldn't just follow hoofprint by hoofprint. Sergeant Foster would know he and the prisoner were well mounted with a good lead. The Mountie would try to figure out where they were headed and ride hard to cut them off.

All right, if he was Sergeant Foster, where would he guess that a deputy U.S. marshal and his prisoner would be headed?

Bitter Creek, of course. There was a jail in Bitter Creek to hold Cotton Younger till a train came by. If the Mountie had gone in with the vigilantes and told them that, Timberline's boys, or maybe a third of them, would be riding directly for Bitter Creek, hoping to keep him from boarding the eastbound U.P. with a prisoner he hadn't paid for.

The next best bet? A run for the railroad right-of-way, well clear of Bitter Creek, with hopes of flagging down a locomotive. He'd be set up nicely for an ambush anywhere along the line if he did that. So the Union Pacific was out. Too many unfriendly folks were expecting him to take Cotton Younger in that way.

As if he'd heard Longarm call out his name aloud, the prisoner rolled over and sat up, muttering, "I got to take a leak. You'll have to take these irons off me, Longarm."

Longarm placed the dismantled Winchester and its parts carefully on a clean, flat rock before he got to his feet. He walked over and hauled the prisoner to his feet. Then he unbuttoned the man's pants, pulled them halfway down his thighs, and said, "Leak away. I gotta put my rifle back together."

"Gawd! I can't just go like this! I'll wet my britches!"

"You do as best you can. I don't aim to hold it for you."

The cow thief turned away, red-faced, as Longarm squatted down to reassemble his rifle, whistling softly as he used his pocket-knife screwdriver.

The prisoner asked, "What if I have to take a crap?"

"I'd say your best bet would be to squat."

"Gawd! With my hands behind me like this?"

"Yep. It ain't the neatest way to travel, but I've learned not to take foolish chances when I'm transporting. You'll get the hang of living with your hands like that, in a day or so."

"You're one mean son of a bitch, you know that?"

"Some folks have said as much. I got my rifle in one piece. You want me to button you back up?"

"I dribbled some on my britches, damn it!"

"That ain't what I asked."

Longarm crooked the rifle through his bent elbow and went back over to pull the prisoner's pants up, buttoning just the top button. "Since there's no ladies present, this'll save us time, when next you get the call of nature. It'll also likely drop your pants around your knees if you get to running without my permission."

"You're mean, pure mean. As soon as I can talk to a lawyer I'm gonna file me a complaint. You got no right to torture me like this."

"You'll never know what torture is until you try to make a break for it. I got some jerky and biscuit dough in my saddlebags. As long as we're resting the mounts, we may as well eat."

He took the prisoner to another flat rock near the hobbled army mounts, sat him down on it, and rummaged for provisions. He cut a chunk of jerked venison from the slab, wrapped it in soft sourdough, and said, "Open wide. I'll be the mama bird and you'll be the baby bird."

"Jehoshaphat! Don't you aim to *cook* it?"

"Nope. Somebody might be sitting on a far ridge, looking for smoke against the skyline. Besides, it'll cook inside you. One thing I admire about sourdough. You just have to get a bite or two down and it sort of swells inside you. Saves a lot of chawing."

He shoved a mouthful into Cotton Younger and took the edge from his own hunger with a portion for himself. After some effort, the prisoner gulped and asked, "Don't I get no coffee? They gave me coffee three times a day in that log jail."

"I'll give you a swallow from the canteens before we mount up again. Tastes better and lasts you longer if you're a mite thirsty when you drink."

He took his Ingersoll out and consulted it for the time. "I'll give the brutes a few more minutes 'fore I saddle and bridle 'em.

I've been meaning to ask: Do you reckon they was really fixing to hang you last night?"

"They never said they was. Pop Wade was sort of a friendly old cuss."

"Somebody told me Timberline was tired of having you on his hands. How'd you get along with him?"

"Not too well. He'd have killed me that first day, if the red-headed lady and Pop hadn't talked him out of it."

"Hmm, that midget's game gets funnier and funnier. Did he really offer you a deal to spring you from the jail in exchange for Jesse James?"

"I told him I'd put him onto Jesse James, but I was only trying to get out of that place. I got no more idea than anyone else where that rascal's hid out."

"Let's see, now. He sends me to get killed. Then, amid the general congratulations, him or Mabel slips you out, they put a barlow knife against your eyelid to gain your undivided attention. It figures. It ain't like they had to transport you out of the valley. They just wanted a few minutes of Apache conversation with you. Once they knew where to pick up Jesse James, you'd be useless baggage to dispose of. Hell, they might even have let you live till the vigilantes found you."

"Damn it, I don't know where Jesse James is hiding!"

"Lucky for you I come along, then. I suspicion you'd have told 'em, whether you knew or not. That Cedric Hanks is a mean little bastard, ain't he?"

"You still think I'm Cotton Younger, don't you?"

"Don't matter what I think. You could be Queen Victoria and I'd still transport you to Denver to stand trial as Cotton Younger."

The owlhoot's expression was sly as he asked cautiously, "Is cattle rustling a federal charge, Longarm?"

"No. It's a fool thing to say. You rustle up some grub or you rustle apples as a kid. You don't rustle cows, boy. You *steal* 'em! If you ride with a running iron in your saddlebags, it's best to be honest with yourself and call it what it is. Cow theft is a serious matter. Don't shilly-shally with kid names for a dangerous, dead-serious *profession!*"

"If I was to admit I was a rustler—all right, a *cow thief* named Jones, would you believe me?"

"Nope. I ain't in a believing business. You don't know what fibbing is until you've packed a badge six or eight years. You owlhoots only lie to decent folks, so you seldom get the hang of it. In my line, I get lied to every day by experts. I've been lied to by old boys who gunned down their own mothers. I've taken in men who raped their own daughters. I've arrested men for the sodomy-rape of runaway boys, for torturing old misers for their gold, for burning a colored man to death just for the hell of it, and you want to know something? Not one of them sons of bitches ever told me he was guilty!"

"Longarm, I know I've done wrong, now and again, but you've got to believe me, I'm only—"

"A professional thief who's done more than one stretch at hard labor. You think I don't recognize the breed on sight? No man has ever come out of a prison without that whining, self-serving look of injured innocence. So save me the details of your misspent youth. I've heard how you were just a poor little war orphan, trying as best he could to make his way in this cruel, cold world he never made. I know how the Missouri Pacific stole your widowed mother's farm. You've told me about the way they framed you for borrowing that first pony to fetch the doctor to your dying little sister's side. You've told me every time I've run you in."

"That's crazy. You never seen me before!"

"Oh, yes, I have. I've seen you come whining and I've had it out with you in many a dark alley. The other day I killed you in a barbershop. Sometimes you're tall, sometimes you're short, and the features may shift some from time to time. But I always know you when we meet. You always have that innocent, wide-eyed look and that same self-pity in your bullshit. I know you good, old son. Likely better than you know yourself!"

"You sure talk funny, mister."

"I'm a barrel of laughs. You just set while I saddle up the mounts. We're almost to the high prairies near the south pass and we have to ride a full day out in the open. You reckon you know how to sit a McClellan with your hands behind you, now? Or do I have to tie you to the swells?"

"I don't want to be tied on. Listen, wouldn't it make more sense to wait for dark before we hit open ground?"

"Nope. We have them others coming at us through the trees right now. I figure we can get maybe ten, twelve miles out before they break free of the trees. I'd say they'll be *here* this afternoon. By then we'll be two bitty dots against the low sun. The course

I'm setting ain't the one they'll be expecting, but there's no way to hide our trail by daylight. If we make the railroad tracks sometime after dark, they'll cut around the short way, figuring to stop any train I can flag down."

"What's the point of lighting out for the tracks if they'll know right off what your plan is?"

"You mean what they'll *think* my plan is, don't you?"

Chapter 15

The moon was high, washing the surrounding grasslands in pale silver as the prisoner sat his mount, watching Longarm's dark outline climb the last few feet to the crossbar of the telegraph pole beside the tracks. He called up, "See anything?"

Longarm called back, "Yeah. Campfire, maybe fifteen miles off. Big fire. Likely a big bunch after us. Leastways, that's what they want me to think. You just hush, now. I got work to do."

Longarm took the small, skeletonized telegraph key he'd had in his kit and rested it on the crossbar as he went to work with his jackknife. He spliced a length of his own thin copper wire to the Western Union line, and next to it spliced in the Union Pacific's operating line.

He attached a last wire and the key started to buzz like a bee, its coils confused by conflicting messages on the two lines he'd spliced into. Longarm waited until the operators up and down the transcontinental line stopped sending; they were no doubt confused by the short circuit. Then he put a finger on his own key and tapped out a rapid message in Morse code. He got most of it off before the electromagnet went mad again as some idiot tried to ask what the hell was going on.

Longarm slid down the pole, mounted his own stolen horse,

and said, "Let's go." He led them west along the right-of-way. He rode them on the ties and ballast between the rails. The horses found it rough going and stumbled from time to time. As the bay lurched under the prisoner, he protested, "Wouldn't it be easier on the grass all about?" Longarm said, "Yep. Leave more hoof-prints, too. Reading sign on railroad ballast is a bitch. That halo forming around the moon promises rain by sunup. *Wet* railroad ballast is even tougher to read."

"What was that message you sent on the telegraph wire?"

"Sent word to my boss I was still breathing and had you tag-ging along. Told him I wasn't able to transport you by rail and where I was hoping to meet up with such help as he might see fit to send me."

"We're headed for Thayer Junction, right?"

"What makes you think that?"

"Well, hell, we're at least ten miles northwest of Bitter Creek and headed the wrong way. You reckon we'll make Thayer Junc-tion 'fore the rain hits?"

"For a man who says he don't know many train robbers, you've got a right smart railroad map in your head. By the way, I've been meaning to ask: Where *did* you figure to run a cow you stole in Crooked Lance? It's a far piece to herd stolen cows alone, ain't it?"

"I keep telling ever'body, I was only passing through! I had no intentions on the redheaded widow's cows."

"But you had a running iron for changing brands. A thing no cow thief with a brain would carry a full day on him if it could be avoided. So tell me, were you just stupid, or did you maybe have one or two sidekicks with you? If there were sidekicks who didn't get caught by the vigilantes, it would answer some questions I've been mulling over."

"I was riding alone. If I had any friends worth mention in that durned valley, I'd have been long gone before you got there!"

"That sounds reasonable. I sprung you solo. A friend of yours with the hair on his chest to snipe at folks would likely be able to take out Pop Wade, or even the two I whupped some civilization into. That wasn't much of a jail they had you in, Younger. How come you didn't bust out on your own?"

"I studied on it. We're *doing* what stopped me. I figured a cou-ple of ways to bust out, but knew I'd have Timberline and all them others chasing me. Knew if they caught me more'n a mile from the Widow Stover and some of the older folks in Crooked Lance, they'd gun me down like a dog. Timberline wanted to kill me when they drug me from the brush that first day."

"He does seem a testy cuss, for a big man. Most big fellers tend to be more easygoing. What do you reckon made him so down on you, aside from that running iron in your possibles?"

"That's easy. He thought I was Cotton Younger, too. Lucky for me he blurted the same out to the widow as she was standing there. When he said I was a wanted owlhoot who deserved a good hanging, she asked was the reward worth mention, and the rest you know."

"Timeberline's been up here in the high country for half a dozen years or more. How'd he figure you to be a member of the James-Younger Gang?"

"The Vigilance Committee has all these durned reward posters stuck up where they meet, out to the widow's barn. That's their lodge hall. Understand they hold a meeting there once a week."

"Sure seems odd to take the vigilante business so serious in a town where a funeral's a rare occasion for an all-day hootenanny. While you was locked up all them weeks, did you hear tell how many other owlhoots they've run in?"

"Pop Wade says they ain't had much trouble since the Shoshone Rising a few years back. Shoshone never rode into that particular valley, but that's when they formed the vigilantes. They likely kept it formed 'cause the widow serves coffee and cakes at the meetings and, what the hell, it ain't like they had a opera house."

"Kim Stover's more or less the head of it, eh?"

"Yep, she inherited the chairmanship from her husband when the herd run him down, a year or so ago. Pop Wade's the jailer and keeps the minutes 'cause he was in the army, one time."

"And Timberline's the muscle, along with the hired hands at his and other spreads up and down the valley. You hear talk about him tracking anyone else down since he took the job?"

"No. Like I said, things have been peaceable in Crooked Lance of late. Reckon they're taking this thing so serious 'cause it beats whittling as a way to pass the time. You figure it should be easy to throw them part-time posse men off our trail, huh?"

"They'd have lost us long ago if we only had to worry about cowhands. I'm hoping that Mountie joined up with 'em, along with Captain Walthers and the bounty-hunting Hanks family. Mountie'd be able to follow less sign than we've been leaving."

"Jesus! You reckon this rough ride down these damn tracks will throw him off?"

"Slow him, some. Hang on, we're getting off to one side. I see a headlamp coming up the grade."

Longarm led his mounted prisoner away from the track at a jogging trot until they were well away from the right-of-way. Then, as the sound of a chuffing locomotive climbed toward them on the far side of a cut, he reined them to a halt and said, "Rest easy a minute. Soon as the eastbound passes I'll unroll my slicker and a poncho for you. I can smell the rain, following that train at a mile or so down the tracks."

"We're right out in the open here!"

"That's all right. The cabin crew's watching the headlamp beam down the tracks ahead of 'em. Folks inside can't see out worth mention through the glass lit from inside. Didn't your cousin Jesse ever tell you that?"

Before the prisoner could protest his innocence again, the noisy Baldwin six-wheeler charged out of the cut and passed them in a haze of wet smoke and stirred-up ballast dust. Longarm waited until the two red lamps of the rear platform were fading away to the east before he put Captain Walthers's poncho over the prisoner and started struggling into the evil-smelling stickiness of his own tightly rolled, oilcloth slicker. He smoothed it down over his legs, covering himself from the shoulders to ankles, but didn't snap the fasteners below a single one at the collar. He'd almost been killed, once, trying to draw his gun inside a wet slicker he'd been fool enough to button down the front.

In the distance, the locomotive sounded its whistle. Longarm nodded and said, "They've stopped the train to search for us. Means one of 'em flashed a badge or such at the engineer. Means at least five minutes for 'em to make certain we didn't flag her down for a ride. I'd say the searching's going on about six or eight miles from here. Must be the Mountie leading."

He heard a soft tap on his hat brim and smiled thinly, saying, "Here comes the rain. Hang on."

He led off, south-southwest, away from the track and up a gentle grade in the growing darkness of the rain-drowned moonlight. The prisoner called out, "Where in thunder do you think you're going? The railroad hugs the south edge of the gap through the Great Divide!"

"We're on the west side of the divide now. All this rain coming down is headed into the Pacific, save what gets stuck in the Great Basin 'twixt here and the Sierra Nevadas."

"Jehoshaphat, are we bound for California?"

"Nope, Green River country, once we cross some higher ground."

"Have you gone plumb out of your head? There's no way to get from here to the headwaters of the Green, and if there was, there's nothing there! The Green River's birthed in wild canyon lands unfit for man or beast!"

"You been there, Younger?"

"No, but I heard about it. It's the wildest, roughest, most tore-up stretch of the Rocky Mountains!"

"Not quite. We got to ride over *that* part before we *get* to Green River country."

Chapter 16

Longarm took advantage of the remaining darkness to cover most of the gently rolling Aspen Range between the U.P. tracks and the mighty ramparts of the Green River Divide. Morning caught them winding up a trail fetlock-deep in running rainwater. They were above the hardwoods now, and rode through gloomy corridors of sombre, dripping spruce. Longarm took a deep breath, and while the smell of the rain-washed timber was pleasant, the air was a mite thin for breathing. He knew he was good for a run up Pikes Peak to even thinner air, but he had to consider the horses. He led slowly on the upgrades and resisted the temptation to trot when the trail, from time to time, ran downhill a few yards.

Even covered with waterproof canvas and oilcloth, they were both damp and chilled to the bone by now. Somewhere above them the sun was trying to break through, but the sky was a fuzzy gray blanket of wet, dripping wool. Off through clearings in the timber, silver veils of rain whipped back and forth in the morning breezes like the cobwebs of a haunted pagan temple. From time to time one of the mountain gods roared majestically in the sky and another spruce died in a blinding lightning flash. More than once that morning lightning whip-cracked down too closely for comfort, but Longarm took little notice of things he couldn't do

anything about. Folks who were afraid of lightning had no business riding in the high country. Electrical storms went with the
territory.

Somewhere in the dripping tanglewood they crossed the Utah
line.

There was no signpost, no natural feature. Someone back in
Washington had drawn a line with a ruler on the map. Half of the
jumbled peaks and ridges had never been properly surveyed by a
white man. The way the Rockies had been thrown together here
made little sense to the Indians, who said Lord Grizzly and the
Great Spirit had wrestled in the Days of Creation and left the
Shining Mountains as their trampled footprints in the torn-up
earth of their Great Buffalo Grounds.

Longarm reined in near a giant potato of lichen-covered granite that leaned toward the trail, and helped the prisoner down,
saying, "We got to spell the mounts on foot for a while. I'm going
to build a fire and dry our bones a mite."

"Could I have these cuffs in front of me for a change? My
shoulder sockets are sore as hell."

"I'll study on it. Just stand against the rock and dry off some
while I find something dry enough to light."

He did think about the prisoner's discomfort as he peeled
damp bark from spruce branches and dug dry punk from under the
soaked forest duff at the base of the rock. Unless the prisoner was a
superb actor, he was neither bright nor given to sudden courage.
He'd let them hold him for nearly a month in a ramshackle log jail
guarded by old Pop and unskilled cowboy jail guards. Longarm
took a spare cartridge, pulled the slug with his teeth, and sprinkled
loose powder into the dry punk between his whittled frizz-stick kindling and struck a match to it. There was a warm, smoky *whoosh*
and Longarm put his face near the ground to blow into the smoldering beginnings before he leaned back, squatting on his boot heels
almost atop the little Indian hand warmer and suggested, "Put your
hands in front of you, if you want."

"Don't you have to unlock these blamed cuffs, first?"

"'Course not. Ain't you ever worn irons before?"

"Not often enough to know how to unlock 'em with no key."

"Hell, scootch down on your heels till your hands are on the
ground. Then just haul your ass and feet over the chain between
your wrists. That'll leave your hands in front of you when you
stand up."

The prisoner looked puzzled, but slid down the rock, fumbling about under the poncho and grunting as he got his knees up against his chin and struggled. Then he suddenly grinned and said, "I done it! My hands is in front of me! Why'd you have me chained like this so long when you must have knowed all the time a man could work his hands to a more comforting place?"

"Wanted to see how educated you were. You got a lot to learn if you intend to follow your chosen trade serious."

The prisoner moved closer to the fire, putting his numb, linked hands out from under the poncho to warm them as he grinned and asked, "Are you starting to believe I ain't one of the James-Younger Gang?"

"Don't matter what I believe. My job's to take you in. Save the tales for the judge."

"Wouldn't you let me go if I could get you to believe my real name's Jones?"

"Nope. They never sent me to find out who you were. Like I said, you could be named Victoria Regina and I'd still deliver you to Denver, Lord willing that we ever get there."

"You're a hard man, Longarm."

"Hell, you don't know what hard can get to or you'd know better than to wander about with a running iron and a name like Jones. I know a dozen deputies who would have gunned you by now just 'cause it's easier and safer to transport a dead man. The papers on you said dead or alive, as I remember."

"Jesus, meeting up with you has given me second thoughts on stealing cows for a living. When they find out I'm not Cotton Younger and cut me loose, I reckon I'll go back to washing dishes!"

Longarm didn't answer. The boy was a born thief, whether he was Cotton Younger or some other reprobate. There was maybe one chance in a hundred that he was telling the truth and that this had all been a fool's errand. The odds of the prisoner living to a ripe old age hadn't changed worth mentioning. If they didn't hang him this year for being Cotton Younger, they'd hang him sooner or later anyway. He was a shifty-eyed and probably vicious thief, no matter how it turned out in Denver.

The prisoner glanced up and said, "Smoke's rising over the top of this rock shelter. You reckon anyone can see it?"

"Not unless they're close enough to smell it. The whole sky is filled with drifting gray."

"How much of a lead do you reckon we have, Longarm?"

"Can't say. We took the two best mounts I knew of and they're bound to be held back by the slowest pony in the posse, 'less they like to ride after an armed man all strung out. I suspicion we're a good fifteen miles or more out front. We'd be farther if somebody wasn't leading who knows his business."

"Yeah. They'd have had to be cat-eyed and hound-nosed to follow us along the railroad tracks like they done."

"Hell, they didn't follow us by reading sign. They followed us by *knowing*. I'd say they sent a party in to Bitter Creek and another down the track, covering all bets. They got more riders than they need, so they ain't riding bunched together. They'll be split into half a dozen patrols, sweeping everywhere we'd be likely to head."

"Jesus, how you figure to shake 'em, then?"

"Don't. Not all of 'em. No matter which fork we take, at least half of 'em will be following us up the right one. Ought to whittle 'em down some if we keep offering choices."

"I see what you mean. How many men you reckon you can hold off if any of 'em catch up?"

"Not one, if he's better than me. Any number if they don't know how to fight. I doubt if they'll dare split up into parties of less than a dozen. I'm hoping the Mountie won't make me shoot him. Man could get in trouble with the State Department, shooting guests."

"He'll as likely be riding off with someone in the wrong direction as on our trail, won't he?"

"Nope. The only ones likely to follow the right trail are the *good* trackers."

He threw another faggot on the fire, watching it steam dry enough to burn as he mused, half to himself, "The cooler heads among the party will likely stay attached to Sergeant Foster. So if push comes to shove we'll be up against Timberline, the Hankses, maybe even Captain Walthers. He's likely riled about me stealing his walker and would know the Mountie knows his business."

"If we get cornered, you could give me a gun and I'd be proud to side you, Longarm."

"Not hardly. I never sprung you from that jail to shoot U.S. or Canadian peace officers. Don't like getting shot all that much myself."

"Hell, you don't think I'd be dumb enough to try to gun *you*, do you?"

"You'll never get the chance from me, so we'll most likely never know."

"Listen, you can't let 'em take me, handcuffed like this! You'd have to give me a chance for my life!"

"Son, you had that chance, before you took to stealing from folks."

"Gawd! You mean you'd let 'em kill me, if it comes down to you or me?"

"If it comes down to you or me? That's a fool question. I'd boil you in oil to save myself a hangnail, but don't fret about it. We're both a long way from caught up with."

It didn't stop raining. They rode out of the storm that afternoon by getting above the clouds. The slanting rays of the sun warmed and dried them as they rode over the frost-shattered rocks where stunted junipers grew like contorted green gnomes on either side. Cushion flowers peeked at them between boulders, not daring to raise a twig high enough for the cruel, thin winds to bite them off. Surprised, invisible ground squirrels chattered at them from either side of the trail, which now was little more than a meandering flatness between patches of treacherous scree or dusty snow patches. The air was still, and drier than a mummy's armpit, but only warm where the sun shone through it. Each juniper's shadow they rode through held the chill of the void between the planets. They passed a last wind-crippled little tree and knew they'd reached the timberline. It wasn't a real line painted over the shattered scree, it was simply that after you got high enough on a mountain, nothing grew tall enough to matter.

Longarm led them to a saddle between higher, snow-covered peaks to the east and west, and at the summit of the pass, reined in for a moment.

There was nothing to see back the way they'd ridden but the carpet of pink-tinged clouds, spread clear to the far horizon with an occasional peak rising like an island above the storm below them.

The prisoner asked, "See anybody?"

Longarm snorted, "We'd be in a hell of a fix if I did. Let's ride."

The other side of the pass was a mirror image of the one they'd just ridden up. The prisoner looked down into the carpet of cloud spread out ahead of them and groaned, "Hell, I was just getting comfortable."

"We ain't riding for comfort. We're riding for your life, and Denver. How long you figure to live once we get there ain't my worry."

"How far do you reckon Denver is, Longarm?"

"About four hundred miles, as the crow flies. We ain't riding crows, so it's likely a mite farther."

"Four hundred miles across the top of the world with half of it chasing us? Jehoshaphat, I wish I was back in that fool jail!"

"No, you don't. They would have buried you by now. By the way, you made a deal with that midget to save yourself from a necktie party. You mind telling me what it was?"

"I told you. He said he'd get me out if I'd tell him where Jesse James was hiding."

"I remember. Whereabouts did you say that was?"

"Hell, *I* don't know! I'd'a said most anything to get my ass out of there!"

"Well, your ass is out. What did you aim to tell Cedric Hanks?"

"I told you. He said he'd get me out if I'd tell him some yarn."

"Spin her my way, then. I listen as good as anyone."

"Oh, hell, I dunno. I'd'a likely told him the stuff as is going around the barrooms. You ask any two men where the James boys went after that big shoot-out in Minnesota and you get three answers."

"Which one do you reckon makes most sense?"

"You heard about them lighting out to Mexico?"

"Sure, and I don't like it much. The James boys has gotten by all these years by hiding out amid friends and kinfolks they grew up with.

"They have to be somewhere in or damn near Missouri. Surprise me if they was even far from Kansas City. Clay County's been pretty well searched over, but they'll be somewhere in the Missouri River drainage when we catch up with 'em. That fool raid they made up into Minnesota likely taught 'em the value of hiding out with folks they can trust to keep a secret."

"I did hear one story about Saint Joe. Where is that from Kansas City?"

"Up the river a few hours by steamboat. I heard it, too. Sheriff of Buchanan County wires that nobody's held up anybody in or about Saint Joe."

"Well, I hear tell Jesse and Frank is trying to go straight. You see, Cole Younger was the real brains behind the gang, and with him in prison—"

"You just lost me, boy. Why do you fellers always spin that same old yarn about being led astray by wicked companions? Goddam James boys has been robbing and killing folks since before they knew why boys and gals were different. If you'd told that midget that Jesse James is reformed after fifteen years of shooting at everybody but his mother, he'd have laughed before he killed you. Though, come to think of it, the Hankses were figuring to kill you anyway."

The light began to fade again as they rode down into the clouds beyond the pass. The top of the storm was only cold and damp, but they were back in rain before they rode under man-sized timber again. The prisoner asked. "When are we fixing to make camp?" and Longarm shot back, "We made it, over on the other side."

"You aim to just keep riding into the night as she falls?"

"Nope. We'll rest the critters, along about midnight. If it's still raining, we'll build a fire. If it ain't, we won't."

"Gawd, you're fixing to kill me *and* the horses the way you're pushing us!"

"Ain't worried about you. The critters and me know how hard we can push."

"Listen, you said by now we don't have more'n a third or so of the bunch from Crooked Lance trailing us."

"Maybe less. Day or so on a cold, wet trail can take the first flush off the enthusiasm. More'n one will have given up by now, I suspicion."

"We've passed a dozen good places to make a stand. I mean, that Winchester of yours might discourage anybody."

"You want me to bushwhack fellow peace officers?"

"Why not? They're out to kill us, ain't they?"

"That's their worry. It wouldn't be neighborly of me to blow holes in anybody wearing a badge. And I don't want to hurt any of them fool cowhands either, if it can be helped."

"Longarm, these fool horses ain't about to carry us no four hundred miles in country like this!"

"I know. It gets even rougher where we're headed."

Chapter 17

The Green River is born from countless streams in the Uinta Range, a cross-grained spur of the Rockies, rubbing its spine against the sky near where Wyoming, Utah, and Colorado come together on the map. As Longarm had thought before, those lines were put there on the map by government men who'd never seen the country and wouldn't have liked it much if they had.

The Green makes a big bend into Colorado in its upper reaches, then turns toward the junction with the brawling Colorado River near the southern border of Utah. To get there, the Green runs through canyon lands unfit for most Indians to consider as a home. The Denver & Rio Grande's western division crossed the Green halfway to Arizona's Navajo lands at a small settlement called, naturally, Green River. The lack of imagination implied by the name was the simple result of not having to name any other towns to the north or south in Longarm's day.

They didn't follow the river when they reached it. For one thing, the cliffs came right down to the boiling rapids along many a stretch. For another, Longarm knew the men trailing him might expect him to try this. So he led his prisoner the shorter way, across the big bend. The shorter way was not any easier; the route took them through a maze of canyons where the floors were choked with brush and the steep, ugly slopes of eroded shale smelled like hot road tar where the sun beat down on it.

They'd been riding for three full days by now and Longarm figured they were nearly a hundred miles from Crooked Lance. Anyone who was still trailing them wanted pretty badly to have the prisoner back.

It was a hot and dusty afternoon when they hauled over another pass, and looking back, spied dust in the saddle of a shale ridge they'd crossed several hours before.

Longarm tugged the lead and muttered, "That Mountie's damn good," as he started them down the far side. Captain Walthers's big walker had proven a disappointment to him on the trail. The army man had chosen it for show and comfort, not for serious riding over rough country, and while the bay he'd gotten from the remount section was still holding up, the walker under him was heaving badly and walking with its head down.

The prisoner called out, "I might have seen a dot of red back there. That'd be the Mountie's jacket, right?"

"Yeah. I saw it, too. Watch yourself, and if that bay starts to slide out from under you, try to fall on the high side. This shale is treacherous as hell."

"Smells awful, too! What in thunder is it?"

"Oil shale. Whole country's made out of it. Gets slippery when the heat boils the oil out of the rock."

As if to prove his point, the walker he was riding suddenly shot out from under him and forward, down the slope. Longarm cursed, tried to steady his mount with the reins, and seeing that it was no use, rolled out of the saddle as the screaming horse slid halfway down the mountain.

Longarm landed on one hip and shoulder, rolled to his feet, and bounced a few yards on his heels, before he caught a juniper bush and came to a standing stop. He looked quickly back and saw that the bay had stopped safely with the prisoner still aboard. He yelled, "Stay put!" and started down the slope of sharp, slick shale in the dusty wake of his fallen mount.

The walker was trying to struggle to its feet at the bottom of the rise, screaming in dumb terror and pain. Longarm could see it hadn't broken any bones. It had simply gutted itself on the sharp rocks after sliding a full two hundred yards down the trail!

He drew his .44 as he approached the dreadfully injured gelding with soothing words. The animal got halfway to its feet, its forelegs out in front of it and its rump high, as its bloody intestines writhed over the cruel, sunbaked surface. Then Longarm fired, twice, when he saw the first round hadn't completely shattered the poor brute's brain.

Swearing blackly, he stepped over to the quivering carcass and got his Winchester and other possessions free, glad it was the captain's saddle he didn't have to mess with cleaning. He put the rifle and supplies on a rock and walked up to where the prisoner watched with a silly grin on his face.

Longarm said, "It ain't funny. Guess who gets to walk?"

"Hell, I don't aim to stay up here like this with the ground under hoof greased so funny!"

Longarm helped him down and led both him and the bay to where he'd piled the other things. As he lashed everything worth carrying to the surviving mount's saddle, the prisoner asked, "You figure we got enough of a lead on them other fellers, with one pony betwixt us?"

"No. Riding double or walking, we ain't got till sunset before they make rifle range on us."

"You don't mean to leave me, do you?"

"Not hardly. Just keep walking."

"Listen, Longarm, if you was to turn me loose afoot I'd be willing to take my chances. I could cover my boot prints, I reckon, if you just rode on, leaving 'em a few horseshoe marks and a turd or two on the trail."

"Didn't carry you all this way to lose you, Younger. You see that half-bowl in the cliffs across the creek we're headed down to?"

"Sure. It looks to be a blind alley, though. A rifleman could doubtless make a good stand in there, but the walls behind him would be sheer."

"I know. We'll dig in there, behind such rocks as we'll have time to fort up in front of us. 'Bout the time they make it to the dead horse, I'll spook 'em with a few rifle rounds and they'll fan out ever' which way, diving for cover. By then it'll be getting dark."

"What's to stop 'em from working around behind us, up on the rim rocks?"

"You want to climb a shale oil cliff in the dark? They won't have us circled tight before, oh, a couple of hours after sunup."

He led the handcuffed man across the ankle-deep creek and up the talus slope beyond to the amphitheater some ancient disaster had carved from the cliff face. He sat the prisoner down beside the tired bay he'd tethered to a bush and proceeded to pile slabs of shale between them and the valley they faced. The dead walker was a chestnut blob across the way. It was just at the range Longarm was sure he could handle. Any man who said he knew where a bullet was going once it got past three hundred yards, was a liar.

The prisoner said, "If you'd take these cuffs off, I could help."

"You want to help, take the horse upslope as far as you can and tie him to something, then come back."

"Won't he be exposed up there?"

"Sure. Out of range, too. They'll spot him, but so what? They'll know we're here. Might save me a round if they grow cautious before I have to waste good lead just funning."

"Won't they know, once you miss a couple of times, that you don't mean to kill nobody?"

"Don't aim to miss by all that much, and if it comes down to real hard feelings, I've been known to draw blood, in my time."

The prisoner led the bay away, and by the time he returned, Longarm had erected a breast-high wall of slabs.

He said, "Look around for some sticks, dry grass, and such. You can work as well with your hands together."

"There ain't enough dry weeds and cheat-grass here for a real fire, Longarm. The thing you had in mind was a fire, wasn't it?"

"Get moving. I got some shifting to do here on this breast-work."

"I'm moving, I'm moving, but you are pure loco! What in thunder do we want with a fire, not saying we could build one?"

Longarm didn't answer. He was a fair hand at drywall construction and figured his improvisation would stand up to anything but a four-pound cannonball, and he knew they wouldn't be bringing along heavy artillery.

He saw the prisoner was doing a shiftless job at gathering dry tinder, so he went to work himself, gathering an armful of bone-dry weeds and cheat-grass stems. He threw it in a pile a few yards back from his stone wall.

The prisoner added his own smaller offering and Longarm started putting chips of shale on the tinder, with smaller fragments first and some fair-sized slabs topping off the cairn.

The prisoner watched bemusedly as Longarm struck a match and set the dry weeds alight. As the acrid blue smoke of burning cheat curled up through the rocks he said, "I can see you're trying to cook them rocks. What I can't figure out is why."

Then a thicker smoke, coiling like an oily serpent, slithered up and through the shale slabs to catch a vagrant tendril of breeze and float skyward like a blob of ink against the blue of the sky.

Longarm said, "Oil shale burns, sort of. Learned it from a friendly Ute last time I passed this way."

"That's for damn sure! Look at it catch! Burns with a damn black smoke, though. You says there's Utes in this neck of the woods?"

"Utes, if we're lucky, Shoshone if we ain't."

"You figure they'll see this smoke signal and come running?"

"They'll more'n likely come creeping, wondering who's here in their hunting grounds. Not many white men have ever been this way and Indians are curious cusses."

"Won't the white boys trailing us see the smoke, too?"

"If they've got eyes they've seen it by now. They won't know if it's us or some Shoshone fixing to lift their hair."

"Hot damn! It may just turn 'em back, don't you reckon?"

"Not hardly. Men willing to chase a man with my rep and a Winchester don't scare so easy. If they read this smoke as Indian signals, it might slow 'em to a cautious move-in, though. I'm hoping they won't be here too long before sundown. If they climb up behind us in good light, we're in one hell of a fix."

"What's to stop 'em doing it tomorrow just after sunup?"

"Tomorrow is another day, and like I keep saying, you eat the apple a bite at a time."

"Yeah, I figure you got maybe twelve to fifteen hours before your apple's all et, too! Man up there on the rim above us could save ammo and likely kill us just by chucking down some rocks! You reckon you could pick a man off against that skyline up there?"

"Doubt it. It's about a quarter-mile straight up. Things look closer than they really are in this clear air of the high country."

"But he'd have no trouble shooting down, would he?"

"Not hardly. Likely miss his first few shots, but we'll have no cover, and like you said, a fistful of rock could do us in, thrown down from that height."

"Gawd, you're pretty cheerful about it all, considering!"

"Well, losing that horse threw me off my feed for a few minutes back there, but we're in pretty fair shape again."

"The hell you say! Can't you see the fix they got us in, Longarm?"

"Yep. They'll likely figure it the same way and move in slow and careful, like I want 'em to. Hate to have to hurt anybody who don't deserve a hurt, this close to the end of our game."

"Longarm, I am purely missing something or you are out of your fool head! We are boxed in here with our backs to a quarter-mile-high cliff! You got a rifle and a pistol to hold off Gawd knows what-all in the way of white folks, and likely a tribe or two of Injuns!"

"Yep. Nearest Utes are about a ten-hour ride away. Boys from Crooked Lance should get here sooner."

"Then what in tarnation are you grinning about? You look like a mean old weasel some dumb farmer just put to work guarding his henhouse for the night!"

"I'll allow some chicken-thieving tricks have crossed my mind since we lost that horse back there. I was worried we might have thrown 'em off our trail, too, till I spied that Canadian's fool red coat on the far horizon. You reckon they wear them red tunics to make a good target or to impress the Cree, up Canada way?"

"Back up. What was that about not trying to throw 'em off our trail? Are you saying you could have lost 'em in the mountains?"

"Hell, can a jaybird suck robin's eggs? I'll allow that Sergeant Foster's a fair tracker, but I've been tracked by Apache in my time, and lost 'em good."

"In other words, you've been playing ring-around-the-rosie with them Crooked Lance vigilantes all this time?"

"Sure. Hadn't you figured as much? Hell, a pissant like *you* could have lost 'em by now! We've been over some rough ground in the last few days, boy. You mind when we crossed that ten-mile stretch of bare granite yesterday? Had to drop some spent cartridges along the way, pretending we'd been shooting birds for provisions. They know I pack .44-40 ammo, so . . ."

"But *why*, Gawd damn it? I thought your mission was to bring me in to Denver safe and sound!"

"I aim to. But I'm a peace officer, too. Can't see my way to leave folks disturbing the peace and carrying on like wild men on federal range land, can I?"

"You mean you aim to arrest somebody riding with that posse of vigilantes?"

"Nope. If things go as I've planned, I aim to arrest the whole damn kit and caboodle!"

Chapter 18

It was getting late when Longarm spied the red tunic of Sergeant Foster on the skyline far up the other wall of the valley. The Mountie had others with him. One rider was too tall in the saddle to be anyone but Timberline. Another distant figure had to be the midget, Cedric Hanks. Longarm looked for anyone riding sidesaddle, but the little detective had apparently left Mabel behind. He counted a good dozen-and-a-half heads up there and the sunlight flashing on glass told him Foster was sweeping the valley floor with field glasses. He'd probably seen the dead horse down on the far side of the creek. He had to have seen the big black mushroom of oil smoke still rising behind them.

Longarm turned to the prisoner at his side and said, "Lie down behind this barricade and stay put. I'll be too busy to keep more'n a corner of my eye on you and I get testy if folks interfere when I'm working."

"Longarm, we are boxed in here like mice in a cracker barrel with the cat peering over the top!"

"Just do as you're told and hush. They're moving down, sort of slow. I'll tell you what's going on, so's to rest your mind. Don't you raise your fool head, though. I only aim to have my own to worry about!"

"What are they doing now, then?"

"What you'd expect. There's only one trail down from the top, so they're riding down in file, and slow. Likely having as much trouble with that shale as we did . . . yep, pony just slipped some, but its rider steadied it nicely. Looks like that redheaded Kim Stover. She sure sits a horse pretty."

"Jehoshaphat! Ever'body from Crooked Lance is coming to pay us a call with guns, and all you can talk about is how pretty that redhead is!"

"Hell, she *is* pretty, ain't she? I'd say Pop Wade must be laying for us with some of the others in Bitter Creek. Don't see Slim Wilson. He'd have led another bunch along the tracks west of Thayer Junction, most likely. The big hoorahs are sticking with the Mountie. All except Captain Walthers. He's with one of the other scouting parties. That's good. I was wondering what he'd say about me gutting his walker."

Longarm removed his Stetson and placed it on a rock atop his wall, peering through a loophole he'd left below the highest course of shale slabs. He moved the muzzle of his Winchester into position and levered a round into the chamber as the band of riders across the way reined in and began to dismount, just up-slope from the dead horse. He nodded and said, "Good thinking. They see this wall in front of the smoke and have the range figured. Yep, I see some of 'em's fanning out, working the rocks for cover."

"Longarm, we don't stand a chance here!"

"Sure we do. They daren't come much closer. They'll stay on the other side of the creek for now."

The Mountie, Foster, approached on foot until he was well within range at the edge of the stream. He took off his hat and waved it, calling out, "I see you, Longarm! You've made a big mistake, Yank!"

Longarm didn't answer.

"You can see that it's eighteen to one! You want to parley or have you gone completely mad?"

Longarm called back, "What's your deal, Foster?"

"Don't be an idiot! You know I'm taking Cotton Younger back to Canada!"

"Do tell? Speaking of idiots, I just saw one wearing a red coat! You really think the others will let you ride north with him, Foster?"

"Yes. We've made our own compromise. The people of Crooked Lance are only interested in the reward for Jesse James. They say the prisoner is mine, once we get a few facts out of him!"

"Sure he is. Why don't you just move back out of range for a spell?"

"We've got you trapped in there, Longarm!"

Longarm didn't answer. Foster wasn't saying anything interesting and it was a far piece to holler.

A rifle suddenly squibbed from among the rocks across the way and Longarm's hat flew off the wall as Foster spun on his heel and ran for cover, shouting, "Stop that, you damned fool!"

Longarm considered speeding him on his way with a round of his own, but it didn't look like the Mountie could run much faster. The shot they'd put through the crown of his hat had sounded like a Henry deer-load, not a .30-30. Longarm marked the rock its smoke was drifting away from and intended to remember it. Timberline and the girl were behind that other big boulder to the left of it. Likely one of the hands had gotten silly. The midget, Hanks, was behind that low slab, and was almost certainly too slick to be taken in by the old hat trick.

Someone else fired from behind another rock, so Longarm bounced a slug off it to teach him some manners, moving to another loophole with his gun since the one he'd fired from proceeded to eat lead. Longarm counted and marked each of the smoke puffs as they fired at the place he'd just been. A woman's voice was screaming at them to stop firing, but the prisoner at his side was spooked too badly to listen. He was suddenly up and running—running in a blind panic up the slope toward the sheer cliff of the amphitheater. Longarm yelled, "Hang it all! Get *back* here, you fool!" But it was too late. The handcuffed prisoner staggered, fell to his hands and knees, and rolled over. Then he was up again and running back to Longarm, eyes wide and mouth hanging open, in a rattle of small-arms fire!

Something hit the prisoner hard enough to stagger him, but he kept coming and in another few seconds was stretched out behind the wall, sobbing and carrying on like a cat whose tail had been stomped.

Longarm snorted, "Jesus H. Christ! Of all the fool stunts! Where'd they hit you?"

"All over! I've been killed!"

The gunfire died away as cooler heads prevailed across the

way. The big lawman crawled over to the prisoner and rolled him onto his back. He whistled thoughtfully and sighed, "Damn it, you *did* get hit, boy! The one in your shoulder ain't worth mention. But the one in your side don't look so good. You feel like throwing up?"

"I just want to be someplace else! *Any*place else! I'm too young to die!"

"You just hold on and lie still, then. You ain't bleeding too bad. I'll stuff some wadding in the wound and wrap it tight for you."

"Gawd, I'm so thirsty, all of a sudden! Can I have a drink of canteen water?"

Longarm had been afraid he'd say that. He shook his head and said, "You're gut-shot, you poor, dumb son of a bitch! What ever made you do a fool thing like that?"

"I was scared! I'm still scared! You reckon I'm fixing to die?"

"Not for a few hours."

"You said you was fixing to bandage me. Ain't you aiming to?"

"No. Best to let the gas escape as it forms. You just lie there quiet. That fool Mountie over yonder's waving his hanky at me and I'd like to see what he wants."

Longarm called out, "That's close enough, Foster!" and the Mountie halted, holding a white kerchief in his hand as he called back, "That wasn't my idea, Longarm. Did they kill him?"

"Nope. But you're starting to piss me off. Why don't you all settle down and make some coffee or something? You know you daren't rush me before dark and somebody figures to get hurt with all this wild shooting."

"Longarm, it's not my job to have a bloodbath here. Why can't you listen to reason?"

"Hell, I'm about as reasonable as anyone for a hundred country miles. You'd best ride home to Canada before they turn on you, Foster. You ain't taking my prisoner, now that I have him. Not without killing a deputy U.S. marshal for your durned old queen!"

"Damn it! That's what I'm trying to prevent! This gunplay's not my idea, Longarm, but your only chance is to hand the prisoner over."

"You're not only pissing me off, you're starting to bore the shit out of me! It's tedious talking in circles and we've all had our say. So ride on out, or join in and be damned to you!"

The Canadian lawman walked back to the boulder that Timberline and the girl were behind. The wounded prisoner gasped, "What's going on?"

"Beats me. They'll likely jaw about it for a spell. How are you feeling?"

"Terrible. It don't look like I'm gonna make it to Denver, does it?"

Longarm didn't answer.

"It's funny, but I ain't as scared now as I was. You reckon it's on account of I'm dying?"

"Maybe. Most men are more scared of it when it's coming than when it actually arrives. You might make it, though. I've seen men hit worse and they've pulled through."

"They say a man knows when he's sinking, but I can't tell. It's funny, but I'd rest easier if I knew for sure, one way or the other."

"Yep, I know what you mean. You got anything you'd like to get off your chest while there's still time, old son?"

"You mean, like a deathbed confession?"

"Must be some comfort to such, since we get so many of 'em."

The wounded man thought awhile, breathing oddly. Then he licked his lips and said, "You might as well know, then. My name ain't Jones and I ain't from Cripple Creek."

"I figured as much. You're Cotton Younger, right?"

"No, my name is Raymond Tinker and I hail from Omaha, Nebraska."

"You ain't dying, boy. You're still shitting me!"

"It's the truth. I told ever'body my name was Jones 'cause I done some bad things in Nebraska."

"That where you started stealing cows?"

"Nope. Learnt to change brands about a year ago. What I done in Omaha was to cut a man."

"Cut him good?"

"Killed the old son of a bitch! He had it coming, too."

"Maybe. What was his name?"

"Leroy Tinker. The mean old bastard whupped me once too often."

"You say his name was Tinker? Was he any kin to yourself?"

"Yep, my father. I told him I was too big to take a licking, but he never listened. Just kept comin' at me with that switch and that silly grin of his. He was still grinning when I put a barlow knife in his guts."

Longarm took another look through the loophole. The sun was low. If anyone had considered moving up or down the valley to scale the cliffs around them, the light would fail them before they got halfway to the top. He glanced at his smudge fire of oil shale. It was still sending up thick clouds of inky smoke. No need to put more shale on it. It'd burn past sundown.

The youth calling himself Raymond Tinker groaned and said, "You must be thinking I'm one ornery cuss, huh?"

"That's between you and the State of Nebraska. Patricide ain't a federal offense."

"You don't believe me. You think I made it up to get out of being Cotton Younger!"

"The thought crossed my mind. We'll settle it in Denver."

"You know I won't live long enough to get there, don't you?"

"Don't hardly matter. Either way, I aim to take you there."

"How—how do you transport a dead man, Longarm? I know it's a dumb thing to worry about, considering, but I'd sort of like to know."

"Well, if you want to die on me, I can't stop you. It's cool up here in the high country, so you'll likely keep a few days before you get rank."

"Ain't there no way to keep me from stinking after I go? I smelled a dead man once. I'd hate to think of myself smelling like that."

"It don't figure to bother you. I was at Shiloh, and the dead were rotting under summer rains. None of 'em sat up to apologize for the way they smelled, so they likely didn't care."

"That ain't very funny, Longarm."

"Never said it was. Shiloh was no joking matter. If I can't pack you in ice, some way, I'll just remember you said it wasn't your own idea. You got any other old murder charges you'd like to unload, Raymond?"

"Nope. Never killed nobody but my father. Is changing brands a federal matter?"

"Not unless it's a cavalry horse's brand. You're turning out to be a big disappointment to me, old son."

"I know, but it just come to me that I'm getting you killed for no good reason. I mean, after I die, you can hand me over to them others and just ride out, right?"

"Wrong. For one thing, you ain't dead yet. For another, you're my prisoner, not theirs. You and them don't seem to get my point, no matter how many times I say it. I was sent to Crooked Lance to bring you in. That's my intention. Dead, alive, Younger, Jones, Tinker, or whomsoever, you can give your soul to Jesus but your ass belongs to me!"

Chapter 19

Sundown came without an attack from across the way. To make sure nobody had foolish nighttime notions, as soon as it was completely dark, Longarm sneaked out and built another fire stack of oil shale well to the front of his breastwork, working silently in the dark. He pulled the slug from a cartridge with his teeth and laid a trail of gunpowder toward the breastwork. It took him four cartridges to make it back to cover.

He struck a match and set the powder trail alight, rolling aside with a chuckle. Someone fired at the match flare as he'd expected.

The powder carried his flame to the shale pile and in a little while the space out in front of him was illuminated in smudgy orange oil light. It left the slope across the creek black as a bitch, but he hadn't been able to see anything that far, anyway, and anybody creeping in was asking for a bullet between the glow of his or her eyes. Longarm was of the opinion that anyone that foolish didn't deserve to go on breathing.

The prisoner coughed and asked, "What's going on?"

"Nothing. They'll likely wait us out till sunup before they make the next move."

"Be a good chance for you to make a break, wouldn't it?"

"Not hardly. Only way out of here is forward, into at least a dozen and a half guns."

"You couldn't scale the cliffs back there?"

"Not with you. And if I did, where would I go?"

"Longarm, I thought my pa was stubborn, but you got him beat by a mile. Don't you know they'll be shooting down on you an hour or less after sunup?"

"Take 'em longer than that. Be nine or ten before they can work up the cliffs behind me."

"Then we'll both be dead, huh? I feel all empty-like below the belt line now. I doubt I'll last till sunup."

"Why don't you try? I'll never speak to you again if you up and die on me, boy."

The dying man laughed bitterly and said, "You've been joking, but joking softer since I got hit. What's the matter, do you feel sorry for me now?"

"Never was mad at you. Just doing my job."

"You never cussed me out for killing my own father. I've been ashamed to tell anybody, even the friends I rode with."

"You rode into Crooked Lance with friends, Raymond?"

"No. I never lied about that part. I've been alone since my partner got caught up near the Great Northern line. I was working my way south to meet some other rustlers . . . all right, cow thieves, in Bitter Creek. You was right about that running iron being foolish, but I never expected to get caught with it."

"Most folks don't. Tell me about your friends in Bitter Creek. Does one of 'em pack a .30-30 rifle?"

"Don't suspicion so. I can't tell you their names. It's against our code."

"The rifle's all I care about. You reckon them other cow thieves waiting to rescue you in Bitter Creek would be serious enough to gun some folks? Say a Missouri sheriff's deputy or a deputy U.S. marshal?"

"Hell, they likely took off like big-ass birds when I got caught. Don't you reckon?"

"Maybe. That's part of the cow thief's code, too. I want you to think before you lie to me about this, boy. I won't press you about who these friends of yours was if you'll tell me one thing true. Was any one of 'em from Missouri?"

"No. I ain't giving anything away by telling you one was from Nebraska like me. The other was a Mormon boy from Salt Lake City."

"Hmm, if I buy that, neither would have reason to pick off folks who knew their way around Clay County. You'd best rest a mite. I don't like the way you're breathing."

Longarm sat silently in the dark, digesting what the dying youth had told him. He assumed that most of what his prisoner had told him might be true. But *someone* had gunned two lawmen from Missouri and at least one man who knew the James boys on sight.

It couldn't be Frank or Jesse James. He'd managed to get at least a glimpse of everyone in or about Crooked Lance and the James boys were not only better at holdups than acting, but were known to Longarm at a glance. He'd studied the photographs of both men more than once.

The prisoner gasped, "Longarm, do you reckon there's really a place like hell?"

"Don't know. Never planned on going there if I could help it."

"If there's a hell, it's likely where I'm headed, for I was birthed mean and grew up ugly. The good book says it's wrong for a boy to love his mama, don't it?"

"Hell, you're supposed to love your mama."

"All the way? I mean, like sort of fooling with her?"

"Are you telling me that's what you and your pa had words about?"

"Hell, no, he never caught us. Ma and me was careful. We only done it when he was off hunting or something."

"But you did commit incest, huh?"

"I don't know what we committed, but I purely screwed her ever' chance I got. She showed me how when I was about thirteen. Said I was hung better'n Pa. You reckon I'll have to answer for that where I'm headed?"

"Don't know. What you want is a preaching man, old son. I don't write the laws. I just see that they're obeyed."

"Well, couldn't you *pretend* to be a preaching man, damn it? I mean, I'd take it kindly if you'd say a prayer over me or something. It don't seem fitting for a man to just lie here dying like this without somebody says somethin' from the good book."

Longarm searched his memory, harking back to a West Virginia farmhouse where gentle, care-worn hands had tucked him in at night. He shrugged and began, "The Lord is my shepherd, I shall not want . . ."

By the time he'd finished, the invisible form at his knees had stopped breathing. Longarm felt the side of his prisoner's throat for a pulse and there didn't seem to be one. He sniffed and muttered, "Never thought I'd miss a poor little pissant like you, but you left me with a long, lonesome night ahead of me."

But the night did pass, and in the dim, gray light of dawn nothing moved across the way, though once, when the breeze shifted, Longarm thought he smelled coffee brewing.

It reminded him he had to keep up his own strength, so he gnawed jerked venison, washed down with flat canteen water, as he watched for movement across the creek.

If they tried to talk some more it meant more precious time. If they didn't, it meant more than one of them was working around behind him. How long would it take to work to the top of a strange cliff a quarter of a mile high? It was anybody's guess.

The sun was painting the opposing cliff tops pink when Foster showed himself once more. He called out, "Longarm?"

"We're still here, as you likely figured. What do you want?"

"Timberline and some of the others are working up to the rim rocks above you. You haven't a chance of holding out till noon!"

"I can try. What's your play, pilgrim?"

"I've been talking to Kim Stover and some of the cooler heads. If you give up now, we can probably work out a compromise. Frankly, this thing's getting uglier than we intended."

"I'll stand pat for now, thanks."

"Longarm, they're going to kill you. Even if they don't shoot to kill from up there, you're taking foolish chances. We can't control things from down here. Once men get to shooting . . ."

"I know. Why don't you ride out with the gal before you both get in deeper? I can promise you one thing, Mountie. You won't make it back to Canada with a dead U.S. deputy to answer for!"

"I can see that, damn it! That's why I'm willing to compromise! If you'll come back to civilization with me now, I'll abide by a legal ruling in Cheyenne about the prisoner. If they say he's mine, I take him. If they give him to you, I give up. Agreed?"

"Hell, no! I got the jasper, and possession is nine-tenths of the law. I don't need no territorial judge to say who he belongs to. The prisoner belongs to *me*!"

"Longarm, you're acting like a fool!"

"That makes two of us, doesn't it?"

Kim Stover called over to Longarm, "Please be reasonable, Deputy Long. I don't want my friends to get in trouble!"

"They're already in trouble, ma'am! This ain't coffee and cake and let's-pretend-we're-vigilantes! You folks wanted the fun without considering the stakes. I'll tell you what I'll do, though. You and any others who've had enough of this game can ride out peaceable, and I won't press charges."

"What are you talking about! You're in no position to press charges! We're trying to save your life, you big idiot!"

"Well, I thank you for the kind thoughts, ma'am, but I'll save my own life as best I can."

Foster yelled, "I'm moving Mrs. Stover out of range, Longarm. You're obviously crazy as a loon and the shooting will be starting any minute now!"

Longarm watched them go back to their boulder, then rolled over on one elbow to gaze up at the cliffs above him. The prisoner's face was pale and cold now, and the eyes were filmed with dust. Longarm pressed the lids closed, but they popped open again, so he went back to watching the skyline.

His eyes narrowed when, a good ten minutes later, a human head appeared as a tiny dot up above. Another, then another appeared beside it. Longarm suddenly grinned and waved. One of the figures staring down at him waved back. Longarm went to the still-smoldering shale-oil smudge fire, and keeping his head down, used his saddle blanket to break the rising column of smoke into long and short puffs. The next time he looked up, the dots on the rim rock had vanished.

He crawled back to the breastwork, tied his kerchief to the barrel of his Winchester, and waved it back and forth above the wall until Foster hailed him, calling out, "Do you surrender?"

"No, but you're about to. Tell the folks around you not to get spooked in the next few minutes. Some friends of mine are moving in behind you and some old boys shoot first and ask questions later when they see Indians. Tell 'em the ones coming in are Utes. They won't kill nobody, 'less some damn fool starts shooting!"

"What in the devil are you talking about? It's my understanding the Utes are not on the warpath!"

"'Course they ain't. They're on the Ouray Reservation, about a ten-hour ride from here, when they ain't investigating smoke on the horizon. The Ouray Utes are wards of the U.S. Government, so I thought I ought to send for 'em. Some of 'em don't speak our lingo, so make sure nobody acts unfriendly as they come in to disarm you."

"Disarm us? You can't be serious!"

"Oh, but I am, and so are they. I just sort of deputized the whole damn tribe. You said eighteen-to-one was hard odds? Well, I figure I now have you outgunned about ten- or twelve-to-one. So don't act foolish."

"My God, you'd set savage Indians against your own race?"

"Yep. Had to. Only way I could do what I aimed to be doing."

"What's that, get away from us with my prisoner?"

"Hell, I could have done that days ago. The reason I led you all down here was to put you under arrest."

"Arrest? You can't arrest *me*!"

"If you'll look up the slope behind you, you'll see that I've just done it."

The Mountie turned to stare openmouthed at the long line of armed Indians on the skyline and the others coming down the trail on painted ponies. He saw white men getting up from behind rocks, holding their hands out away from their gunbelts as they tried to look innocent. A pair of Ute braves had Timberline on foot between their ponies. To avoid any last-minute misunderstandings, Longarm got up from behind his little fort and walked over to them, waving his Stetson.

An older moon-faced Indian on a stocky pinto rode it into the creek and waited there, beaming broadly as Longarm approached. He said in English, "It has been a good hunt. Just like the old days when we fought the Sioux and Blackfoot in the high meadows to the north. What is my brother from the Great White Father doing here? Do you want us to kill these people? They do not seem to be your friends."

"My blood brother, Hungry Calf, is hasty. Is the agent over on your reservation still my old friend, Caldwell?"

"Yes. He is a good man. He does not cheat us as the one you arrested that time did. We did not bring him. Agent Caldwell is good, but he says foolish things when we ride out for a bit of fun."

"I'd like to have all these people taken to the reservation, Hungry Calf. I'm arresting them in the name of the Great White Father."

"Good. We will take them to Agent Caldwell, and if he gives us his permission, we will hang them all for you."

"Tell the other *Ho* not to harm them in any way. Most of them are not bad people."

"Ah, but some of these *saltu* have broken the white father's law. Can we hang them?"

"You won't have to. You *Ho* have herds of longhorns now. You know how a hand cuts the critters he wants from a rounded-up herd?"

"Of course. Herding longhorns is less fun than hunting, but we are now fine cowboys, if what Agent Caldwell says is true. We shall drive them all in together, then my brother can cut the bad ones out for the branding, It should be interesting to watch. I have never herded white people before."

Chapter 20

It took Longarm and his Ute allies most of the day to get the out-raged whites over to the Ouray Reservation, to the east. One of the Indians was kind enough to pack the dead prisoner, wrapped in a tarp, across a pony. When they rode into the unpainted frame buildings at the government town called White Sticks, as the sun went down, a tall man in a dusty black suit came out with a puzzled smile.

Longarm rode up to him and smiled back, saying, "Got a dead man with me, Mister Caldwell. Can I store him in your icehouse for a few days?"

"God, no, but I'll bury him under ice and sawdust in a shed till you want him back. Who are all these other folks, Longarm? What have you and my Indians been up to?"

"I'm citing them for helping me make some arrests. They'll be bringing in some others before morning. I deputized some of Hungry Calf's young men to round up the others headed this way."

Foster rode over to protest, "See here! I am on Her Majesty's business under an agreement with the State Department!"

Longarm said, "He don't work for the State Department, Sergeant. You're on land controlled by the Department of the Interior and they don't *like* State all that much. Ride back and take charge of the others, if you're all so anxious to help. Tell 'em to make camp and sort of stay put, for now, while I make arrangements with my friends. You do have your own grub, don't you? These *Ho* friends of mine don't have all that much to give away."

Interested despite his outrage, Foster asked, "Why do you call them *Ho*? This is the *Ute* reservation, isn't it?"

"Sure it is. Ute is what others call 'em. They call themselves *Ho* 'cause it means *folks* in their own lingo. They call you *saltu* meaning *strangers*, for reasons you can likely figure out. So don't mess up and nobody will get hurt."

Caldwell said, "Longarm is delicate about Indian niceties. He calls Apaches by their own name of Na-dene. Calls a Sioux a Dakota."

"All but the western Sioux," Longarm corrected. "They say *La*-ko-tah."

The Mountie sniffed and said, "All very interesting, I'm sure. Do you have a telegraph connection here, Agent Caldwell?"

"Sure. Wired into Western Union."

"May I use it to notify Her Majesty's Government I've been abducted by Ute Indians?"

Caldwell glanced at Longarm, who nodded and said, "Why not? He's a guest."

Longarm saw that the Mountie wasn't going to explain things to the others, so as Foster and Caldwell went inside the headquarters building to send the message, Longarm ambled over to the large group of whites around the Indian campfire they'd helped themselves to. Longarm saw that his Ho friends had given them back their sidearms, as he'd told them to, and had hidden their horses someplace as he had instructed.

Timberline had been squatting on his heels next to Kim Stover, who sat cross-legged on a saddle blanket near the small fire. The tall foreman smiled thinly and said, "I'd better never see you anywhere off this reservation, Longarm. You've pushed me from obliging a lady to *personal*!"

Longarm figured Timberline was just showing off for the red-head, so he ignored him and announced for all to hear, "I'm holding the bunch of you overnight on what you might call self-recog. The Indians won't pester you 'less you try to reclaim a horse."

The midget, Cedric Hanks, piped up from across the fire, "You've no right to hold us here! We're white folks, not Utes!

Your writ don't apply to us here! The Bureau of Indian Affairs has nothing to say about the comings and goings of such as we."

"You may be right, Hanks. When that Mountie's through, I'll wire my office for a ruling. Meanwhile, you'd all best figure on a night's rest here in White Sticks. I'll see, later, about some entertainment. Hungry Calf likes to put on shows for company. By the way, I got some Ho out looking for your wife and the others. We'll sort it out once all the interested parties are together."

"You say they have a telegraph line here? I'd like to send some wires."

"You don't get to. Reservation wire's for government business only. The Mountie rates its use because he's a real peace officer with a government. Private detectives are just pests. As for the rest of you, since some of you put all that effort into keeping the Western Union line to Crooked Lance out of order, you got no reason to send messages into a busted line."

Kim Stover asked, "Do you have any idea who among us might have cut the wire to Crooked Lance, Deputy Long?"

"Got lots of ideas. But I'm trying to work out proof that would hold up in court. There's more'n one reason to cut an outlying cow town off from communications. Friends of the prisoner one of you shot might have wanted things quiet while they made a private play to spring him. Then again, the Eastern meatpackers might not want folks with a hard-scrabble herd in rough range to be abreast of the latest beef quotations back East. I'll save you asking by telling you. When I left Denver, range stock was selling for twenty-nine dollars a head at trackside."

The girl smiled for a change, and said, "Oh, that *is* a good price! We had no idea the price of beef was up!"

"I figured as much. We're going into a boom on beef after the bad times we've been having. They've been having bad crops and politics over in the old countries. Queen Victoria and Mister Bismarck are buying all the tinned beef they can get for their armies. France is bouncing back from the whupping the Prussians gave 'em a few years back and is carving slices out of Africa with an army that has to be fed. I'd say the hungry days are over for you cow folks."

Timberline's voice was almost friendly as he finished counting on his fingers and observed, "Jesus! Figuring all our herds consolidated, we got near fifty thousand dollars worth of beef up in our valley!"

"I know. You'll be able to build your schoolhouse without ob-structin' justice and such. As long as we're on the subject, that prisoner of yours . . ." Then Longarm caught himself and de-cided he'd said enough, if not too much, for now.

He was saved further conversation by the arrival of Hungry Calf at the fire. On foot, the chief looked much shorter than he had while astride a pony, for the Ho were built like their Eskimo cousins in the northlands they'd wandered down from before Columbus took that wrong turn to India. Hungry Calf's arms and legs were a bit shorter than most white mens'. Yet his head and torso were bigger than Longarm's. Given legs in European pro-portion to his body, he'd have been as tall as Timberline instead of being a head shorter than Longarm. It was just as well he was friendly. A hand-to-hand set-to with the bearlike Hungry Calf would be one hard row to hoe.

The Indian said, "The people are happy to have something new to talk about. The maidens would like to have a fertility dance to entertain our guests."

Longarm nodded and said, "That's right neighborly of my brother's people. You tell 'em it's all right. Then come back. I'd like a few more words with my Ho brother."

As the Indian waddled off in the darkness Longarm turned back to the crowd of mostly young male cowhands and said soberly, "I want you all to listen up. The Indians are trying to be neighborly, and some of them young squaws can be handsome-looking to a healthy man, so I'd best warn you, Indians on a reser-vation are wards of the state and you're not allowed to trifle with 'em."

One of the Crooked Lance riders snorted, "That'll be the day! This whole durned camp smells like burning cow— excuse me, Miss Kim."

"Burning cow pats is what you're smelling, sure enough. I don't want anyone here to get close enough to smelling any squaws to consider himself an expert on the subject. If the Indian agent catches you at it, it's a federal charge. If the squaw's old man does, it can get more serious. So you let 'em flirt and shimmy all they want, and keep your seats till the entertainment's over, hear?"

As he started to leave, Kim Stover asked, "Is this . . . fertility rite liable to be . . . improper?"

"You mean for a white lady to watch? No, ma'am. You'll likely find it sort of dull, considering the message."

He excused himself and walked a few yards toward the clustered outlines of the agency. Hungry Calf materialized to say, "The one in the red coat is standing around the ponies. Can my young men kill him?"

"No. Just have them watch him, without hindering him in any way. I want to know whatever he does, but he's allowed to do it."

"What if he steals ponies? Can we kill him then?"

"No. The Great White Father will pay you for anything he steals from my Ho brothers."

"Hah! I think my brother is baiting some kind of trap! Can Agent Caldwell tell you the message he sent on the singing wire!"

"He doesn't have to. I know."

"Longarm has strong medicine. He knows everything. We know this to be true. When that other agent was cheating my people, none of us suspected it, for the man was cunning. Longarm's medicine unmasked his trickery, even after his written words on paper fooled the other agents of the Great White Father. The red coat is a fool. We shall watch him, cat-eyed, through the night, until he does what Longarm knows he will."

Longarm thanked his informant and went over to the agency, where he found Caldwell seated at a table with his vapidly pretty white wife. As Longarm remembered, her name was Portia.

Portia Caldwell remembered him, too. She literally hauled him inside and sat him in her vacated chair, across from her husband, and began to putter with her cast-iron stove, chatting like a magpie about fixing him something to go with his coffee.

Longarm grinned across the table at his host and said, "I'll settle for maybe a slice of that apple cobbler you're famous for, ma'am. What I came to ask about was the disposition of the remains I had packed in."

Caldwell grimaced and said, "I might have known you'd want to talk about it at the table. Is it true the dead man was kin to Jesse James and wanted in Canada on a very ugly charge I'd as soon not repeat in front of my wife?"

"You read the sounds of the Mountie's key as he was sending, huh? Who'd he wire, Washington or Fort MacLeod?"

"Both. He said he'd gotten his man, whatever that means."

"It's Mountie talk. You got the—you know—properly guarded?"

"Couple of Utes are keeping an eye on the shed it's stored in. You don't expect anyone to try and steal a—preserved evidence?"

Portia Caldwell shoved a big bowl of apple cobbler in front of

Longarm, saying, "For heaven's sake, I know there's a corpse in the smokehouse! I'm an army brat, not a shrinking violet. I saw my first body when my mother took me to visit Daddy, three days after Gettysburg!"

Caldwell grimaced again and said, "She says the worst smell was when they burned the dead horses. Ain't she something?"

"You're lucky to have the right woman for your job. The Shoshone try to steal any of your charges' ponies, lately?"

"No, we're having trouble with a few Apache bands to the south, as always, but I'd say the day of real Indian Wars is over, wouldn't you?"

"Maybe. I filed a report from a 'breed informant a few months ago. If I was you, I'd keep an eye peeled for a wandering medicine man called Wava-something-or-other. They say he's a Paiute dream-singer who has a new religion."

"Paiute? Nobody's ever had much trouble from that tribe. They maybe shot up a few wagon trains back in '49, but, hell, every young buck did that in them days just for the hell of it. Most of the fighting tribes despise the Paiute."

"Well, this one young jasper I've heard of bears watching, just the same. He ain't trying to stir up his own people. He wanders about, even riding trains, selling medicine shirts."

"Medicine shirts? What kind of medicine?"

"Bulletproof. Not bulletproof *iron* shirts. Regular old buckskin shirts with strong medicine signs painted on 'em. I ain't certain if this young Paiute dream-singer's a con man or sincere, but, like I said, we're keeping an eye on him."

Portia Caldwell asked, "If you know who he is, why can't you just arrest him, Longarm?"

"On what charge, ma'am? If there was a law against religious notions I'd have to start with arresting Christian missionaries, which just might not be such a bad idea, considering some I've met."

"But this Paiute's selling crazy charmed shirts he says can stop a bullet!"

"Well, who's to say they can't, as long as no Indian does anything to get his fool self shot at? The danger as I see it ain't in *wearing* a lucky shirt. It's in wearing it on the warpath."

Caldwell shook his head and said, "My Ute are a pragmatic people. Besides, who'd buy medicine made by another tribe?"

"The Pine Ridge Dakota, for openers. This Paiute priest, prophet, or whatever has been selling his shirts mail-order."

"Oh, the damned Sioux can't be serious about it. They've been whipped too many times. And besides, why should they think the magic of another tribe would be any good to them?"

"Don't know. I ain't a Dakota. Sitting Bull has said much the same about the crosses and bibles the Catholic mission at Pine Ridge has been distributing."

"That's not the same. Christianity is not an Indian superstition."

"You're right. It's what us whites call good medicine."

"Longarm, if you intend to start another religious argument—"

"I don't. I'm outnumbered two-to-one, hereabouts. I've passed on my information. You B.I.A. folks can do what you've a mind to with it."

"I thank you for it, and I'll keep an eye peeled for those crazy bulletproof medicine shirts, but I'm certain we've seen the last of Indian uprisings in this century."

"Maybe. 'Bout thirty, forty years ago another white man collected some information on another kind of Indian. He was an Englishman named Burton, but he was sensible, anyway. He told Queen Victoria's Indian agents about some odd talk he'd picked up from some heathen informants. They told him they knew better. British India had seen the last of Indian risings, too. Couple of years later the Sepoy Mutiny busted wide open and a couple of thousand whites got killed."

He excused himself and got up from the table to let them ponder his words of cheer as he left. Outside, the night was filled with the monotonous beat of a dog-skin drum as Longarm sauntered back to where he'd left his "guests."

A circle of Ho women were around the fire, arms locked, as they shuffled four steps to the left, followed by four steps to the right. Longarm hunkered down by the widow Stover's blanket and observed, "I told you there wasn't all that big a shucks to it, ma'am."

"How long do they keep that up?" she asked.

"Till they get as tired of it as we already are, I reckon. I've seen it go on all night."

"Is that all there is to it? Neither the beat nor the dance step varies. If you could call dragging your feet like that dancing."

"Indians set great store by repeating things, ma'am. The number four is sacred to the spirits. They think everything either should or does happen in fours."

"Where'd they get such a fool superstition?"

"Don't know. Where'd *we* get the notion of the Trinity and everything happening in threes?"

"I'm not a Roman Catholic, either. You said this was a fertility rite. I expected something . . . well, more pagan."

"Oh, they're pagan enough. But Indians don't act dirty about what comes natural. That drum beat's calculated to heat things up, if you'll listen to it sharp."

"What is there to listen to? That fool medicine man just keeps whacking it over and over, bump, bump, bump."

"You missed a beat. He hits it four good licks and starts over. The normal human heart beats just a mite slower than that drum. After a time, though, everybody listening sort of gets their own hearts going with that drum. Hearts beating faster heats the blood and, uh, other things. The fertility part just comes natural, later, in the lodges."

"You mean we're likely to see an all-night Indian orgy?"

"Nope. You won't see or hear a thing. They don't show off about such matters."

"Well, if it's all the same to you, I'm bored as well as tired and I'd like to get some sleep."

"I figured as much. If you'll allow me, I'll take you over to the agent's house and they'll bed you in a spare room."

"Oh? That's right thoughtful of you and your friends. I was afraid I'd have to spend another night on the ground in my blankets."

"No need to, ma'am. If you ask her, Portia Caldwell might work out a bath for you, too. Let me help you up."

He rose, hauling Kim to her feet, and took her by an elbow to guide her toward the agency.

Timberline suddenly appeared in front of them to demand, "Just what do you think you're up to, damn it?"

"Don't think nothing. I'm carrying this lady over to the agency to put her to bed."

The big ramrod swung, saying something about Longarm's mother that he couldn't have possibly been informed about. Longarm ducked the roundhouse and danced backward, drawing his .44 as he sighed and said, "Now that's enough, old son."

"Damn it, if you was any kind of man at all you'd fight me fair."

"If I fought you with fists I'd be more fool than any other kind of man worth mention. You're too big for me and I'm too fast on the draw for you, so I suspicion we ain't able to have a fair fight, either way."

Kim Stover got between them and soothed, "Don't be silly, Timberline. He was only taking me over to stay with the married couple at the house."

"Oh? I thought—"

Longarm knew what he'd thought, but a man was wasting time to jaw with a fool. So he said, "We'd best get over to Portia Caldwell, ma'am. I got other fish to fry this night."

Timberline tagged along, muttering under his breath, but he didn't do or say anything until they had all reached the porch of the agency. Kim Stover turned to him and said, "You'd best stay out here, Timberline."

"I mean to see you're safe, little lady."

"Safe? I'm under arrest, thanks to going along with this foolishness. If you're talking about this other man trifling with me, nobody knows better'n you I can hold my own on any front porch."

"I ain't leaving you alone with him."

Longarm said, "Yes you are. I'll go along with some showoff for the diversion of a lady, but she's just asked you to git, so you'd best do it."

Timberline didn't move away, but he stopped following as Longarm escorted the redhead up the steps. As he was about to knock, she put a hand on his sleeve and said, "One moment, sir. You didn't disagree when I just said I was under arrest!"

"Ain't polite to correct a lady, ma'am."

"May I ask what I'm under arrest for, now that you have your prisoner and the rest of us are left out in the cold?"

"You ain't half as cold as my prisoner is on that bed of ice, ma'am."

"I'm right sorry he got killed, but you know I never fired a shot at anyone!"

"Somebody did. Hit him twice, too. I ain't charging you with killing him, ma'am. Let's say you're a material witness."

"Dang it, *I* don't know whose bullets hit that boy! Half the men with me were shooting at Cotton Younger!"

"I know. Obstruction of justice and killing a federal prisoner under a peace officer's protection could be taken seriously, but I'd be willing to overlook past misunderstandings, if that was all that happened."

"You mean you're still investigating the missing lawmen and the killing of Sailor Brown?"

"Don't you reckon I ought to?"

"Of course, but none of us knows anything about any of that!"

"There I go, correcting ladies again, but you're wrong, ma'am. Somebody either with you or headed this way knows more'n they're letting on."

"That may well be, but I don't see why you're holding me or the other innocent folks."

"Funny, Hungry Calf did, and he ain't been herding cows as long as you. What we're having here is a tally and cut, ma'am. My Indian deputies are still rounding up the herd. I suspicion some will come in willingly on their own. By this time tomorrow I hope to be done marking and branding."

"And then my innocent friends and me will be riding out?"

"Maybe. Depends on who gets arrested. I'd best knock now. I've other chores to tend to."

As he knocked, the redhead demanded, "Are you accusing *me* of . . . something?"

The door opened. Longarm introduced the two women, and before he had to answer more questions, left them to work things out.

Timberline was still waiting, and this time he had his old hog leg out and pointing. Longarm said, "Oh, put that fool thing away, kid. No gals are watching."

"God damn you! I ain't scared of you!"

"That makes us even. You'd best get back to the dance. The squaws'll be passing drinks and tobacco in a while. They ain't supposed to have no liquor, but you'll likely get some passable corn squeezings."

Timberline kept the pistol trained on Longarm as the lawman walked right past him. Timberline called out, "Stand still, God damn it! I ain't done with you!"

Longarm kept walking. Timberline followed, blustering, "Turn around, God damn it! I can't shoot no man in the back!"

Not looking back, Longarm said, "Not here, you can't. Quit showing off without no audience, Timberline. We both know you're stuck on a reservation filled with friends of mine. You got no horse.

You got no nerve to go with your brag. You keep pestering me and you'll have no gun. I'm coming to the conclusion you ain't grown up enough to wear sidearms, the way you keep carrying on."

Timberline holstered his gun, muttering, "One day we'll meet where you ain't holding all the winning cards, Longarm."

Longarm didn't bother to answer. He went near, but not all the way, to the fire, and took up a position where he could watch, standing back from the glow and the shifting shadows. He didn't watch the dancers. Once you watched the first eight steps of most Indian dances you'd seen about all that was about to happen. He watched the vigilantes and the little bounty hunter, Hanks, long enough to see that they didn't seem to be up to anything interesting, either. Foster wasn't near the fire. Across the way, Timberline had hunkered down by some of his sidekicks, scowling fiercely.

A soft female voice at his side asked, "Has Longarm a place to sleep this night?"

Longarm turned to smile down at a pretty, moon-faced girl of perhaps eighteen summers. Like other Ho women she wore a shapeless, ankle-length Mother Hubbard of cotton, decorated with quillwork around the collar. Longarm said, "Evening, Dances-Humming. Is my brother, your husband, well?"

"This person is no longer the woman of Many Ponies."

"Oh? Something happen to him?"

"Yes, he got older. This person is not a woman for a man who'd gotten old and fat and lazy. Many Ponies was sent home to his mother's lodge."

Longarm nodded soberly. He knew the marriage laws of the Ho well enough not to have to ask foolish questions. Some whites might say they were sort of casual about such things. He considered them practical.

On the other hand, while the man he knew as Many Ponies might be getting fat, he was big for a Ho and inclined to brood. The girl called Dances-Humming, while very pretty, had learned English from the last agent, the one arrested for mistreating the Indians. If there was one woman to be trusted less than a Larimer Street play-pretty, it was a squaw who spoke perfect English.

He said, "How come you ain't dancing with the other gals?"

"This person is tired of the old customs. They mean so little when our men grow fat and drunk on the Great White Father's allowance."

"Some healthy young cowboys, over by the fire?"

"This person has seen them. None of them look interesting. The last time you were here, this person was younger and you laughed at her childish ways. Since then, this person has learned how white women make love. Would you like to see how Dances-Humming can kiss?"

"Like to. Can't. It's against the law."

"The Great White Father's law, not ours. Come, we can talk about it in my lodge."

Longarm was about to refuse, but a sudden suspicion made him reconsider. Dances-Humming giggled and took his hand, tugging him after her through the dim light. He allowed himself to be led, muttering, "Sometimes there's nothing a gent can do but lay down and take his beating like a man."

Dances-Humming's lodge was not a tent. Like most of her people on the reservation, she'd been given a frame cabin neatly placed along the gravel street leading to the agency. The B.I.A. furnished whitewash, with the understanding that the Indians would paint their cabins. They never did so, not because they were shiftless, but because they thought it was silly to paint pine when the sun soon bleached it to a nice shade of silver gray that never needed repainting.

Dances-Humming led him inside and lit a candle stub, bathing the interior in warm, soft light. The cabin was furnished with surplus army camp furnishings. The walls were hung with painted deerskins and flat gathering baskets woven long ago. Dances-Humming seldom worked at the old skills. Reservation life was turning her and her people into something no longer Indian, but not yet white. Prostitution had been unknown when the various bands of Ho had roamed from the Rockies to the Sierras in a prouder time.

Dances-Humming sat on a bunk, atop the new-looking Hudson Bay blanket. She patted the creamy wool at her side and said, "Sit down. This person's guest looks puzzled."

"I reckon I am. Last time I was here you said something about a knife in my lights and liver."

"This person was angry. You arrested a man who had been good to her and they made her marry an old man. But that was long ago, when this person was a foolish child."

She suddenly drew her legs up under her and was kneeling in the center of the bunk. She pulled the loose Mother Hubbard off over her head and threw it aside. She laughed, stark naked, and asked, "Has not this person grown into a real woman?"

Longarm said, "That's for damn sure!" as he stared down at her firm, brown breasts in the candlelight. Then he sniffed and said, "My medicine don't allow me to pay a woman, Dances-Humming."

"Did this person ask for presents? What do you take her for, a whore?"

Longarm did, but he didn't say so. He said, "If Agent Caldwell caught us, he'd report me to the B.I.A."

"No, he wouldn't. He owes his job to you. Besides, how is he to know?"

"Well, you might just tell him."

"Why would this person do that?"

"Maybe to get a white man who riled you in trouble. You did say you'd *fix* me, last time around."

Dances-Humming cupped her breasts in her hands and thrust the nipples out at him teasingly, asking, "Is this the way you're afraid this person will fix you?" Her voice took on a bitter shade as she added, "You are a white man with a badge. Do you think they'd take this person's word against yours?"

He saw that there were tears in her sloe eyes and sat beside her, soothing, "Let's not blubber about it, honey. You're just taking me by surprise, is all. I mean, I didn't know we were friends."

"You men are all alike when it comes to a woman's mind! Don't you know that a woman is a cat? Don't you know why a woman, or a cat, spits most at those who ignore her?"

"Ignoring you would be a chore, considering."

"Good. Let's kiss and make up, then, shall we?"

Without waiting for an answer, Dances-Humming was all over him, bare bottom in his lap as she rubbed everything else against him while planting a wet, openmouthed kiss full on his lips. She had his back to the wall now and was fumbling at his buttons, complaining with her mouth on his, "You white men wear so many clothes! Don't they get in the way at times like these?"

"They sure as hell do!" Longarm said, pushing her clear enough to start undressing himself, as he added, "Snuff that candle. You ain't got curtains on the windows!"

She laughed and leaped from the bunk, a tawny vision of desire as she bent to put the light out. By the time she crawled up on the bunk beside him, Longarm had gotten rid of most of his duds. The first thing he'd removed was his gunbelt, and he'd shoved it between the bunk and the wall, the grips of the .44 handy.

She wrestled playfully with him as he finished undressing and they were both laughing when, at last, their nude bodies melted together.

Dances-Humming was hotter than a two-dollar pistol and moved it like a saloon door on payday, but there was something wrong. Longarm had been with enough women to know when they were taking pleasure as well as giving it. The little squaw made love like a professional, and since that way's calculated to pleasure a man, Longarm enjoyed it.

After a time, as they rested with him still inside her, he ran his hand down between their moist warm torsos to tickle her wetness. She stopped him, asking, "What is the matter, didn't you enjoy it?"

"You know I did, honey. I'm trying to make you come."

"Why? This person didn't ask it."

"Well, hell, it's common courtesy! Don't you *want* to come, honey?"

"I already did, before. You can just do as you wish. This person does not mind. She is tired."

Longhorn frowned, wondering why she was lying. She'd acted like she was going crazy a minute ago, but he'd been with too many others to be fooled. While she wasn't getting paid like a whore, she was doing it like a whore. He'd wondered where she'd gotten that new blanket.

He said, "Well, if you're tired, you're tired. I'll just be on my way, soon as I can find where I threw my boots."

She stiffened and said, "You can't leave now! It's too early!"

"Maybe nine o'clock, maybe ten. I thank you for the hospitality, but I can see I ain't wanted, so—"

"Don't go! I'll let you play with me! I'll do anything, anything you want!"

"Uh-uh. Your Indian powwow stuff is slipping, too. I'd better get it on down the road, honey."

He swung his bare legs over the edge and sat up, bending over to reach for his socks. Dances-Humming reached for the holstered .44 against the wall, drew it, and placed the muzzle against the back of Longarm's head as she pulled the trigger.

The gun clicked twice before he'd reached around and taken it from her, saying, "First thing they ever told me was not to leave a loaded gun where a whore could get at it, Dances-Humming. I took the liberty of unloading it before leaving it there to bait you."

She tried to back away as far as possible, but she only got as far as the corner. She sat there, knees drawn up, and trembling as she gasped, "I don't want to die!"

"Well, not many folks do. Did the man who put you up to this say how you were to get away with killing me, or are you just dumb?"

"I didn't think! I had to—I *have* to keep you here, no matter what!"

"Well, blowing my brains out my nose was a piss-poor idea, honey. You weren't gonna sing that same old song about the wicked white man trying to rape an Indian lady defending her honor, were you?"

"I don't know! There wasn't time to think!"

"You'd better *learn* to think, girl! If I'd been as dumb as you, we'd both be in a pickle. I'd be dead and you'd be explaining things to Hungry Calf and the other chiefs. I'll allow an Indian agent will believe most anything, but you'd last less than five minutes when the elders got to asking what happened."

She buried her face in her hands and began to bawl like a baby.

Longarm reached out and put an arm around her, soothing, "Oh, hush, no harm's been done."

"Are you going to tell on me?"

"Don't reckon I need to now. You do see how another wicked white man led you astray, don't you? I swear, Dances-Humming, you do get led astray more'n any Ho gal I've met. You sure you didn't have an Apache grandmother? No, that don't figure. Apache blood would have left you smarter. You see, honey, if folks can't be smart, they have to be good. Dumb and wicked is a fearsome combination."

"If you won't beat me, I'll tell you who paid me to keep you here all night."

"I don't aim to beat you, and I know who paid you. As long as he never paid you to kill me, what the hell."

"What are you going to do when you leave here? Are you sure you'll be able to kill him? He said he would be very cross with me if I let you out tonight."

"Well, I'll tell you what we'd best do. Since I'm supposed to spend the night here, I'd just as soon. You did say you didn't want me to tell Hungry Calf and the others, didn't you?"

"Don't tell them! I'll do anything."

"I know. I'm going to have to tie you up. Not that I don't trust you, you understand, but I'd never in this world be able to fall asleep with you running about maybe looking for knives and such."

"I wouldn't try again to hurt you. This person is afraid."

"That makes two of us. I'll tie you gentle, but I'll tie you fast. You want to do anything, first?"

She started to protest, but she knew he meant it, so as Longarm rummaged through her things for a rope she pulled a chamber pot from under the bed and relieved herself. From the long, hissing sound, he knew she was badly frightened.

He found a length of cotton clothesline, tested it with a few snaps, and decided it would do. He brought the coil to the bunk and sat down, fishing in his pants for his jackknife. Dances-Humming rose to her feet and stood before him, resigned to his will.

Longarm cut the rope into four sections and got up, pulling the top blanket from the bunk. He threw it out in the middle of the floor and patted the quilted surface as he said, "Climb aboard and pick out a comfortable position; you'll be in it for some time."

"I sleep best on my stomach."

"There you go, then. Facedown, hands above your head. I'll give you a little slack, but I'll hear you if you get to jerking it, and I'll whup your bare ass for it."

The treacherous little squaw lay across the mattress on her belly and Longarm lashed a wrist to each head post of the bunk while she sniffled and protested. He tied her ankles to the posts at the foot of the bunk, leaving her some slack to shift a bit. Then he sat down with his back to her and started pulling on his socks. She asked. "Why are you getting dressed?"

"To keep from freezing before morning, of course. I'll throw the blanket over you, directly. Then I'll hunker down in a corner in my duds, facing the door."

"It's so early. Even Many Ponies used to make love to me more than once a night."

"Honey, you are full of shit as well as frigid. You won't get out of them ropes by stirring up the love potion pot. I'll allow it figures to be a tedious cold night, but what the hell."

"Won't you do it one more time? Now that this person has less fear, she remembers how nice you felt inside of her. She was too worried to let herself go before. This time will be different."

"Oh, hell, I got my socks on and you're hogtied just right, and facedown to boot!"

"I can raise myself high enough. See?"

He saw indeed, as the moonlight now lancing through one window shone on the firm, plump hemispheres of her tawny buttocks. He ran his free hand over her flesh, soothingly, and sighed, "Don't know as it's right to do it to a gal tied up with ropes. Read someplace about this French feller who liked to do it that way, and the book said he was touched in the head."

"Untie me, then."

"In a pig's eye! You don't want to get humped. You only want to have them ropes off you!"

"That's not this person's reason. Feel the way she's gushing with her need!"

He explored the crevice between her writhing buttocks and warm brown thighs with his fingers, noting, "You're drooling like a woman in love and that's a fact."

"Do it! For some reason this person is excited by the ropes!"

Longarm got up and climbed aboard the bunk, resting his weight on all fours as he positioned his knees up and to either side of her hips. It was awkward in this position, but as Dances-Humming felt his erection in the wet crevice between them, she moved herself into line and took advantage of the slack bondage to engulf him with a hungry sigh.

"Oh, it feels so . . . *interesting* this way!" she giggled, as Longarm, getting the hang of it, began to rock back and forward on his knees. It was well for him that he was a practiced horseman with well-developed riding muscles; even so, his thighs began to cramp by the time it was too late to stop. The Indian girl began to gyrate wildly as she literally screwed herself on and almost off, biting her lip as she groaned delighted words in her own language, for Dances-Humming was not a white man's love toy now. She reverted to her birthright as a natural, hot-blooded girl who a missionary, in his ignorance, might describe as "primitive."

This time she didn't fake an orgasm. She had one, then another and another as the man who'd mastered her pounded and pounded her from the rear. Longarm gasped, "Oh, Jesus H. Christ!" and let her rip. It felt funny as hell to come with both legs fixing to bust.

He was tempted to untie her and make a night of it, now that they'd become better acquainted, but he knew he'd need his strength come sunup and he still didn't trust her far enough to spit.

He climbed off and got dressed, throwing the Hudson Bay blanket over the crooning, sex-drugged little squaw.

He bent and kissed her on the ear. Then he went to a corner and slid down to squat Mexican style with his holster pulled around between his thighs. He reloaded the .44. Then he crossed his arms over his raised knees and lowered his head to them, trying to think if he'd left any loose ends.

He couldn't think of any. His saddle and possibles were stored in the agency, along with Kim Stover. If any of the others got in trouble with squaws or corn squeezings it wasn't his duty to worry about it. Agent Caldwell and the tribal council were getting paid to keep things down to a roar, hereabouts.

It was already getting chilly, as the thin air of the high country surrendered its stored sunlight to the stars. He knew he'd have a frozen ass by daybreak, but he'd been cold before, and he aimed to rise early and to be wide awake as soon as he did so.

He might have dreamed. He must have dreamed, for he was thinking about how cold it was out here on the picket line tonight with the enemy just across the river and no picket fires allowed this close to the front by order of the general when, somewhere, a rooster crowed, and he sat up, blinking the cobwebs from his brain and shivering in the icy dawn.

He sat still for a moment, gazing across the little cabin at the girl on the bunk. She was watching him from under the edge of the blanket, her sloe eyes unreadable. Longarm nodded and said, "'Morning."

"This person has been trying to understand you. Even for a white man, you act crazy."

"It was your idea to do it that way. I'm damned if I can see what that French feller got out of it. Can't change position worth a damn."

"This person wasn't talking about that. It was very exciting to be taken as a captive. Now the tales of the old women make more sense. What makes no sense at all is the way you acted after you made this person tell you the truth."

"Would you rather I'd have spanked you?"

"No. Many Ponies tried to beat me once. I sent him home to his mother's lodge. I thought you'd go after the man who paid me to betray you."

"And miss all the fun we had? Along with being dumb, you lack the imagination of your people, Dances-Humming. The Ho are famous hunting and fighting folks. The Dakota call 'em their favorite enemies; it's hard as anything to outwit the Ute band of the Ho."

He got up, stretching and moving his holster over to his left hip as he came over and removed the blanket to untie her. Dances-Humming rolled over and writhed invitingly on her back, asking, "Would you like to do it the old-fashioned way this time?"

"I'd like to. Can't. Got too many chores to tend to. I'll be leaving now, with some parting words of advice. If you repeat 'em to the B.I.A. I'll have to call you a liar, but you ain't making it as an Indian, gal. If I was you, I'd move down to Salt Lake and take up the trade near the U.P. station. You're a pretty little thing, and you could make your fortune off railroad roustabouts and whisky drummers looking for what you're so good at. You stay here on the reservation, selling half-ass treachery along with what you're good at, and some night one of the decent folks hereabouts will surely cut your throat."

He left as she was still protesting her inborn goodness.

Outside, the air had a bite to it, but tasted crisp and clean. The girl's cabin, like most Indian dwellings, was unventilated and smoke-scented, for folks living close to nature with few warm clothes valued warmth more than their tears, and Indians could put up with more smoke than you'd think was good for their eyes.

As he walked toward the agency, he wondered if Caldwell would notice the squaw-smell clinging to his unwashed hide. He probably wouldn't. The whole little town smelled Indian. It wasn't a bad smell, just different. White towns smelled of coal smoke, unwashed wool, and horse shit. Indian villages smelled of burning dung, greased rawhide, and the dry, corn-husk odor of Indian sweat. By now, Caldwell and his woman smelled that way themselves.

As he approached the agency, a young Ho fell in beside him

and said, "I am called Spotted Bear. Hungry Calf had me watching the dead man in the smokehouse."

"I know, brother. How long ago did the man in the red coat steal the body?"

"Many hours ago. He took his own and one of our ponies, too. He rode out just after midnight, but his sign is easy to read. When shall we go after him?"

"We're not going to trail him, brother. I'll see that the owner of the stolen pony gets paid double. You and your friends did well."

The Indian smiled at the compliment. "We did as you asked, but we don't understand it. Wasn't it your plan to let the red coat do a bad thing so you could kill him?"

"No. He was not a bad man. Just a fool pest I wanted to get rid of. I knew he wouldn't leave without the dead man as a present for his she-chief, so I let him steal the body."

"Does the crazy red coat's she-chief eat human flesh?"

"No. She wants the dead man's, uh, scalp. She thinks he did a bad thing to one of her people."

"Oh. What did the dead man do to the red coat's tribe?"

"Nothing. But he don't know that. He's likely huggin' himself right now for being so all-fired foxy. We can forget about him. He's a good woodsman, and since he thinks we're tracking him, he'll make sure nobody sees him again till he gets where he's going. Did anybody else try to get away during the night?"

"No. All the white men are sleeping in their blankets by the fire. Some of them had firewater and got drunk. The reservation police are watching them, but your orders were not to interfere, just watch, is this not so?"

"You are a good and clever warrior, Spotted Bear. I'll leave you now. I don't want the other white men to know we're close."

As the Indian dropped back, Longarm went on up to the agency. He smelled ham and eggs, so he knew the Caldwells were early risers, like their charges.

Someone had been watching from a window, because the door opened as he came up the steps and Caldwell said, "We've been looking for you. Sent a Ute out to fetch you when the wire came, but he said he didn't know where you were."

"I sleep private. What wire are we talking about?"

Caldwell handed him a piece of yellow paper, explaining,

"This came in right after the Mountie telegraphed his own report. Your own outfit was likely listening in."

Longarm held the telegram up to the light and read:

TO: DEPUTY LONG OURAY RESERVATION STOP #ONE WHAT
ARE YOU DOING IN UTAH TERRITORY STOP #TWO WHAT
HAPPENED TO KINCAID STOP #THREE DO YOU NEED
ASSISTANCE STOP.

Longarm chuckled and folded the telegram away, following the agent inside. He nodded to the two women seated at the breakfast table and when Portia Caldwell invited him to some ham and eggs, he said, "In a minute, ma'am. I have to send a message to my chief. If he doesn't find one waiting for him at his office, he'll be hard on the help."

Caldwell took him into an office where a sending set sat under a rack of wet-cell batteries. Longarm sat down at the table and began to tap out his reply, routing it through the Bureau of Indian Affairs to the Justice Department and thence to the Denver office. With the salutations out of the way, he sent:

ANSWER TO #ONE MY JOB STOP ANSWER TO #TWO LIKELY
DEAD STOP ANSWER TO #THREE NO STOP SIGNED LONG.

Agent Caldwell, who'd sent some Morse in his time, had listened in. He said, "If that don't confuse your boss, it pure confuses me! Would you mind letting me in on just what the hell you're up to, old son?"

"Cutting and branding, like I said. Just got rid of that feller from Canada, and by the way, you can use your smokehouse again. Sergeant Foster rode off with the body."

"You let the Northwest Mounted steal a U.S. federal fugitive?"

"No. I let him think he did. That owlhoot was just a poor shiftless thief who never did anything Uncle Sam's interested in. Got at least a couple of birds with one shot, too. By slickering the Mountie into vanishing off into the blue with the evidence, I can forget who might have to answer to Utah for killing him. I'd be obliged if we kept all this between us, though. Might be a few birds left to that shot I just mentioned."

"What was that about Kincaid?"

"He's another deputy, turned up missing. I'm looking for the one that bushwhacked him on his way to Crooked Lance. Been snooping around for Mexican heels and a .30-30 deer rifle amongst the folks I brought over here yesterday evening. Ain't found anybody that fits yet. But we'll have more company soon. Let's see about them ham and eggs. I've worked up a real appetite, likely from the mountain air."

Chapter 21

A band of mounted Indians brought in Mabel Hanks and the six riders from Crooked Lance who'd been with her when she tried to cut Longarm and his prisoner off at Bitter Creek. They'd given up there, and followed sign as far as the scene of Tinker's death before being jumped and captured by Longarm's Indian allies.

Mabel rode in dusty but trying to look elegant, sitting sidesaddle under her feathered hat, which the Indians admired immensely. Her little husband came over as Longarm helped Mabel dismount, stealing a feel of the holstered, man-sized S&W she wore around her corseted waist. Cedric Hanks said, "You shouldn't have let 'em take you, damn it!"

"Oh, shut up! What were we supposed to do, make a stand in a dry canyon against all these Injuns? What's going on hereabouts? It looks like you-all had a firefight where these jaspers surrounded us."

Cedric shrugged and said, "They surrounded us, too. This lawman's pretty slick, but he lost his prisoner. Damned if I can figure what he wants with the rest of us."

Mabel glanced at Longarm and asked, "Is that right? Did the prisoner get away after all the work we did?"

"Didn't get away, ma'am. He's on his way to Canada, dead. That Mountie rode off with the body."

"And you're still standing here? What's the matter with you? He can't be more'n a few miles off. Why ain't you chasing him?"

"Got bigger fish to fry. Besides, I've transported dead ones before. Gets tedious to smell after a day or so on the trail. I figure packing a rotting cadaver all the way to Canada is punishment enough for being more stubborn than smart. You and these boys hungry? The agent sent some husked dry corn over from the stores and the Indians will sell you jerked beef and coffee. For folks as aimed to track me and mine from hell to breakfast, you didn't store much grub in your possibles."

"We thought you was making for Bitter Creek, like you said."

"I figured you might. Where's Captain Walthers? Following the tracks across the Great Salt Lake Desert?"

"How should I know? The army man peeled off along the way. He rode off talking dark about a telegram to the War Department."

"That's good. Why don't you set a spell and make yourselves to home? I'll be over at the agency if you need anything. Anything important, that is. I don't split firewood and the Indians will show you where to get water, answer the call o' nature, or whatever."

He walked away, leaving the newcomers to jaw about their position with those already gathered, worried and restless, around the campfire.

As he crunched across the gravel, Hanks fell in at his side, protesting, "Not so fast, dammit. You got no right to hold Mabel and me. We ain't done nothing. Hell, the other night, I thought you and me was fixing to spring Cotton Younger together!"

"So did I, till I got a better grasp on the situation. You were right about Mabel being riled with me, but what the hell, she had her reasons."

"I don't know what you're talking about. Did Cotton Younger say anything to you 'fore he passed away? You must know it wasn't my idea to shoot him before he told us where the James boys was hiding!"

"He died sort of sudden," Longarm lied.

"Jesus, didn't you get anything out of him? How come you let that Sergeant Foster steal him? Wasn't your orders to bring him in dead or alive?"

"Yep, but I just explained all that. They'll likely rawhide me some for losing the body, but not as hard as they would have for gunning a guest of the U.S. State Department, and Foster was a serious cuss. Besides, what can you really do to a dead owlhoot? He can't talk and hanging him without a fair trial seems a mite un-civilized. I reckon they could hold a trial, if the jury had clothes-pins on their noses and the judge didn't ask how he pleaded, but as you can see, it'd be a waste of time and the taxpayers' money."

"You're funning me, Longarm. I'll bet you got it out of him. I'll bet you know where Jesse James is hiding! I know you mar-shals from old. You wouldn't take that Mountie pulling the wool over your eyes unless you was on to something bigger than old Cotton Younger!"

"Well, you just go back to your woman and study on it. I've had my say about the missing cadaver and this conversation's over."

He left the bewildered little man standing there and continued to the mission. The sun had topped high noon and he found the Caldwells and Kim Stover out back, seated in the shade behind the kitchen shed as the harsh, cloudless light made up for the cold night before by baking the dusty earth hot enough to fry eggs on.

Agent Caldwell started to ask more questions, but his wife, Portia, looked knowingly at Kim and said something about mak-ing the rounds of the village, adding something about sick Indian kids.

Caldwell muttered, "I don't remember any of the Utes being sick," but he let her lead him off after she'd tugged firmly on his sleeve a time or two.

Kim Stover smiled wanly and said, "She's quite the little match-maker, ain't she?"

Longarm sat on the kitchen steps near her camp chair in the shade and said, "She's got a lot of time on her hands, out here with no other white women to talk to."

"She was advising me on the subject. I reckon we sort of told the stories of our lives to one another, between supper and break-fast. She doesn't think I ought to marry up with Timberline."

"I never advise on going to war or getting married, but the gal who gets Timberline ain't getting much in the way of gentle. He rides good, though. Must know his trade to be working as ramrod for a big outfit. Maybe he's out to marry you for your cows."

"I know what he's after, and it ain't my cows. Ben and me didn't have much of a herd when he died. It's thanks to Timberline my herd's increased by a third since then. I know you don't like him, but he's been very kind in his own rough way."

"Well, maybe he don't like my looks. How'd he add to the size of your herd? Not meaning to pry."

"He didn't steal them for me, if that's what you're getting at. Timberline's been honest and hardworking, for his own outfit and all the others in Crooked Lance. He's the trail boss and tally man when we drive the consolidated herd to market because the others respect him. More than once, when the buyers have tried to beat us down on the railside prices, Timberline warned us to hold firm. Working for an Eastern syndicate, he always knew the going and fair price."

"That figures. His bosses back East would wire him the quotations on the Chicago Board. That's one of the things I've been meaning to get straight in my head, ma'am. You folks needed that telegraph wire. When did it first start giving you trouble?"

She thought and said, "Just after we caught that cow thief, Cotton Younger. We wired Cheyenne we had him and they wired back not to hang him but to hold him till somebody came to pick him up. Right after that the line went dead. Some men working for Western Union fixed it once, but it went out within the week. Timberline and some of the others rode up into the passes to look at it. They said it looked like the whole line needed to be rebuilt."

"Were any of those other lawmen in Crooked Lance while the line was up that one time? More important, did any of them send a message from your father-in-law's store?"

"I wouldn't know. I don't speak to him or to his two awful women. My ex-mother-in-law said bad things about me that weren't true. Her snippy daughter backed her."

"Do tell? What did they say against you?"

"Oh, the usual small-town gossip about a woman living alone. My sister-in-law's a poor old maid who likely doesn't know what grown folks do in the dark. Her mother can't know much better. All her man thinks about is money. You notice they only have one child, and she was born long enough ago to be getting long in the tooth now. Poor things are spiteful 'cause they never get no . . . you know."

"Ummm, well, they did seem sort of lonesome, now that you mention it. They gossiped about you and Timberline, huh?"

"Oh, that's to be expected, even though he's never trifled with me. What they suspicioned was even more vicious!"

"You mean they had more'n Timberline about your door-yard?"

"They as much as accused him of Ben's death. When he was killed in a stampede they passed remarks about how Timberline had never liked Ben as much as he seemed to like me."

"That's a hard thing to say about a man. Anybody go along with it?"

"'Course not. You may as well know I took it serious enough to study on it, too. I questioned all the hands who were on the drive with my late husband. Talked to hands who weren't fond of Timberline as well as his own Rocking H riders. Them two old biddies should be ashamed of themselves!"

"Just what happened to your man, if you don't mind talking about it?"

"It was a pure accident, or, more rightly, Ben was a pure fool. They were driving in rough country when the herd was caught by a thunderstorm. A lightning flash spooked the herd and they started to stampede. My husband rode out wide to head 'em off and turn the leaders. Riding in fallen timber at a dead run. They say Timberline shouted a warning to him. Called him back and told him not to try, but to let 'em run, since the running was poor and there was a ridge ahead that would stop 'em."

"That sounds like common cow sense, ma'am. What happened then?"

"Ben's pony tripped over a log and went down. The herd ran over him and the pony, stomping both flat as pancakes. Later, my in-laws allowed it was Timberline's fault. They said he'd put Ben on the point, knowing it was dangerous."

"Well, somebody has to ride the point, though some trail bosses tend to pick unmarried men for it."

"Ben knew cows as well as anyone. Nobody got him killed. He got himself killed trying to prove he was the best cowboy in the valley."

She looked away as she added bitterly, "He had to prove he was good for *something,* I reckon."

Longarm sat silently, mulling over what she'd told him. He had to admit the boss bully of Crooked Lance hadn't done much more wrong than any other trail boss would have, and even if he'd had a hankering for another man's wife, Timberline didn't look like a man who could scare up thunder and lightning with a wave of his hat.

Longarm's groin tingled slightly as he mulled over her words about the Stover women. The one in his room had moved her tail from side to side like a fish. In the livery stable, had it been the same one? It was hard to tell. Nobody does it the same way standing up. Had he laid the mother, the daughter, or *both* of 'em? And did he really want to know?

Kim Stover was asking, "When are you going to let us ride out? I asked the Caldwells, and while they're friendly enough, I couldn't get a straight answer from either one."

"That's 'cause they don't know, ma'am. They're likely as puzzled about it as yourself."

"Don't *you* know?"

"Well, sure. Ain't ready to say just yet."

"Portia Caldwell said you were given to sly ways, but I think you've passed sly and ridden into ridiculous! You've lost Cotton Younger. You know everything we do. What are you waiting for now?"

"The full cast assembled, ma'am. By now, Captain Walthers has intercepted the wires sent from here and will know where we are. He should be riding in directly, madder than a wet hen and likely leading a troop of cavalry."

"Good Lord! Are you waiting for the whole world to ride onto this reservation?"

"No, ma'am, just all my suspects. If you're getting bored, I'd be proud to take you for a ride in the hills or something."

"I'll pass on the something. Every time Timberline takes me for a ride we wind up wrestling."

"I don't wrestle with gals, ma'am. My offer was meant neighborly."

"I'll still pass on it. Timberline's enough to handle. You've got a very sneaky habit of saying one thing and meaning another!"

Chapter 22

Captain Walthers rode in from the west late that afternoon. The Indians had not rounded him up. It would not have been a well-advised move, for the captain rode in full uniform at the head of two troops of U.S. Cavalry under fluttering red and white guidons.

Longarm was waiting for him on the front porch of the agency, along with Caldwell and some of the others, including Kim, the Hankses, and Timberline.

Captain Walthers rode directly up and stared down grimly without dismounting. "I have two questions and a squadron to back them up, Longarm. Where is my horse, and where is my prisoner?"

"Both dead. Your walker slipped and gutted himself on sharp shale, so I had to shoot him. My office will pay damages, of course."

"We'll settle that later. What's this about my prisoner, Cotton Younger, wanted for desertion in time of war?"

"The man I lit out with is dead and gone, whether you wanted him or not."

"What do you mean, gone? Where's his goddamned body? Sorry, ladies."

"He was killed by one of these vigilantes. I don't know which one. That Canadian peace officer, Foster, made off with the remains last night. He's likely got a good start on you by now."

"He stole a man wanted by the War Department? Which way did he ride out?"

"Headed for Canada, most likely. You'd be wasting your time trying to catch him, Captain. He's a hell of a tracker and has a day or more of lead on you. I doubt I could find him myself now."

"I'll see about that. I'm charging you with horse theft, Deputy."

"Why make more of a fool of yourself? I said we'd pay for the critter and my defense at any trial would be that I requisitioned the nearest mount at hand to save a man from a lynch mob. As a peace officer, I have the right to do such things as the need arises."

"Why didn't you ask me to help you, then?"

"You'd only have got in my way. As it was, I had a hell of a time making it here before these others caught up."

The army man turned to the Indian agent and asked, "Aren't you the law hereabouts?"

"I sure am, soldier."

"I demand you arrest that man for obstructing me in my duties!"

Caldwell's face was calm as he answered, "I demand you flap your wings and lay an egg, too, but I don't suppose you have to if you don't really want to."

"You don't intend to let a few past misunderstandings between the army and the Bureau of Indian Affairs obstruct justice, do you?"

"I sure do, soldier. Once upon a time, when I had some Navajo all set to ride back peaceable, some hotheaded second lieutenant charged in with his troop and— Never mind, some of our men have acted like idiots, too, in the past. Suffice to say, I don't reckon your office and mine owe one another favors."

"I see. You intend to side with the Justice Department in this jurisdictional dispute."

"No, I intend to side with Longarm. He's a friend of mine. I never met *you* before."

Captain Walthers turned in his saddle to address a burly, middle-aged noncom, saying, "Sergeant! Arrest that man!"

The sergeant looked thoughtful and replied, "Begging the captain's pardon, but we're on Indian land."

"God damn it, Sergeant, are you afraid of Indians?"

"Ute Indians? Yessir, and Fort Douglas might just like to know our plans before the captain starts an Indian war without their say-so."

"I am surrounded by maniacs!" the captain protested to any-one who wanted his opinion. Then he scowled down at Caldwell and demanded, "Would you sic your tame Utes on us if we just took this sassy deputy off with us?"

Caldwell shrugged and said, "I don't know how *tame* they might be if you tried to arrest their blood brother, soldier. It's my duty to try and keep them off the warpath and if they got unruly, I'd have to chide them for . . . whatever. You'll notice I've told my wife to stay inside until this is settled. I've told these other folks to take cover, but nobody listens to me around here. Not even the Indians, when they get riled up about things."

The sergeant leaned toward the captain to murmur, "Sir, some Utes are covering us from those houses on our left flank. Just saw some movement off to the right."

"Damn it, the War Department's going to get a full report on this entire matter!"

Caldwell asked mildly, "Would you like to send a telegram on my agency wire, Captain? It'll be dark soon. You and your men are welcome to spend the night on my reservation."

Walthers hesitated as Longarm cast an anxious glance at the sky. The damned sun *was* getting low again. That was the trouble with soldiers. They moved like greenhorns riding snails.

He suddenly brightened and asked, "Hey, Captain? As long as you and your troopers will be riding back to Fort Douglas in the morning, what do you say to helping me transport some prisoners to the Salt Lake railroad depot? From there I'll make connections over the divide and down to Denver, and—"

"What prisoners are you talking about? Are you holding that army deserter after all?"

"No, the one we were all fighting over in Crooked Lance is dead and gone. I'm figuring on arresting the killer of Deputy Kincaid, once I tie up a few loose ends so—"

"You ask the *army* to help you, after the way you've thwarted me at every turn?"

"Well, it would be neighborly, and we are working for the same government, ain't we?"

"How would you like to flap your wings and lay an egg, Longarm?"

"I thought it was funnier the first time I heard it. Does that mean you won't help me?"

"I'd join the Mexican army first! As soon as my men and their mounts are rested I'm going back to Fort Douglas to file an official complaint, and you—you can go to the devil!"

"I'll tell Marshal Vail you were asking about him. You're leaving me in a bit of a bind, though. Can't deputize these Indians to transport prisoners off the reservation. Yep, it figures to be a chore."

For the first time since riding in, Captain Walthers looked pleased as he asked, "You don't say? My heart bleeds for you, Longarm, but I just can't reach you. I hope you sink, you—never mind. Ladies present."

The captain wheeled and rode off to find a campsite for the night as his troopers followed, some of them grinning and one corporal tipping his hat to the ladies as he swung past.

Kim Stover asked, "What was that about you making some arrests?"

Longarm looked around, as if worried about being overheard, before he confided, "I'm going to have to ask a favor, ma'am. Timberline?"

"I'm listening, but I don't feel up to doing favors, either."

"Just listen before you go off half-cocked. It's a long, hard ride back to Crooked Lance, the way we've all come. On the other hand, it's an easy downhill ride from here to Salt Lake City."

"What in thunder do I want to go to Salt Lake City for?"

"A ride, of course. Free ride on the railroad back to Bitter Creek, from where you'll be only a spit an' a holler from Crooked Lance. Wouldn't you like to save Miss Kim here, and the others, a long hard ride for home?"

"Maybe, but what's the tricky part?"

"I aim to deputize you as a U.S. marshal's deputy. You'll get a dollar a day, vittles, and a free ride almost home in exchange for doing nothing much."

Kim Stover's eyes widened as she smiled hopefully.

Cedric Hanks said, "Hell, why not deputize *me*? He's only a cowboy, big as he may be! Me and Mabel are professionals!"

"I thought abut it," Longarm soothed, "but my boss ain't partial to private detectives since he had a set-to with Allan Pinkerton's Secret Service, during the war. As for your wife, I've never heard of a female working for the government."

Timberline's suspicion had faded to anticipation as he asked, "Would I get to wear a badge?"

"Not on temporary duty. As a peace officer, I'm empowered to deputize posses and such, but I won't need more'n one hand to help me herd my suspects in."

Mabel Hanks asked, "Who on earth are you talking about, Longarm? Who are you fixing to arrest?"

"Ain't sure yet," Longarm lied. "We'll work it out come morning, after the troopers and that pesky captain leave."

Longarm didn't spend the night with Dances-Humming. For one thing, he couldn't trust her. For another, he wasn't sure he should take his clothes off. He spent the night in the agency in a spare room next to Kim Stover's. As he lay across the bed, fully dressed, he could hear the redhead moving about on the other side of the thin wall. Once he heard her using the chamber pot. It shouldn't have made him think of what it did, but the redhead had a nice shape and it was hard not to picture what he caught himself seeing clearly in his mind.

He knew his boast had been spread around by now. Timberline had strutted off like a rooster, feeling important most likely. Hungry Calf's young men were watching to see if anyone tried to make a break for it. They had instructions not to try and stop him—or her. The killer—or killers—of Deputy Kincaid and that Missouri lawman were dangerous as hell, but wouldn't get far once they made their play.

He could hear the bedsprings under the woman in the next room. She seemed to be tossing and turning as if she found it hard to fall asleep, too. Longarm lay there, puffing his cheroot and blowing smoke rings at the ceiling as he thought about Kim Stover, mostly to keep awake.

There was a soft tap on his door. Longarm frowned and rolled quietly to his feet. He slid over to the door and asked, "Yeah?"

A man's voice said, "It's Captain Walthers. I'd like a word with you."

Longarm muttered, "Shit," and opened the door.

The army man didn't come in. He said, "Some of those hands were talking to my troopers by the fire. What's going on here, now?"

"You mean Timberline helping me transport a prisoner or two? You already said you wouldn't do it."

"I don't owe you spit, but I'll admit I'm curious. Do you really have anything nailed down, or are you trying to bluff someone into making a break for it?"

"I owe you an apology. You ain't as dumb as you seem. I didn't think it was possible, anyway."

"I figured you were bluffing. Unless your suspect's awfully dumb, he'll figure it out as well. There's hardly a chance of getting away from here. Anybody can see that. You let the Mountie get away with our prisoner because you weren't expecting it. By now, you'll have your Utes watching every route out of the reservation, won't you?"

More to pass the time than in any hope of learning anything, Longarm said, "Maybe the one, or ones, I'm after ain't as smart as you and me."

"It's not my mission, but I've put a few things together. Your friend, Kincaid, had worked in Missouri, as had the other missing lawman and the old man who apparently came to help Cotton Younger. That means your man is from Missouri, probably well-known there. He had to kill the three of them because they might have recognized him on sight."

"You aiming to help me, or are we just jawing?"

"Unless you can nail a prisoner with a military charge, I have no authority to help you. Cotton Younger was the only possible member of the James-Younger Gang wanted on an army warrant, and thanks to you, his corpse is halfway to Canada by now!"

"You do go by the book, don't you? It's no wonder Cotton Younger deserted your old army. It's gotten chickenshit as hell since I was in the service. 'Course, in those days we were fighting, not lookin' up rules and regulations. It's been nice talking to you, Captain."

He closed the door softly in Walthers's face. While he wanted to annoy the captain, he didn't intend to disturb the lady next door.

He chuckled as he heard the angry boot heels stamping off. If he couldn't use the infernal soldiers, at least he might get rid of 'em by rawhiding their leader every chance he got.

He sat on the bed and pondered whether to get some sleep or not. The Indians would awaken him if anything important happened. He knew he might have a hard day ahead of him, too.

A tiny beam of light caught his eye. He saw that it came from a chink in the pine paneling between the rooms. He shrugged.

She was likely under the covers, anyway. He lay back and tried to doze, but sleep refused to come. He muttered, "What the hell, curious is curious."

He got up and tiptoed to the wall, putting an eye to the peephole. He was almost too late. Kim Stover had just turned from the dressing table and was headed back for the bed, stark naked. Longarm held his breath as she crossed the room and snuffed the light before getting under the quilts. Then he went back to his own bed, grinning.

He'd been right as rain. She was red-haired all over.

The army column rode out just after breakfast, taking their own sweet time, as always.

Hungry Calf found Longarm eating beans by the pony line and said, "Nobody left last night. What does my brother think this means?"

"Means I was wrong, or that I'm up against somebody smarter than I figured. Are your young men watching the soldiers?"

"Of course. It is fun to scout them from the rimrock. Just like the old days. Both you and Agent Caldwell said it would be a bad thing to attack them. Could we just frighten them a little?"

"No. I just want to know when they're clean off the reservation and out of my hair. I'd like to have that snoopy captain at least half a day's ride away from me before I make my next move."

"We will do it, but the way you white men do things is very boring. Do you always take so much time to take an enemy at a disadvantage?"

"Some of us do. Lucky for us, your folks never got the hang of it."

"If you know who you're after, why don't you just kill him?"

"Like you said, our ways are boring. I have to be able to prove my suspicions in a court of law. Sometimes, when a bad white man is very clever, he refuses to fight. He just says he didn't do it. Then I have to get twelve other white men to see if he lies."

"Can't you choose these twelve from among your friends?"

"Not supposed to. How long a ride is it to Salt Lake City, maybe with some kicking and fussing along the way?"

"Two days, as white men ride. Maybe three, with trouble. The big town you speak of is sixty, maybe seventy of your miles."

"Good roads?"

"Yes. Wide wagon trace. Plenty water. Easy riding. Just far. Didn't you ride that way the last time you were here after bad white men?"

"No, took the hard way home. That's how I knew about that holdout in the oil shale country. With all the folks and the fooling about, I'll figure on a seventy-two hour ride. It's gonna be a tricky bitch, but I'll manage."

Hungry Calf wandered off and Longarm spent the morning trying not to go out of his head from inaction. By noon, more than one of the people in White Sticks had pestered him for an idea of when he intended, for God's sake, to *do* something.

A little past noon he wandered over to the crowd around the cold campfire. His scouts had told him the army troops were long gone, and he saw that Kim Stover had joined her Crooked Lance friends, along with the Hankses and Timberline.

He moved into position, took a deep breath, and let half of it out as he said flatly, "Cedric Hanks and Mabel Hanks, you are under arrest. Anything you say may be used as evidence against you."

Everyone looked more than startled, but the midget leaped to his feet as if he were about to have a running fit. Mabel started to reach under her duster as Longarm's .44 came out. "Don't do it, Mabel. I'd hate to gun a lady."

Cedric gasped, "Longarm, have you been drinking, or were you always crazy? You are reaching for straws! We ain't done a thing you can fine us ten dollars for!"

The others were on their feet now, moving to either side as the little detective danced in front of Longarm, protesting his innocence.

Longarm said, "Deputy Timberline, disarm them prisoners."

The big ramrod grinned and started to do so. "Hot damn! But what are we arresting 'em for, pardner?"

"The murder of Deputy Kincaid is enough to hang 'em. We'll get the details of the other killings out of 'em in the Salt Lake City jail!"

Cedric Hanks pointed a pudgy finger at his wife and blurted, "It was her that took that shot at you in Bitter Creek, God damn it! But we were only trying to scare you!"

Mabel gasped and said, "It was his idea! I only wanted to be friendly, remember?"

"I remember it fondly, Mabel. You wore them same high heels

when you smoked up the law office in Bitter Creek that night. A .30-30 is a light as well as an accurate weapon, too. I'll allow you made good time, beating me back to the hotel like that. Then you and Cedric made up that fool story about someone running down the hall when I caught him trying to sneak in for another try at me."

"Longarm, you know I had my head against that panel while you were—"

"Watch it. There are ladies present and you're talking about your wife."

"Hang it, I couldn't have overheard what I overheard unless—"

"You had your head next to my keyhole. Where did you folks bury Kincaid and the other lawman, Hanks?"

"Bury? We never laid eyes on either. We was in Bitter Creek till after you reached Crooked Lance. Hell, we met you on the train, halfway to Cheyenne!"

"So what? It's a short run and the trains run both ways from Bitter Creek. You were laying for me. Just like you laid for them others sent for Cotton Younger!"

"Hell, there was a whole mess of you sent! You think we'd have been dumb enough to try and stop you all?"

"No, just the smart ones. You used me to do what you aimed to do all along. I'll allow you got me to spring your friend from the Crooked Lance jail. Or if that wasn't it, you were trying to get one more lawman out of the way. We'll settle the details when we carry you before the judge."

"Longarm, you don't have a thing on us but hard feelings for some past misunderstandings. Hell, you don't even have no *bodies* to show that judge!"

Longarm chuckled and said, "Sure I do. I got both of yours. You mind your manners, and I'll try to deliver 'em both alive!"

Chapter 23

"I feel sorry for the poor thing," Kim Stover said as she sat by Longarm on a log, a day's ride from Ouray Reservation.

They'd made camp for the night at a natural clearing near a running brook of purring snowmelt from the Wasatch Mountains. The hands had built a roaring white man's fire of fallen, wind-cured timber, and the Hankses were across from Longarm and Kim Stover. The midget's left hand was handcuffed to his partner's right, for the female of the species in this instance was likely deadlier than the male.

Longarm chewed his unlit cheroot as he studied his new prisoners across the way. Then he shrugged and said, "Nobody asked her to marry up with the little varmint, ma'am."

"Oh, I'm not feeling sorry for her! It's the poor little midget she's obviously led into a life of crime."

"Nobody gets led into a life of crime, ma'am. Though most everyone I meet in my line of work seems to think so. Folks like to shift the guilt to others, but it won't wash. The man who murdered Lincoln had a brother who's still a fine, decent man. An actor on the New York stage. I'd say his baby brother led himself astray. Most folks do."

"I can see your job might make you cynical."

"No might about it, ma'am. It purely does!"

"Just the same, I'd say that woman was the cause of it all. She's hard as nails and twice as cold. She's been spitting at you with her eyes all day."

"She's likely riled at me for arresting her and the midget."

"There's more to it than that. A woman understands about these things. I can tell what's passed between the two of you!"

"Oh?"

"Yes. She obviously feels scorned by you. Tell me, did she flirt with you when first you met?"

"Well, sort of."

"There you go. And being a man who'd be too much of a gentleman to take the likes of her seriously, you likely laughed at her pathetic attempts to turn your head."

"Now that you mention it, I did have a chuckle or two at her expense."

"She's been flirting with Timberline and some of the others. I told him what she was and he said I was probably right. You don't reckon she'd be able to seduce any of our party, do you?"

"Not with her husband handcuffed to her and the key in my pocket."

"I know most of the boys pretty well, but some of 'em are young and foolish, and she's not bad-looking, in her cheap, hard way. You're probably well-advised to keep them chained together. She'd do anything to get away."

"I'd say you were right on the money, ma'am. But we got Timberline and over two dozen others guarding 'em. So I reckon they'll be with us as we ride into Salt Lake City."

"Which one do you reckon will hang for the murders, the trollop over there or her poor little husband?"

"Don't know. Maybe both of 'em, if they get convicted. They're both sticking tight as ticks to their innocence."

"You think the woman did the shooting, don't you? It took me a few minutes to figure out what you meant about that .30-30 rifle. Won't you need that as evidence?"

"I could use it, but I made a dumb move back in Crooked Lance when I jawed about it in front of everybody. I suspicion the rifle's as well hid as the bodies, by now. They both packed S&W .38s till Timberline took 'em away."

"He's so easy to please. I do think Timberline's starting to like you, Longarm."

"Well, most boys like to feel important in front of a pretty gal. He's never really gone for me, serious. Them few brags and swings were sort of like walking a picket fence. Not that I blame him, all things considered."

"I thank you for the compliment."

"Just stating the facts as I see 'em, ma'am."

"Stop flirting. You know it flusters me. There's something else I've been wondering about."

"What's that, ma'am?"

"If there is one thing I've learned you're not, it's a fool, Longarm. You played a foxy grandpa on that Mountie, didn't you?"

"Did Portia Caldwell give away anything about government business while the two of you jawed about me?"

"She didn't have to. I figured out why you were so calm and collected when Sergeant Foster rode off like a thief in the night with the body of that man we'd been holding. He wasn't Cotton Younger at all, was he?"

Longarm laughed and said, "You weren't behind the kitchen door when the brains got passed out, Miss Kim. I told you all in Crooked Lance you were wasting a lot of time by holding out on everybody over that fool reward. If you'd sent him on to Cheyenne right off, we'd have all known it sooner."

"But the Mountie still thinks he's packing the real Cotton Younger off to Canada? Oh, my, that's rich!"

"Might be getting ripe, too. I wonder if he'll smoke him, salt him, or just hang tight and tough it through. Hell of a long ways, considering it's summer."

"You waited until Captain Walthers came and left, satisfied that another man had his deserter. You are the sly one, but why did you do that?"

"Why? Had to. Had to whittle it down to where I was the only lawman left. These jurisdictional matters can be a real pain, as you may have noticed when you were still in the game."

"I'm sorry, now, that we were so dumb about it all. I know we'd have been tricked out of the reward some way, even if we had been holding the real Cotton Younger. Would you mind telling me who we *were* holding, all that time?"

"He was almost who he said he was. His real name was Tinker, 'less his dying confession was another lie. Doesn't seem likely, though, considering some of the other things he confessed to. There was no reward on him. So despite our past misunderstandings, you'll have to settle for the rising beef market."

"I feel like such a fool! Imagine, holding an innocent boy and almost seeing him hung improper!"

"Don't be too hard on yourself, ma'am. I don't go along with improper hangings, but it turned out all right in the end. As for him being innocent, he wasn't Cotton Younger, but he wasn't all that innocent, either. Your friends were right to grab him as a cow thief, 'cause that's what he was. He wasn't out for your particular cows, but he wasn't packing that running iron for fun, either."

"Some of the boys are worried about the fact that one of them shot him before we got, well, more friendly-like. I told them you'd said you'd forget about it when we all rode into Salt Lake City. Can I take it I told 'em true?"

"Well, I never forget much, but I overlook a few things. My report will say he got shot trying to escape, which is close enough to the way it happened. No way on earth we'll ever know just whose round finished him, and most of you were shooting at him, as I remember it."

"You're very understanding. I'm truly sorry if I seemed snippy when first we met. But one thing puzzles me. When you first rode into Crooked Lance, you said you weren't going back without Cotton Younger."

"I know what I said, and I meant it. But as you see, it wasn't Cotton Younger you were holding. It ain't my fault I can't make good my brag. The man we were all fighting over answered Cotton Younger's description, but he was somebody else. Meanwhile, half a loaf is better than none, and I *am* taking in the killer of Deputy Kincaid. So it'll most likely pay for my time and trouble."

"Longarm, who do you think you're bullshitting?"

"I beg your *pardon*, ma'am?"

"Come on, I've gotten to know you, and you are not the wide-eyed country bumpkin you pretend to be! You have no intention of going back to Denver without Cotton Younger, have you?"

Longarm laughed and said, "That's true enough, if I can lay my hands on the cuss, but who do you suggest I pick to fit my warrant?"

"I don't know how I know this. Maybe it's because there's something sort of smug crawling around in them innocent eyes

when you don't think I'm looking. But I think you're too satisfied
about a job well done. I think you know where Cotton Younger is!"

Longarm's mouth went dry as he forced himself to meet her
level, questioning gaze, but his voice was calm as he shrugged
and said, "You have a lively imagination, ma'am. I told you the
man we all thought was Cotton Younger, wasn't. That don't leave
us with anyone who answers to his description, does it?"

"I thought maybe you had your eye on one of the hands from
Crooked Lance."

"Do tell? What makes you say that?"

"The midget and the woman likely gunned those other lawmen, like you said. If they were sent out to free the man they
thought was Cotton Younger, that makes sense. The other man,
the man who was a member of the James-Younger Gang could
have only been killed by the *real* Cotton Younger!"

"Keep talking."

"Don't you see? The Hankses are private detectives who'd do
anything for a dollar. That old man pretending to be a Canadian
would have been valuable to them as an ally. Why would they
have gunned him?"

"Beats me. Why would Cotton Younger have done it, if Cotton
Younger wasn't the man in your jail?"

"That's simple. The real outlaw's been hiding out in Crooked
Lance all this time. You know we're way off the beaten track, and
ordinarily, no one would ever look for anyone there. Then a man
answering to his description got picked up by us vigilantes and
you know the rest. All hell broke loose. Old Chambrun-what's-his-
name came busting in to free his kinsman, learned we had the
wrong man, and started to light out. That's when the real Cotton
Younger might have killed him, to shut him up for good. The
Mountie saw through the fake Canadian accent. No telling how
many ways a reckless old outlaw could have been caught, later,
knowing the whereabouts of a wanted man who aims to lay low
in Crooked Lance for keeps!"

Unfortunately, she was hitting damned close to home, considering she hadn't heard the dying Sailor Brown's last, wondering
protest about being gunned unexpectedly.

Longarm chuckled and said, "You'd have made a great detective yourself, Miss Kim. But you're forgetting something. Nobody hereabouts fits Cotton Younger's description. Timberline's
too big and the midget is a mite short. I don't know exactly what

color hair you and that other gal might have started out with, but even if it should be cotton-blonde, the feller I'm after is a man." He didn't think he should tell her how he knew that both she and Mabel Hanks were definitely female, so he added, "I've looked all the others over, more'n once. There ain't one in a whole score of riders that would fit the wanted posters for Cotton Younger, real or otherwise."

"Half the men in Crooked Lance aren't here."

"I know. If there's anything to your suspicions, I might look the entire population of Crooked Lance over with a hand lens some day. But I aim to carry my prisoners in as I catch 'em, not as I'd like 'em to fit wishful thinking."

"Then, in other words, you're saying I'm just running off at the mouth!"

"Well, I do see some points you've raised that will have to be answered. If ever we get that odd-matched pair to talk. To tell the truth, I don't *know* just what they were up to."

"You don't? Then why did you arrest them?"

"I told everybody at the time. For the murder of Deputy Kincaid. You eat the apple a bite at a time, ma'am. It ain't my job to get all the details out of 'em."

"But you said you didn't know what they were up to!"

"I meant I didn't know *why*. They might have been out to set the prisoner free. They might have been after the reward, just like they said. It don't matter all that much. You heard 'em admit they took a shot at me in Bitter Creek. That's against the law, no matter how you slice it. Just why they did it and who they're working for will come out in the wash. Since the midget is the brains, and she's the brawn, he'll no doubt tell a few tales on her to save his neck, before it's all over."

"Brrr, they are a pair, ain't they? What was that he said about having his head to some plywood, listening to you talk to somebody in Bitter Creek?"

"Oh, I don't remember just who I was talking to, ma'am. After his wife took a few shots at me I caught him listening, is all."

"Oh, I got the impression he was listening in on you and that slut of his. I'm trying to remember just what it was he said."

"Well, don't you worry your pretty head about it, Miss Kim."

This redhead was too quick-witted to be let out without a leash! A muzzle wouldn't hurt, either! How many of the others had she been to with her infernal speculations?

She suddenly blurted out, "Oh, I remember. He said he was listening when you and that hussy were . . ."

"What, ma'am?"

"You told him to hush, 'cause there were ladies present. Meaning me, I take it, since I'd hardly call Mabel Hanks a lady."

"I thought he was fixing to cuss. He was pretty riled when I arrested him."

"Longarm, were you and that awful woman—? Oh, I can't believe it!"

"That makes two of us. You do have a lively mind, and a mite dirty, meaning no disrespect. The woman is his wife, Miss Kim. Allowing for her being no better than you think she is, what you're suggesting is mighty wild, if you ask me!"

"I'm sorry, but it did cross my mind. She's not bad-looking, and you are a man, after all."

"Heaven forbid I'd be *that* kind of man, Miss Kim! Do I look like the sort of gent who'd trifle with a woman with her husband listening, watching, or whatever?"

She laughed a sort of earthy laugh and said, "As a matter of fact, you do. But I can't see you loving up a gal who'd just shot at you, with her husband next door, listening, or not. Nobody would do a thing like that but a very stupid man, which I'll allow you ain't."

"There you go. I knew you'd drop them awful notions, soon as you reconsidered 'em a mite!"

Chapter 24

Somewhere, somebody was hollering fit to bust, so Longarm woke up. He rolled, fully dressed, from under his canvas tarp and sprang to his feet, Winchester in hand, and headed over toward the smoldering embers of the fire in the direction of the confusion.

He found Timberline kneeling over Mabel Hanks, shaking her like a terrier shakes a rat as he thundered, "Gawd damn it, lady! I don't aim to ask nice one more time!"

Longarm saw the open handcuff dangling from the one still locked to Mabel's right wrist and said, "Let her be, Timberline. Even when she's talking she don't tell the truth worth mention."

He shoved a pine knot into the embers and waited, squatting on his heels, until it was ablaze. Meanwhile, everyone in camp converged around Timberline and his smirking captive. As Longarm got to his feet with the torch held out to one side, Kim Stover asked, "What happened? Where's the midget?"

"Damned if I know. My own fault. I locked that bracelet as tight as she'd go, but he has a wrist like an eight-year-old's and we hardly arrest enough that young to mention."

He fished the key from his pants and handed it to her. "When Timberline gets through shaking her teeth loose, get him off her and cuff her to a sapling till I get back."

"Are you going after him in the dark?"

"I don't aim to wait till sunup."

He found a tiny heel mark in the forest duff and started away from the clearing. A couple of the hands fell in beside him, anxious to help.

He said, "Go back and check to see if he lit out with anybody's weapon. I have enough to worry about, tracking him, without having to keep you fellers from getting shot."

"How do you know he has a gun, Longarm?"

"I don't. But I never track, trusting to a man's good nature. Put out them embers and keep together. He ain't got a mount. He may decide he needs one and you likely know by now, he's a slippery little imp!"

He left them to debate the matter and started ahead, making out a scuff mark here and a heel print there, until he came to the bank of the stream.

"Wading in water so's not to leave tracks, huh? Poor little bastard. Don't you know how cold it gets up here at night?"

He assumed his quarry would come out on the far side. Nine out of ten did. A distant, steady roar, far up the slope, told him there was a waterfall within a mile. Taking into account the size of the strides Cedric took, a mile in icy snowmelt seemed about right. Longarm shoved the sharp end of the pine knot in the mud beside the stream, leaving it glowing there as a distraction visible for a good distance. Then, swinging wide, he ran up the slope through the trees. He ran until his lungs hurt, and ran some more, making no more noise than he could help in his soft-soled boots over spongy, fallen fir needles.

He was out of breath by the time he reached the waterfall, and anyone making better time would have to have longer legs. The midget's only chance was that he'd been gone longer than Longarm figured.

He hadn't. After Longarm had squatted near the lip of the falls for about five minutes, he heard a splash downstream and the crunch of a wet boulder turning under foot. He waited until a barely visible movement caught his eye across the falls. Then he said conversationally, "'Evening, Mister Hanks. Going someplace?"

The darkness exploded in a flashing roar of brilliant orange. Longarm knew, as something smashed, hard, into the wood above his head, that the little bounty hunter had stolen someone's saddle rifle.

He fired back, rolling away from where he'd just been, as another shot flared across the stream, followed by the patter of little running feet.

Longarm ran across the slippery lip of the falls, calling out, "Hold on, old son! You're turning this into serious business!"

His quarry fired again, aiming at the sound of Longarm's voice. The shot went wild, of course, since Longarm knew enough to crab sideways after sounding off. He fired back, not really expecting to hit a savvy gunfighter in the dark by aiming at the flashes. He noticed that the little man had fired and crabbed to his right both times as a broken twig betrayed his next run. He kept running uphill, too. It figured. A man that size hadn't seen army training or he'd know more about dismounted combat in the dark. The first thing you learned from old soldiers was that most men crab to the right and instinctively run uphill when they're lost in the dark.

Longarm got behind a tree and called out, "Cedric, I'm pure tired of chasing you! You drop that thing and come back here!"

A bullet thudded into the trunk. The ornery little cuss was shooting to kill. So Longarm let out a long coyote wail and gasped, "Gawd! I'm hit! Somebody help me! I'm hit in my fool leg!"

Then he moved quietly off to one side and waited.

Something crunched in the dark. What seemed like ten years later, Longarm heard another sound, closer. The little cuss was *serious*!

Longarm decided to end it.

He fired blindly in the direction of the last sound, moving to his left as he levered the Winchester and watched the bright wink of the other's rifle. Then Longarm fired, not at the flash, but to its left as he was racing. He heard a thump and the sound of a metal object sliding downhill over roots and pine needles, followed by some thrashing noises and a low, terrible curse.

Then it became very quiet.

Longarm counted, "One, Mississippi, two Mississippi . . ." to a hundred. Then he moved in, knowing that not one man in a thousand plays possum through a hundred Mississippis.

He heard harsh breathing, which was either somebody dying or damned fine acting. So he circled uphill and approached quietly from the far side.

In the almost total darkness Cedric Hanks was only an inkblot against a blackboard. Longarm moved in, squatted, and put his Winchester's muzzle against the blur before he said, quietly, "I'm fixing to strike a light. One twitch and this thing goes off."

"You've done me, you big bastard!" the midget groaned.

Longarm held the match well out to the side, anyway, as he thumbnailed its head aflame. Then he whistled and said, "Smack in the chest. You're right, mister. You're dead."

"You big bully! I never had a chance."

"Sure, you did. You could have stayed put. What made you make such a fool play, Hanks? Your best bet would have been to face the charge in court. As your wife, Mabel, didn't have to bear witness against you, and vice versa."

"That bitch woulda sold me to save her own twitching ass! Why'd you put that light out? I can't see a thing."

"Nothing to look at," Longarm soothed, holding the lighted match closer to the little man's glazing eyes. He said, "Mister Hanks, you are done for and that's a fact. Before you go, would you like to give me Mabel's ass?"

"You already had it, you son of a bitch! Everybody's had her. She was always sayin' mean things about my size. How tall I am, I mean."

"She's a tartar, all right. Did she gun Kincaid, or was it you?"

"I don't know who she might have gunned in her time. You know who broke her in? Her own stepdaddy. Ain't that a bitch?"

"Yeah, but let's stick to serious crimes. When did you learn the man in Crooked Lance wasn't the real Cotton Younger?"

"Don't josh me, dammit. You know he was Cotton Younger."

"Let's try it another way. Who sent you out here? Who were you working for?"

"I told you, dammit, we was working it on our own, for the reward!"

"Then why did you and Mabel try to get rid of me?"

"It was her idea. She said she'd seen you once before, when one of the other gals in this . . . place she worked, pointed you out. She knew you were fixing to steal our chance at the reward. Shit, you know the rest."

"After she missed me on the streets of Bitter Creek, you worked out that old badger game to take me in bed, huh?"

"Sure. If you ask me, she enjoyed the screwing part best. I was to creep in and do you after she'd wore you out. I told her you

looked like a hard man to wear out that way, but she said she'd
give it her best."

"All right, how'd you do Kincaid? Fall in with him on the trail
and maybe finish him off as he was dozing restful in her arms?"

"I told you, I never seen this damn Kincaid!"

"What about that lawman from Missouri?"

Cedric Hanks didn't answer.

He couldn't.

Longarm closed the dead man's eyes and got to his feet, heading down the slope. The little man would have been a messy load
to carry. The cowhand who'd been careless about leaving firearms
about could fetch him when he came to pick up his rifle.

Longarm made plenty of noise and called out, "It's me, coming in!" as he approached the campsite. As others crowded around,
asking all sorts of questions, he called out, "Let's get some light
on the subject. It's all over."

Someone kicked ashes off the banked coals and threw some
sticks of kindling on. They blazed up. Longarm looked at Mabel
Hanks, kneeling by an aspen sapling with her wrist chained to it,
and said, "I'm sorry, ma'am. Your man is dead. Before he passed
on, he named you as the murderer of Deputy Kincaid. He died
before I could find out about the others, but—"

Then Mabel Hanks was screaming like a banshee and fighting
her handcuffs like a chained grizzly as she glared at him insanely,
calling him a mother-loving son-of-a-whore for openers.

The she really started talking dirty.

Longarm saw Kim Stover staring at the raging woman, openmouthed, and suggested, "You'd best go off and stop your ears,
ma'am. I suspicion she's a mite overwrought."

"For God's sake, she should be! You just said you killed her
husband!"

"Yes, ma'am. He was trying to kill me, too. I was a mite better
at it."

Longarm had studied women, but the longer he'd been at it the
harder it was to figure them out. After having called Mabel all
sorts of things, Kim Stover went over to comfort her, as the more
recent widow shouted, "He was twice the man you were, you son
of a bitch!"

Timberline sidled up alongside Longarm, asking softly,
"What was that about her killing them fellers?"

"Let's put it this way: What he said to me was sort of fuzzy, but what I'll remember to the judge might put her away for a spell."

"Hot damn! You aim to railroad her, right?"

"Now, that's putting it unfriendly, Timberline. Let's say I'm worn out tying up all the loose ends of this case and, what the hell, I know for sure she shot at me. I'll allow it ain't neat, but at least it's enough to satisfy a grand jury and let me get on to something more worthy of my time. I don't really care if they convict her or not. I just want to be rid of this whole infernal mess!"

"You reckon any of us will get called as witnesses?"

"Why? Did any of you see her gun Kincaid or anyone else?"

"Hell, nobody but that old tattooed man ever *got* to Crooked Lance!"

"There you go. We'll just deliver the gal to the Justice Department and let them worry about her."

"You still need me as a deputy? I mean, what the hell, one old gal don't seem to rate all this guarding, if you ask me."

Longarm shrugged and said, "We'll be in Salt Lake City by tomorrow afternoon, deputized or singing Dixie. It would be a favor if you were with me when I took her to the federal courthouse. I'll likely need a witness, transporting a female prisoner as I just did."

"A witness? Federal courthouse? You just said you wouldn't need us in court. I wish you'd make up your mind."

Longarm laughed and explained, "Not as a witness against her. As a witness for me, just while I sign her in. You've heard the mouth on her, and half the women a lawman brings in sing that same old tune of rape."

Timberline's eyes widened. Then he grinned lewdly, and exclaimed, "Hot damn! I never thought of that! A man *would* get some golden opportunities in your line of work, wouldn't he?"

"People suspicion as much. A lawman with a lick of sense won't trifle with female prisoners, though. Usually, I like to bring 'em in with at least one deputy, making it two words against one. You won't have to sign statements or anything. They'll record you as my deputy and, of course, you'll get a check from the Justice Department that you can cash in Bitter Creek when you and the others get off there."

"Well, we're all headed to Salt Lake City, anyways. What's this thing about recording me?"

"You'll be in our files as a sometime law man. It won't interfere with your job at the Rocking H. We just like to keep a record on who's for or against us."

"Hell, that sounds good. Can I go on calling myself Deputy Malone?"

"Well, it wouldn't be official, once I drop you off the payroll, but I doubt if you'd get arrested for it. Malone's your last name, huh?"

"Yeah, but you can call me Timberline like everybody else. They been joshing me so long with that fool name I've gotten used to it."

One of the hands came over with a worried look and said, "I can't find my saddle rifle. Anybody see a Henry .44-40?"

Longarm said, "Didn't see it, but I know where it is. Get a tarp or a waterproof groundcloth and some latigos or twine. Got another package up the slope I'd be obliged if you'd wrap for me, seein' you're wearing leather chaps. My wool britches are soiled enough as it is."

Timberline followed Longarm and the cowhand up the slope to where their torchlight revealed the missing rifle ten yards from the toadlike body of the midget. Cedric Hanks had been ugly in life. Glaring up at them in death he looked like something that should have been carved on the parapets of Notre Dame. Timberline grimaced and said, "Funny, he looks so ugly for such a tiny thing. Didn't it bother you, Longarm? Picking on somebody so much littler than you?"

"Why should it? Never bothers *you*, does it?"

"Hey, I thought we'd made up!"

"Couldn't resist getting in a lick for fun. As to who was picking on who, the midget had the advantage as well as the choice to make it a serious fight."

"Advantage? Poor little turd didn't come up to your belly-button!"

"Making me the bigger target. As you can see, we were both throwing .44-40 balls at one another, so if anything, I had to aim better, since there was so much less to hit. He likely became a gunslick in the first place when he noticed that while God created Man, Sam Colt and other gunsmiths made them equal."

Timberline watched the cowboy roll the little corpse up in the groundcloth as he shuddered and said, "My head tells me you're likely right. But I'm glad it wasn't me that killed him. Looks like Windy's wrapping up a baby!"

"Let's get back with him. It's too late to think of bedding down, 'cause the sun's creeping up on us. We'll get an early start. We can eat right away and break camp by first light."

He turned and walked toward the campfire winking up at him through the trees, feeling more morose about the killing than he'd really let on to the men behind him. It didn't bother him that the man he'd killed had been so small. It bothered him that he'd had to kill at all. He'd trained himself not to show the sick feeling these affairs left in his stomach. He'd steeled himself to eat his next few meals mechanically, tasteless as they might be. He knew why so many men in his line of work wound up with bleeding ulcers, or like poor Jim Hickock, got to be ugly drunks toward the end.

He wasn't given to probing the dark shadows of his own mind, but he knew one night he'd dream about that ugly little gargoyle, as he had again and again, about the others he'd had to kill. It wasn't as if he felt guilty. He couldn't remember shooting anyone who hadn't deserved it. At least, not since the war. As a matter of fact, he wasn't sure *why* he should feel so drained after a gunfight—and disappointed.

Maybe it was just the waste. People lived such a short while at best. Man was born with a death's-head less than an inch below the soft skin of his face. By the time he was old enough to talk, he knew the graveyard waited just up the road ahead. What was it that made some men *rush* the process?

He remembered that first one in the dawn mists of Shiloh, shouting fit to bust as he charged through the spring greenery into another boy's gunsights. He remembered the kick of the old Springfield against his shoulder as the world dissolved in gray blue smoke for a long, breathless moment and how, as the smoke cleared, that other boy had been lying under a budding cherry tree with a surprised look on his face, and how the cherry blossom petals had fluttered down like gentle, pink snowflakes as the body stopped twitching. The first man he'd killed had been fourteen or so. A farm boy, from the looks of his dead hands as they lay, half open, near the stock of his musket in the cherry blossoms. It was later, when the kitchen crew brought the evening grub up to the line, that he'd noticed the ball of fuzzy, gray nothingness in his gut. He hadn't been able to eat a thing. By the second evening of the battle, he'd been hungry as a bitch wolf and pinned behind a stone wall without so much as a plug of tobacco to chew on. He'd learned, by the time they marched him beyond Shiloh Church through the sniper-haunted forests, not to let his feelings show.

But he still wondered sometimes, late at night, who that other boy had been, and why he'd been in such an all-fired hurry to end the life he'd hardly started.

Chapter 25

"The City of the Saints" lay at the base of the Wasatch Range, staring out across the desert to the west. Salt Lake City had grown some since Longarm had been there a few short years before. The outlying houses now extended into the foothills and the party had to ride for more than an hour through the town before they could get to the part they were headed for.

Little kids came out of the somber Mormon houses along the gravel road to stare at the big party riding in. Some of the kids threw sassy words or poorly aimed horse turds at them before scooting behind a picket fence. Longarm didn't know whether they were just being kids, or whether the Mormons were still telling them bedtime stories about how cruel the outside world could be. As long as they didn't improve their aim or throw something solid, it wasn't worth worrying about.

Timberline was leading the mount that Mabel Hanks, handcuffed to the saddle horn, was sitting. Mabel had simmered down to a sullen silence, with a *just-you-wait!* look in her smoldering eyes.

Longarm found himself riding alongside Kim Stover, who seemed sort of quiet herself, since breaking camp. Longarm thought he knew what was bothering her, so he didn't say anything.

They were riding in at an easy walk, for they were too far from the center of town to lope the rest of the way in and Longarm had warned his Wyoming companions not to make sudden motions in sight of the sometimes-truculent Mormon folk they were paying a call on.

After perhaps five minutes of silence, the redhead said with a disgusted tone in her voice. "I'd as soon you'd ride with someone else, Deputy Long."

"Oh? Well, you can drop back if you've a mind to, Miss Kim. I'm up here near the head of the column 'cause I know the way to Main Street and will likely be dismounting, first, at the Federal Building."

"If it's all the same to you, I mean to head direct to the depot."

"I never try to change a lady's mind, but I did offer you and yours a free ride up to Bitter Creek. I figure it'll take an hour or so to do the paperwork on my prisoner. Then I'll be free to see about getting all these hands and horses fixed with transportation."

"You're not taking that woman back to Denver?"

"Nope. They never sent me to get her. I'll let the Salt Lake office do the honors. Maybe ride back to Denver in one of them fancy Pullman cars. Be nice to stretch out between clean sheets for a change and I'm overdue for a good night's rest."

"I should think you'd enjoy another night with Mabel Hanks. But I suppose you've tired of her, eh? You men are all alike."

Longarm rode in silence for a time before he sighed, observing, "I might have known you gals would have your heads together on the only subject womenfolk never get tired of jawing about."

"Don't look so innocent. She told me—everything."

"She did? Well, why are you keeping it a secret? Where did she say she buried Kincaid and that other feller from Missouri?"

"Damn it, she didn't talk about any murders. She told me about you and her, in Bitter Creek."

"Well, I know I can hang the sniping in Bitter Creek on her. I was hoping she'd let her hair down to another woman on the details of her life of crime."

"Don't pussyfoot with me, you animal! She says you had your way with her in—in a fold-up bed. She said that's why her poor little husband tried to kill you. He was defending her honor."

Longarm fished a cheroot from his vest pocket and lit it without comment.

After a time, Kim asked, "Well?"

"Well what, ma'am?"

"Aren't you going to deny it?"

"You reckon you'd believe me, if I did?"

"Of course not. Her description was, well, vivid."

"Funny, ain't it? Ten aldermen of the church could swear a man was tuning the organ of a Sunday, and if one woman told his wife he'd been at a parlor house instead—"

"Then you do deny it!"

"Ain't sure. Maybe I'd better study on it before I say one thing or t'other. I don't aim to have you think I'm all that wicked. On the other hand, I wouldn't want you to put me down as a sissy."

Despite herself, the redhead laughed. Then she recovered and said, "I don't think she could have made that up about you folding her up in the wall when her husband busted in on you."

"By golly, that's a good touch I'd *never* have come up with! Next time the boys are bragging in the pool hall, I'll see if I can get them to buy such an interesting yarn."

He puffed some smoke ahead of him, and addressing an invisible audience, pontificated, "That story about the one-legged gal in Dodge was right interesting, Tex. But did I ever tell you about the time in Bitter Creek I made mad gypsy love to this gal married to a midget?"

"It does sound sort of wild. Are you suggesting she told me a lie? Why would any woman lie about such a thing?"

"Don't know. Why do men swap stories about Mexican spitfires and hot-blooded landladies? Old Mabel's likely practicing up for when we carry her before the federal district judge, up ahead. Wait'll she gets to where you helped hold her down while Timberline and all them other riders behind us took turns with me at—whatsoever."

"Oh! Do women play such tricks on you when you arrest them?"

"Not *all*. Only three out of four. Some ladies who shoot folks are sort of modest."

"She *is* a murderess and the wife of a gunslick, isn't she? I hadn't considered that angle."

"I know. Most folks are more partial to dirty stories."

"Look, I'm sorry if I've wronged you, but damn it, she made it sound so *real*!"

"Do tell? Who'd she say was better at it, me or the midget?"

This time her laughter was less forced. She recovered and grinned. "I daren't repeat what she told me. As a woman who's been married, I'm not sure all the . . . details were possible."

Longarm didn't answer.

After a while, Kim said, "Yes, I see it all now. She's been trying to drive a wedge between us. I'd forgotten she was facing the rope. Tell me, do you think they'll really hang her?"

"If she's found guilty."

"Brrr. It seems so . . . so awful to think of a *woman* hanging."

"Ain't much fun for anybody. Mary Surratt was a woman, and they hung her for conspiring to kill Abe Lincoln. Some folks figured she was innocent, too."

"Oh, my, what an awful thought! Doesn't it bother you to think of innocent people getting hung?"

"A mite. But since I've never hung nobody, it ain't my worry."

"I can't believe you have no pity for her. Even after what she did."

"I feel pity for everybody, ma'am. Mostly, I feel pity for the victims more'n I do the killers. Deputy Kincaid and likely that other feller had families. They'd likely expect me to do the right thing."

"An eye for an eye and a tooth for a tooth, eh? Isn't there something else about *mercy* in the good book?"

"Sure there is. I've read things written by philosophers. They say two wrongs don't make a right. They say the death penalty don't really stop the killings out our way. They *say* all sorts of things. But when it's their own son or daughter, husband or wife who's the victim, you'd be surprised how fast they get back to that old 'eye for an eye!' "

"Someday, we may be more civilized."

"Maybe. Meanwhile, we don't hang folks because they've killed someone. We hang 'em in order that someone else won't get killed. I've read what Emerson and them have to say about reform. Maybe some killers *can* be reformed. I don't know what makes a man or woman a killer. But I do know one thing. Not one killer has ever done it again, after a good hanging!"

It was a long time before she broke the silence once more to say, "I think I understand you better, Longarm. I'm afraid I had some cruel thoughts about you. I thought maybe you were bringing Mabel Hanks in for those killings just to, you know, wipe the slate. I can see you're a proud man, and a man sent on a mission that fell apart when it turned out we'd captured the wrong man. I thought, just maybe, you were out to nail just anyone, in lieu of Cotton Younger."

"Not quite, ma'am. Don't think I could get anyone to buy Mabel Hanks as Cotton Younger. She ain't built right."

Chapter 26

The Federal Building was near the Mormon Temple grounds on the tree-shaded Main Street of Salt Lake City. A crowd of curious onlookers gathered as the big party of strange riders stopped in front of the baroque outpost of far-off Washington.

Longarm dismounted and told some of the hands to keep the crowd back as he and Timberline helped the handcuffed woman down from her horse. A worried-looking bailiff came out to watch as they led Mabel Hanks, sputtering and cursing, up the stone steps.

Longarm noticed Kim Stover tagging along at his side and muttered, "You'd best wait out here, ma'am."

"I've ridden too long a way to miss the ending, Longarm. I promise not to say anything or get in the way."

He saw there was no sense in trying to stop her, so he dropped it. He nodded to the bailiff and said, "I'm Deputy Long. Denver office. You likely got the wire I sent from Ouray Reservation about this suspect. Where do you want her?"

"Judge Hawkins ain't arrived yet, Deputy. We'd best get her to his chambers and I'll send over to his house for him. Ought to be just finishing breakfast by now."

Longarm followed the uniformed man inside, along with Timberline, Kim, and Mabel Hanks, who kept swearing at them.

They went up a flight of marble steps with iron railings to the second floor, where the bailiff ushered them into a deserted courtroom and then into the judge's smaller, private chambers beyond.

When he had left them alone there, Kim asked, "What happens now?"

Longarm said, "We wait. Waiting is the worst part of this job."

Timberline asked, "Do we have to sit through a trial, like?"

Longarm said, "No, just a preliminary hearing before the judge. He'll set her bail and a date for the trial. She'll likely spend a month or more waiting 'fore it gets serious."

Kim asked, "Won't you have to attend the trial, Longarm?"

"Sure. They'll send me back from Denver when it starts. But like I said, we're getting to the slow part. By the time it's all wrapped up you two will be up in Crooked Lance, fighting the buyers over the price of beef. Sometimes I wish I'd stayed a cowboy."

Mabel Hanks suddenly spat, "I'll never swing for it, God damn your eyes! This is a raw pure railroad job you're pulling on me, Longarm!"

"Oh, I don't know. I disremember if you said Cedric killed Kincaid."

"You know he didn't. The poor little mutt wouldn't hurt a fly, you big bully!"

"Let's save it for the judge. It's tedious to remind you over and over about them .44-40 slugs he was throwing my way in his innocence."

As if he'd been announced, Judge W.R. Hawkins came in wearing everyday duds and a frown. He was dabbing at some egg stains on the front of his vest as he sat behind his imposing desk and asked, "What's all this about, Deputy Long?"

Longarm saw that the others had all found places to perch, so he lowered himself to a chair arm and asked, "Don't we rate a proper hearing with some bailiffs and all, Judge? Ought to have a matron for this lady, too. It's a long story and I'd like to get the cuffs off her."

"Just give me a grasp of what we've got and we'll work out the niceties as they come up. I'm holding regular court in less'n an hour."

Longarm shrugged, fished the key from his pants, and tossed it over to Timberline. "Unlock her and sort of stand over there by the door, will you? I reckon Mabel knows enough to be a good girl, but we gotta do things proper, court in an hour or no."

He waited till Timberline had carried out his instructions before he began to tell the whole story from the beginning. After a few minutes he started to describe the sniping in Bitter Creek. "Hold on, now," Hawkins cut in. "Did you *see* this lady firing at you from across the street?"

"Not exactly, but we found high-heel prints, and a .30-30 is a womanly rifle, Your Honor."

"Hmmph, I've seen many a cowboy in high heels, and as for a .30-30 being womanly, I hunt deer with one myself! Are you saying I'm a sissy or that I took a shot at you in Bitter Creek?"

"Neither, Your Honor. I'm saying it's circumstantial evidence."

"Damn *slim*, too! Keep talking."

Longarm told the rest of it, with a few more interruptions from the judge. When he got to the part about the Mountie stealing the corpse of Raymond Tinker, the judge laughed aloud and said, "Hold on! Are you saying that fool Canadian, backed by them rascals in the State Department, is packing the wrong man all the way back to Winnipeg in high summer?"

"Yessir, he seems to take his job right serious."

"By jimmies, I can't wait to tell the boys at the club that part. But you lost me somewhere, Deputy Long. You say it looks like this lady killed at least two, maybe three men. What have you to say for yourself, ma'am?"

Mabel Hanks said, "He's full of shit! This whole thing's nothing but—a lovers' spat!"

"A lover's *what*?"

"You heard me, Your Honor. He's just mad at me 'cause I wouldn't leave my husband for him. I'll admit he turned my head one night. He is good-looking and, well, I'm a poor, weak woman. But I saw the error of my ways in time and went back to my true love. He *said* he'd fix me for spurning his wicked advances, and as you see, he's trying fit to bust!"

Longarm found something very interesting about his fingernails to look at as the judge raised an eyebrow and observed, "Now, this is getting interesting! What have you to say for yourself, Deputy Long?"

"I'm a poor, weak man? The question before you ain't no morals charge, Your Honor. So I'll save a lot of useless talk by offering no defense to her wild allegations. I brought her in for killing folks, not for . . . never mind."

Hawkins stared at the woman thoughtfully for a long, hard moment. Then he nodded and said, "I've known Deputy Long long enough to suspect he wouldn't hang a lady for spurning his wicked advances, ma'am. However, since you aren't represented by an attorney, it's the duty of this court to cross-examine in your behalf."

He turned to Longarm and said, "Leaving aside your improper reasons for arresting this lady, what in thunder do you have on her?"

"I'll admit it's mostly circumstantial, Your Honor, but—"

"But me no buts. If she killed Kincaid and that other lawman, where are the damned bodies?"

"Your Honor, you can see we'll never find body one, 'less the killer tells us where they're hidden. We do have the body of Sailor Brown, and this woman and her late husband were in Crooked Lance when somebody gunned him."

"As was a whole valley filled with folks, damn it. What on earth is wrong with you? Where did you leave your brains this morning? Don't you remember Sailor Brown was a wanted man with papers on him? Hell, anyone who did kill him could come forward to claim the reward!"

Longarm looked surprised and asked the prisoner, "How about it, Mabel? As you see, there's no charge to the bushwhacking of the old man. Can't you 'fess up just a little and help us clear things up a mite?"

"Oh, go to hell! You'll not trick me again. You told me you'd marry up with me in Bitter Creek, remember?"

"Now, that, Your Honor, is the biggest lie she's told so far, and since we first met, she's told some lulus!"

"Let's get back to the murders she's accused of. Frankly, I'm surprised at you, son. You've never brought a prisoner in with such flimsy evidence to back your charges."

"I'll allow the killer was tricky, Your Honor, but I'm doing the best I know how."

"This time your best isn't good enough. Holding her for killing folks we can't even say for sure are dead won't keep her overnight! You got anything, anything at all, you can *prove*?"

Longarm looked uncomfortable as he suggested, "Maybe if we sent her into another room to be searched for evidence . . . Miss Kim might be willing to help."

Timberline, leaning against the door, spoke up, "We patted her down for shooting irons, remember?"

"I know, but we never really stripped her down for a proper search. Why don't we send the two of 'em in the next room? There's no other way out of here and who knows what we'll find stashed in her corset?"

The judge frowned and said, "Deputy Long, you are starting to tread on the tail of my robes! What are you up to, son? You know I can't order a search unless I order this other lady to search for some *thing*."

Longarm said, "What I'm hoping Miss Kim will find on her will be, uh, documentary evidence, Your Honor. She and her husband were bounty hunters. There were no reward papers or telegrams in their packs when I arrested 'em both."

"That's better. What am I to tell this other lady to look for in the way of papers?"

"Letters, telegrams, anything tying 'em in to someone in Missouri. Maybe someone named James or Younger."

The judge nodded and Kim got to her feet, saying, "Let's go, Mabel. It'll only take a minute."

"Damn it! I don't have nothing on me!"

"That may be so, dear. Why don't we get it over with?"

The judge got to his feet and opened the door to his dressing room. The two women went in, with some grumbling on Mabel's part, and Hawkins shut the door. His voice was ominous as he said, "Now that we are alone, let me tell you something, Deputy Long. I think you are wasting my time! You've been a lawman too long to bring a prisoner in on such flimsy evidence! Have you just gotten dumb, or was there anything at all to that fool woman's story about you bedding down with her?"

Longarm grinned and said, "Hell, she's just a no-account adventuress, Your Honor. She did take that potshot at me in Bitter Creek, but you're right. It'd be a waste of time to prove it and her midget husband probably put her up to it. He was the dangerous one of the pair. Without him, she'll likely end her days in some parlor house. Not that she won't give right good service in bed."

Judge Hawkins looked thunderstruck as he almost roared, "You *knew* you didn't have the evidence to hang her?"

"Sure," Longarm said. "She never gunned them lawmen. *He* did." He pointed to where Timberline stood, stiffened against the door, slack-jawed. Longarm added, conversationally, "Don't do anything foolish, Mister Younger. We both know I can beat you to the draw nine times out of ten!"

Timberline gasped, "What are you saying, damn it! I thought I was your deputy!"

"Oh, I deputized you as the easiest way to bring you in without having to fight a score or so of your friends, Mister Younger. You might say the nonsense with Mabel Hanks was a ruse. It was you I wanted all the time. Your Honor, may I present the Right Honorable Cotton Younger from Clay County, Missouri, and other parts past mention?"

Just then the door flew open and the two women sailed out, fighting and fussing. Mabel had a firm grip on Kim Stover's red hair and Kim was holding firm to the corset around her otherwise naked body as they landed in a rolling, spitting heap between Longarm and the man against the door.

Longarm muttered, "Damn!" as Timberline opened the door and crashed backward out of the chambers.

Longarm drew as he leaped over the catfight on the rug and came down running. As he left the room, a bullet tore a sliver from the jamb near his head and he fired across the deserted courtroom at the smoke cloud in the far doorway.

He ran the length of the courtroom and dove into the hallway headfirst, landing on his belly and elbows as he slid across the marble floor beneath the first shot fired his way at waist level.

He rolled and fired back at the tall, dark figure outlined by the window at the end of the long hallway. The target jacknifed over its gunbelt and feinted sideways for the stairs—still trying, with a .44-40 slug in the guts!

Longarm leaped to his feet and ran to the stairway, hearing a series of bumps and the clatter of metal on the marble steps.

The man called Timberline lay on the landing, sprawled like an oversized broken doll. His gun lay beyond, still smoking.

As Longarm went down two steps at a time, a bailiff appeared on the steps, coming up. Longarm snapped, "Go down and bar the doors. He's got a score of friends outside!"

Federal bailiffs were trained to obey first and think later, so this one did as he was told. Longarm knelt to feel for a pulse. Then he stood up again and began reloading his warm double-action, muttering, "Damn it to hell! Now we'll never know where Jesse James is hiding!"

Chapter 27

It seemed simple enough to Longarm, but Judge Hawkins made him repeat the whole story in front of a court reporter and Kim Stover and a few of the more stable folks from Crooked Lance he'd decided to let in.

The hearing was held in the outer courtroom, with Timberline—or rather, Cotton Younger—stretched out under a sheet on the floor. The coroner said it had been the fall down the steps that finished him with a broken neck, though he'd have died within the hour from the bullet wound.

As the court reporter put it down on paper, Longarm explained, "The late Cotton Younger rode into Crooked Lance five or six years ago, wanted dead or alive in lots of places and worn out with running. He took the first job offered him, at the Rocking H, and discovered he had a good head for cows. They promoted him to foreman and he became a respected member of the valley community. He had a fine lady he was interested in, and maybe, if things had gone better for him, he'd have stayed straight and we'd have never known what happened to him."

Kim Stover cut in to insist again, "Timberline *couldn't* have been Cotton Younger! He doesn't answer those wanted-poster descriptions at all!"

"That's true, ma'am. He's a head taller now than his army records showed. But you see, he ran off from Terry's Column as a *teenager*. It sometimes happens that a boy gets a last growing spurt, along about twenty or so. He was tall when he rode into Crooked Lance. Taller than most. The rest of you probably didn't notice another saddle tramp at first. By the time it was important just how tall he really was, he was five or six inches taller. Must have been some comfort to him, when his real name came up in conversation, but as you see, he still dyed his hair."

"Where would he get dye like that?"

"It wasn't easy. He likely used ink. His hair was too black to be real. Not even an Indian has pure black hair. Natural brunettes have a brownish cast to their hair in sunlight. His was blue black. I noticed that right off. Noticed a couple of slips, too. He knew the old man I found on the mountain had been shot, before I said one word about his being dead. Another time, he referred to Sailor Brown as the old tattooed man. I don't remember mentioning what I found under his beard to anyone in Crooked Lance, but a boy who'd ridden with him would have known about Brown's tattoos."

Judge Hawkins said, "I'll take your word for it you shot the right man, Deputy Long. Finish the story."

"All right. Cotton Younger was hankering after the widow Stover, here. Don't know if he had anything to do with her being a widow, so let's be charitable. Kim Stover and her friends liked to play vigilante when the cows were out minding themselves on the range. So when they spied the late Raymond Tinker just passing through, they grabbed him, searched him, and found him with a running iron.

"Cotton Younger was just showing off as usual and there's no telling what they'd have done with the cow thief, if the poor stranger hadn't answered to the old description of Cotton Younger!"

"That's the corpse you pawned off on the Mountie, right?"

"Yessir. Had to. Once word was out that a sidekick of Jesse James was being held in Crooked Lance, every lawman in creation converged on the place to claim him for their own.

"While I was whittling away some of the competition, the other dead man, here, was sweating bullets. You see, he didn't *want* lawmen sniffing around. Sooner or later, any one of us might have unmasked him as the *real* Cotton Younger. He got word by wire that Kincaid and another lawman from Missouri were riding in. He busted up the wire and laid for 'em. He knew anyone from Missouri might recognize him on sight, and by now, he was trying to pass the cow thief off on us as the real article."

"What about Sailor Brown? I thought he was a *friend* of Cotton Younger."

"He was. Or, that is, he used to be, in another life. Brown rode in with me, pretending to be some crazy old French Canuck, and aiming to get his old pal out. He never got to *see* the man in jail, but it didn't matter. When a bunch of us rode over to talk to this lady here about the fool notions her friends had on holding Tinker for the reward money, Sailor Brown took one look at what everybody called Timberline and knew what was up. He was also wanted himself, and the Mountie rattled him some by talking French to him. Brown didn't savvy more'n the accent. So Brown was riding out, likely laughing about how his young friend had slickered us all, when said young friend put a bullet in him."

"To make certain no one in the outside world would ever learn of his new identity, right?"

"There you go, Your Honor. That takes us to the midget, Cedric Hanks, and the lady being held over in that jail cell as a material witness. They were what they said they were—bounty hunters. They knew they didn't have the weight to ride out with the prisoner. They only wanted him to tell 'em where the James boys were, so they could collect on that much bigger bounty. They were playing their tune by ear, pumping the rest of us for information, obstructing us as best they could. Sort of like a kid tries to fix a stopped clock by hitting it a few licks and hoping."

"You say the midget was the more vicious of the pair."

"No sir, I said the smartest and most dangerous. I've sent a few wires and gotten more on 'em to go with what the railroad detective first told me. Little Cedric had a habit of collecting his bounties the easy way and was probably in on more killings than we'd ever be able to prove. So it's just as well he made things simple for us by acting so foolish. He was at least a suspect when he got killed trying to escape, so my office says I'm not to worry about it overmuch."

"I intend to hold his wife seventy-two hours on suspicion anyway, before we cut her loose. She said some mean things about this other lady and she'd best cool off until Miz Stover's out of Salt Lake City."

Longarm turned to the redhead and said, "I've been meaning to ask about that set-to before. I went to all that trouble to get Cotton Younger in here peaceable, pussyfooted to get you gals out of the room before I announced his arrest, and there you two were, rolling and spitting like alley cats between us, and he was able to make a break for it!"

Kim Stover blushed and looked away, murmuring, "If you must know, she passed a very improper remark and I slapped her sassy face for it. I suppose I shouldn't have, but she sort of blew up at me. After that, it's sort of confusing."

"I'd say you were winning when the bailiffs hauled you apart. You're gonna have a mouse over that one eye by tonight, but she collected the most bruises."

"She bit me, too. I daren't say where."

Judge Hawkins took out his pocket watch and said, "I think we've about wrapped this case up, and damned neatly, too, considering. By the way, Deputy Long, do you know a Captain Walthers from the Provost Marshal's office?"

"Yessir. They've heard about this over at Fort Douglas, have they?"

"Yes. I just got a hand-delivered message, demanding Cotton Younger as an army deserter."

"You reckon they'll get him, Your Honor?"

"Justice Department hand over *spit* to the War Department? I turned the fool message over and wrote, 'Surely you jest, sir!'"

"They won't think that's funny, Your Honor."

"So what. I thought it was funny as all hell!"

Chapter 28

The train ride from Salt Lake City to Bitter Creek took about nine hours—a long time to go it alone and far too short a time sitting across from a very pretty redhead with a black eye.

They'd wound up things in Salt Lake City by midafternoon. So the sunset caught them more than halfway to where Kim Stover and the others were getting off. They'd had dinner in the diner alone together, since the others were considerate, for cowhands, and Kim had stated that she was mourning Timberline's demise, and was ready to forgive and forget where Longarm was concerned. He'd asked a friendly colored feller for some ice for her eye, but all it seemed to do was run down inside her sleeve, so she'd given up. He thought she was as pretty as a picture in the evening light coming in through the dusty windows, anyway.

She was studying him, too, as the wheels under the Pullman car rumbled them ever closer to the time when they would have to say good-bye.

She licked her lips and said, "Your cigar is out again."

"It's a cheroot. I'm trying to quit smoking."

"Don't you allow yourself any bad habits?"

"Got lots of bad habits, Miss Kim. I try not to let 'em get the better of me."

"Is that why you never married?"

He looked out at the passing rangeland, orange and purple now, and said, "Soldiers, sailors, priests, and such should think twice before they marry. Lawmen should think three times and then not do it."

"I've heard of lots of lawmen who've gotten married."

"So have I. Knew a man who let 'em shoot him out of a circus cannon for a living, too. Didn't strike me as a trade I'd like to follow. He left a wife and three kids, one night, when he missed the net."

"A woman who thought enough of a man might be willing to take her chances on widowhood."

"Maybe. More to it than that. A man in my line makes enemies. I've got enough on my plate just watching my own back. Could run a man crazy thinking of a wife and kids alone at home while he's off on a mission."

"Then you never intend to settle down?"

"After I retire, maybe. I'll be pensioned off before I'm fifty."

"Heavens! By the time *I'm* fifty we'll be into the twentieth century!"

"Reckon so. These centuries do have a way of slipping by on us, don't they?"

"You mean life, don't you? I'm staring thirty down at medium range and there's so much I've missed. So much I never got to do. My God, it does get tedious, raising cows!"

"Well, the price of beef is rising. You'll likely wind up rich and married up with someone, soon enough."

She suddenly grimaced and marveled, "My God, if you hadn't come along when you did, I might have married Timberline, in time! There's not much to choose from in Crooked Lance, and a woman does get lonesome."

"I know the feeling, ma'am. Reckon we were both lucky, the way it all came out in the wash."

"You mean *you* were lucky. You must be pretty pleased with yourself, right now. You got the man they sent you after, solved the murder of your missing partner, and made fools of your rival law officers. I'll bet they're waiting for you in Denver with a brass band!"

"Might get a few days off as a bonus. But I got a spell of travel ahead, first. This train won't be in Cheyenne till the wee, small hours. This Pullman car is routed through to Denver, but we'll likely sit in the yards for a spell before they shunt it on to the Burlington line. Be lucky if we make Denver by noon."

She looked up at the ornate, polished paneling and said, "I never rode in a Pullman before. How do they fix it into bedrooms or whatever?"

"These seats sort of scootch together over where our legs are, right now. A slab of the ceiling comes down to form an upper bunk, with the stuff that goes on this bottom one stored up there. They run canvas curtains around these seats. Then everybody just goes to bed."

"Hmm, it seems a mite improper. Folks sleeping all up and down this car with only canvas between 'em."

"The wheels click-clack enough to drown most sounds. I mean, sounds of snoring and such."

"Be a sort of unusual setting for, well, honeymooners, wouldn't it?"

"Don't know. Never had a honeymoon on a train."

"I never had one at all, damn it. What time do you reckon they'll start making these fool beds up?"

"Later tonight. Maybe about the time we're pulling into Rawlins."

"That's a couple of stops past Bitter Creek, ain't it?"

"Yep. We'll be getting to Bitter Creek before nine."

"Oh."

The train rumbled on as night fell around them and the porter started lighting the oil lamps. Kim Stover rubbed at a cinder or something in her good eye and said, "I reckon I'll walk up to the freight section and see to my pony."

Longarm rose politely to his feet, but didn't follow as she swept past him and out. And likely out of his life, forever, a bit ahead of time.

He sat back down and stared out at the gathering darkness, wondering why he didn't feel like dancing.

He'd pulled off a fine piece of work, with no loose ends worth mentioning and no items on his expense voucher they could chew him out for, this time. Not even Marshal Vail would blanch at paying for that horse he'd lost, considering the laugh they'd had on the War Department. So why did he feel so let down?

It wasn't on account of shooting Cotton Younger. He'd been keyed up and braced for it ever since he'd noticed that funny blue shine to that too-black hair.

"Come on, old son," he murmured to his reflection in the dirty glass. "You know what's eating at you. You can't win 'em all! This time, you got into damn near ever skirt in sight. Includin' some you'll never know the who-all about! So just you leave that redheaded widow woman alone. She's the kind that needs false promises, and that ain't our style!"

The train ate up the miles in what seemed no time at all. Longarm couldn't believe it when the conductor came through, shouting, "Next stop Bitter Creek! All out for Bitter Creek!"

He glanced around, wondering if she was even coming back to say good-bye. It didn't seem she was. But, what the hell, mebbe it was better this way.

He got to his feet and walked back to the observation car as the train slowed for Bitter Creek. He was out there, puffing his cigar, as the train pulled into the station.

He stared over at the winking lights of the little cow town as, up near the front, the sounds of laughter and nickering horses told him they were unloading from the freight section. He started to lean out, maybe for a glimpse of red hair in the spattered, shifting light. But he never . . .

Someone fired a pistol into the air with a joyous shout of homecoming. Even though they had a long, hard ride ahead, the Crooked Lancers were a lot closer to home than he was. Then again, he didn't have a home worth mentioning.

As laughter and the sound of hoofbeats filled the air, the train restarted with a jerk. He stood there, reeling backward on his boot heels as they pulled out of the place where it had all started. Some riders waved their hats and a voice called out, "So long, Longarm!"

He didn't wave back. He threw the cheroot away and watched the lights of Bitter Creek drop back into the past. As they passed a last, lighted window on the edge of town, he wondered who lived there and what it was like to live anywhere, permanently.

Then he shrugged and went inside. The observation car was dimly lit. The bartender had folded up and closed down the bar for the night. He walked the length of the train back to his own seat, noticing that they'd started making up the Pullman beds and that the centers of each car were now dim corridors of swaying green canvas that smelled like old army tents. After a short while he got up and went to his own berth and parted the curtains to get in.

Then he frowned and asked, "Where do you think you're going, Miss Kim?"

The redhead was half undressed on the bunk bed. So she just
smiled shyly and said, "We'd best whisper, don't you reckon?
I'm sort of spooked, with all these other folks outside these canvas hangings."

He sat down as she moved against the window side to make
room for him. He took off his gunbelt, saying softly, "You got
lots of cows expecting you, Kim."

"I know. They'll keep. You warned me when we met I was
destined to get in trouble with the law."

"Before I take off my boots, there's a few things you should
know about me, honey."

"Hush. I'm not out to hogtie you, darling. I know the rules of
the . . . *game* is sort of wicked-sounding. Let's just say I was hoping for at least two weeks with you before I go back to punching
cows. You reckon we'll last two weeks?"

"Maybe longer. Takes most gals at least a month before
they've heard all a man's stories and start nagging him about his
table manners. I reckon that's why they call it the honeymoon."

"You must think I'm shameless, but damn it, I'm almost thirty
and it's been lonesome up in Crooked Lance!"

"Don't spoil the wonder by trying to put words to it, honey.
We got lots of time to talk about it between here and Denver."

And so they didn't discuss it as he took off his boots, removed
his clothes, and finished undressing her in the swaying, dimly lit
compartment while she tried not to giggle and the engine chuffed
in time with their hearts.

A good two hours later, as the night train rolled on for
Cheyenne, Kim raised her lips from his moist shoulder and murmured, "Will you tell me something, darling?"

He cuddled her body closer and asked, "What is it, kitten?"

"Am I as good in bed as that hussy, Mabel Hanks?"

He didn't answer.

She raked her nails teasingly through the hair on his chest as
she purred, "Come on. I know you had her. She told me something
about you that I thought at the time she had to be making up."

"That why you tagged along?"

"Partly. But I'm afraid I might be in love with you, too. But,
yeah, it pays to advertise. I thought she was just bragging, but I'm
glad she was right about you."

He decided silence was his best move at the moment. But she moved her hand down his belly and insisted, "Come on. 'Fess up. Am I as good as Mabel?"

"Honey, there ain't no comparison. You're at least ten times better."

"Then prove it to me. Let's do it some more."

So they did. But even as her lush flesh accepted his once more, he found himself wondering. Did this make it Kim Stover and her mother-in-law, Kim Stover and her sister-in-law, or all *three* of the Stover women?

Longarm
on the Border

Chapter 1

Even before he opened his eyes, in that instant between sleep and wakefulness, Longarm knew it had snowed during the night. Like the hunter whose senses guide him to prey, like the hunted whose senses keep him from becoming prey, Longarm was attuned to the subtlest changes in his surroundings. The light that struck his closed eyelids wasn't the usual soft gray that brightens the sky just before dawn. It had the harsh brilliance that comes only from the pre-sunrise skyglow being reflected from snow-covered ground.

Opening his eyes only confirmed what Longarm already knew. He didn't see much point in walking across the ice-cold room to raise a shade at one of the twin windows. The light seeping around the edges of the opaque shades had that cold, hard quality he'd sensed when he'd snapped awake.

Longarm swore, then grunted. He didn't believe in cussing the weather, or anything else he was powerless to change. He was a man who believed that swearing just wasted energy unless it served some purpose besides relieving his own dissatisfaction.

Last night, when he'd swung off the narrow-gauge after a long, slow, swaying trip up from Santa Fe to Denver, he'd noted the nip in the air, but his usually reliable weather sense hadn't warned him it might snow. For one thing, it was just too early in the year. It was only the first day of September, and the Rocky Mountains' winter was still a couple of months away.

Longarm hadn't been thinking too much about the weather last night, though. All that had been in his mind was getting to his room, taking a nightcap from the bottle of Maryland rye that stood waiting on his dresser, and falling into bed. On another night, he'd probably have followed his habit of dropping in at the Black Cat or one of the other saloons on his way home, to buck the faro bank for a few turns until he relaxed. He'd started to cut across the freightyard to Colfax instead of taking the easier way along Wynekoop Street. What he'd seen happen in New Mexico Territory had left a sour taste in his mouth that the three or four drinks he'd downed on the train couldn't wash away.

There was little light in the freightyard. The acetylene flares mounted on standards here and there created small pools of brightness, but intensified the darkness between them. Longarm was spacing his steps economically as he crossed the maze of tracks, sighting along the wheel-polished surface of the rails to orient himself, when he sensed rather than saw the man off to his left. He couldn't see much of anything in the gloom, just the interruption of the light reflected on the rail along which he was sighting.

"Casey?" Longarm called.

He didn't think it was Casey, who was the night yard super, and more likely to be in his office, but if it was one of Casey's yard bulls patrolling, the fact that he'd called the boss's name would alert the man that Longarm wasn't a freight car thief.

A shot was his answer, a muzzle flash following the whistle of lead uncomfortably close to his guts. Longarm drew as he was dropping and snapshotted as he rolled, throwing his own lead at the place where he'd seen the orange blast. He didn't know whether or not he'd connected. He hadn't had a target; his shot was the equivalent to the buzz a rattlesnake gives when a foot comes too near its coils.

Faintly, the sound of running footsteps gritting on cinders gave him the answer. Whoever'd tried to bushwhack him wasn't going to hang around and argue. For several seconds, Longarm lay on the rough earth, sniffing coal dust, trying to stab through the dark with his eyes, straining his ears to hear some giveaway sound that would spot a target for him. Except for the distant chugging of a yard mule cutting cars at the shunt, there was nothing to hear.

Longarm didn't waste time trying to prowl the yard. Being the target of a grudge shot from the dark wasn't anything new to him, or to any of the other men serving as deputy U.S. marshals in the unreconstructed West of the 1880s. Longarm guessed that who-ever'd been responsible for the drygulch try had been skulking in another car of the narrow-gauge on the trip up from New Mexico. God knows, he'd stepped on enough toes during his month there to have become a prime target for any one of a half-dozen merci-less, powerful men. Any of them could've sent a gunslick to trail him to Denver and waylay him. The attack had to have originated in New Mexico Territory, he decided. Nobody in Denver had known when he'd be arriving.

Brushing himself off, Longarm had hurried on across the freightyard and to his room. He'd hit the sack without lighting a lamp, dropping his clothes to the floor as he shed them, bone-tired.

On the dresser, the half-full bottle of Maryland rye gleamed in the light trickling around the windowshade. Its invitation was more attractive than the idea of staying in the warm bed. Longarm swung his bare feet to the floor, crossed the worn gray carpet in two long strides, and let a trickle of warmth slip down his throat. As he stood there, the tarnished mirror over the dresser showed his tanned skin tightening in goosebumps raised by the room's chill air.

Crossing the room to its inside corner, Longarm pulled aside a sagging curtain. He grabbed a cleaner shirt than the one he'd taken off, and a pair of britches that hadn't been grimed with coal dust from the cinders he'd rolled in last night at the freightyard.

He wasted no time in dressing. The cold air encouraged speed. Longjohns and flannel shirt, britches, wool socks, and he was ready to stomp into his stovepipe cavalry boots. Another short snort from the bottle and he turned to check his tools. From its usual night resting place, hanging by its belt from the bedpost on the left above his pillow, Longarm took his .44-40 Colt double-action out of its open-toed holster. Quickly and methodically, his fingers working with blurring speed, he swung out the Colt's cylinder, dumped its cartridges on the bed, and strapped on the gunbelt.

He returned the unloaded pistol to the holster and drew three or four times, triggering the revolver with each draw, but always catching the hammer with his thumb instead of letting it snap on an empty chamber and perhaps break the firing pin. Each time he drew, when Longarm had returned the Colt to the holster he made the tiny adjustments that were needed to put the waxed, heat-hardened leather at the precise angle and position he wanted it to ride, just above his left hip.

Satisfied at last, he dripped a bit of oil on a square of flannel and swabbed the Colt down before reloading. He checked each cartridge as carefully as he did the fresh round he put into the cylinder to replace the one he'd fired last night. Then he checked out the .44-caliber derringer soldered to the chain that held his pocket watch on its other end. He put on his vest, dropped the watch into its left breast pocket, the derringer into the right-hand pocket. Longarm always anticipated that trouble might look him up, as it had in the freightyard. If it did, he aimed to be ready.

Longarm's stomach was growling by now. He quieted it temporarily with a short sip of rye before completing his methodical preparations to leave his room for the day. These were simple and routine, but it was a routine he never varied while in civilized surroundings. Black string tie in place, frock coat settled on his broad shoulders, Stetson in its forward-canted angle on his close-cropped head, he picked up his necessaries from the top of the bureau and stowed them into their accustomed pockets. Change went into one britches pocket and jackknife in the other; his wallet with the silver federal badge pinned in its fold was slid into an inner breast pocket. Extra cartridges went into his right-hand coat pocket, handcuffs and a small bundle of waterproofed wooden matches in the pocket on the left.

As he went out of the room, Longarm kicked ahead of him the soiled clothing that still lay on the floor. Hoh Quah, his Chinese laundryman, would pick it up and bring it back clean that evening. He closed the door and between door and jamb inserted a broken matchstick at about the level of his belt. His landlady wasn't due to clean up his room until Thursday, and Longarm wanted to know the instant he came home if an uninvited stranger might be waiting inside—somebody, for instance, like the unknown shadow who'd failed to pick him off last night. Anybody who knew his name was Custis Long could find out where Longarm lived.

Not only the rooming house, but the entire section of the un-fashionable side of Cherry Creek where it stood was still asleep, Longarm decided when he stood on the narrow veranda looking over the street. The night's unexpected snowfall, though only an inch or less, made it easy for him to see whether anyone had been prowling around. He took a cheroot from his breast pocket and chomped it between his teeth, but didn't light it, while studying the white surface.

There was only one set of tracks visible. They came from the house across the street, and the toes were pointed in the safe direction—for Longarm—away from the house, toward the Cherry Creek Bridge. Just the same, Longarm didn't step off the porch until he'd flicked his gunmetal-blue eyes into the long, slanting shadows between the houses. He didn't really expect to see anyone. The kind of gunhand who'd picked the safety of darkness once for his attack would be likely to wait for the gloomy cover of hoot-owl time before making a second try.

His booted feet cut through the thin soft snow and crunched on the cinder pathway as Longarm walked unhurriedly to the Colfax Avenue Bridge. He turned east on the avenue. Ahead, the golden dome of the Colorado Capitol Building was just picking up the first rays of the rising sun.

George Masters's barbershop wasn't open yet, and Longarm needed food more than he did a shave. He didn't fancy the cold, free lunch he knew he'd find at any of the saloons close by, so he went on past the barbershop another block and stopped at a little hole-in-the-wall café for hotcakes, fried eggs, ham, and coffee. The cheroot went into his pocket while he ate. The longer he held off lighting it, the easier it'd be to keep from lighting the next one.

Leaving the restaurant twenty-five cents poorer but with a satisfactorily full stomach, Longarm squinted at the sun. Plenty of time for a shave before reporting in at the office. He walked at ease along the avenue, which was just coming to life. The day might not be so bad in spite of the weather, he decided, feeling the warmth from his breakfast spreading through his lean, sinewy body. He grinned at the bright sun, glowing golden in a crystal sky. Deliberately, he took a match from the bundle in his pocket, flicked it into flame with a thumbnail, and lighted the cheroot.

Smelling of bay rum, his overnight stubble removed and his brown mustache now combed to the angle and spread of the horns on a Texas steer, Longarm walked into Marshal Billy Vail's office before eight o'clock. It gave him a virtuous feeling to be the first one to show up; even Vail's pink-cheeked, citified clerk-stenographer wasn't at the outside desk to challenge him. The chief marshal was already on the job, of course, fighting the ever-losing battle he waged with the paperwork that came from Washington in an ever-mounting flood.

Vail looked pointedly at the banjo clock on the wall. "This'll be the day the world ends," he growled. "What in hell happened to get you here on time for once?"

Longarm didn't bother answering. He was used to Vail's bitching. He felt his chief was entitled, bound as he was now to a desk and swivel chair, going bald and getting lardy. Deskwork, after an active career in the field, seemed to bring out the granny in a man, and Longarm decided he might bitch about life, too, under the same circumstances.

Vail shoved a pile of telegraph flimsies across the desk. "I guess you know you raised a real shit-stink down in New Mexico. You better have a good story to back up the play you made there. I've got wires here from everybody except President Hayes."

"Don't go feeling lonesome," Longarm replied mildly. "Chances are the word ain't got to him yet. Maybe you'll get one from him, too, before the day's out. You want me to tell you how it was?"

"No. In fact, I'm not sure I want a long report in the file telling exactly what happened. Think you can write one like you handed in after that Short Creek fracas a few years back?"

Vail was referring to a report Longarm had turned in about his handling of another political hot potato that had consumed a month of time, resulted in eight deaths, and upset a hundred square miles of Idaho Territory. The report had read simply, "Assigned to case May 23. Completed assignment and closed case July 1."

"Don't see why not," Longarm considered for a moment before he went on. "I figured things might be hottening up down around Santa Fe, at the capital. Some gunslick tried to bushwhack me when I got off the narrow-gauge last night."

"Hell you say." Vail's tone held no surprise. "You get him?"

"Too dark. He ran before I could sight on him."

"Well. Keep your report short, so I won't have to explain things I don't know about. Besides, I want you out of this office before that pot down there boils over clear to Washington."

"Suits me, Chief, right to a tee. There's snow on the ground and more in the air, and you know how I feel about that damned white stuff."

"If it'll cheer you up any, the place you'll be going to is just a little cooler than the hinges of hell, this time of year." Vail pawed through the untidy stacks of documents on his desk until he uncovered the papers he was after. "Texas is yelling for us to give them a hand. So is the army."

"Seems to me like they both got enough hands so they wouldn't need to come running to us. What's wrong with the Rangers? They gone to pot these days?"

Vail bristled. As a one-time Texas Ranger, he automatically resented any hint that his old outfit wasn't up to snuff. Huffily, he said, "The Rangers got more sense than to bust into something that might stir up trouble with Mexico. Here's what Bert Matthews wrote me from Austin." He read from one of the papers he'd uncovered. "He says, 'You see what a bind we're in on this one, Billy. If one of my boys sets foot across the border and gets crossways of Diaz's rurales, we'd risk starting another war with them. Whoever goes looking for Nate Webster's got to have federal authority back of him and can't be tied to Texas. That's why I'm looking to you to give us a hand.' "

Longarm rubbed his freshly shaved chin and nodded slowly, "I hadn't looked at it thataway. Makes sense, I s'pose. Who's this Nate Webster fellow and what'd he do?"

"He's a Ranger, and as far as Bert knows he didn't do anything except drop out of sight somewhere on the Mexican side of the Rio Grande. Bert don't think it was by accident, because just a little while afterward two black troopers who deserted from the 10th Cavalry and the captain of their outfit, who went looking for 'em, all three disappeared across the river, too."

"Wait a minute now. That Rio Grande's a damn long river," Longarm observed. "It's goin' t'take a while to prowl it all the way down to the Gulf of Mexico. I got to have some place to start looking from."

"You have, so simmer down. I wouldn't be apt to send you if it wasn't that all four of them men disappeared from the same place. Little town called Los Perros. Dogtown, I guess that'd translate into. You ever hear of it? I sure as hell never did, but it's been a spell since I left Texas."

Longarm shook his head. "Name don't ring a bell with me, but you know about the only time I was in Texas, how long I spent there, and all. Where's this Los Perros place at, in general?"

"It's supposed to be about where the Pecos River goes into the Rio Grande."

"Rough country, in that part," Longarm said thoughtfully. "If it's there, though, I reckon I can find it. Only, I aim to take the long way gettin' there. I better circle around New Mexico instead of going the straightest way. I show my face in old Senator Abeyeta's country before the old man wears his mad off, I'd have to fight my way from Santa Fe clear to El Paso."

"You steer clear of New Mexico Territory, and that's an order," Vail agreed. "You've stirred up trouble enough there to last awhile."

"Now, don't get your bowels riled up, Chief. I'll figure me out a route. Just let me think a minute." He leaned back in the red morocco leather chair, the most comfortable piece of furniture in the marshal's office, and began thinking aloud. "Let's see, now. I take the Kansas Pacific outa here tonight and switch to the Missouri Pacific at Pueblo. That gets me to Wichita, and I make a connection there with the Indiana–Great Northern or the Southern Pacific to San Antonio. Pick me up a horse and some army field rations at the quartermaster depot there, ride to Fort Stockton, or whichever other fort's nearer to Los Perros. That'll beat jarring my ass on the Butterfield stage, and it'll get me to spittin' distance of the border a lot faster."

"Tell my clerk," Vail said impatiently. "He'll write your travel vouchers and requisition your expense money. Here. Take these letters and read 'em on the train. They'll give you the whole story as good as I can. Now get the hell outa this office before I get a wire from the attorney general or the president telling me to suspend you or fire you outright."

"Which you can't do, if I ain't here," Longarm grinned. "All right, Chief. By the time I close this case and get back, things ought've cooled down enough to get me off the political shit list."

During the three train changes and four days and nights it took Longarm to reach his jumping-off place deep in Texas, he spent his time catching up on lost sleep and studying the letters Marshal Vail had gotten from the Texas Rangers captain and those sent to Ranger headquarters by the post adjutant at Fort Stockton. He was looking for some sort of connection that might tie the four disappearances together, but there didn't seem to be any.

Ranger Nate Webster had been working on a fresh outbreak of wholesale rustling involving what had come to be called the "Laredo Loop" along the Texas border. Cattle stolen from central

Texas ranches were hustled across the Rio Grande's northern stretches, their brands altered, and bills of sale forged to show that the steers had been Mexican-bred and bought from legitimate ranchers in the Mexican states of Chihuahua, Cohuila, or Nuevo Leon. Then, driven south through Mexico, the rustled herds were brought back across the river at Laredo and sold there to buyers. As Laredo was the only point on the border except El Paso, nearly a thousand miles north, where a railroad crossed the Rio Grande, it had long been a center for livestock sales. Even with Mexican cattle selling well below the market price for Texas beef, the profits were huge. Nate Webster's investigation had led him to Los Perros. He'd been heading there when he'd last reported to ranger headquarters in Austin. That had been early in July, and he hadn't been heard from since.

Soon after the Ranger made his last report, the two troopers from the all-black 10th Cavalry, the "buffalo soldiers," as they'd been named by the Indians, who saw in the blacks' hair a resemblance to buffalo manes, had deserted from Fort Lancaster. This small outpost was one of a string of almost a dozen forts, a day's ride apart, that had been built paralleling the Rio Grande to forestall the threat of invasion during the U.S.-Mexican War in 1846. The two men had left a trail that the Cimarron scout summoned from Fort Stockton had had no trouble following. He'd followed it to Los Perros. Captain John Hill, the Charley Troop commander, had gone with the scout. Hill had sent the Cimarron back to report and had himself followed the deserters' trail across the Rio Grande. Like Webster, like the deserting troopers, Hill had vanished on the Mexican side of the river after leaving Los Perros.

"Dogtown," Longarm muttered to himself, drawing on four-year-old memories of the last case that had taken him to Texas. "Los Perros. Mouth of the Pecos. Wild country. Big enough and rough enough to swallow up four hundred men, let alone just four, without a trace being left. I better start trying to remember what little bit of the local lingo I learned."

Then, because it was his philosophy that a man couldn't cross rivers before he tested them to see how deep and cold they ran, Longarm ratcheted back the rubbed plush daycoach seat, leaned back and went to sleep again, the smell of old and acrid coal dust in his nostrils. A little stored up shut-eye might come in handy when he hit the long trail on horseback from San Antonio to the Rio Grande.

At the I-GN depot in San Antonio, Longarm swung off the daycoach and walked up to the baggage car to claim his gear. He'd left everything except his rifle to the baggage handlers; it would have been tempting fate to leave a finely tuned Winchester .44-40 unwatched in a baggage car or on a depot platform between trains. The rifle had ridden beside him all the way from Denver, leaning between the coach seat and the wall.

As always, he was traveling light. He swung the bedroll that contained spare clothing as well as a blanket and groundcloth over one shoulder, draped his saddlebags over the other, and picked up his well-worn McClellan saddle in his left hand to balance the rifle in his right. Then he set out to find a hack to carry him from the depot to the quartermaster station.

"All the way to the quartermaster depot?" the hackman echoed when Longarm asked how much the fare would be. "That's a long ride, mister. Cost you fifteen cents to go way out there. It's plumb on the other side of town and out in the country."

"We got to go by Market Plaza to get there, don't we?" Longarm asked. When the hackman nodded, he went on, "I'll pay the fare, even if it does seem a mite high, provided you'll stop there long enough for me to eat a bowl of chili. I got to get rid of the taste of them stale butcher-boy sandwiches I been eating the last few days."

"Hop in," the hackman said. "It's my dinnertime, too. Won't charge you nothing extra for the stop."

Counting time taken for eating, the ride down Commerce Street and then north on Broadway to the army installation took just over an hour. The place was buzzing with activity. After more than five years of debating, the high brass in Washington had finally decided to turn the quartermaster depot into a large permanent cantonment, and everywhere Longarm looked there were men at work. Masons were erecting thick walls of quarry stone to serve as offices; others were busy with red bricks, putting up quarters for the officers. A few carpenters were building barracks for the enlisted men on a flat area beyond the stables, where the hackman had pulled up at Longarm's instructions.

Not until he'd been watching the scene for several minutes did Longarm realize what had struck him as odd. There was only a handful of soldiers working around the quadrangle the buildings would enclose when all of them were completed. The hackie lifted Longarm's saddle and saddlebags out of the front of the carriage; Longarm got out and paid the man. He stood with his gear on the ground around his feet until the hack drove off. Then he slung his saddlebags and bedroll over his shoulders, picked up the saddle, and started for the nearest uniforms he could see, a clump of soldiers gathered around a smithy's forge a few yards from the stable buildings.

Longarm singled out the highest-ranking of the group, a tall lantern-jawed sergeant. "I'm looking for the remount duty noncom," he told the man.

"You found him, mister. That's me. Name's Flanders."

"Mine's Long, Deputy U.S. Marshal Custis Long, out of the Denver office. I need to requisition a good saddle horse for a case I'm here on."

"Be glad to oblige, Marshal. Soon as you show me a badge or something to prove you're who you say you are."

Wordlessly, Longarm took his wallet from the pocket of his Prince Albert coat and flipped it open. The sergeant studied the silver badge pinned in the fold for a moment, then nodded. He measured Longarm's muscular body with his eyes.

"How far you going to be traveling?"

"To the border."

"You're a sizable man, Marshal Long. You plan to pack much more gear than what you've got here?"

"Nope. This is all the horse'll have to carry."

"Follow along, then. I guess we can fix you up."

Longarm followed the sergeant around the stable to a small corral where a dozen or so horses were milling. The *rat-a-tat* of carpenters' hammers nearby was obviously making some of the animals nervous, for they were walking around the corral's inner perimeter. The others stood in a fairly compact group near the center of the enclosure. Most of them were roans and chestnuts, but there was one dappled gray a hand taller than the rest. It stood out like a peacock among sparrows.

"Don't try to palm off any of them walking nags on me," Longarm cautioned the sergeant. "Last thing I need's a nervous mount."

"Maybe you'd rather do your own picking," the man suggested.

"Maybe I better, if it's all the same to you."

Longarm was still carrying his Winchester. He tilted the muzzle skyward, levered a shell into the chamber, and fired in the air before the sergeant knew what he intended to do. Two of the horses at the corral's center reared, three others bolted for the fence. Most of those that had been fence walking either shied or bucked. The gray was among the handful that did not react to the shot. Longarm studied the dapple through slitted eyes. A light-coated horse made a man stand out, more than a roan or chestnut would, but he told himself that could be good as well as bad. He pointed to the animal.

"I'll take the gray, if he stands up to a closer look. Bring him over here and let me check him out," he told the sergeant.

"Now, I'm real sorry, Marshal Long. That's the only one I can't let you have."

"Mind saying why? Is he an officer's private property?"

"Well, yes and no."

"Make up your mind, Flanders. Either he is or he ain't."

"He ain't an officer's private property, Mr. Long. Thing is, Miz Stanley, that's Lieutenant Stanley's lady, she's took a liking to Tordo, there. Rides him just about every afternoon. She'd be mighty riled if I was to—"

Longarm interrupted. "This lieutenant don't own the horse?"

"No, sir. Except, we was going to ship Tordo up to Leavenworth for their bandsmen, seeing we got no band here, and the lieutenant stopped us because his lady'd took a shine to the nag."

"I suppose Miz Stanley'd be just as well off if she took her exercise on another horse, wouldn't she?"

"No, sir. Begging your pardon, Mr. Long, she'd want Tordo."

"Happens I want him, too. He's the best-looking of that bunch out there. Now, bring him here and let me check him over. You can give the lieutenant's lady my regrets next time she wants to ride."

Longarm's tone carried an authority the sergeant was quick to recognize. He opened his mouth once, as though to argue further, but the deputy's blued-steel eyes were narrowed now, and the soldier knew he was looking at a man whose mind was made up. Reluctantly, the sergeant walked over to the gray and put a hand on its army-style clipped mane. He started back to where Longarm waited. The horse, obedient to the light pressure of the man's hand on its neck, walked step for step with the sergeant.

"Seems to be real biddable," Longarm commented.

"Tordo's a good horse, Mr. Long. Can't say I blame you for picking him out."

Longarm checked the gelding with an expert's quick, seemingly casual glances and finger touches. Teeth, eyes, spine, cannons, hooves, were all sound. His inspection lasted barely three minutes, but when it was finished Longarm was satisfied with his choice.

"He'll do, Sergeant. Make out the form for me to sign while I saddle him. Or is this the kind of post where commissioned men do all the paperwork?"

"No, sir. Most of the officers are out on a field exercise, anyhow. I've got the forms over yonder in the stable. I'll have 'em ready by the time you're fixed to ride. If you don't want to bother saddling him yourself, I'll call a trooper to do it for you."

"Thanks, but I'd as soon do it myself, Flanders. You go on and take care of the forms."

Longarm saddled the dapple with the same economy of motion that marked all his actions. He'd finished cinching the girth, had sheathed his Winchester in the scabbard that angled back from the right-hand saddle fender, and was knotting the last rawhide saddle string around his bedroll when a woman's voice spoke behind him.

"I don't know who you are, but that's my horse you're saddling."

Without turning around, Longarm replied, "No, ma'am. It's the U.S. Government's horse."

"Don't be insolent! Now, take that saddle off at once and find yourself another mount! I'm ready for my afternoon canter."

Longarm finished knotting the saddle string and turned around. He doffed his Stetson as he spoke. "Beg pardon, ma'am, but I ain't about to do that. I need this one in my work."

"Really? Just who are you? And what sort of work do you do?"

"I'm Custis Long, ma'am. Deputy U.S. marshal from Denver. And I'm on a case, which is all I need to say, I guess." Longarm realized he was speaking arbitrarily, which wasn't his usual way with a woman, but this one was being just too damned high-handed.

His abrupt manner surprised and puzzled her, that was clear from the expression on her face. Longarm took the moment of silence to inspect her. He wondered if she kept one full black eyebrow higher than the other when she wasn't angry. He couldn't give her a good mark for beauty, he decided, her features were a mite too irregular. Her nose arched abruptly from the full brows down to wide nostrils now flared with displeasure. Her lips were compressed, but that didn't hide the fact that they were on the full side. Her chin was thrust out aggressively. Her eyes were dark, and her hair was dark, too. It was caught up in a bunch of ringlets that dropped down the back of her neck to her shoulders.

She was wearing a cavalry trooper's regulation campaign hat, though it didn't have the regulation four dents in the crown. A soft, plain white blouse was pulled tightly over upthrust breasts. Her feet, in gloss-polished riding boots, were spread apart to show she had on a split skirt that dropped nearly to her ankles. Her hands were planted on her hips, and from one wrist a riding crop dangled by its looped thong.

Longarm's unconcealed inspection didn't cause the woman to drop her eyes, or even seem to embarrass her. When she found her voice, she said firmly, "Mr. Long, there are ten or fifteen other horses over there in the corral. One of them will be just as satisfactory as Tordo for your use."

"I'm sorry if it makes you mad, ma'am, but the plain fact of it is, where I'm heading for, my life might depend on my having the best horse I can throw my saddle on."

As though he hadn't spoken, she went on, "I'll find Sergeant Flanders and tell him to get you another horse. Meanwhile, you will take that saddle off Tordo at once!"

"I ain't about to do that, ma'am. Let's see, you'd be Lieutenant Stanley's wife, I guess?"

"What difference does that make?"

"Not one bit, Miz Stanley. Except it ain't going to do you no good to call the sergeant. He told me you'd be mad, after I'd made up my mind which horse I wanted. It didn't matter to me then, and it don't matter to me now."

She stamped a booted foot. "Mr. Long, if you don't take that saddle off Tordo right this minute, I'll—"

"You'll do what?" Longarm had held his temper, but he was getting angry, too, now. "I need this gray for my business. You just want him for funnin'. It's a government horse, and I figure my claim's a lot better'n yours is. Now, I can't waste my time arguin' with you. I got my job to tend to."

As Longarm turned to mount the gray, she moved cat-quick, raising the riding crop to slash at him. As fast as she acted, Longarm reacted faster. He caught her arm as it came down and held it

firmly while he took the crop off her wrist and tossed it to the
ground. She brought up her free hand to slap his face, but Longarm grasped it before the blow landed. For a moment they stood
there with arms locked, anger flowing between them like an elec-
tric current where flesh touched flesh. Then she relaxed, and Longarm released her.

They were still glaring, eye to eye, when Sergeant Flanders
came hurrying up. His arrival broke the tension. He said, "Now,
let's don't you and the marshal go having words, Miz Stanley. I
hope you won't blame me, but Marshal Long can carry his claim
for whatever he needs clear up to Colonel Tompkins. I told him—"

"It's all right, Sergeant," she broke in. "Mr. Long's explained
to me that you told him I always rode Tordo."

"Looks like I've convinced the lady I need him more'n she
does, Sergeant," Longarm said. "Now, if you'll give me that form
you got, I'll sign it and be on my way." He took the requisition
Flanders had in his hand, rested it on the saddle skirt, and scrawled
his name on the proper lines. Handing the form back to the sergeant, he said, "Now, if you'll show me where the commissary's at,
I'll swing by there and pick up some rations and be on my way."

Flanders pointed to a sprawling warehouse-like building a
short distance away. Longarm nodded and swung into the saddle.
Touching his hat brim to the woman, he rode off, leaving them
looking at his back as he made his way to the commissary. He
didn't turn to look at them.

Chapter 2

While waiting for the rations he'd drawn to be assembled, Longarm had gotten directions to help him find the road he'd take out of San Antonio. After he'd reached the end of the town, he'd have to rely on the army ordnance maps he'd picked up at the same time. He rode due west from the quartermaster depot. The houses of San Antonio lay to his left; the city was just changing the direction of its expansion from west to north. The line of closely settled streets stopped nearly two miles from the depot, though there were a few scattered dwellings, mostly small truck farms, between the body of the town and the military installation.

Longarm was taking his time, getting acquainted with the habits of the gray horse. Tordo had been trained well. The animal responded to the pressure of a knee and the touch of a boot toe with as much readiness as it did to the rein. For the most part, after he'd satisfied himself that the dapple could be trusted, Longarm let the horse pick its own way across the grassy, tree-dotted, saucerlike plain that sloped gently to the banks of the San Antonio River, which now lay just ahead.

He'd reached the riverbank and was looking for signs of a ford when thudding hoofbeats caught his attention and he turned to look behind him. Mrs. Stanley, mounted on a roan that must have been her second choice of the horses in the corral, was overtaking him fast. Subconsciously, Longarm noted that she sat the horse well, holding easily to the saddle as the roan loped toward him. He reined in and waited. She drew alongside and brought her mount to a halt.

"If you're looking for a ford, the best one's only about two hundred yards upstream," she said. "If you don't mind company, I'll ride with you a little way."

"You'll be wasting your time, if you're scheming to talk me into swapping horses," Longarm warned her. "Otherwise, I'll be right pleased to have you ride alongside me for a spell, Miz Stanley."

"I promise that I won't try to persuade you." She seemed to have gotten over her fit of anger; her voice was light and pleasant. "I really rode after you to apologize for the way I acted back at the corral. I don't usually behave so thoughtlessly."

"Wasn't no need to come apologizing, ma'am. I don't hold grudges over things that don't amount to a hill of beans."

"Just the same, it was childish of me. I understand why you'd need the best horse you can find, in your job. It must be a dangerous one."

"I reckon it is, sometimes." Longarm wasn't given to dwelling on the danger of his work. In his book a job was a job, and a man did it according to his best lights.

"Here's the ford," she said, pointing to the spot where the river's olive green water took on a lighter hue as the stream spread to run wide and shallow over a pebble-covered underwater limestone shelf. Turning their horses, they splashed through water only inches deep and rode up the shallow bank on the opposite side.

"Guess you must ride this way pretty often," he suggested after they'd covered a few hundred feet on the west bank of the river.

"Almost every day. Riding's about the only relaxation I have in this dull little town. Especially now, when my husband's away on a training exercise."

"Funny. I never figured San Antone was so dull."

"I don't suppose it would be, for a man. You've got the gambling places and dance halls and saloons. But all I've got is the company of other army wives, and we get bored with one another after a few gossipy afternoon teas. At home, now, it's a different thing."

"Where's home to you, Miz Stanley?"

"New York. It's never dull there. We have the Broadway shows—musicals or dramas—tea dances at the big hotels, receptions, opera, always something interesting."

"I can see it'd be different. Can't rightly say much about New York; I never visited back there, myself."

"You should, sometime. It's a different world." She pointed to a thickly wooded area that lay just ahead of them, where trees in closely spaced groves dotted a wide stretch of grassland that ended on their right, at the foot of a high white bluff. "Of course, you won't see things like that in New York. The nearest thing to open country there is Central Park. Somehow, that area ahead reminds me of it; perhaps that's why it makes me feel at home when I see it."

"Seems like I recall this place from when I was in San Antonio before. San Pedro Springs, they call it, don't they?"

"Yes. It's one of my favorite spots. On Sundays and holidays it's overrun with families having picnics, but on days like today it's as deserted as the Forest of Arden."

"Can't say I been there, either. Matter of fact, I never got out to San Pedro Springs but once, when I was here last time."

Mrs. Stanley seemed compelled to talk. "Sometimes I bring my lunch out here and stay all day. I've found arrowheads and pieces of old Mexican army equipment from the Texas-Mexican war of fifty years ago."

"You interested in history, then, Miz Stanley?"

"Not especially. But it gives me something besides garrison gossip to think about."

They were approaching an especially large grove of hackberry and pinoak trees bordered by a heavy growth of low-branched chinaberry trees that formed a wide, dense belt around the taller growth. Longarm kneed the dapple to turn it and skirt the edge of the grove, but the lieutenant's wife was reining in.

"There's the most beautiful spring in the middle of this grove," she said. "I just can't pass by it without stopping for a sip of water."

Longarm thought the excuse was flimsy, almost as thin as her story of having ridden after him to apologize. His work took him to army posts quite regularly and he'd met bored, restless army wives before. Almost from the time they'd crossed the river he'd been getting the groin twitches he felt whenever he was with an attractive woman who was obviously making herself available to

him. He pulled rein and swung out of his saddle before she was
quite ready to dismount.

"I'm pretty thirsty myself," he told her. "We'll just go get
some of that spring water together."

He moved to help her from her horse. She was riding sidesaddle, with her right leg hooked over the horn, and had to swing the
leg high over the pommel to free it. Longarm caught her booted
foot in one hand and steadied her to the ground. His free arm
passed up the backs of her thighs, over the soft bulge of her buttocks to her waist. She was beginning to tremble before both her
feet were on the ground. The trembling increased as he pulled
her to himself and sought her lips. They locked together, tongues
entwined. Longarm felt himself growing erect as she rubbed her
hips against him.

She felt the swelling beneath his britches, pulled away, and
panted, "Hurry! Let's go into the grove! I want you right now, this
minute!"

Taking him by the hand, she pulled him into the shelter of the
brush. They'd taken only a few steps into the screening growth
when she stopped and began fumbling with the buttons of her
riding habit. The thought flashed through Longarm's mind that
this was going to be clumsy and uncomfortable, but the woman
had other ideas. She let the skirt fall, slid her drawers down to follow the skirt, and went to her knees on the soft, cushioning grass.

"From behind!" she urged. "Like a horse mounts a mare! Be
my stud! Now, right now!"

She dropped to her elbows. Her inviting, round, white buttocks gave speed to Longarm's fingers as he worked the buttons
of his fly free and knelt behind her. He penetrated deeply, to his
full length, withdrew until he almost lost her, then slammed
fiercely to her again. The novelty of the situation was almost as
exciting to him as it seemed to be to the woman. He thrust lustily,
ramming hard, not trying to tease her or hold back. She whimpered deep in her throat, a sound like the whinnying of the mare
she was pretending to be. The whimpers became moans and the
moans changed to groans of pleasure. Longarm grasped her with
a hand on each side of her hips, callused fingers digging into soft
flesh. Her buttocks writhed against him as he drove fiercely into
her, stroke following quick, full stroke. Then, in a sudden, gasping crescendo of quick, sharp cries, he felt her body sag and grow
limp. Longarm held her up as he pounded home the few thrusts

he needed, and pulled her firmly against him until his own climax pulsed and passed.

He lowered her gently to the turf. She lay on her side for a moment, ribs heaving. When she rolled over on her back to look up at him, kneeling there by her, she saw his frock coat gaping open to show the holstered Colt above his left hip.

"That's the first time I've been made love to by a man wearing a pistol and a long coat," she grinned. "But I loved it!"

"Me, too," he agreed. "Maybe it was a mite hasty, but it was sure fine."

"Damn it, I couldn't wait. The minute I felt your hands touching me when you helped me dismount, I started itching for you."

"We won't be in a hurry, next time," he promised. "You get out of that tangle of clothes you're in. I'll go get my bedroll, and we can stretch out and be comfortable together."

When he'd tethered the horses and returned with the bedroll, Longarm found Mrs. Stanley standing a little deeper in the shelter of the trees, in a clearing where a spring bubbled gently to form a small, grass-edged pool. Except for her boots, the lieutenant's wife was naked. Her clothes were hung neatly over the bottom branch of a spreading pinoak.

"I couldn't get my boots off," she told him. "You'll have to help me."

"I'll be pleased to help you do just about anything, ma'am."

"Start out by calling me anything but 'ma'am,' then."

"I damn sure ain't going to call you Miz Stanley, not now. But that's all of your name I know."

"It is, isn't it? My name's Cynthia. My best friends call me Cyn, which tells you something about me, I suppose."

"Unless I disremember, I told you my name when you was giving me hell back at the corral."

"Yes. Custis. Custis Long," she sighed happily. "And I'll admit, you're long where it counts the most."

They spread the bedroll and Cynthia sat down while Longarm yanked off her boots. He hung his coat and vest on the pinoak beside Cynthia's garments, and deposited his holstered pistol within easy reach, at the edge of the spread blankets. Then he worked his own stovepipe boots free and sat beside her. She offered her lips, and when the first clinging kiss exhausted their breath, Longarm began moving his mouth and tongue across her shoulders and down to her full, upthrust breasts, seeking the dark puckering aureoles that were thrusting up at him. She stopped him with a hand under his chin.

"Not fair, Custis. You've still got most of your clothes on. Here, I'll help you undress. That'll be part of my pleasure."

His undressing was prolonged, interrupted by kisses that started as soon as Cynthia had helped him shed his shirt and pulled down the top of his longjohns. At once she sank her teeth like a cannibal into his shoulder, biting almost hard enough to draw blood. Longarm's calloused hands caressed her breasts roughly. She began to moan again. Cynthia fumbled loose the strained buttons of his fly to release the erection she'd been helping along by passing a squeezing hand along its swelling length. He kicked off his longjohns and britches and rolled on top of her. She spread herself to receive him, legs raised high, hips rolling and rising to meet his slow, deliberate thrusting. Longarm was not hurrying now, but prolonging the sensation. Twice when he felt her nearing climax he slowed to a stop, plunging full into her hot, wet depth, holding her tightly and pushing hard, but without motion. Each time after her breathing eased and her moans slackened to silence he began thrusting again, controlling himself, until the third time she began to cry and quiver. He knew she was ready now, and speeded his tempo, bringing her up with him until they exploded together in the long, dazed bursting of ultimate sensation that left them both limp and motionless.

After they'd begun to breathe normally, she whispered, "If you think I'm a shameless bitch, you're right, Custis. But not with everybody. It takes a certain kind of man to bring out the bitchiness in me, and you're that kind."

"Can't say I'm sorry, Cyn. You're some armful of woman. But I reckon you know that."

"I like for you to tell me." Her hand, exploring his chest, hesitated and stopped at a puckered scar. She sat up, looked, and said with a gasp of surprise, "My God! What kind of life do you lead?"

"About a normal one, for a man in my line of work. But we don't need to talk about them souvenirs. Let's just lay back and rest awhile. We've got plenty of time."

Cuddled together, they grew warm and dozed, sprawling languidly as the shade from the towering trees that surrounded the clearing and hid them crept across the grass.

Cynthia awoke first. Longarm became aware of hands moving

warmly over his skin, exploring his body, of the moist tip of her tongue tracing his eyelids and ears and trailing along his cheek, before it slid into his mouth. Her busy hands had already brought him to a half-erection before he was awake, and when he became aware of her soft stroking the erection peaked. He rolled to face her, his movement pinning one of her legs under him. She brought the other leg high up on his ribs and guided him into her, squirming with sensuous pleasure as he entered slowly and went deep deliberately. When he began to move his hips, she clamped her legs tightly around him to stop him from moving.

"No," Cynthia said. "Not for a while yet. I just want to feel you in me—all of you. Just to hold you here without moving, while you kiss and fondle me."

"I always try to oblige a lady."

"You still think I'm a lady, Custis?"

"Sure. Only you're a woman, too. Ain't often you'll find both of 'em together."

He lay still as she'd requested, except for the movements of his hands over her breasts and belly and along her hips and down them, to knead and squeeze her soft cheeks. The caresses she gave him in return, long deep kisses, sharp nips on shoulders and chest, had their effect. Longarm could feel himself building to a tremendous orgasm. He moved his hips experimentally, questioningly. She relaxed the grip of her thighs enough to let him make a few short beginning thrusts. He moved to rise on top of her, but she pushed her hand against his chest.

"Please, Custis. The way we did the first time. Be my stallion again while I'm your mare. Only slower, take longer."

Cynthia went to her hands and knees again and Longarm mounted her as she had asked him to. He went in fast, with one single, brutal stab. She whimpered and shuddered and came almost at once, but Longarm was in full control of himself now, and so of her. His back arched over her quivering body and he gave her no time to relax from her first quick orgasm, but set a rhythm, easy at first, pounding home hard, neither slowing nor stopping, until her limp muscles tightened and she came to life again beneath him. He felt no urge to hurry; she'd asked him to take longer. Even when Cynthia began moaning, her juices flowing freely, running down his thighs as well as hers, he neither hurried nor stopped. He was holding her tightly, as he had the first time, a hand clamped on each hip, but when she started to whimper again, deep in her throat, he leaned forward and grabbed her full breasts, using them like reins to ride her hard, to pull her back against him. Groans began to pulse from her throat, and Longarm felt himself getting close. Cynthia's writhing stopped, her body tensed under his, and now he went faster for a few tremendous lunges, before his own spasm took him, lifting him out of awareness of anything but the woman under him and the flow he was gushing deep inside her.

Awareness returned as they lay curled together, spoon fashion, on the rough blanket, her back to him. The sun was red and low, and could be seen only through the treetops now as it neared the horizon.

"If you're going to get home tonight, we better be stirring," Longarm said. "It'll be dark in another little while."

"What're you going to do, Custis? Travel on tonight?"

"Nope. I aim to camp right here and start fresh at daybreak."

"Then I'll stay with you. If you'd like for me to, that is. All I've got to go home to is an empty house and a lonesome bed."

"I'll be real proud if you want to stay. It'll be a dark camp, though—no fire, and hardtack and jerky for supper."

"Who cares about food? We'll be too busy to miss supper."

Cynthia proved as good as her word. They slept when they'd exhausted one another, and awoke to come together again in the bright silver light of the full moon. The night passed quickly. When false dawn showed, Longarm got up, leaving Cynthia asleep, and groped into his clothes in the half-light. His movements woke her, and when he came back from the edge of the grove, where he'd gone to check the horses and relieve the pressure on his night-filled bladder, he found her lying on her back, gazing at the sky.

"Why didn't you wake me up one last time?" she asked.

"Figured it'd be better if I didn't. It's time I left."

Cynthia sighed. "I guess I knew you'd say something like that. Damn you men, anyhow. You've always got some kind of duty that spoils a woman's pleasure."

"It's how the world was made. Nobody's been able to change it."

"Will you be coming back this way?" Cynthia stood up and walked to the tree where her clothes hung. "And when?"

"Can't say to either one. When I do come back, I'll find you."

"No good-byes, now, Custis. You go ahead. No kisses, no last waving. Look back at me if you want to, but that's all. I'm superstitious about saying good-bye."

While they talked, Longarm had been folding and rolling his bedding, a tight, neat roll of blankets protected by a waterproof ground cloth with his slicker on the outside, where it'd be handy. He stood up and threw the roll over his shoulder. At the edge of the clearing, he turned once to look back. Cynthia stood with her shoulders squared, breasts high and proud in the dawn light. He smiled, and she smiled in return. Then Longarm turned and pushed through the high, whipping growth of chinaberries to where the dapple stood, saddled and ready to ride.

Tordo was feisty with morning freshness, and Longarm let the animal trot, stepping high, until he'd settled down to the day's work, and slowed to a walk. The sun grew warm on Longarm's back and sent the shadows of man and horse in long black streaks ahead of them. They moved across the rising lip of the saucerlike depression in which San Antonio lay. The long, hot days in the saddle that lay ahead were as far as Longarm planned. There seemed no use in making schemes until he got to Los Perros, the town that was still a mystery to him, and found out more about the border jumpers.

Chapter 3

Dusk found Longarm a long ten miles from the Butterfield stage-coach station at the Medina River, where he'd planned to spend the night. He hadn't wanted to push Tordo on his first day out, and the big dapple was still stepping high when Longarm decided to make a dry camp instead of stumbling through the dark until moonrise to reach the river. In rattlesnake country, he'd learned it wasn't a good idea to choose a sleeping place in pitch-blackness, and he'd seen plenty of big rattlers sunning themselves that day. He scouted around to make sure there weren't any rattler dens close by before hobbling the gray and spreading his bedroll.

After he'd fed Tordo, he sat Indian style on his blankets while he chewed leathery jerky and crumbly hardtack and washed it down with a few sips of water. While he puffed the one cigar he was allowing himself every day, he used the last remnants of light to read the ordnance map, memorizing his route and studying the area of the Rio Grande where he was going. Before turning in, Longarm changed the plan he'd framed in Denver. Instead of going to Fort Stockton and backtracking from there, he'd bear farther south and go directly to the outpost from which the soldiers had departed—Fort Lancaster. Satisfied that he was on the trail at last, Longarm crawled under the top blanket. At least, he told himself as he dozed off, he wouldn't have to fight bedbugs all night, as he'd probably have done in one of the bunks at the stage station.

Midmorning breakfast at the Butterfield station on the bank of the Medina, and a good ration of grain for the dapple, set Longarm and Tordo back on the trail in high spirits. He pushed the horse into a lope for a mile or two, then nudged it into a run, testing its gait and wind and responsiveness to his commands. This was something he hadn't taken time to do the day before, while he was still getting acquainted with the animal. When he'd reaffirmed his opinion that he didn't have to worry about the gray, Longarm slowed their pace to a walk. He got to the Sabinal stage depot in time for a twilight supper, and pushed on across the stream before stopping for the night.

On familiar ground now, thanks to intensive study of his map, Longarm began cutting his time by leaving the road when it made curves and zigzags and pushing across country. In this way he could beat the time the stagecoaches made. The vehicles had to swerve to avoid hills and valleys; he could cross them. On the afternoon of the third day, with the Frio River behind him and the Edwards Plateau looming against the skyline to the northwest, Longarm rode into Uvalde. As he'd suspected it would be, the sheriff's office was in the back of the courthouse. He walked in and introduced himself to Sheriff Frank Purdom.

"I know your backyard don't exactly reach to the border," he told the sheriff, "but I was wondering if you'd heard anything about a little town right on the Rio Grande, somewheres close to the mouth of the Pecos. It's called Los Perros."

Purdom stroked his sideburns. "Los Perros? Can't say I recall it, but that don't signify much. There's plenty of squatter towns along the river that don't have names anybody's ever heard of, ten miles away from 'em."

"Figures," Longarm nodded. "Figures, too, if the place had a bad reputation, you'd likely have heard it mentioned."

"I imagine so," Purdom agreed. Then he added, "I'll tell you something, though, Marshal Long. We got enough mischief to handle right here in our own county, so we don't reach out for trouble."

"Sensible. That mischief—would it include a fresh rash of rustling?"

"There's always a certain amount of cattle thieving, you know that. I will say that here lately there's been bigger herds than usual drove off. Why? You onto something I oughta know about?"

"No. I was just wondering if you might've got an idea the old Laredo Loop's at work again."

His question surprised the sheriff. "Where'd you hear about the Laredo Loop? You never said you was from Texas, and I know all the old boys in the marshal's force around here."

"Now, I don't lay claim to knowing anything. Far as being from Texas, the only time I was here was on a gold smuggling case a few years back, but that was way south of here. I was just curious. I heard about the Laredo Loop then, and I got to wondering about it."

"I see." Purdom shook his head. "I just don't know. We don't work the Mexican side anymore. Back in old Juarez's day, us and the rurales got along pretty good. With that bastard Diaz running things there now, it's all changed."

"So I've heard." Longarm stood up. "Well, I still got riding to do between here and dark. Anything special to watch out for between here and the border?"

"Nothing that comes to mind." Purdom surveyed his visitor's well-worn boots and skintight britches, his eyes stopping for a moment at the slight bulge made by the holstered pistol in the left side of his frock coat. "You look like you can handle yourself. If I was you, I'd shed that coat, though. You say you're strange to these parts, so just keep in mind you're going into right dry country, when you head west. Don't pass by any good water without letting your horse drink, and topping off your canteen. Do that, and you'll make it."

As he rode out of Uvalde, Longarm discovered the sheriff had neglected to tell him that besides being dry, the country was also about ten degrees hotter than hell's hinges. Even though he'd taken time before leaving the town to fold his coat and tie it neatly inside his slicker, he'd been on the road only a short-time before sweat began welling out. The sun was like a bright gold coin that had been heated in a furnace until it was almost at the melting point. The character of the land changed suddenly. Grass and bright green foliage gave way to bare, stony earth, olive-hued mesquite, and gray green cactus. The sparse plants looked as though the beating sun had bleached out all their color. The month might well have been July instead of September.

He looked at the baked countryside, at the low humps of the

Edwards Mountains to his right, and wondered why they were named on his ordnance map as mountains. Nobody who'd ever seen the Rockies could call those little chunks mountains, he was sure of that. He rode on after fishing his bandanna from his pocket and folding it into a triangle, which he tied loosely around his neck to catch the drops of sweat that trickled off his chin. The heat leached out his energy, and when he reached the Nueces River just as the sun was turning to bright orange above the horizon's jagged rim, Longarm decided to stop for the night. The map told him this would be his last sure water before he reached Fort Lancaster, still eighty miles ahead.

"Tordo," he told the dapple as he tethered the horse by the rock-strewn riverbank, "you better drink good tonight and before we hit the trail in the morning. We got two damn dry days ahead."

Dry they were, indeed. The autumn rains hadn't started yet, and the only watercourse shown on Longarm's map was Sycamore Creek, which had neither sycamores along its bank nor water in its bed. Longarm had expected that, because the map also bore the notation, *dry in summer*. He poured water from the canteen into his cupped palm and sloshed it into Tordo's mouth, let the horse rest a short while, then kept pushing on at a carefully measured, energy-saving gait that brought him in sight of Fort Lancaster late in the afternoon of the third day out of Uvalde.

"You men are sure as hell out in the middle of nowhere, here," Longarm remarked to the fresh-faced young lieutenant who'd found himself in command of the fort when Captain Hill had disappeared.

"It's desolate, all right," Lieutenant Bryant agreed. His eyes followed those of his visitor in scanning the bare, beaten earth of the parade ground outside the orderly room window. Distorted by heat shimmer from the earth, the U.S. flag hung limp on the flagpole, its thirty-eight stars hidden in its folds. On both sides of the hoof-pocked center area, on worn adobe walls of the narrow barracks buildings, the sun picked out seams and water-cut runnels that had turned the hardened clay into a jigsaw puzzle of lines, like those on the faces of very old men. A few troopers, with the sleeves of their gray flannel field shirts rolled high, lounged in the scant shadows at the ends of the structures.

"If a man was stuck here long at a time, I'd bet he'd get right randy," Longarm suggested. "Want to go find himself a woman."

"It happens. Makes problems for us when it does."

"Like them two that skipped?"

"I'll tell you something odd, Marshal. Those are the only two outright desertions we've had during the two years I've been here. Oh, there've been some who wandered off without authorization— overnight, a day or two. Most of them are men who go looking for a woman in one of the shanty towns along the river, or maybe at the Apache resettlement camp south of here."

"Only them two didn't come back, and when your captain went looking for 'em, he disappeared, too."

"You're certainly not suggesting that Captain Hill deserted?" Lieutenant Bryant sounded horrified.

"Don't get miffed, son. I didn't mean it that way." Longarm judged that this was the time to ask the question that had been puzzling him since he'd been assigned to search for the missing cavalrymen. "You got any ideas why them two troopers took off like they did? And wasn't it sort of funny your captain felt like those two men were important enough for him to go chasing himself?"

Lieutenant Bryant thought for a long time before he replied, "I'm sure you need to know this, Marshal, but I hope you'll keep it confidential. Captain Hill didn't want to cause any scandal, or do anything that'd harm the way the ranchers feel about our troopers."

"Go ahead and spill it, Lieutenant. If you knew me at all, you'd know I don't flapjaw. It's my business to find things out. If you don't tell me what you're trying to set on, I'll just go dig it up anyways."

"Yes, I suppose you will. Well, Captain Hill felt he had to bring those men back to face court martial. The troopers deserted because they'd raped a rancher's wife."

"White woman, of course?" When Bryant nodded, Longarm went on, "And I bet down here in Texas, your black buffalo soldiers ain't exactly what you'd call popular."

Bryant retorted sharply, "They're damned good soldiers, Long. I don't care what civilians might say or think about them."

"Nobody said they wasn't. And rape ain't exactly something that comes with the color of a man's skin. But I can see you got a real problem. Don't worry. I don't aim to make it worse."

"Thanks. Now, how can I help you, Marshal?"

"About the biggest help you can give me is to trot out that Cimarron scout that went down to the border with the captain."

"Sorry, sir. He was called back to Fort Stockton. By now, he's out in the field somewhere."

"Well, hell!" Longarm didn't try to hide his disgust. "How'm I going to find out what Captain Hill was aiming to do when he went border jumping? He must've had some idea in his head about where them two troopers was heading for."

"He did. I can help you there. Tinker reported to me—Tinker's the Cimarron's name—when he came back from Los Perros alone. He said the captain had found out, I don't know how, that the troopers were going south into Mexico until they got far enough from the border to feel safe. I suppose they thought we wouldn't follow them or try to bring them back, with conditions as they are now in Mexico."

"Um. How'd the captain find all this out?"

"From asking around Los Perros, Tinker said."

"It's for sure all three of 'em dropped out of sight after they left Los Perros, then?" Longarm rubbed his face. The sweat was making his stubble itchy. He reminded himself that he'd have to find out if there was a barber at the fort, and, he remembered, if the sutler there had his kind of cheroots; he was down to three. He said, "I guess that's my next stop, then. What d'you know about the place, Lieutenant?"

"Los Perros?" Bryant shook his head. "Not much. I've stopped there a few times, when a patrol took me close to it. Captain Hill didn't like the men to go there, so I tried to set an example."

"Suppose you tell me as much as you can. Whatever you seen's pretty certain to be a help to me. I like to know what's in a hole before I jump in."

"There's not much to tell, Marshal Long. The place isn't really a town, just a bunch of shanties. Jacales, they call them around here. Shacks made out of scrap wood and tree limbs and tin, whatever the people can pick up, I suppose. Two or three houses built of good solid lumber. A saloon, of course, with gambling tables."

"Whorehouse upstairs?" Longarm broke in to ask.

"Strangely enough, no. I think there was at one time, but when Captain Hill started discouraging the troopers from going to the town, the girls scattered out."

"I've traveled around some," Longarm observed, "and I've found out it's got to be a real piss-poor town that can't support a whorehouse."

"That's Los Perros," Bryant smiled thinly. "As far as I can see, it doesn't support anything except the saloon. No stores, nothing."

"How big a place is it, then?"

"Not big at all. Only perhaps twenty or twenty-five Americans and a couple of hundred Mexicans and border breeds."

Longarm nodded. He'd seen a few border settlements such as the one the lieutenant had described when he was breaking the gold-smuggling case. He said, "That really ain't what I'm after. What kind of people are they? They go by the law, or what? And this fellow I heard runs things, what's he like?"

Bryant thought for a moment. "Marshal, I can't tell you a lot about the people. Some of them have little truck gardens, not big enough to be farms. They sell produce to the ranches and to the fort, here. Some have little goat herds or they keep chickens. They scrape out a living, somehow. And I don't know what the Americans do, if they don't work at the saloon or for the sheriff."

"That's one I'm interested in. He's the big boss, ain't he?"

"Yes. Tucker's his name, Ed Tucker. And I don't think he was ever elected sheriff, he just took over the job."

"Got any idea where he's from?"

"I'd guess from the South, judging by the way he talks."

"Is he old enough to've fought in the war?"

"Oh, yes. I'd guess he's pushing fifty, maybe past that."

"Mean, or easygoing?"

Again the young officer hesitated before answering. "Maybe not mean, but he's sure not easygoing. I mentioned that Captain Hill unofficially discourages our men from going there. Since the captain began doing that, anybody in an army uniform gets a cool reception."

"How many men has he got backing him?"

Bryant shook his head. "That's something I can't tell you, Marshal. I've only seen Tucker two or three times. I'd say he's got a lot of curiosity, or maybe it's suspiciousness."

"How's that?"

"Well, I went to Los Perros once looking for the Mexican who supplies the fort with eggs. Tucker stopped me, asked what I was doing, and when I told him, he tagged along with me until I left. The next time, I was in the saloon. It was a hot day, and getting late, and I was going to bivouac my patrol a little way out of town. I thought if I let them stop for a beer or two, they wouldn't be so tempted to sneak back at night for a drink." Bryant looked earnestly at Longarm. "It wasn't exactly according to the captain's ideas, but there weren't any official standing orders—"

"I understand about the army, Lieutenant," Longarm broke in. "Go ahead."

"Tucker came into the saloon while we were there. He came up to me and said I'd better keep my men on a tight rein, that their uniforms wouldn't keep them out of his jail if they made trouble. That was about all."

"Damn it, you must've noticed something more, or heard talk. It'd be a big help to me if I knew whether the sheriff had two or three men to back him, or two or three dozen. I'll remind you about something. When I go in to a place, I'm by myself. I don't have a squad of troopers with carbines and sabers to back up my play."

"I wish I could help you more, Marshal Long. The plain fact is, I just don't know any more to tell you."

Longarm sensed the young officer's disappointment. "Guess if you don't know, you don't. It ain't your fault. Wasn't your job to go prying into what goes on in Los Perros. Leastwise, it wasn't the times you was there."

"What're you planning to do, Marshal? About Captain Hill and the deserters?"

"Whatever I got to do to find 'em. And to find me a Texas Ranger that dropped out of sight about the same way they did. Last place he was heard from was Los Perros, too."

"You think there's some kind of connection?"

"Don't know yet, son. Might be, might not be. All I can say right now is about what you told me a minute ago. I just plain don't know. But I sure as hell intend to find out, soon as I can get to Los Perros and start digging."

"If there's anything I can do—"

"Just happens there is." Longarm smiled. "I been eating outa my saddlebags the past few days. I washed as best I could when I made a stop where there was water, but I ain't fond of shaving with cold lather. If you was to offer me some cooked supper and a hot bath in a tub, and maybe dig up one of your troopers who knows how to shave a man without cutting his guzzle in two—"

"Of course. I—I suppose it'd be all right if you stayed in the captain's quarters. His orderly can look after you. And you're more than welcome to join us at our mess, such as it is."

"I'd appreciate that, Lieutenant. Man's going out looking for trouble, he always feels better if he goes clean-shaved and with a full belly. And I can smell trouble waiting for me in Los Perros."

Chapter 4

Longarm reined in at the edge of the sandy draw and looked across the white expanse at Los Perros. Remembering the lieutenant's description, he had to agree that the young officer had been right when he said it wasn't much of a town. The Rio Grande dictated the settlement's shape: long and narrow. Los Perros stood on a sandspit, and Longarm could see that when rains upstream swelled the river, the sandspit would become an island. Now, the sandy wash on the Texas side of the river was dry. Beyond the town, the green current ran in a narrow channel, and Longarm judged it was both deep and swift.

Los Perros stretched out, a long, thin, straggling shamble of houses. Most of them were patchwork jobs, put together from spliced short boards. Some of the planks bore the faded imprint of words: "Silver's Cuban Tobacco Twist," "Aunt Miranda's Dark Molasses," "Winchester Arms Co.," showing that they'd come from salvaged packing cases. Some of the shanties were pole shacks, made by driving tree limbs into the ground in a square and nailing to them sheets of metal made from straightened-out kerosene containers, or the red-painted metal cannisters in which army gunpowder was once shipped. The roofs of most of the houses were rusted sheets of metal that came from only God knew where, to wind up on a sandspit on the Texas border.

A few structures were solidly constructed from planed boards, and even these were in need of paint. Longarm spotted the saloon at once; it was Los Perros's biggest building, two low stories tall, with a false front that made it look higher than it really was. A short distance from the saloon, another solid house rose above the low roofs of the jacales. This one had been painted, though there were patches of bare wood showing now where the paint was peeling off. Another decent house stood on the opposite side of the saloon, and a third could be seen behind the bar's false front. On the near side of the sandspit a new house had been started, though no one was working on it now.

There were no streets that Longarm could see. The houses stood higgledy-piggledy, and sandy trails wound between them. A few people were moving in the town. Most of them seemed headed in the general direction of its center. All but a few were on foot, though the hats of three or four who rode burros or horses could be seen bobbing along at a higher level than the heads of the pedestrians.

Instead of crossing the draw at once, Longarm nudged the dapple with his heel and turned to move along the sandy margin. He wanted a look at the town from one end, and wanted as well to get an unobstructed view of the river channel that divided Mexico from Texas. At the end of the sandspit he reined in and looked back. Now he could see the place from another angle, and decided it was a bit bigger than he'd thought at first; there were houses on the sloping western side that had been invisible from his earlier broadside vantage point.

Sloping ground led to the river. A lone fisherman, his pole propped in a forked stick, sat at the shore's edge. In its channel the Rio Grande rolled smoothly, its water an opaque greenish brown. The surface, unbroken by ripples, told Longarm the water was both deep and swift. The bank on the Mexican side rose sheer from the water. The rough, stone-studded rise was crowned with a thick growth of chamizal, a mixture of scrub mesquite, catsclaw, and broad-leafed pear cactus. It looked tangled, impenetrable, and unfriendly, as scrubby and shabby as the town itself.

"Well, old son," Longarm muttered under his breath. "It sure as hell ain't much to look at, and I don't reckon it'll improve when I get closer."

He angled across the draw to the humped center of the sandspit and rode into Los Perros, moving in the general direction of the saloon. Before he reached the building's tall false front, Longarm entered an open space, not a formal square or plaza typical of so many Southwestern towns; this one had no well-defined perimeter. The buildings that marked its roughly circular area were set askew, at odd angles to one another, giving the enclosure a ragged, unplanned look. The saloon, across from the spot where Longarm sat on Tordo, seemed to be the area's chief focal point; the second was a well, located a bit off-center, and half a dozen yards from the well a single, man-high post a foot in diameter had been set in the hard earth. The plaza, if it could be called that, was obviously about to be the scene of some kind of public occurrence. People kept arriving to join the crowd already stirring within it.

Longarm was less interested in the buildings and other permanent features of the place than he was in the people standing and moving around. Most of them were men, though a handful of women clustered at one side, shrilling at children who darted like so many small, brown, active beetles between the legs of the men. It was not a prosperous-looking group. The men were generally dressed in the loose raw cotton blouses and trousers of borderland peons; their heads were covered with wide-brimmed straw sombreros, their feet stuck sockless into huaraches of braided leather. Black was the predominant color among the women: black dresses that swept the ground and black rebozos that covered the wearers' heads and shaded their faces so that Longarm couldn't tell which were young, which middle-aged, and which old and wrinkled.

Against clothing dominated by monotones, the few men wearing charro outfits stood out like peacocks in a flock of pigeons and crows. The charro suits glistened with gold or silver embroidery on waist-length, fawn-hued jackets and on towering felt sombreros, and along the seams of skintight pants that were tucked into tall, shining, high-heeled boots. Equally conspicuous were the men, fewer in number, who wore the regulation outfits of border ranch hands: tight Levi's faded from indigo to sky blue by repeated washing with lye soap, denim shirts of blue or gray or tan, stitch-traced high-heeled boots, and broad-brimmed Stetsons, creased Texas style, a single deep dent running up the front from brim to crown.

Longarm was suddenly very conscious of his Prince Albert coat and his cavalry-style, forward-tilted Stetson. He was also aware that the eyes of just about everybody in the plaza seemed to be watching him. He looked around for a hitching rail and saw only one, in front of the saloon, and guided Tordo at a slow walk around the edge of the plaza, twitching the reins when necessary to keep the dapple from breaking up a group of people.

He noticed now that here and there around the plaza's rim, tiny threads of smoke were beginning to rise from the improvised stoves of food vendors. Longarm recalled that any event in a settlement along the border drew food stalls to feed the crowds, as well as vendors carrying trays of sweets, buns, and candied cactus and sweet potatoes. It had been a long time since breakfast. Longarm watched for a tray bearer, spotted one, and reined up. For a nickel he got three puffed buns crusted with colored sugar on top, and munched them as a prelude to the lunch he'd look for later. He sat Tordo long enough to finish the last bun after he got to the hitching rail, then dismounted and looped the gray's reins around the crossbar.

He'd taken three or four steps away before he remembered the Winchester in his saddle scabbard. In almost any place except Los Perros, Longarm would have left the gun where it was. Nowhere in the West would a saddled horse or its gear be touched by anybody except its owner. Los Perros impressed Longarm as being a town where normal rules and customs were ignored. He went back, slipped the rifle from its scabbard, and tucked the butt into his armpit. Then he joined the crowd that by now had grown to sizable proportions. The center of interest seemed to be near the well. He dodged his way in that direction and stopped eight or ten paces from the well.

One of the men wearing the clothes that identified him as a ranch hand stood alone, a short distance from where Longarm stopped. The marshal stepped up to him and asked, "What's the fuss about?"

"Everybody's waiting for the whipping to commence."

"Whipping?"

"Sure. Sheriff Tucker's got the right idea. Instead of lockin' a lawbreaker in jail, havin' to feed him and keep him, the ol' sheriff sees he gits a good whipping, then he's turned loose."

"Who's getting whipped today?"

"Don't recall his name. Some saddle tramp that pulled a knife on one of the sheriff's deputies and cut him a little bit."

"Maybe I'm wrong, but I thought public whipping was outlawed in the United States," Longarm observed. "Seems to me that was done when the slaves got freed."

Turning, the stranger faced Longarm squarely. "Mister, here in Los Perros nobody gives a billy-be-damn for the U.S.A. If you're a Yankee bluenose, this ain't no place for you."

Longarm was more interested in getting information than he was in protesting an implied insult. He let the comment slide by and asked, "I suppose this drifter stood trial, didn't he? And the judge said he was guilty?"

"Sure. It was all handled legal and proper."

"Who was the judge that tried the case?"

"Hell, we ain't got but only one judge in Los Perros—Sheriff Tucker. If you wasn't a stranger here, you'd know that."

"Seeing I am a stranger who don't know beans about your town, maybe you can tell me how come a man can be sheriff and judge all at the same time."

"Maybe you better ask Sheriff Tucker about that. It's just the way things has always been here, I guess."

"I see."

Before Longarm could ask another question there was a stir in the crowd and a murmur of voices. Longarm and the stranger craned their necks to see what was happening. A knot of men was coming around the corner of the saloon building. Their leader was an imposing figure. He stood high and wide in fancy, heeled boots with colored stitching and wore a tall-crowned Stetson creased in a Dakota peak, but his width competed with his height and detracted from his overall appearance. His stomach hung over his trousers top and rolls of fat forced him to wear his gunbelt too low. Even then, the fat crowded the butt of the old-fashioned ivory-handled revolver that dangled in a tooled leather holster. A gold badge was on the big man's left shirt pocket.

Longarm realized he was getting his first look at Sheriff—and apparently, Judge—Ed Tucker, the man who occupied the catbird seat in Los Perros. Longarm would have been more impressed if Tucker had been a bit on the lean side, and if he hadn't reeled ever so slightly as he strode in front of the little group that trailed him. Still, Longarm thought, he'd reserve judgment until he'd had a chance to study Tucker's face, which was concealed by the shadow his broad-brimmed Stetson cast in the noonday sun.

One of the four men walking behind Tucker was obviously the prisoner. He was shirtless, and wore handcuffs that caught the

sun and reflected silver. Longarm paid less attention to him than
he did to the other three. Each of the two men flanking the prisoner held one of the handcuffed man's arms. The one bringing up
the rear carried the whip, a broad leather thong, over his shoulder. All three of the men, who could only be sheriff's deputies,
had the cocky walk of hard cases. Longarm knew the breed; he'd
seen them and tangled with them before.

Old son, he told himself silently, looks like you're going to be
on the short end of the odds, if it comes out them fellows had
anything to do with the army men and the Ranger who dropped
out of sight.

By now the sheriff and his men were pushing through the suddenly thickened crowd in the center of the plaza. They wasted little
time in ceremony when they reached the cleared area around the
well and post. The two who'd escorted the prisoner lashed the
man's hands high on the post and stepped aside. The sheriff stepped
forward.

"Jed Morton," he proclaimed loudly, "you been tried and convicted of attemptin' manslaughter. You been sentenced with mercy,
because the man you tried to kill didn't die. Instead of hangin' you
up by your neck till you're dead, the court's been good to you. All
you're goin' to git is fifty lashes." He nodded to the man holding
the whip. "All right, Spud. Go ahead and lay it onto him."

Stepping aside, the sheriff made room for the man carrying
the whip to move into position beside the prisoner. He whirled the
lash experimentally, the wide leather thong whistling through the
still air, then brought it down on the prisoner's back with a loud,
flat thwack. The man flinched, but did not cry out.

Though he'd never heard of Jed Morton and didn't know
whether the man was innocent or guilty, Longarm twitched in sympathy as the whip fell. He'd heard of fifty-lash whippings in the old
days, and knew they usually meant death to the one receiving them.
He made no move to protest. He knew any interference he offered
might get in the way of carrying out his assignment. He'd reminded
himself sternly during the few seconds before the whip wielder began the punishment that this was no business of his.

Again the whip whistled and landed, but as before, Morton
did not cry out. The third blow brought a sigh from deep in his
throat, though, and the fourth lash, landing on the weals raised
by the earlier blows, produced a louder sigh, a moan of pain. Spud,
the whipper, continued the punishment. Longarm, his stomach

muscles tightening, lost count of the blows after the sixth or seventh had fallen. Morton was moaning steadily now, a throaty monotone that rose only slightly in volume as each new slash cut into his tattered back. His skin had split after the first few lashes, and blood spattered each time the whip swung. The spectators nearest the whipping post pushed back to avoid the flying drops.

There was an unearthly air hanging over the plaza. The crowd was deathly silent. The only sounds heard were the whip's whistling, the wet, flat noise as it splatted home, and the fading moans of the man tied to the stake.

Longarm's gorge was rising. He felt that he'd stood all he could. Morton was almost unconscious now, hanging limply by his bound wrists. Still the wet, ugly splat of new blows sounded with monotonous regularity. In spite of his resolution not to interfere, Longarm had had a bellyful of the spectacle. He elbowed through the packed crowd until he stood in the front rank of spectators. Spud was raising the whip for another cut at Morton's bloodstained back when, without seeming to aim, Longarm fired. The heavy rifle slug ripped into the ground between Spud's feet. Spud leaped back, letting the whip drop from his hand.

"That's enough," Longarm announced. His voice was flat; he did not need to raise it to be heard in the stillness that hung like a shroud over the plaza. "The show's over."

He shifted the rifle, bringing its muzzle high enough to cover Sheriff Tucker and the two deputies beside him. All three men had started forward when the shot rang out. Now, as the Winchester's muzzle stared into their faces with its single menacing, unblinking black eye, they took a step backward.

"Who in hell you think you are?" Tucker called.

"I'm the man who stopped this sorry damned circus," Longarm replied levelly. He raised his voice only a little. "That's all you need to know right now."

"You got no right!" Tucker's throat and jaws worked with repressed fury. "You're interferin' with the law's due process! I can put you in jail for this!"

Still in the same low, level tone, Longarm invited, "Come ahead." He shifted the rifle to swing it in a short arc that menaced the sheriff and his two deputies in turn. "If you're ready to pay what it'll cost you."

None of them moved. Tucker repeated his question: "Just who are you, anyhow?"

"I told you once, that's enough." Longarm still kept his voice at a conversational pitch. He might have been discussing the weather, or the price of steers. Addressing the deputies, he said, "You two. Get that man down off the post."

There was a steeliness in Longarm's tone now that the men recognized as the voice of authority. They neither argued nor made any threatening gestures as they moved to obey. Rather, they very carefully kept their hands in front of them, at chest level, while they walked to the stake and untied Morton. When they'd freed him and were supporting his unconscious form, they looked questioningly at Longarm, waiting further orders.

From the moment the Winchester's blast had shattered the silence of the plaza, the crowd had been frozen and motionless. Now people began to stir, those closest to the whipping post pushing back to widen the circle in which Longarm held the sheriff and his men. The spectators remained silent, though, and now the eerie quiet was making itself felt, stretching the nerves of the little group in the plaza's center.

Longarm felt the tension building and moved to take charge before it broke. He ordered, "Take that poor devil someplace where his back can be tended to."

For the first time, the deputies looked to Tucker for instructions. He said, "I guess the jail's as good a place as any. Haul him over there, boys. Tell Wahonta I said to take care of him."

When the deputies turned to Longarm for confirmation of the sheriff's instructions, he nodded. "Do what he told you to. We're going to be right in back of you, me and the sheriff, to make sure nothing happens to him on the way there."

Spud, the man who'd handled the whip, asked sullenly, "What about me?"

"You come along with us," Longarm replied. "And bring that whip with you." He turned to Tucker. "All right. Let's march. You lead out."

Silently, the crowd parted to make an aisle for the group. The deputies carrying the unconscious Morton led the way, with Spud behind them. Behind the three deputies came the sheriff. Longarm walked just far enough to the rear to keep the muzzle of his Winchester out of Tucker's reach. He didn't want gunplay on the crowded plaza. The deputies in the lead headed for the saloon, and for a moment Longarm wondered if the jail and sheriff's office were part of that building, but they veered around one side of it and went to a smaller structure the saloon building had hidden from view. It was built of the sturdiest timbers Longarm had seen in Los Perros.

As an afterthought, when they started around the saloon, Longarm called to Spud. "You. That gray over at the hitch rail's my horse. Get him and lead him along with us. The rest of you hold up right here till he brings the critter up."

As in most of the towns he'd seen wherever his cases took him, Longarm found that the Los Perros jail also included an outer office for the sheriff and a lean-to or ell for his living quarters. As they entered, Sheriff Tucker let out a bellow.

"Wahonta! Git out here with some hot water and rags! There's a hurt man I want you to tend to!"

Judging by her name and appearance, Longarm placed the girl who responded to the summons as an Apache. She looked surprisingly young, though as was always the case with women of the Southwestern Indian tribes, her age was hard to judge. She had the Apache stockiness of build, short legs, wide hips and shoulders, and the square tribal face that would broaden and flesh out as she grew older. Yet she had about her the bloom of extreme youth as well as the quick, springy step of the very young. Longarm guessed what her relationship with the sheriff was, and made a mental note to confirm his hunch when he had time. Right now there were more important things to do.

He said to the men carrying the prisoner, who was beginning to twitch and moan, but still wasn't fully conscious, "One of you at a time, take off your gunbelts and hang 'em on those pegs on the wall." In sullen silence, the deputies obeyed. Spud wore no gunbelt. "Now all three of you take that fellow back in the jail and put him on a bunk." Tucker, after a moment of indecision, started to follow his men. Longarm said, "Not you, Sheriff. You stand right where you are." To Wahonta he said, "You go in, too. Fix up that man's back as good as you can." The Apache girl looked questioningly at the sheriff, who nodded. Then she followed the men into the first cell.

Longarm swung the Winchester's muzzle in Tucker's general direction. "Lock 'em up."

"Now, wait a minute—" Tucker began.

Longarm cut him short. "Lock 'em up, I said!"

Tucker glared, but took a key ring from the wall peg on which it hung and locked the cell door. It was crowded in the cell, even with Morton stretched out facedown on the cot that was the cubicle's sole piece of furniture. Longarm held out a hand for the key ring. The sheriff handed it over.

"Now, then," Longarm told the thin-lipped Tucker, "let's you and me go in there"—he indicated the door by which Wahonta had entered—"and have us a little private confab."

Chapter 5

Sheriff Tucker pushed his hat back on his head as he and Long-arm went into the ell attached to the jail building, and Longarm got his first really close look at the man's face. It wasn't one to inspire confidence. Tucker's eyes were narrow slits set in puffs of fat. His lips were a wide, crooked slash that turned down at the corners above a once-firm chin that was now half-buried in a set of double chins bulging below it. He wore a Burnside beard—a heavy mustache that crept around his cheeks and clean-shaven jaw to merge with full, flowing muttonchop whiskers. His nose veered back and forth between brow and tip, evidence that the sheriff had at one time been a man prone to indulge in fistfighting. Longarm revised Lieutenant Bryant's estimate of Tucker's age. He'd bet the man would never see fifty again, and might well be past fifty-five.

Tucker asked again, "Who in hell are you, to come bustin' into town like you did and get in the way of the law bein' enforced?"

"I might just argue with you about that whipping being according to law," Longarm replied. "Fellow I was talking to before it got started said you're sheriff and judge both, here in Los Perros."

"Well? What if I am? Somebody's got to keep the damn town in line."

"Makes me wonder just whose laws you're talking about, though. Your own, or the state's, or the U.S.'s."

"We don't worry about little things like that around here. We do what we got to, to keep things quiet."

"What kinda things?"

"Damn it, man, you know what I'm talkin' about. Lawlessness in general."

Choosing his words carefully, Longarm said, "The way I look on it, laws made up to suit special cases is worse'n no law at all."

"An expert on the law, are you?" Tucker challenged.

"Nope. Never claimed to be that. Let's just say I got my own ideas. And when push comes to shove, I figure my ideas are as good as the next man's."

"You still ain't told me who you are."

"Name's Custis—"

Before Longarm could finish, the sheriff spoke quickly. "Custis? Now, that's a real fine old Virginia name. Fought on the side of right during the war, I suppose?"

"I suppose." Longarm didn't need to ask which side Tucker meant. The sheriff's Southern accent told him that.

"Who'd you fight under?"

"Depends on when. I rode with more'n one, while I was serving."

"Did you now? You want to name me names?"

"I disremember things like names, sometimes. Especially when I figure somebody's getting too nosy."

"Look here, Custis, it ain't nothing to be ashamed about, being on the side that lost. Hell, I'm real proud to say I rode with Quantrill, back then."

Tucker's naming of the notorious guerrilla fighter, far more outlaw than soldier, told Longarm perhaps more than the sheriff had intended. It also changed his mind about revealing that he was a deputy U.S. marshal, at least for the time being. Letting Tucker think he was a bullying opportunist with more brass than brains might serve his purpose better. Instead of commenting on the sheriff's revelation of his past history, Longarm merely nodded.

"Now, you might wonder why I told you about myself," Tucker went on. "Fact is, I got a good thing goin' here, have had for a pretty fair spell, and I don't aim to let some owlhoot drifter mess things up for me. Which is what you come close to doin' when you busted up that whippin'."

"Maybe my stomach ain't as strong as it used to be," Longarm offered mildly.

"I don't know about your stomach, but I got to say I like your nerve. Ain't many men'd have enough sand in their craw to call a play the way you did."

"That wasn't much, Sheriff. I didn't look for sensible men to argue with a cocked and loaded Winchester, no matter how fast they might be with a Colt."

"You feel like tellin' me why you showed up in Los Perros?" When Longarm said nothing, but just continued to look at the sheriff with his steel-blue eyes, Tucker asked, "You're on the dodge, ain't you? Law's after you someplace up the line—San Antone, maybe, or El Paso. Fort Worth? Galveston?"

"Now, seeing as you're the law here, or say you are, you don't expect me to answer a fool question like that, do you?" Longarm was curious to find out how far he could prod the sheriff before he'd balk.

"Not unless you got less brains than I give you credit for." Tucker paused, studying Longarm closely. "If it'll make you feel any better, I ain't interested enough to find out. But it's got to be that, or you're lookin' for somebody that's got your dander up, on the prod to gun him down."

"Let's leave it stand that I'm just traveling."

"If that's how you want it." The sheriff frowned thoughtfully. "It could be something else, a-course. You might be carrying a badge. Or you might've been with a bunch that got busted up, and lookin' to make a new connection."

"Like I said, Sheriff, let's say I'm just traveling."

"You'll be plannin' to move on, then." Tucker wasn't asking a question. Longarm understood that, and got the warning message that the statement implied.

"Sooner or later," he said.

"I guess you know you only got two choices."

"Which are what?"

"Move on, or throw in with my boys and me."

"You saying you'd pin a deputy's badge on me, after what I done out there a while ago?"

"Shucks, Custis, I'm a big enough man to overlook that. I was about to tell Spud to hold up, anyhow. It wasn't in my mind to let him kill Morton. Except he had to be give a good lesson to."

"Fellow I was talking to, the one told me about Morton's

trouble, he didn't say it wasn't a fair fight that got your deputy hurt."

"That don't signify." Tucker's voice hardened. "Thing is, my man got cut so bad I had t' send him clear down to Laredo for him t' be doctored. Most people in Los Perros, they know they can't hurt one of my boys without they pay for it. Them as don't got t' be reminded. That goes for you, too, Custis."

"Join up or move on? Is that the way of it?"

"Clear as I can say it. You do one, I take good care of you, money and all the rest. You do anything else, then you better keep on travelin'. For your own good."

"Suppose I tell you I'd like to sorta nose around a little bit and see what Los Perros is like before I make up my mind?"

Tucker thought about this for a moment, then nodded slowly. "All right, that's fair enough. You stay around a few days, see what you see. Only don't go pullin' no more stunts like the one I'm lettin' you git away with."

"Now, I didn't come here to get crossways with you, Sheriff. Or with anybody else, far's that goes. I got mighty tender toes, though. I'd imagine you're smart enough to tell them deputies of yours not to step on 'em."

"Don't worry about that. They're my boys, they do what I tell 'em to. Nothing else." Tucker frowned, then added, "Except maybe for Spud. He's been actin' a little bit uppity, now and again. Not enough so I got to whip him into line, but he'd be the only one that might give you a bad time."

"That's my problem, though, ain't it?"

"I'd say so. Don't look for me to take sides, though, Custis. Even if he is my boy, when I tell him to leave you be and he don't, that's his lookout."

Longarm marked down the possible ill feeling between Tucker and Spud as a hole card that might fill a thin hand for him if it was needed. He said, "Looks like we understand how it stands between us, Sheriff. Now let's go see what's happening to that poor devil your man Spud just about beat to death. And I guess all of 'em oughta be glad to get let out of that cell. They'll be getting a mite restless by now."

Longarm's guess was a good one. The Apache girl, Wahonta, was still tending to Jed Morton's back; Morton lay facedown on the cot, groaning now and then. The three deputies were crowding up to the bars, impatient to be released.

"Took you two long enough to settle whatever it was you went to talk private about," Spud grumbled as the sheriff unlocked the cell door.

"Cool off, Spud," Tucker advised. "You wasn't hurt a bit, no more'n Ralston or Lefty." The others grunted, but said nothing. Tucker led them to the office area, where he sat down behind the battered desk and motioned for the others to find seats, too. "Now," he said, "this gentleman here's Mr. Custis. He's made a right hand-some apology to us for gittin' hisself crossways of our law, and him and me have settled any differences there might've been."

"Now just a minute—" Spud began.

Tucker cut him short. "You shut up, Spud. If you hadn't been so damn heavy-handed with that whip, this dustup never would've happened."

Spud glowered, but kept quiet.

"Mr. Custis figures to stay in Los Perros for a little while," the sheriff continued. He shifted his eyes from Longarm to Spud as he spoke. "He ain't lookin' for trouble with nobody, and I told him we wasn't goin' to hold no grudges for him buttin' in on us. You all understand what I'm tellin' you?"

All three of the deputies had their gazes fixed on Longarm. He kept his face impassive, meeting their stares without flicking an eyelid.

Tucker concluded, "Now. That's all I got t' say."

When it was clear that none of the deputies was inclined to argue with their boss, Longarm spoke up. "I aim to get along with everybody. Now, if you gentlemen feel like you want to join the sheriff and me, I'm standing the drinks."

It didn't appear that the general population of Los Perros could afford saloon prices, Longarm thought. Except for Tucker, the deputies, and himself, the cavernous, shabby place was echoingly empty. The scarred floor gave indications that booted feet did walk on it in numbers at times, however, and the array of bottled goods available, as shown by the display in front of the mirror behind the bar, seemed adequate. From inside the building, the exterior outlines of the structure made sense. The bar area covered about two-thirds of the available space. A small enclosed area—offices, maybe storerooms, Longarm thought—filled the rear portion. Above this was a balcony, and though the stairs to it ended in a blind turn, Longarm was sure there were rooms opening onto a corridor over the offices or storage area. He absorbed the layout in one quick, sweeping glance as the group crossed to the bar. An aproned barkeeper appeared from nowhere. Longarm tossed a gold eagle on the scarred pine that in Los Perros substituted for the mahogany or walnut of more civilized places.

"Name your pleasure, gentlemen," he said.

For himself, Longarm ordered his standard Maryland rye, and realized as he sipped it with relish that this was his first drink since he'd gotten off the train in San Antonio just a week ago. He felt for a cheroot to go with the drink, and remembered that the sutler at Fort Lancaster hadn't been able to replenish his dwindling supply. There were only three left in his pocket. It seemed to him the occasion called for celebrating, so he fished out one of them and lighted it. The heavy smoke and sharp tang of the whiskey did a lot to make him feel more at home in the alien surroundings.

Ralston, the deputy standing at Longarm's right, asked, "You going to be around Los Perros for a while, Custis?"

"Awhile. And I aim to stay out of trouble while I'm here."

"Hell, I don't blame you much for butting in today. I was just about sick, listening to that poor son of a bitch groan, and them whacks Spud was dealing with the whip."

"It didn't seem to bother Spud any," Longarm commented, carefully keeping his voice neutral.

"Nothin' like that bothers Spud." Ralston looked down the bar. He was standing on Longarm's right. Lefty, the other deputy, stood on his left, and beyond Lefty was Tucker. Spud, the last man in the line, was engaged in a whispered conversation with the sheriff. Dropping his voice, Ralston said to Longarm, "I'd look behind me when I was out at night, if I was you, Custis. Spud took that deal today right personal. He was saying some pretty ugly things he'd like to do to you while we was all locked up together."

"Thanks, Ralston. I'll remember that. Maybe I can return the favor someday."

"Ah, forget it. I didn't say nothing, anyhow."

Raising his voice, Longarm called, "There's another round or two of drinks to come out of that eagle on the bar. Sing out for refills."

He thought about Marshal Billy Vail, back in Denver, and could imagine his chief's face changing color if he was to see government expense money being spent on whiskey for a bunch

of toughs in Los Perros. His thoughts were interrupted by Sheriff
Tucker calling his name.

"Custis! Come on back to the office with me. I just saw Miles
Baskin stick his head outa his door. He's a man you'll want to
know, if you're goin' to be in town awhile."

Baskin turned out to be a somewhat colorless individual.
His lean face was adorned with the walrus mustache that was
the trademark of a saloonkeeper, but this was the only outstand-
ing feature of an otherwise nondescript face. His eyes were colorless, his nose unremarkably straight, and what his lips looked like
was a secret guarded by the overhanging mustache. As he hadn't
been involved in the dispute that had flared in the plaza, Baskin
greeted Longarm pleasantly enough.

"I don't know what brings you to Los Perros, Custis, but any
new customer's welcome in my place," he said. "Hope you'll
drop in often."

"I was hoping I might do better'n drop in. I see you got some
rooms upstairs, and I'm going to need a place to sleep. You happen
to have one vacant, or are they all full up?"

"I don't keep whores in them, if that's what you're getting at,"
Baskin said. "You can have your choice for two bits a night. We
don't get many travelers stopping off here."

"Fine. I'll pick one out later on. I don't guess there's a livery
stable in town, is there? I got a horse that's going to have to be
stabled and fed."

"No," the saloonkeeper said. Then, as an afterthought, "Ed,
seeing Custis is a friend of yours, why don't you let him put his
animal in the corral with your spare ones?"

"Well, I—" Tucker stopped, smiled, and went on, "I guess it'd
be all right. One more nag won't work old Joselito to death."

"Looks like I'm all fixed up then," Longarm said. "That calls
for a drink, if you gents feel like stepping out to the bar."

"No need for that," Baskin told him. He opened a wall cabinet
and took out a bottle. "I keep enough back here to take care of my
friends when they drop in. What's your pleasure, Custis?"

"Maryland rye, if you got it handy."

"Just happens I do." The saloonkeeper reached in and brought
out a second bottle. He put the bottles and glasses on the table
that he used for a desk. "Drink up, gentlemen."

After his first sip, Longarm decided that the quality of
Baskin's private stock was a lot better than that of the liquor sold

over his bar. He remarked, more to fill the silence than for any other reason, "Looks like business is slack for you today."

"It's quiet," Baskin agreed. "Things will liven up tomorrow, though. Ed'll tell you that."

"Oh? What's the occasion?"

"Why, it's the big Mexican holiday," Tucker said. "*Dieciséis de Septiembre*, their Independence Day. They'll be swiggin' mescal and pulque and dancin' in the plaza out there till all hours. But my boys'll be on hand to keep things from gittin' too wild."

"Now, wait a minute, Ed," Baskin interjected. "Did you for-get—"

Tucker said quickly, "No, damn it, Miles, I ain't forgot. We can talk about that later on."

"If you gents need to talk private business, I'll excuse myself," Longarm offered.

"It's nothin' important," the sheriff assured him. "Just a little somethin' I told Miles I'd give him a hand with." He turned back to the saloonkeeper. "And I'll take care of it, don't worry."

"You go on and settle your business," Longarm told them. "I'll step on back to the bar and finish my drink with your deputies, Sheriff."

Spud, Lefty, and Ralston were standing where he'd left them, and Longarm noticed that the ten-dollar gold piece he'd put on the bar had disappeared. The thought passed through his mind that with bar whiskey a dime a shot, the three must've done some real two-fisted drinking during the few minutes he'd been with Tucker and Baskin, but he didn't say anything. It was worth a lot more than ten dollars to him to wash away the anger the plaza incident had sparked.

He said, "Well, it looks like I'm all fixed up. Room upstairs, a place for my horse in the sheriff's corral. Now, if one of you gentle-men'll just be kind enough to show me where the corral is, I'd bet-ter unsaddle him and get settled in."

Ralston, the friendliest of the three, volunteered, "Come on, Custis. It's just a step or two. I'll show you the layout."

"I'd appreciate it."

Longarm followed Ralston out of the saloon and around the building to the sheriff's office. Tordo stood at the hitching rail. Just outside the office door, the Apache girl was wiping out the basin in which she'd brought the water to minister to Jed Morton's back. She paid no attention to the two men.

As he slipped the dapple's reins free of the rail, Longarm asked the girl, "How's the man you were tending to?"

"Him all right." Her eyes, turned to Longarm as she spoke, were jet black and opaque. "Him be sore four, five days. Not hurt bad."

"Thanks for fixing him up, Wa—Wawayna, is it?"

"Wahonta." When she corrected him, Longarm thought the girl almost smiled. She added, "You welcome," and turned to go back into the office.

Ralston warned, "Don't get no ideas about the 'Pache gal. She's private property."

"Yours?"

"No. Times when I get horny, I sorta wish she was. Well, hell, you'll find out soon enough. She's Ed's girl. So be smart and keep outa her way." They started around the building to the corral. Ralston added, "Keep outa Spud's way, too. He holds on to a mad a long time."

"But you and Lefty don't?" Longarm was loosening Tordo's saddle girth. He didn't look up from his job.

"I can't say about Lefty, but I already said I don't hold you no bad feelings because of today."

Longarm set his saddle where some others rested on the top rail of the corral, tossed his bedroll over one shoulder, his saddlebag over the other. He chalked up his purchase of drinks for the deputies as a wise investment, one that was already paying dividends. The return he was getting from Ralston alone was making it worthwhile. He said, "You mentioned it. Don't worry about Spud. I'll be careful not to let him get behind me. Especially in the dark."

"You've got his style tagged, all right. You take the way he's trying to cut—" Suddenly, the deputy seemed to realize he was letting his mouth run away with his good sense. He stopped short.

Longarm was curious to know what he'd started to say, but decided it'd be better to wait instead of prodding. He could get the man talking again, later on. There was also a growing void in his stomach that was yelling to be filled up. He remembered that he'd had only those three buns at noon, and lunch had slipped his mind in the general ruckus.

"I'll pick up my rifle from inside, and go see about that room," he told Ralston.

"I'll walk on back with you, I guess. Nothing else to do right this minute."

Side by side they walked back to the saloon. Lefty and Spud

no longer stood at the bar; except for the aproned barkeeper the place was empty. Longarm said, "Hate to leave you by yourself, Ralston. You been real helpful. I'll remember it. Right now I'm going to see if this place has got such a thing as a bathtub. I need to soak the trail dust off my hide. When I'm dirty, I feel about as mean as your friend Spud acts. See you around town, tonight or maybe tomorrow."

As he went up the stairs, Longarm could feel Ralston's questioning gaze on his back.

Chapter 6

There was still daylight in the western sky when Longarm glanced out the window of the room he'd selected. He felt a lot better now, more like going downstairs in search of food. For a dime, he'd been provided with a big wooden tub of hot water in which he'd soaked and soaped away the travel grime. He'd felt so good that he'd tipped the mozo who'd brought the tub another dime.

Fresh underwear and socks and a clean shirt added to his well-being. The porter who'd attended to the tub had assured Longarm that his wife was *"una lavandera maravillosa,"* who'd be glad to wash the dirty garments Longarm had removed and return them the next day. After the mozo left, Longarm wasted no time getting ready to seek his supper. He dressed quickly, though not so fast that he neglected his invariable routine of checking his Colt and derringer. He'd had the foresight to bring a bottle of Maryland rye up from the bar; he had enjoyed a few sips while he was soaking, and another as he dried himself, and the whiskey had whetted his growing appetite.

As always, hunger took second place to safety. Longarm paused long enough after locking the door to his room to break a match and wedge half the stick between door and jamb. He didn't want to risk being surprised on his return by Spud or one of the surly deputy's friends.

One look at the free-lunch counter that stood at the end of the saloon's bar only confirmed what his quick glance earlier had hinted. The slices of darkening curled-up bologna, discolored rat cheese, brine scummed pickles, and hard-boiled eggs with chipped shells were enough to stop a man's appetite dead in its tracks. Baskin's free lunch offering not only didn't compare with those of the Windsor Hotel bar or the Black Cat Saloon, but were less appetizing than most of those he'd seen when cases had taken him into the cheap, shoddy bars in Denver's Lowers.

Recalling the food stalls that had been setting up for business at the time he'd first entered the Los Perros plaza, he stepped through the batwings onto the narrow veranda that ran the width of the saloon's front and looked around the almost deserted open area to see if any of the native vendors were still in operation at their stalls.

Old son, he told himself, maybe you're in luck. Looks like you don't have to depend on that slop inside to fill your belly. That grub out there might not be much better, but it'll at least be hot.

Though the plaza wasn't nearly as crowded as it had been when Los Perros's residents were gathering in anticipation of the whipping, there were still a few people around. Taco and tamale vendors stood beside the small charcoal fires that kept their iron pots hot. In addition, a half-dozen stalls—bare planks supported on trestles to make rough counters—dotted the margin of the plaza. People stood at most of them, eating. Longarm stepped to the ground and strolled idly around, going from counter to counter, trying to find the one at which the food looked most appetizing. As he walked, the tang of stewing hot red peppers mingled with the fainter smells of beef and garlic to set his juices running.

All the stalls seemed to be family affairs, operated by women. All of them offered about the same menu: chili con carne, tamales, frijoles, enchiladas, and steaming tortillas, served in thick ironstone plates that held the heat in the food. While the patrons stood at the counters, the women cooked and served them. The distribution of labor, he noted, was very consistent. The younger girls filled the plates from pots that rested on improvised stoves bent from metal sheets; the older girls served the food; the mothers cooked the tortillas; the grandmothers made them, starting with small balls of moistened cornmeal, slapping the balled meal into thin round sheets, rotating the meal cakes between wrinkled palms until they were paper-thin and ready to be cooked, greaseless, on the top of the metal stove. The very youngest children worked at one side of the serving area, grinding raw dried corn kernels on stone *metates* into a meal almost as fine as flour.

Approaching darkness was bringing out lanterns on the counters of the stalls before Longarm finished his leisurely inspection tour. He hadn't found anything different at any of the stalls; all he'd succeeded in doing was making himself hungrier by watching others eat. He stopped at a counter where a girl was trying to get a lantern lighted. Darkness had brought a breeze, and every match she struck fizzled out before she could touch it to the wick. Longarm took one of his waterproofed matches from his pocket and thumbnailed it into flame. Cupping the match expertly in his hands, he touched the wick with it. The kerosene-soaked fabric ignited, and he guided the girl's hand in lowering the glass chimney quickly, before the wind whipped the flame out.

"*Ay!*" the girl breathed. "*Muy bueno! Gracias, señor, por su ayudo.*"

Longarm scraped up enough of his scanty Spanish to reply, "*De nada, señorita.*"

"*Pues, habla Español?*" the girl asked, bringing her eyes up to meet his. "*Ve que esta extranjero.*"

"*No hablo mucho,*" Longarm replied. "*Conoce Inglés?*"

"A little bit, I speak," she said. "You are stranger, no?"

"I'm a stranger, yes, and hungry."

"*Porqué no come? Mira—*" she indicated the pots on the stove behind the counter, shook her head, and said, "Excuse, *señor,* I forget. Look, we got good *chili colorado, chili verde,* we got tamales and frijoles, and *mi abuela,* her *tortillas* they very fine. So, what you wan' to eat?"

"Everything you just said sounded pretty good. Maybe you can fix me up a plate with a little bit of everything on it?"

"*Un poco de todas? Sí.* I fix you."

She moved back to the stove, almost dancing, Longarm thought, her steps were so light and graceful. Moving with unconscious poise, she ladled food from the pots crowded together, peeled the cornmeal husks from four tamales, and put them on top of the beans and chili con carne swimming on the plate. Finally, she grabbed a stack of smoking tortillas from the cloth-covered platter where they were being laid by the woman cooking them—

obviously, Longarm thought, her mother. She laid the tortillas on the other food and danced back to where he waited.

"You eat now," she commanded with a smile that showed flashing white teeth between firm crimson lips. "Is no good when it get cold."

Longarm looked for utensils. There was no fork, no spoon, no knife. He asked, "How'm I going to eat without tools?"

"Tools?" She frowned, then her eyes widened. *"Ah, sí, cuchara, tenedor. Pues, señor, no tenemos."* Seeing that he didn't understand her, she added, "Here, I show you."

Picking up a tortilla, the girl pulled a strip off one side and folded it between her fingers and thumb to form a scoop. She pushed the edge of the tortilla into the food, lifting meat and beans in it, and held it to his mouth. Longarm was too surprised to do anything but make a single bite of the tortilla strip and the chili and beans it contained.

"You see?" the girl giggled. "Is easy, no?" She handed him the remainder of the tortilla. "You do, now."

Longarm's fingers were as dexterous as any man's, but he had trouble forming the strip he tore off into a scoop of the proper shape. He made a try or two, but the tortilla always opened out and let the food drop back on the plate before he could lift it.

"No, no," she said. "Do like so. Here."

She took his hand in both of hers and bent his fingers into the proper curves to support the thin tortilla while he scooped up a portion of chili and beans and got them in his mouth. Her hands on his were warm and light, and reminded him somehow of a butterfly he'd caught many years ago, when he was a boy in West Virginia. All at once he was aware that the girl was less a girl than a pretty young woman. He became purposely clumsy, so that she had to keep helping him.

"What's your name?" he asked. After being helped to several bites, he'd picked up a tamale and was eating it.

"Lita."

"Let's see, that'd be short for—Adelita, maybe?"

She smiled. "No, *señor*. Guess some more."

"Carmelita?"

"No, no! Ay, nunca advenirse. Mi nombre completa es Estrellita."

"Now, that's a right pretty name, I'd say."

"Y usted? Que se llama?"

Longarm remembered how the sheriff had shortened his name in time to reply, "Custis."

"Cos-tees?" she tried, frowning.

"No. Custis." He stressed the "u," which she'd turned into an "o".

"Ah, sí! Coos-tees. Is nice."

Lita's mother had been keeping an eye on the pair. From her place at the stove, she called, "Lita! *Paradese hablando con el gringo!"*

"Callate, mama!" the girl replied. *"No daname hablar un poco con un extranjero!"*

"Cuidado, chica!" the woman said. *"Los gringos quieren solamente una cosa de mujeres!"*

"No hay que tal!" the girl shot back. *"Dejame in paz!"*

Longarm's rusty and slight knowledge of Spanish kept him from understanding the exchange, but he caught the woman's warning. He thought, all women are alike wherever a man goes. They see a fellow making up to their daughter, they're damn sure all he wants is to get in her drawers.

Lita didn't seem bothered by the scolding, which stopped as soon as her mother saw she was wasting breath. She went back to cooking tortillas, casting an occasional suspicious look over her shoulder while Lita continued to help Longarm eat his dinner.

He wasn't sure which he enjoyed most, the food or the girl's help in eating. He found Lita a delight to watch. She was at that point when a girl has just become a woman, with a woman's awareness of a man. Lita was small, but fully rounded in all the right places. Her full gathered skirt didn't hide a saucy pair of buttocks when she danced from counter to stove, and her blouse was cut low; its rounded neckline gave Longarm a view of the valley between full breasts each time she leaned toward him across the counter. Her cheeks were high in a face that was neither oval nor triangular, but a blending of the best of both. Dark eyes, full lustrous brows, and dark red pouting lips under a straight flared nose completed his picture of her.

"You like?" she asked, when his plate had been cleaned of the last peppery trace of chili sauce.

"Yep. It was real good. *Muy bueno.*"

"You wan' some more? Is plenty on stove."

"No, thanks, Lita. I'm as full as any man's got a right to be."

"Maybe you come back, some time?"

"You just bet I will. Now how much do I owe you?"

"*Ah, quince centavos,* Coos-tees. Like you say, feefteen cents."

"It's worth double that." He dug into his pocket and passed her a half-dollar. "Here. You keep whatever's extra, for helping me."

"*Gracias,* Coos-tees. I think you a nice man."

"And you're a right pretty girl. I'll be back to eat with you again, real soon. Maybe tomorrow."

"I think I will like that. *Vaya con Dios,* Coos-tees."

There being no place else to go in Los Perros, Longarm went back to the saloon. The place had lost the deserted look it had had in the afternoon. Poker games were in progress at two of the four felt-covered tables, and there was a respectable lineup along the bar as well as a scattering of men sitting at the round tables that dotted the floor. Most of the men had on the clothes that marked them as ranch hands: faded Levi's, boots, wide-brimmed felt hats. He found a place at the bar at the edge of a knot of men and ordered his usual rye. He sipped it slowly while listening to the backwash of gossip from the group beside him.

To Longarm's disappointment, gossip was all he heard. Much of the chatter consisted of complaints: bedbugs in the bunkhouse, hard beans in the cookshack. He listened until he'd finished his drink, then ordered a refill and wandered over to watch the poker games. So far, he'd heard nothing useful. Rustling had been mentioned once or twice, but casually, not in terms of a major new outbreak. Nothing had been said about either the army or the Texas Rangers.

That wasn't too unusual. Longarm had worked before at picking up cold trails. He'd learned that as time went by, incidents that were prime conversational fodder when they happened were forgotten. Captain Hill had been missing since June, Nate Webster since July. If their vanishing had been discussed then, it had been forgotten by September. Questioning would refresh memories, but Longarm wasn't quite ready yet to start asking questions.

Standing between the two poker tables that were busy, Longarm watched silently. Spud was in the game at one of the tables, and although he'd seen Longarm, he'd ignored him. The game at the other table was uninteresting, a friendly affair with two-bit antes, bets of fifty to seventy-five cents, and raises about as big as the bets. The game at the table where Spud sat was for blood, and small change wasn't being mentioned by any of the players in it.

There was room for six, and all seats were filled. Spud was at the dealer's left, and after he'd begun paying attention to the game, Longarm thought there was something vaguely familiar about the house man. He couldn't associate him with any case he'd handled, or match his face with the descriptions or pictures on any of the wanted circulars he'd looked at lately. He heard the other players call the man George, but that didn't ring a bell, either.

Three of the other men at the table were ranch hands, judging by their clothes. Two were in their thirties, old enough to have cut their teeth on poker in bunkhouse and trail-ride games. The third was a fresh-faced young cowboy who wore the expression of one who'd been sliding deeper and deeper into the hole that waits for gamblers trying to buck a game out of their depth. The remaining two players were Mexicans, dressed in embroidered charro suits; they played with skill, folding when their cards didn't justify a draw, raising moderately but not extravagantly when they stayed in the pot.

There was no friendly banter or "dealer's choice" about the game these seven played. George, who was banker as well as dealer, stuck to five-card draw, the game that demands the greatest skill and judgment from a player. The house man wasn't a fast-shuffle artist, Longarm decided after he'd watched a few hands, nor did he use the standard gaffs such as rubber- or spring-loaded sleeve holdouts, palmed cards, or other devices professionals use to give themselves an unbeatable edge. As far as Longarm's skilled eyes could tell, it was an honest game, for which he gave Miles Baskin good marks. He hadn't expected a straight game in Los Perros.

During the short time Longarm had been looking on, the pile of chips in front of the young cowhand had shrunk steadily, and the young fellow had been getting nervous in inverse ratio to the diminishing of his stake. Now, as the dealer flicked cards around the table, the youth grabbed each one as it hit the felt in front of him, looked at it quickly, and added it to the fan forming in his hand. He'd begun growing tense after he'd picked up the third card; his nerves tightened visibly after he'd seen the fourth, and then he relaxed after looking at the final card.

"Openers?" the dealer asked the table at large.

Shaking his head, Spud put his cards facedown on the table.

The man to his left, one of the charro-suited Mexicans, also passed. The ranch hand who had the next call opened for a modest dollar. "Just to keep the deal from being wasted," he remarked.

Wordlessly, the second Mexican tossed a white chip into the pot. After a moment's hesitation, but before the play passed him by, he added a second white chip.

"Cost you two dollars, Billy-Bob," George announced. "Spud, if you and Gonzales want in, you better be making up your mind."

"Plenty of time," Spud remarked. "I'll see what Billy-Bob does."

Billy-Bob put in his two whites; so did the other ranch hand in his turn. The dealer followed suit; after he'd fed the pot he riffled the depleted deck and looked questioningly at Spud and Gonzales. Both of them tossed their second white chips into the growing pile in the table's center.

"Who wants cards?" George asked.

"It ain't worth it, but I'll take the two I paid to see," Spud said. He got the cards, looked at them, and stacked them on the table in front of him.

"One," Gonzales requested. He threw his discard on the pile Spud had started before sliding the new card into his hand.

"Two for me," said the ranch hand who'd opened. He tossed out his discards, looked at the new ones without comment or change of expression, and squeezed the fanned-out cards into a stack that he cradled protectively in his hands.

Instead of speaking, the Mexican held up two fingers, tossing his discards out and sweeping the new ones into his hand in a single motion. He laid his cards down, his face bland and unruffled.

"I—I'll play what I got," Billy-Bob announced. His voice was a bit higher-pitched than usual and he was clenching his cards tightly between pressed palms.

"Luke?" the dealer asked the last man.

"Since I paid for 'em, you better gimme two." He got the requested cards, looked at them, added them to his hand, and tossed all the cards on the discard heap.

"I'm drawing two," George announced. He did so, discarded and stacked the discards neatly, then looked across the table. "You bought the bet when you raised, Gonzales."

"Five." Gonzales tossed a red chip in the pot.

The ranch hand and the second charro followed suit.

"And five," Billy-Bob said as soon as their chips had clattered to the table. He tossed in two reds from the small stack of chips he'd been clicking nervously.

There weren't enough chips in the young fellow's stake to drag the betting out, Longarm thought.

"Ten to me, then, gents," George said. "And you, too, Spud. If you're staying in, that is."

"Oh, I'm in," Spud replied. He threw in the chips, then leaned back in his chair, smiling to show that he hadn't a worry in the world.

George raised his eyebrows at Gonzales, who added another red chip without speaking. Then the dealer's eyes moved to the next player. "Fiddler?"

"Reckon I'll just cut my losses before I get tempted." The ranch hand slid his hand to George, who added it to the deadwood.

"Aleman?" George asked. The Mexican shrugged and fingered his chips for a moment. Impatiently, George repeated, "Aleman?"

"I find myself forced to raise," Aleman announced. "But only a small amount. Five more dollars, *señores*."

Defiantly, Billy-Bob tossed in the red chip, then added his last blue. "And ten more," he said, making an almost visible effort to keep his voice steady.

Wordlessly, George tapped the tabletop with his five stacked cards and added them to the discards. In equal silence, Spud added a red and a blue chip to the pot. Holding up two fingers, Gonzales dropped a red and two blues in the table's center. Aleman threw in two blues, his face still bland and unreadable.

Longarm hadn't been keeping close track of the betting, but it had registered subconsciously. He estimated that there was something just over a hundred dollars in the pot, three or four months' wages for the young cowhand whose raise had escalated the betting.

"Damn it!" Billy-Bob said. "I wanta raise, but all I got is enough to call!"

On impulse, Longarm flipped a double eagle onto the table in front of Billy-Bob. The youth looked up, startled. He identified Longarm as his unexpected benefactor and said, "Thanks, mister. I'll pay you back outa the pot."

"Win it first," Longarm told him.

Billy-Bob tossed the twenty-dollar gold piece in the pot. "I guess I don't need to buy chips with this." Then he added his last two reds to the growing heap on the table. "And up ten more."

"I got too much in there not to look, now," Spud observed. He fed the pot a pair of blues. "But all I'll do is call."

Gonzales announced regretfully, "That will not be good enough, *señor*." He put in three blue chips. "The game becomes more costly."

"*Sí, amigo*," Aleman agreed. "I also raise. Ten more dollars."

"Hell's bells!" Billy-Bob exploded. "You men are freezing me out!" He looked at the house man. "Unless I can play the pot short."

"Not a chance." George shook his head. "There's a house rule against short-played pots. Baskin says they give him too much trouble."

Billy-Bob looked pleadingly at Longarm.

"Sorry, friend," Longarm said. "I kept you in the game once, but that's as far as I go."

"Come look at my hand," Billy-Bob invited.

Longarm shook his head. "Nope. I didn't mean to, but I seen what one of these other men's holding, after I staked you. If I look at your cards now and put up money for your bet, it'd be just like you was playing with a marked deck."

"He's right," George said approvingly. "But there's sure not any house rule that says the rest of you can't make a side pot, if you want to. High hand out of the three'd take the side pot, Billy-Bob's hand would just count in the main pot."

"I won't get sucked into a three-way pot with them two greasers," Spud announced angrily.

Gonzales straightened up at the insulting word, but subsided when Aleman hissed a remark in a voice too low for Longarm to hear.

Gonzales said, "If the *caballero*"—he made the word sound like the sort of insult Spud had hurled at him as he indicated the deputy—"if the *caballero* objects, then the *joven* must find the chips with which to call or raise."

"Damn it, I got too much in that pot to be raised outa it," Billy-Bob protested. He appealed to the man on his left. "Luke, will you stake me? You know I'm good for it, if I happen to lose."

Luke sighed. "I guess it's only money. All right, Billy-Bob. I'll stake you if you promise you won't do nothing but call from here on in. You make any raises, I pull out."

Billy-Bob started to object, but caught Longarm's headshake

out of the corner of his eye and settled back into his chair. "We got a deal, Luke. All right. I'll just call any raise that's made."

Somehow, the dispute had shattered the game's mood. Spud glared angrily at the two charros and they glared back. He looked with equal anger at Billy-Bob, who raised his chin defiantly.

George tried to make peace. "Billy-Bob's called your raise, Aleman. Luke, you owe the pot two blues for Billy-Bob. Spud, you're short two blues, and Gonzales is shy one, if you're going to let the call stand."

"I'm damn sure goin' to see what everybody's been bettin'," Spud said. He tossed the chips in.

"That will satisfy me, also," Gonzales said.

Aleman shrugged. "I would not want to be the only one who disagrees." He added a blue chip.

"Show 'em down, then, gents," George ordered.

Gonzales said, "These I would like better if they were in sequence, but with an ace at the top, I think they will get respect." He spread out a heart flush.

"They ain't good," Spud told him. "Not against my four tens."

"*Qué lastima!*" Aleman murmured. "I have put too much trust in three treys and two queens."

As Billy-Bob watched the hands being displayed, the grin on his face grew bigger and bigger. Trying to match the calm of the other players and not quite succeeding, he laid his cards down one by one, all spades, in sequence from the five to the nine.

"I guess I got all of you topped," he said, exhaling gustily.

Spud exploded. He kicked his chair aside and swiveled to face Longarm. "Damn you, Custis! You begun this! If you hadn't staked that little cowpoke, he'd've been froze out and I could've run that pot up to a good one!"

"Cool down, Spud!" George commanded. "The gent didn't do anything that was out of line."

Longarm said nothing, but faced Spud with an expressionless face.

"That's twice today you butted into my business," Spud went on. "And that's just about two times too many!"

Longarm remained silent. He kept his features frozen, his hands still.

George was out of his chair by now, moving between Longarm and Spud, saying, "Hold yourself down, Spud! You know the boss don't like dustups in here!"

Over the house man's shoulder, Spud grated, "This ain't the time to settle with you, Custis. But stay outa my way! You hear?"

"Loud as you're yelling, I'd have to be deaf not to," Longarm replied quietly. When Spud began to sputter, he added, "I judge you ain't got any more to say, so I'll bid all you gents good night."

Deliberately turning his back on Spud, but watching the deputy in the flyspecked bar mirror, Longarm walked away.

Chapter 7

Before Longarm got to the bar, Billy-Bob caught up with him, waving the twenty-dollar gold piece that had gotten him over the hump in betting up the pot he'd just won.

"Mr.—Custis, ain't it? I don't know how to say thanks for helping me out. I'd be right proud to buy you a drink if you'll let me," the young cowhand said, handing Longarm the double eagle.

"You don't need to thank me. It'd be a hell of a sorry world if a man couldn't do something for somebody besides himself, once in a while."

"Just the same, I'd be proud to stand up and drink with you."

"Well, I won't say no to your invitation, Billy-Bob. What's the rest of your name, anyway?"

"Larkin. I work for the Bar Z Bar, down on Devils River."

"That's to the southeast, ain't it?" Billy-Bob nodded and Longarm asked, "Your friends Luke and Fiddler work there, too?"

"No, sir, they're from the next spread south, the Arrowhead."

"You been around here long?" They'd reached the bar; without asking, the barkeep set a bottle of Maryland rye in front of them.

"About two years." Billy-Bob cocked an eye at the bottle's label and asked, "Is this what you always drink, Mr. Custis?"

"Yep. I guess it's what folks call a cultivated taste."

"If it's good enough for you, it'll sure do for me."

The young hand poured the whiskey into the glasses the barman had put beside the bottle.

"Not a lot of ranches down this way, are there?" Longarm asked.

"No, sir. Not too many. The range is so poor, a spread's got to be mighty big around here. The Bar Z Bar foreman says it takes fifty acres to feed a steer."

"You folks bothered by rustlers much?"

"Haven't been since I got here. There's an awful lot going on up to the north, I hear. Up along Howard Creek and the South Concho and the Cemeche country."

"That so?" Longarm sipped thoughtfully before he put the next question. "You heard any talk about the Laredo Loop working again?"

Billy-Bob frowned. "I've heard it mentioned, is all. But didn't the Laredo Loop start someplace up above the Pecos?"

"It all began there." Longarm had been recalling, since he'd left Denver, all the stories he could remember about the across-the-border-and-back operation. "On up north from that place they call Vinagaroon. Then this fellow that's made himself a judge, Roy Bean, moved into Vinagaroon and set up some kind of six-shooter law. I got an idea the Loop's back in business, but it crosses into Mexico quite a way south of where it used to."

"You wouldn't be working for the cattleman's association, would you, Mr. Custis?"

"Nope. That kinda job wouldn't suit me a bit. I'm just sort of curious. Billy-Bob, you can do me a favor, if you will. Keep your ears open, and if you hear any talk about the Loop, or about rustlers, pass it on to me."

"Anything I can do to help you, I sure will," Billy-Bob promised. "Will you have another drink?"

"Guess not, but I thank you." Longarm looked across the room toward the poker tables. George, the house man, was sitting by himself, dealing solitaire. The two-bit ante game was still going strong, but the men who'd been sitting in the money game had gone. He told the young cowboy, "I need to go talk to George a minute. Then I'm going to turn in. I had a right early start and a busy day."

"I'll look for you next time I'm in town," Billy-Bob promised.

"Maybe I'll hear something that'd help you. And thanks again for staking me."

"You needed it. I don't suppose you've played as much poker as I have, but for what it's worth, I'll tell you something I've found out. Learning the game's just like eating an apple. You take one bite at a time."

"I guess I see what you mean."

"Sure you do. Just remember to chew every bite up good, and don't bite off more'n you can gulp down without choking. I'll see you later on, son."

I'd be a sight better off if I took my own advice about biting and chewing, Longarm thought as he crossed to where George was sitting. For a while there, today, I came close to getting a bigger mouthful than I could swallow.

George looked up at Longarm's approach and said, "If you're looking for a game, this is about all that's going right now."

"Thanks, but poker's not on my mind tonight. I just wanted to say I'm sorry I busted things up for you a while ago."

"I was glad to see Billy-Bob get some help. That game was too rich for him, anyhow. No, I don't blame you a bit. That Spud's got a real hair-trigger temper. If he didn't work for Ed Tucker, I don't think I'd let him sit in on any game I was dealing."

"Well, he's been building up a real mad at me all day."

"I know. I watched you face down him and Ed's bunch in the plaza earlier today. It didn't surprise me when Spud blew up." George frowned and looked closely at Longarm. "Say, don't I know you from somewhere else?"

"You might. I've got around a little bit. Seems like I've seen you someplace, too."

"I move around. Most of us do; it's part of the trade. And we might've run into one another if you've been in Cheyenne or Helena or San Francisco or Denver in the past few years."

Longarm's memory clicked. "Sure. Denver. You ran a faro table at Big Jim Little's place, just down Holiday Street from Jennie Rogers's whorehouse."

"That I did, for damn near a year. I guess that's where I remember you from. But I can't recall your name. You a miner? Cattleman? You don't look like the kind that sits at a desk or stands back of a ribbon counter."

"I'm traveling now as Custis." Longarm knew that in the half-world of the professional gambler he needed only to use this phrase to warn George that he didn't want his identity revealed if the house man should remember him more clearly.

"I see." George nodded understandingly. "Well. Denver. It's a long way from Los Perros. I don't mean to pry, but the way you acted out on the plaza today, you sure didn't seem bashful."

"Now, I didn't say I'm on the dodge, did I? There's other reasons a man might have for changing handles."

"Sure, sure." The gambler dropped his voice. "I'll just tip you that if it's the law you're bothered about, you're safe in Los Perros as long as you stay on Ed Tucker's good side."

"I gather he's all the law there is here. How'd he work that out, you know?"

George shook his head. "I haven't been here all that long. From what I've heard, he just grew into the job. Had a few men behind him, more or less took over the town."

"That's about how I figured," Longarm nodded. "Tucker and your boss get along pretty good, don't they?"

Suddenly, the gambler's face stiffened and he dropped his confidential tone. "I suppose they do. Baskin would have to, wouldn't he, the business he's in?"

"Oh, I wasn't prying," Longarm said hastily. He stood up. "Well, now that I know I was right when I figured I'd seen you before, I'll sleep easier."

"Oh, come on, the night's early. Stay awhile, and we'll hash over Denver, and Big Jim and Jennie and Mattie Silks, and Vesta King, and all the gorgeous girls they had."

"Maybe tomorrow night, or the next. I started riding before sunup, and it's getting on for late."

"Sure. Later on, then, Custis. Sleep good."

"I almost always do."

Longarm made his way across the saloon's main floor, unworried. He wasn't sure George's memory would put a badge on him, but even if it did, the gambler would almost certainly keep quiet unless it came to a hard-rock showdown with Baskin standing beside Tucker. He started up the stairs, being glad that the place didn't have a gaggle of women taking customers up to their rooms through the night. He hadn't been exaggerating when he'd told George it had been a long day.

Habit kept his feet quiet as he walked along the uncarpeted hall to the door of his room, fishing the key from his pocket as he moved. The habit of walking silently was by now almost an instinct. So was the habit of checking the broken matchstick that he'd wedged between the door and jamb. Longarm looked for the sliver of wood before inserting the key. His hand stopped in midair when he saw the matchstick half was missing. He'd shifted the key to his left hand even before he looked down and saw the splinter of white pine gleaming, a little speck of brightness on the dark wood of the floor.

A half-dozen possibilities flashed through Longarm's mind in as many seconds while he studied the closed door.

It could be Spud, he thought—bushwhacking's about his speed. Or somebody Spud put on me, to do what he don't want to face up to. Tucker, maybe, he'd send a gunslick instead of coming himself.

No, Tucker was doing his damnedest to butter up to me today, as soon as he saw I wasn't going to crawfish.

Might be Tucker's looking for somebody to handle Spud for him—he hinted at that—but Tucker wouldn't wait in my room, he'd wait till we got by ourselves in private, on his grounds.

Spud's still the one it's most likely to be.

One of the corners, I'd say. Or setting on the bed, it's right even with the door. No. That'd put the window in back of him. If he's smart, not the bed.

Me, I'd be along the wall just inside the door, the side it opens along.

Whoever's there, it ain't that big of a shucks, now I know.

Longarm inserted the key delicately, careful not to scrape metal against metal. He recalled that the lock worked easily, and took a full minute, turning the key with infinite patience to engage the wards and pull the lock's square bar out of the strike plate without it scratching. If he made a noise, it was inaudible to his own ears, and he was satisfied that whoever was inside couldn't have been warned.

Leaving the key in the lock, Longarm drew. He turned the knob with his left hand, quickly, and flung the door wide open. As soon as it had swung wide enough to admit him, he dove into his room, rolling when he hit the floor, winding up against the wall away from the bed. His eyes had been sensitized to darkness by his walk down the unlighted hall and his moments of deliberation outside the door. He had no need for the Colt that was ready in his hand. Except for himself, the room was empty.

Well, now, he told himself, leaning against the wall in the

darkness, guess I better be glad there wasn't nobody here. Now I'm the only one who knows what a damn fool I looked like, diving in ass over appetite. But it's a hell of a lot better to look foolish than to be dead.

He got to his feet and closed the door, locking it automatically. He started for the dresser in the dark, groping for the bottle of rye. His fingers encountered cloth. In the darkness, he stood laughing silently, thinking, I plumb forgot that I sent out my clothes to be washed; it was that porter come in to deliver 'em while I was gone. He crossed to the window and pulled down the shade before lighting the lamp, then pushed the lamp as far back on the bureau as it would go, resting against the mirror, so it would cast no shadow on the windowshade. Only then did he pick up the bottle and have a nightcap.

Hanging his gunbelt on the bedpost at the left of his pillow, Longarm emptied his pockets quickly, undressed even faster, and was in bed within five minutes from the time he'd entered the room. He went to sleep instantly, and slept like a baby.

Though he was by nature an early riser, Longarm didn't wake up until the sun was shining yellow against the drawn window shade. He snapped awake instantly and sat up in bed. Though he'd checked the sheets and mattress on moving into the room the day before, he'd learned through unhappy experience that bugs that bite by night have an uncanny way of making themselves invisible during daylight hours; before leaving the room he had spread his own ground cloth and blanket over the bed without turning the linen down. If there'd been any miniature bloodsuckers that his inspection had missed, they hadn't found him to disturb his rest.

Throwing back the blanket, he rolled to his feet and snapped up the shade. He stretched hugely in the sunlight, the solid muscles of his body flexing the last vestiges of drowsiness from his system. Fishing the chamberpot from under the bed, he arced a golden stream until the morning pressure on his bladder was relieved, then padded on bare feet to the dresser for a wake-up shot of rye.

Ten minutes later, his routine of dressing finished, his Colt and derringer checked thoroughly, he strode down the stairway to the bar.

"What does a man do for breakfast here in Los Perros?" he

asked the barkeeper. It wasn't the same man who'd been tending bar the night before.

"Help yourself to hard-boiled eggs and whatever else strikes your fancy." The barkeep jerked a thumb at the free lunch table.

Longarm went over and looked at it. The same food he'd seen there the evening before was spread on the same chipped platters.

"Thanks," he told the barkeep. "Maybe later on."

When he stepped through the batwings and looked at the plaza, Longarm was surprised to see an even bigger crowd milling around than had gathered for the whipping yesterday. Then he remembered the sheriff telling him about the fiesta, Mexican Independence Day. He noticed, too, that it wasn't the same quiet, almost sullen crowd he'd seen the day before. Today, the people of Los Perros wore their best and brightest clothes, and were laughing and happy.

A few streamers of colored paper dancing in the light breeze on the far side of the plaza caught Longarm's eye; he wondered if the food stalls might not be setting up early. He started toward them, pushing through the throng. Somewhere close by he heard a mariachi band tuning up. Before he reached the streamers, Longarm thought he saw a remembered figure. He changed direction, and when the crowd in his way no longer blocked his vision, he saw that it was indeed Lita's family, setting up their trestles and counter.

Lita saw him when he was still a yard or so distant. She was wrestling with a plank twice as long as she was tall, and let it rest across one shoulder to greet him. "Coos-tees!" she exclaimed. "You come to eat again, no?"

"If you got something ready, Lita. But I'll give you a hand with that board, first."

"I can do it. I am strong."

"But I'm stronger." He took the plank and settled it into place across the trestles, completing the serving counter. "Now then. I hope you got something besides chili and frijoles. They're a mite too spicy for breakfast."

"Is not cook yet, the chili. We got bizcochos that Mamacita bake just a little while ago. And we bring hot coffee from our kitchen at *la casa,* so we don't lose customers who don't wait for it."

"If that's what you got, that's what I'll have."

"You wait, I fix."

In a moment, she'd produced three of the same kind of round,

sugar-crusted buns that Longarm had eaten the day before, together with a cup of steaming coffee. Longarm bit into one of the
buns. He hadn't paid much attention to those he'd had the previous day, there'd been too much else on his mind. This bun was
still hot and moist, and tasted of spices and seasonings strange to
him. Accustomed to flat-tasting baked foods—bread, biscuits,
and soda crackers—he thought it was odd, but excellent.

"You like Mamacita's bizcochos?" Lita asked.

"They're right tasty. I guess I could stand 'em for breakfast
now and again." He sipped the coffee. It was laced heavily with
chicory, and reminded him of the French-type brew he had been
served when he was in New Orleans.

Mamacita came up to the counter and expressed her disap-
proval of Lita's attention to Longarm's breakfast needs in rapid-
fire Spanish that was beyond his ability to follow. He didn't need
a translation, though; the expressions on the faces of both Lita
and her mother were easy for him to read. The exchange lasted
only a few moments before Mamacita turned away with a disgusted shrug.

Lita said, "I got to work now. You come to the *baile* tonight,
Coos-tees?"

"Sure. It's the only dance in town, ain't it?"

"Maybe I dance with you then, if you ask me."

"Oh, I'll do that." He swallowed the last bite of the last bizco-
cho, drained his coffee cup, and handed Lita a quarter. "That
enough money to pay for breakfast?"

"Is plenty. You pay too much, like last night."

"Well, like I told you then, anything extra's for you." Longarm
touched a forefinger to his hat and said, "See you at the dance."
Then he started back to the saloon. He wanted his Winchester for
the scouting trip he planned to make.

When he went to the corral for Tordo, he avoided the sheriff's
office. He didn't want to start the day with a run-in with Spud,
and for all he knew the deputy might be on duty. Going directly to
the corral, he saddled Tordo and started south along the river
channel. He wasn't sure what he was looking for, but knowing the
lay of the land was often an insurance of survival. Longarm intended to survive.

By midafternoon, he'd covered the area near Los Perros on the
U.S. side of the Rio Grande as well as the bank of the channel

along which he'd started. That left the northern, upstream, end of the sandspit. He was forced to ride back almost to the center of town in order to avoid the lagoon formed by the backwater where the sandspit split the river. Going north on the spit, the houses of Los Perros straggled to an occasional lonely shanty more quickly than he'd realized they would. He'd thought there would be dwellings all the way to the northern end of the spit that rose like a whale's humped back above the river; the south end was thickly built up. Beyond the northernmost of the hovels, though, the sandspit stretched for at least two miles. He saw why when he'd left the last of the dwellings behind. High-water marks began to show almost at once.

Longarm continued to the point where the river split. Here, the Rio Grande now ran wide and sluggish at low water, over a sandy bottom. Might even be some quicksand here and there, he thought as he surveyed the point from the height of Tordo's back. He recalled that Texas rivers running in sandy beds were notorious for their quicksand. At the place where he'd pulled up the dapple, there was water on both sides of him: the lagoon on his right, the channel on the left. On the Mexican side of the channel the bank began a steep rise that quickly became a steep bluff; under the bluff the water deepened and the current ran as fast as it did along the downstream end of the sandspit.

Longarm could easily see why Los Perros was a no-man's-land, a place where an unscrupulous pusher like Ed Tucker could set himself up a miniature kingdom. In the rainy season, when the Rio Grande ran in flood, Los Perros stood as an island that could be claimed—or disclaimed—by the U.S. or Mexico. It was, he thought, like places he'd encountered elsewhere in the West. He remembered spots in Indian Territory where there were similar no-man's-lands, created by careless or inexpert surveyors who'd mistaken a natural landmark or guessed at longitude and latitude lines instead of making a star sighting to establish them correctly.

Anyhow, Longarm told himself, there wasn't going to be any argument about which country had jurisdiction when the time came for him to produce his badge, as long as there was dry land on the U.S. side of Los Perros.

Tordo tossed his head and snorted, and Longarm read the message; the horse was thirsty. Stopping to let him drink every time there was a wet spot on the ride from San Antonio had imprinted in the animal's mind the notion that he had to drink every time he saw water. Longarm slacked the reins and touched the dapple's side with his toe to wade him out into the river where he could drink easily. The gray waded out, testing the sand underfoot before each step, his instinct telling him that such bottoms could be treacherous. Tordo stopped in knee-deep water to drink.

There was no current to ripple the surface; the river's rushing water passed to Longarm's left. Idly, he looked over the dapple's bent head and gazed at the bottom, clearly visible through the shallow water. For a moment, he didn't take in what he was seeing. Then it sank home that the sand under the surface was covered with a pattern of dents that could have been caused by only one thing: the hooves of steers being waded across the stream.

Waiting until the dapple had drunk his fill, Longarm nudged the horse ahead. The bottom dropped gradually for a distance of at least two hundred yards. Until it started there to slant, Longarm's stirrups had stayed several inches above the surface. He went on until he felt wavelets slapping his boot soles, then reined in. The water wasn't as clear here, roiled a bit by the current, but he could still make out hoofprints in the sand.

To his left, the Mexican bank of the Rio Grande was low. The upward slope began at a point opposite the sandspit's end. To his right, the calm surface of the lagoon lapped at land that was almost level with the water. There were no hoofprints in the sand that stretched back from the lagoon; its surface rippled in windswept ridges.

To Longarm's trailwise eyes, the story was completely clear. Even a light breeze would smooth the loose, soft sand, and beyond it the baked soil was too hard to take prints. The bank on the Mexican side shelved gently from the water, here. At this one point, there seemed to be no quicksand. Driving a herd of cattle across, even at night, would be no trick at all.

Old son, Longarm told himself as he sat on Tordo's back surrounded by the green sun-dappled water, looks like you just fell headfirst into the place where the new Laredo Loop starts out.

Chapter 8

Standing on the veranda of Baskin's saloon, Longarm looked out across the plaza. Los Perros had turned out in full for the fiesta. He was sure that every man, woman, and child was crowded into the irregular circle that served as the town's public arena.

Music from a mariachi band in front of the saloon almost drowned that from a *banda Guadalajara tapatia* on the other side. The twanging of the strings and bell-like marimba notes of the mariachis at times clashed sourly against the brasses and cymbals of the *Guadalajareños*, but if there were discords where the music blended in the plaza's center, this didn't seem to bother the dancers. They twirled and stomped to the rhythm of the music that was being played closest to them.

"I really do like to see my people having a good time," said a voice at Longarm's elbow.

He turned. Sheriff Tucker had come out of the saloon behind him. Longarm agreed, "They're whooping it up, all right."

"Didn't see you at the barbecue at noon today," Tucker said.

"Maybe that's because I didn't know there was one."

"Well, doggone that Lefty! I told him to make sure you got a special invitation. Man like you, Custis, comin' from outside, don't generally find much t'do in a little place like this."

"Oh, I manage to fill up the time. Tell me something, Sheriff. How many ranches would you say there are in a day's ride to the north, up along the Pecos on both sides?"

Tucker pursed his thin lips. "Not too many, that close. There's such poor range hereabouts that most of the spreads have got to be so big it'd take you a day just to ride across one of 'em."

"That's about the way I figured," Longarm nodded. "There sure as hell ain't much grass anyplace I looked at around here so far."

"Sounds like you been sizin' up the range, Custis. You lookin' for anything special?"

"No. Just interested in seeing the lay of the land around these parts, is all."

"You interested in ranchin', then? Funny. I didn't take you for a cattle rancher. Guess I'm goin' to have to change my mind again."

Longarm finally realized that Tucker's sudden expansiveness didn't mean he was getting friendly. The sheriff was drunker than usual. He asked, "How's that? I didn't know you'd made up your mind about me in the first place."

"Well, I did. When you took on Spud and the boys that day you showed up, I put you down in my book as a gunslick on the owlhoot trail. But after I'd thought a bit, that didn't make sense. If you was on the dodge, you'd've laid low, not called no notice to yourself."

Longarm wasn't going to waste the man's loquaciousness. He threw the logical question. "After that, how'd you tab me?"

"I didn't, till now. You had me plumb puzzled. Right now, though, it's popped into my mind you might just be a land agent for one of the big railroads. I keep hearin' there's two or three of 'em that wants to run a line down to the Gulf. If you're interested in land, but not in ranchin', that's all the reason I can see."

Longarm wasn't too surprised at Tucker's conclusion. Everywhere in the West, railroads were adding lines to supplement their major routes, and right-of-way agents were thick. Dropping his voice, he said, "I won't say yes or no. But suppose I was, now. Think you might help me pick up some land on the quiet?"

"You're damn right, I can! What I say is law, anywheres inside of a hundred miles of here." Tucker looked around. "Listen, this ain't the place to talk about a deal, Custis. Let's go back to the office. The boys are all out, keepin' an eye on the fiesta. We can talk private there."

In the sheriff's office, with the outer door closed, Tucker shouted, "Wahonta! Bring the whiskey bottle and some glasses!" When the Apache girl came in with a half-filled bottle and some thick tumblers, he told her brusquely, "Now, go tend to whatever it is you're doin'. We got business to talk."

Longarm's eyes followed the girl as she left. Tucker noticed him watching her. He said, "Maybe she don't look like much to you, but that little 'Pache gal's the sweetest piece of ass I run into in a long time. A-course, I broke her in right. I was the first man ever rode her. She wasn't but only fourteen when I bought her off the resettlement camp south of here, a couple years ago."

"She's a right nice-looking girl," Longarm commented neutrally.

Tucker had poured, now he passed Longarm a glass across the desk. "Now, then. Like I told you, I'm the law here—sheriff, judge, and jury. When I say frog, people jumps. I can get whatever land you're after, Custis, water and mineral rights throwed in. You call the tune, I make 'em play it." He waited for Longarm to take the bait, and when no response followed he added, "Understand, now, I'd look to git a little something for my trouble. A sort of commission, we could call it."

"We could call it that," Longarm agreed. "But I got a better deal than that."

"I'm listenin'."

"Let's just suppose I was after land for a railroad right-of-way. Think you could push the price I'd pay down low enough so I could double what I'd charge the railroad? That way, we'd have a real big piece of cash to split up between us."

Tucker grinned. "That'd be easier'n pissin' in a dishpan. I can set my own price on what land you'd want. And there's ways to fix up deeds and papers so the railroad never would catch on."

"I know all about deeds and papers," Longarm said. "There's one thing that bothers me, though. How about your boys? Spud and Lefty and Ralston, would you have to cut them in on the deal?"

"Hell, no! I let them pick up what they can, cut 'em in on my deals when I feel like it, but you can leave them to me to handle." Tucker splashed more whiskey into his glass.

Longarm said, picking his words carefully, "Meaning no offense, Sheriff, but are you including Spud in that? I guess you heard I had a little run-in with him in the saloon last night, after you told him everything was supposed to be nice and friendly."

"Well, I hadn't heard, but you got to remember, Spud's hot-headed. He's got a real quick temper."

"I noticed that yesterday. Times I wondered if you had him on a real tight halter. He was just about sassing you."

Tucker nodded, his blubbery lips twisted angrily. "I ain't forgot that, Custis." He thought for a moment. "Look here now. You've laid it out straight with me, I'll do the same with you. Spud's been gettin' uppity of late. I got a hunch he's feelin' too big for his britches. Gittin' idees, if you follow me."

Longarm nodded. "Like taking things over, here in Los Perros?"

"Somethin' like that," Tucker agreed unhappily. He drained his glass and refilled it. "Listen, Spud was just a lard-ass boy when I talked Quantrill into lettin' him ride with us. And I put him in as my *segundo* when I took over here. I made him, and I can bust him."

"Suppose you can't?"

Tucker winked across the desk. "You recall I told you I had you tabbed for a gunslick at first? One reason I let you off so light, let you stick around, is so I could watch and see if you might be a man who could he'p me handle Spud, when the time's right."

Longarm leaned back in his chair. "Well, now. I could handle him, but whether I would handle him, that'd depend." He decided it was time to get on another track. When Tucker sobered up, he'd remember their talk, and might just regret it. He asked, "How'd you get to be boss man here, anyhow? I bet it took some doing."

"Sure it did, and here's how I done it." Tucker slapped the heavy ivory-handled Schneider & Glasswick revolver that hung from his gunbelt. The old-fashioned pistol had caught Longarm's eye the day before. He'd noticed it had been modified to handle cartridge loads, and had wondered why the sheriff still carried such an outdated weapon when new Colts were so cheap and plentiful.

Tucker continued, "I used this as free as I had to, just like I did in the war. This is the same gun Quantrill give me, you know that? Had it worked over, but I still hold to it. Maybe because it's the gun I killed my first man with."

Longarm saw that the sheriff was growing maudlin. It was time to cut off their talk. He said, "You let me think about what you've told me. We'll get down to cases later on."

"Wait a minute! Have we got a deal, or haven't we?"

"Maybe. I got to sleep on it. My tail'd be in a worse crack than yours would, if what we was doing leaked out."

"Don't worry about that." Tucker slapped his holster again. "I can shut up anybody that starts to give us trouble."

"I still want to think about it some. We'll talk some more tomorrow." Longarm stood up. "You going back to watch the fiesta?"

"No. I think I'll just stay here and lay up with Wahonta for a while." As Longarm went to the door, Tucker said, "One more thing, Custis. If we get in this deal, it wouldn't do for us to act too friendly. Them railroads swing a lot of steam. If they get a hint there's somethin' funny going on, they might even get them damn federal marshals in here to check up on us."

"Sure. I'll keep that in mind." Longarm opened the door and waved. "Enjoy yourself, Sheriff. We'll talk about things tomorrow."

Walking back to the plaza, Longarm took stock. He was beginning to make tracks to where he wanted to be. He'd found what was pretty sure to be the crossing of the new Laredo Loop, and his hunch was that it would somehow lead him to Nate Webster's trail. He was getting on terms with Tucker that should open the trail leading to information about Captain Hill and the 10th Cavalry deserters. Best of all, just by keeping quiet and letting Tucker's crooked imagination do his work for him, Longarm had repaired the damage done by his impulsive move in stopping the whipping the day he'd arrived in Los Perros. On the bad side, his snap decision to keep his real identity covered might hinder him from asking too many open questions. In a place like Los Perros, there'd be gossip aplenty. Everybody in town probably knew what was going on, and they'd be leery of answering questions put by a man who had no authority to do so. Still, in very little time, he'd made a pretty fair start, good enough for him to take the evening off and spend a little time at the fiesta with Lita. He had mixed feelings about Lita. There were times when she seemed to be little more than a child, and times when a woman showed through. Maybe how he'd act would depend on which side of her showed up strongest when the time came, if it came.

Things had gotten quieter and noisier both, Longarm thought when he entered the plaza. The two bands had reached some kind of truce, and were both playing in the plaza's center, taking turns instead of competing. The sun was low, and the uneven edges of the big open area were already deeply shadowed. Flickering hachones, bottles or funnel-capped cans filled with kerosene into which rag wicks had been inserted, were mounted on poles here and there, turning the plaza into a patchwork of bright spots and shadows.

Longarm started for the stall where he'd had breakfast, thinking he'd probably find Lita somewhere close to it, but before he could push very far through the crowd he was hailed by Lefty, the sheriff's deputy.

"Hey, Custis! I got a bottle in my pocket, come have a drink with me!"

Longarm didn't especially want a drink after the heavy slug he'd downed while talking with Tucker, but he didn't want to do anything that would stretch the taut truce that had been patched up among himself, Lefty, and Ralston. He said, "Don't mind if I do."

Lefty hauled a flask out of his pocket, and Longarm managed to swallow a light swig while appearing to take a heavy one. He gave the bottle back to Lefty, who tilted it and smacked his lips.

"Ah! That's prime stuff!" Lefty pocketed the bottle. "Listen, you don't need to be all by yourself, Custis. Want a partner to dance with? Hell, just ask any of these little greaser gals, they don't care who swings 'em around, long as he's got pants on."

"I'm just walking, Lefty, trying to stay out of trouble. Looks to me like the easiest way to do that is not to horn in on somebody else's girl."

"They ain't goin' to be no trouble," Lefty assured him. "Ed's put the fear o' God in this Los Perros bunch."

"Just the same, I'll walk easy and keep quiet."

"Ah, what's a fiesta, if you don't have a dance or two?" Lefty scanned the crowd, saw a young girl and her escort a few feet away, and waved to them. "Hey, Luis! You and Tina come here a minute!" As they started to obey, he said to Longarm, "I'll tell the gal to dance with you. Luis won't mind."

"Now, wait a minute—" Longarm began, but before he could go any further the couple had joined them and Lefty was making the arrangements he'd insisted on.

"Luis, this is a friend of mine, *Señor* Custis. He's a stranger here, wants to dance a round or two. You don't mind if Tina obliges him, do you?"

"If it is her wish," Luis replied. "I do not own her, *Señor* Lefty."

Lefty turned back to Longarm. "See? It's all fixed. Tina, this *señor* wants to dance with you a little while."

"*Porqué no?*" the girl shrugged. "A *baile* is for dancing, no? Come, *señor.* If you do not know the steps, I show you them."

"Now, hold on," Longarm protested. "When it comes to dancing, I got two left feet. I'm afraid I'd step all over you. But I thank you kindly for offering to show me, *Señorita* Tina."

"*Qué pasa?*" Tina asked Lefty. "*Dice el hombre quiere bailar, ahora el dice no. Qué chiste es?*"

This time it was the deputy who shrugged. "*Por supuesto, es un engano. El me diga quiere bailar.*"

"*Qué cosa!*" Luis exclaimed. "*Bastamente esta tontería! El gringo insulta mi Tina!*"

Longarm caught the gist of this exchange, and said to Luis, "No, *amigo. La senorita es—*" he sought the word he couldn't remember and finally found it—"*es muy linda.*"

"*Cagado!*" Luis exclaimed.

Lefty intervened. "*Cállate, Luis! Hablamos mas tarde. Véte, tu y Tina!*"

Muttering, Luis took Tina's arm and led her away. Lefty said to Longarm, "Damn it, Custis, you like to've fixed yourself with that greaser. He was real put out, claimed you insulted his girlfriend."

"I got the general idea," Longarm said. "Don't blame it all on me, Lefty. I told you, I ain't interested in dancing. Thanks for your trouble, anyhow. Sorry I rubbed your friend the wrong way."

"Ah, he's just a spic I know," Lefty replied. "I guess I was a little too previous. Here, have another swig, and we'll forget it."

To placate him, Longarm took a token swallow, thanked Lefty, and walked on as soon as he could without offending the man further. He was still looking for Lita; the girl Lefty'd tried to get him to dance with couldn't hold a candle to her, he thought as he pushed toward the food stalls. He wondered why the deputy had suddenly become so friendly; the day before, he'd been standoffish, not as hostile as Spud, but a lot less amiable than Ralston. Maybe he'd been told by Tucker to be cooperative, maybe Ral-

ston had talked him around, or maybe he'd just changed his mind
by himself, Longarm thought. Whatever the reason, Lefty's solic-
itude had come as a real surprise.

As he'd half expected her to be, Lita was near the spot where
her family's food stall had been earlier in the day. The stall was
dismantled now, with trestles, planks, stove, and pots piled up
ready to be carried home. A short distance away, Mamacita was
gossiping with a group of women who, like her, were draped in
black rebozos; two of the younger children had curled up at her
feet and were sleeping. Lita stood off to one side, laughing and
chattering with a few girls of her own age. She saw Longarm and
tripped, light-footed, to greet him.

"Coos-tees! I think maybe you forget we going to dance."

"Don't count on me doing much dancing, Lita. Stomping
around to music ain't right in my line."

"Is nothing, to dance. Come on, I show you. You learn real
fast." She tucked her arm in Longarm's and led him to a space
where there was room to maneuver. "Now. You listen to *la musica*
and look how my feet they go. Then you see is easy."

Lita began to dance, facing Longarm and holding his hands,
arms stretched out. To humor her, Longarm began moving his
feet, but they kept getting tangled up. It wasn't as much his clum-
siness that was to blame as it was the sight of Lita's firm young
breasts bouncing unconfined under her thin, scoop-necked blouse.
She stopped and stamped a foot in mock anger.

"Coos-tees! You don' look at my feet, you watching my
tetas!" she exclaimed. "Is not good you look so here! Mamacita
might see."

"I told you I wasn't no dancer," he said. "Why don't we forget
about dancing, and find some place where your mama can't
watch you?"

"No!" Lita's eyes flashed and her smooth round chin set stub-
bornly, though she was still smiling at him. "We don' go nowhere
till you dance with me! You look, now, I show you *mas despacio*,
slow."

Longarm hadn't lied to either Lita or Tina. Though he'd done
a little square dancing as a boy in West Virginia, he'd decided
early that dancing was a time-wasting substitute for the real activity it imitated, and a lot less enjoyable. After making up his
mind on that point, he'd lost interest in becoming skilled on the
dance floor.

He said, "All right, if that's what you want. But you're just wasting your time, trying to turn me into a dancer."

Just as Lita began her second effort to teach him, Longarm saw Tina and Luis dancing their way toward them. Luis was trying to look unconcerned, but Tina's face was cast in a glowering frown. Longarm smelled trouble, and he wasn't disappointed. As soon as the other couple had gotten within a yard or so of him and Lita, Tina broke away from Luis and ran up to Longarm. Without any preliminary scolding, she brought up her hand and slapped his face.

"Gringo cabrón! You make *insulta* to me!" she cried loudly.

Around them, the other dancers stopped to watch. Luis took a step that brought him closer to Longarm. He demanded loudly, "What you do, *Tejano zopilote?* You wan' to take *mi querido* away from me? Just because you big gringo, you think you better as me, no?"

Longarm knew better than to respond to Luis's insults either with words or with action. In that particular crowd, whatever he did could be wrong. The people would help Luis if it came to a fight, whether Luis attacked him or he struck the Mexican youth first. He felt a surge of relief when Lefty appeared from nowhere.

"All right!" the deputy called. *"Ningunes hace maleza!"*

His shout quieted the angry murmurs that were rising, and those nearest shoved back a bit. The spectators in the rear, who hadn't heard Lefty, and knew only that trouble was brewing, kept pushing in, though, trying to see what was going on.

Longarm said quickly, "Look, Lefty, this ain't no fight I picked. All of a sudden, this girl begun yelling, and slapping at me. Said I'd insulted her."

"He call me *puta!*" Tina said loudly.

Her voice low and angry, Lita spat, "You are *puta!*"

Longarm thought Lita was even prettier when she got mad than when she was just having fun.

Lefty asked him, "That right, Custis? You call this girl a whore, right here in front of her friends?"

"I never called her anything!"

"Mientrador!" Luis shouted. "I hear him say it! You get out of my way, Lefty! I wan' to fight him!"

"That's a pretty serious thing to do in these parts, Custis, insult a young lady. Looks to me like I got to do what Luis says, git outa the way and leave you two go at it."

Longarm had seen the setup coming. He wasn't worried about a fight with Luis, but he knew what Luis's friends would do—and, he thought, those friends include Lefty. I can put Luis down with a punch or two, but the minute we start mixing it up, his friends start closing in and out come the knives. Then Lefty can play it any way he wants. He can let 'em carve me, or he can shoot me and say he had to do it, or it was an accident while he was trying to break up the mob. And if I draw on this bunch, five shots won't stop 'em.

He said to Lefty, "You guarantee to stand by, see it's a fair fight? Just Luis and me, none of his compadres buttin' in?"

"Don't worry, Custis. You know these Mexicans ain't no good with their fists. I'd say you can put him down with one punch, and that'll be it. But if I don't let him have a chance at you, this crowd's gonna git outa hand. Hell, you can see that yourself."

"All right. I'll take him on."

"You'll have to shed that gunbelt first. They wouldn't figure it was a fair scrap if I let you keep it on."

"Figured I'd have to do that." Longarm opened his frock coat and unbuckled his gunbelt. He handed the belt and holstered Colt to the deputy. "You take care of it for me."

"Sure. I won't let nobody grab it. The fight won't last but a minute anyhow, if you're the man I take you to be."

When Longarm shed his pistol, the tone of the crowd's rumbling changed. It was no longer as angry and threatening as it had been. There was a sudden jostling in the circle that enclosed Longarm and the others. He looked around to see several very sullen-faced men shoving into the front ranks of the onlookers. If Longarm had any doubt left that the deputy had set him up, it vanished at that point.

Oh-oh, he said to himself, here come the knife hands.

Aloud, he said to Lefty, "Guess I better skin out of this monkey coat, too. If I'm going to fight, I'll do it in style."

Slipping out of the sleeves of his Prince Albert, he folded the coat into a neat square. When he pushed it at Lefty, the deputy instinctively held out the hand with which he wasn't holding Longarm's gunbelt. Longarm shoved the coat against Lefty's chest, forcing him without seeming to into bringing up his entire arm to clasp the coat securely.

"What about your vest?" Lefty asked.

"Oh, I'll just keep it on. But I'll ask you to look after my watch. Don't want it to get busted."

He lifted the watch out of its pocket and ran his fingers along the chain to the pocket on the opposite side. Lefty's eyes were caught by the glitter of the watch. He didn't see the derringer until it was in Longarm's hand. Before the deputy could free his own loaded hands, the muzzle of the ugly little double-barreled derringer was pushing, cold and menacing, into his temple.

"There's two .44 slugs in this little thing." Longarm's voice was low, almost a whisper. "One of 'em will blow whatever you use for brains right outa that ugly skull of yours."

"You don't have to shoot me!" Lefty said. "I'll do just what you tell me to!"

"Good." Raising his voice, Longarm said, "Lita! Get over here, quick!" The girl ran to stand beside him. Longarm said, "Take his gun out and hand it to me. Soon as you do that, strap my gunbelt on me."

Lita moved without hesitating to follow instructions. He held out his free hand and she slid Lefty's pistol into it, butt-first. Then she relieved the deputy of Longarm's gunbelt.

Events had moved so swiftly that the crowd hadn't had time to grasp exactly what had happened. Those closest to the action were frozen into silent motionlessness, their eyes trying to follow everything. The angry mutterings from the more distant spectators began to subside as mob instinct transmitted the feeling that something was going on that should be heeded. In the momentary silence, Lita got Longarm's gunbelt around his waist. The pressure of her soft body, the warm scent that wafted up from the valley between her breasts, all registered on Longarm, but he put them out of his mind and concentrated on the job at hand.

He replaced the watch and derringer in their pockets and settled the gunbelt to his liking. He looked at Luis and said, "I don't like people that lie to me, Luis. I know this *hombre* here put you up to trying to get me. You better tell me about it."

Luis was eager to talk. "*Sí, señor*. It was hees idea. He say so soon you and me start to fight, then my *compañeros* they help out, with they knives."

"About what I figured. You ready to tell the sheriff that?"

"*El jefe? Señor* Tucker?" Luis hesitated only a moment. "*Sí*. I tell him, just like I say it to you."

"Good." Longarm turned to Lita. "You better come along, too. This crowd's going to be upset. After I'm gone, they might take their mad out on you."

"I go where you say to, with you, Coos-tees."

"Now, then." Longarm looked sternly at Lefty. "You're going to walk in front of me and Lita, and shoo people outa our way. If you got an idea I'm too good to backshoot a man, you're right, but I don't count rats like you as men. Now, march!"

With the deputy leading the way, motioning the onlookers aside, a path opened like magic. Longarm kept Lefty in front, Lita on his right, Luis and Tina on his left, as they moved quickly through the crowd of silent spectators, around the saloon, and into the sheriff's office.

Chapter 9

As Longarm had suspected he would be, Sheriff Tucker was still in bed with Wahonta. Tucker came in from the ell in response to Longarm's call, tugging his trousers up over his longjohns. His eyes snapped open wider than anyone had ever seen them do before when he saw the little group.

"Just what in billy-blue-hell's this all about?" he demanded.

"It ain't very important, Sheriff," Longarm answered. He took his Prince Albert from Lefty and slid his arms into the sleeves as he was talking. "Just figured you might want to explain to this deputy of yours that he can go to jail on charges of attempted murder and stirring up a riot, if I feel like pushing charges on him."

"Lefty?" Tucker was incredulous.

"He's the only deputy of yours I see here."

"Now, damn it, Custis, I let it pass by when you begun a ruckus with my men yesterday. I ain't so sure I'm of a mind to be as easy on you, if you're tryin' the same stunt again."

"Maybe you better listen to what this young fellow here's got to say, before you blame me for starting anything," Longarm suggested.

Tucker glared at the young Mexican. "All right, Luis, what you got to say about all this?"

Luis shuffled his feet, head hanging. "He tell you the true, *Señor Jefe. El Señor* Lefty, he wan' me and Tina, we make *alboroto,* and he wan' me I have some *toscos* ready, they should *matarle apuñalados* so soon we start."

"He tellin' the truth, Lefty?" Tucker demanded. "You put him up to startin' a ruckus with the crowd? And havin' his tough friends ready to knife Custis in the fracas?"

"It wasn't my idea, Ed," Lefty pleaded.

"I don't give a hot-pepper shit whose idee it was! I'm askin' you did you do it the way Luis told me?"

"Yeah, but it was Spud's idea!" Lefty confessed. "After Custis cost him that big pot in the poker game last night, and after he'd made fools outa all of us at the whippin', Spud figured we had a right to git even!"

"So you and Spud framed up this scheme to do it," Tucker nodded. "Well, I'm the one who tells you and Spud what you do and what you don't do! You don't get no wild hairs up your ass and go off on your own! And both of you knows that, by God!"

"What the sheriff's trying to tell you, Lefty," Longarm broke in, "is that we settled whatever differences there might've been between us, when we had a private talk a few hours back."

"Is that right, Ed?" Lefty asked.

"Yes, damn you, it is! And you and Spud come close to—" Tucker caught himself before he'd said too much. He changed the direction of his words. "You boys been with me long enough to know that I'm the one that gives orders who you're to take after or let alone."

Longarm had to compress his lips to keep from laughing. When he was sure his voice wouldn't give him away, he said, "Looks to me like your boys are getting outa hand, Sheriff. I'd say they need a good lesson."

"What'd your idea be of a lesson?"

"Is this one here any good with this gun I had the girl take off him?" Longarm held Lefty's pistol out to the sheriff. "If he is, and you'd want to look the other way, I'm just about mad enough to face off with him."

"Well . . ." Tucker sounded doubtful. "That'd be a quick way to settle things, I guess. You sound pretty sure you can take him."

"If he can't use this any better'n he can hang on to it, I don't guess I'd have much to worry about." Casually, Longarm nudged aside the lapel of his coat and rested a hand on the butt of his

Colt. He had an idea that both Lefty and Tucker would recognize the professional's touch shown by his gunbelt and holster. His guess was correct; Lefty took one look and started shaking his head.

"That's a shooter's rig if I ever seen one, Ed. I'd just the same as suiciding myself if I went up against him."

"Now, you can count on me to see it's a fair and square show-down," Tucker told the deputy. It was obvious to Longarm that the sheriff was enjoying watching a man squirm, especially since it wasn't costing him anything.

"No, Ed. I ain't fool enough to take on a deal like that."

Tucker's voice showed his disgust. "You're a damn sorry turd, Lefty. Now, in case you'd forgot, you got a job I told you to do to-night. Git the hell outa here and git on it! When you git back, you and me and Spud will set down and have a little private talk our-selves." He took the pistol that Longarm still held and handed it to Lefty. "Maybe you better practice up with this, just in case you make another mistake like the one you just did."

After Lefty had gone, Longarm told Tucker, "You might as well send these other two kiting." He indicated Luis and Tina. "All they done was what your man told 'em."

"What about the other girl?"

"I'll take care of her."

"I'll just bet you will!" the sheriff chuckled. He waved a hand at Luis and Tina. "Git! Vamoose!" As they left, he took Longarm by the arm and led him to one side, where Lita couldn't overhear. In a half-whisper, he said, "Look here, Custis, Lefty and Spud stepped outa line, but I didn't put 'em up to it. Fact is, you was more'n half right earlier, when you said they was gittin' uppity. After we wind up the deal with your railroad, how'd you like to settle down here and throw in with me?"

"I'd have to think on it, just like I'm still thinking about the other deal." Longarm stared into Tucker's little pig eyes. "I guess you'd look for me to help you get rid of Spud? Maybe Lefty, too?"

"Well, it'd even things up if you was around backin' my play, when the time comes for me to make it."

"We'll talk about it more, later on." Longarm turned to Lita. "Come on. I'll see you get back to where you belong."

When he closed the door of the sheriff's office behind them, Lita said, "I think you a very brave *hombre,* Coos-tees. I like you, *mucho muchissimo!* You better kiss me now." When he hesitated, she asked, "You think maybe I'm still *niña,* leetle girl? You don' look at me like that when my *tetas* jiggle when I show you the dance, no? All right, I show you more!"

Lita pulled Longarm's head down and her mouth found his. Her lips were soft and firm in turn, pulsing and alive. Her tongue darted into his mouth, hot, seeking, probing. He felt the pressure of her breasts on his chest as she clung to him. Then, before he'd expected her to, Lita broke off the kiss.

"So, what you think now, Coos-tees?"

"I think we oughta find a better place than this. Come on." He led her to the corral. There was a new moon, hanging high; it gave little light, and in three hours, four at most, it would be gone. Still, it was bright enough to see Tordo's gray form in the corral.

"You ride a horse?" he asked.

"No. I don' know about a horse. Better I ride with you."

Longarm didn't waste time cinching on his McClellan. His saddle blanket hung over the corral rail beside the McClellan and his bridle; he took the bridle, ducked through the pole fence, and slid the bit into Tordo's mouth. He led the dapple out of the enclosure, tossed the blanket over his back, and lifted Lita on. He leaped on behind her. He'd never ridden the gray without a saddle before, but he trusted Tordo's instincts. Besides, they weren't going very far.

During the short ride to the sandspit north of Los Perros, far enough beyond the last of the houses to ensure privacy, he held Lita close to him. He left the reins slack, guiding the dapple with the pressure of his knees, while his hands explored her breasts under the thin, low-necked blouse. He bent his head now and then to nuzzle her neck and bare shoulders. There was a smell of spice— cinnamon or cloves, he thought, or perhaps something he couldn't name—that clung to her skin. Her hair, long and black and shining in the moonlight, brushed back across his cheeks as Tordo moved over the last stretch of hard earth before the thudding of his hooves was swallowed by soft sand. They rode almost to the end of the sandspit before Longarm reined in and jumped to the ground.

He reached up and lifted Lita from the dapple's back. His hands spanned her waist, and he felt the quick pulsations of her breathing as he held her briefly while lowering her to the ground. Her head came only to his shoulders; she had to stand on tiptoe to bring her mouth up to meet his. He felt her hands travel across his shoulders, slipping off his coat and vest, then she was fumbling at his gunbelt. He let go her soft buttocks to help her, and eased the gun carefully down to his coat, where it would not touch the sand. Then his hands went back to pull her close to him once more, her soft body nestling close, her hips undulating as she felt him grow hard against her.

"*Chíngame!*" she urged, whispering. "I think I die if you don't!" Her hands became busy with Longarm's britches, freeing his belt, fumbling open the buttons below it. She sensed his hesitation. "Don' worry, Coos-tees, I been with men before." She'd liberated his erection now, and added with a sigh, "But not a man like you!"

Her hands flashed swiftly in the soft moonlight, grasping her full skirt and pulling it high. She wore nothing underneath it. Longarm got a glimpse of her dark pubic hair as she brought a leg up to straddle him, squeezing her thighs around him tightly. Holding him between her moistly warm thighs, she moved her hips gently back and forth. Longarm began to believe that Lita was, as she'd insisted, no longer a little girl.

For a few moments they clung, kissing, while Lita moved her hips, rubbing him slowly. She began to gasp. Longarm picked her up by the waist and lifted her off the ground. Lita spread her legs and guided him into her hot throbbing depth, wrapped her legs around his waist and locked them behind his back, to pull him into her fully. She screamed then, a light, breathy cry of delight. Longarm braced his legs by spreading them and supported her buttocks with his hands, squeezing their soft, firm muscles. Her body twisted, her gasps became a sobbing laugh of pain and pleasure as with his hands he moved her back and forth. He felt the vibrations begin deep in her body. They spread, her muscles undulating, until she was trembling. Her head fell back, the laughing sobs rising from her taut throat as she let ecstasy take her and shake her until, still trembling, she gave a final gasp and went limp in his hands.

He supported her gently, still buried deeply in her, still rock-hard and unsatisfied. "Hold on around my neck," he told the girl as soon as he felt her muscles become firm again. Lita clasped her hands behind his head, and Longarm moved with short careful steps to where Tordo stood, only a few feet away. Whisking the saddle blanket off the gray's back, he managed to unfold it and after a fashion to spread it on the sand.

Longarm's britches had slipped down when he took the few steps needed to reach the blanket and place it on the ground. He sidled along its edge, Lita still locked close to him, her hot wetness urging him to hurry. He was holding himself back, not wanting to enjoy his orgasm alone, giving Lita as much time as he could manage to be ready to share it with him. He dropped to his knees on a corner of the blanket and in the same unbroken motion lunged forward, pinning her beneath him, stabbing even deeper into her than he'd been while they were standing up.

"Madre de Dios! Que verga!" she cried out. *"Qué cosa maravillosa! Es mas qué chorizo, es un grifo de caballo! Dame todo, Coos-tees! Ándale! Ándale!"*

Longarm obeyed her demands. Although he didn't understand the words, her tone told him that Lita needed no more time. He thrust fiercely and she splayed her legs wide to engulf him, her hips rocking. Her trembling began almost at once. Longarm was past being ready, but after the interruption of moving, it took him a few minutes to reach a peak again. He rocked faster and faster, racing Lita's beginning orgasm, until he caught up and pushed hard one last time, and held himself deep within her while her cries broke the cool night air, until his shaking ended and he fell aside, leaving the girl sprawled on the rough wool beside him, both of them limp and spent.

They lay, not moving or talking, watching the moon as it waned imperceptibly, then began playing the game of undressing one another. The night breeze was soft on their naked bodies. Lita lay with her head cradled on Longarm's shoulder. Now and then she'd rub her cheek on his skin, or he'd raise a hand to caress her breasts, his hard fingertips gentle as they traced the puckered tips of her dark rosettes. As their vigor returned the kissing began again, and their hands on each other grew more inquisitive. Longarm rubbed his palm down the smooth warm flesh of Lita's stomach and combed his fingers through her bush to feel the fresh moisture stealing out between her thighs. She spread them for him, and his fingers explored more deeply. Lita's hands were cradling and hefting him, curling around, weighing, feeling his erection begin to grow.

"Es muy hermoso, su grifo, Coos-tees. But I like it more inside me, not in *mis manos.* You wan' I show you how I like?"

"Sure. If you like it, I will, too."

Her hand went to his hip, lightly pulling, and he responded by turning on his side. Lita was lying on her back; she threw her legs across his body and used her heels to pull herself close, then to pull even closer when he was inside her. She moved with measured slowness, sighing now and then, a small healthy gust of breath, and Longarm lay quite still, contented to feel her inner pulsing wrapping him in soft sensation. She shuddered gently, relaxed, and lay motionless for several minutes. Then she began a slow rotation of her hips, digging her heels into his back, and moved this way until another shudder seized her, quicker this time than before. Once more she lay quiet. Longarm stretched a hand and grasped her breast, its firm smoothness resilient and alive under his palm. He cupped his hand gently, moving it to find the other breast and caress it.

Lita began to quiver. She pulled away and brought her legs up in the air. In the brush between them the waning moon caught glints like dewdrops. "Go in me, Coos-tees!" she gasped. *"Al frente! Con su grifo de caballo! Chíngame duro, presteza! Duro! Duro!"*

Longarm didn't know all the words this time either, but no interpreter was needed. He lunged into her swiftly and fiercely, ignoring her cry of pleasure or pain, arched his back above her and pushed hard, driving deep, the flood building in him forcing him to speed, to thrust, until it crested and burst and Lita's cries of *"Duro! Duro!"* faded to a long, choking moan, and then to silence.

Longarm relaxed, lying heavily on top of her, too spent to move. Lita did not object, but bore his weight with little breaths of pleasure. The moon had gone by now, and the night lay dark and still around them. After a long while, he rolled off and lay by her.

"Tu es mucho hombre, Coos-tees," she murmured, nibbling at the lobe of his ear. "You still think I am *niña,* now?"

"If I ever mistook you for a little girl, I sure know better," he replied. "You're *muy mujer,* Lita."

"I make you feel good, no?"

"You make me feel good, yes. How you feel?"

"You wait a little while, I show you."

Longarm's chuckle was cut short before it got out of his throat. Distantly, the quiet was broken by an irregular thudding of many hooves and the muted blats of cattle protesting being night-driven. He sat up quickly, there was no mistaking the sound.

Lita sat up, too. "What is it, Coos-tees? What you hear?"

"Hush a minute. I'm trying to figure which way they're coming from."

"They come from the *nordeste,* from *los ranchos grandes de Tejas,*" she said casually, as though surprised that Longarm didn't know such a simple fact.

"How do you know?"

"*Por supuesto,* Coos-tees, everybody know this thing. Is happen *muchos veces.* Maybe three, four weeks was *otro hato de ganados* go *sobre del rio.*"

"You mean everybody in Los Perros knows there's cattle being drove across to Mexico pretty regular?"

"*De verdad. Porqué?*"

"Because them steers are rustled, Lita. They're stolen from ranches up along the Pecos and above there."

"*Sí. Esta conozco.* Why you don't ask me, you wan' to know?"

"Because I didn't realize you knew about it." Longarm stood up, pulling Lita to her feet. "Come on, put your clothes on. We got to get out of here."

"*Porqué?* You tired *hace chinga?*"

"No, I ain't tired. If I had my druthers, I'd stay here all night with you. But I got business to look after."

By now, the movement of the cattle herd was much louder. Longarm judged the first riders hazing the steers would be getting to the ford within fifteen or twenty minutes. Dark as it was, there'd be no chance of him and Lita being seen, but the rustlers might have guards, outriders, ahead of the herd, or flanking it, and there was no place on the sandspit for them to hide.

He told Lita, "I'll carry you back to town. I got to go pick up my gear anyhow, get the horse saddled proper." He was pulling on his clothes as he spoke.

"Coos-tees. You go away, now?"

"For a spell. I don't know how long."

"But you come back, no?"

"Sure. I'll be back, soon as I can. You ain't seen the last of me yet, Lita." Then, in sober afterthought, he added, "At least, I hope you ain't."

Longarm dropped Lita off at the spot she pointed out, a shanty a short distance from the plaza. He rode to the corral and in swift silence, working by feel, saddled Tordo. Then he made short work of collecting his bedroll, saddlebags, and rifle from his room. Within little more than half an hour he was back at the sandspit, in time to hear distantly the splashings of the last few steers being driven across the river.

There wasn't enough light for him to tell how many men were riding herd. By the same token, the rustlers wouldn't be able to see him, either, sitting at a safe distance from the crossing, getting his clues from sounds alone. He waited until the hoofbeats and splashings and blattings subsided, and the rustlings in the chamizal on the Mexican side of the border were barely audible. Then he nudged Tordo ahead and across the Rio Grande in pursuit of the stolen herd.

Chapter 10

Following the rustlers was easy, even in the dark. The cattle cut noisily through the belt of chamizal that extended only a mile or two beyond the river, then angled south and west. Longarm stopped in the brush to let the steers and their drivers get safely ahead of him, for after the chamizal ended there was no cover. Past the strip of brush, the land ran level for a score of miles before it rose at the beginning of the foothills of the Serranias de Burro, farther west. It was a harsh plain, as Longarm saw when daybreak came, a place of scanty vegetation, rolling gently between river and foothills, dotted by groves of mesquite scrub and cactus, cut by dry arroyos and an occasional shallow canyon in which there might run a thread-thin stream, more creek than river.

For once, Longarm was pleased with the glacial slowness shown by the army's procurement branch. The ordnance map he carried in his saddlebags dated from the U.S.-Mexican War of 1846, and had been prepared for troops being staged to invade Mexico from the Texas border. It covered the area he was traveling through in very good detail. Studying it, he could figure what he'd do if he was driving a stolen herd to Laredo, and was able to ride unworried at a distance from the rustlers.

There were no settlements within more than sixty miles of the

Burro foothills, no people to see the moving cattle—or the lone rider following them. Somewhere to the south, probably along the Zarro or San Carlos River, he was pretty sure there'd be a ranch used by the ring that ran the new Laredo Loop. They'd need such a place, where brands could be altered and bills of sale forged to allow the cattle to be returned to Texas and sold at the Laredo railhead without questions being raised.

As he'd expected, the rustlers turned the herd almost due south after angling in from the border. Longarm's map had led him to the most likely place ahead of the slower-moving herd; he'd gotten to the shallow valley he'd guessed would be their path just before sunup. Finding a cut in which to hide the dapple, Longarm had waited an hour before the steers passed by, a good three-quarters of a mile distant, too far to see anything except the dust cloud they'd raised in passing. He'd leaned back, resting against a convenient rock, while he chewed jerky and hardtack and sipped from the canteen. He'd given up wishing for a cheroot. After having failed to find any at Fort Lancaster or Los Perros, he'd reminded himself philosophically that he'd intended to give up the damned things, anyhow.

Stomach filled, he'd dozed. There was no great hurry. The herd would leave an easy trail to follow, and he'd had a busy day and night. When he woke up, he was sweating; the sun was blazing clear in a bowl of cloudless blue. The trail ahead promised to be a hot one, and his map told him it led through a baked, water-scarce land. He was splashing water from his cupped hand into Tordo's mouth when the riders passed. Sunlight glinting from a bit or strap buckle, or perhaps from the silver conchos of a hatband, alerted him to their approach. Their path was too close for comfort, he thought. He led the gray deeper into the narrow arroyo and clamped a hand over his muzzle. He wasn't sure whether Tordo had the habit of whinnying at the approach of strange horses; he'd never been with the gray in a situation like this before. The restraining hand eliminated a needless risk.

There were four riders. Longarm watched their backs as they loped their mounts in a direction that would take them straight to the ford, and wished he could've seen their faces. Old son, he told himself, those hombres backtracking has got to mean just one thing. They've left the steers with two or three men up along the trail, and there'll be another herd crew taking over to push the critters on to their headquarters. And that's the place I want to find.

Mounting, he set Tordo to a trail-burning lope, picking up the broad path of droppings and faint hoofprints that the steers had left. He kept a close watch for dust ahead of him, but saw none. Instead, after he'd covered four or five miles, he saw the thin line of smoke from a small fire rising from a canyon half a mile ahead. Neither riders nor steers were visible. Longarm risked riding almost to the rim of the canyon before dismounting. He looped Tordo's reins over a mesquite limb and took his rifle from the scabbard that hung slanted in front of the saddle. Dodging from one area of scant cover to the next, he worked his way slowly to the rim.

A small creek, little more than a series of bathtub-sized pools connected by a trickle that in places narrowed to a hand's width, ran through the canyon. Steers straggled along the creek. Some drank from the pools, some looked for graze on the barren soil, others just stood staring vacantly into nowhere. Longarm couldn't see all the brands, but he noted that at least five were represented in the herd. It was a typical rustler's herd, small enough to be moved quickly and quietly by just a handful of men.

At one of the pools upstream from where the herd milled, two men squatted beside a tiny campfire. A tin skillet sat canted on a boulder near them, beside the tiny blaze that had drawn Longarm to the spot. Their horses were unsaddled, tethered to a bush a few paces from the fire. The men were eating from tin plates.

Their backs were to him, so Longarm took his time studying the way the land lay. There were no boulders or rock outcroppings near the fire big enough to give the two any kind of cover. Their rifles were with their saddles, beside the tethered horses. He had the advantage of both position and surprise, and the need for information outweighed the easier alternative of dogging the rustled herd to the gang's headquarters. Longarm sighted quickly and sent a slug from the Winchester into the skillet.

Amid splinters of rock and with a metallic clanging that started the steers jumping and running aimlessly, the skillet bounced three feet into the air. The men dropped their plates and leaped to their feet, hands reaching for revolver butts.

"Get your hands up! First one that touches his gun's a dead man!" Longarm shouted. He was still hidden by the boulder behind which he'd crouched to survey the camp.

His call stopped the rustlers' hands in midair. Slowly their arms went up, and they turned carefully to face the direction from which the command had come. Longarm wasn't too greatly surprised to see that one of the pair was Lefty. He'd been very sure, after Lita's revelation of the night, that Sheriff Tucker was involved in the rustling ring, and Tucker had sent Lefty off with a reminder of a job that waited for him.

When he was sure that both men were frozen into position, Longarm stood up and stepped from behind the boulder. Keeping the men covered by his Winchester, he began to pick his way across the bare, rock-strewn ground down the sloping canyon sides.

Lefty's companion said something to the deputy when Longarm had closed half the distance between them, but Longarm was too far away to hear the remark or Lefty's answer. He called, "Keep your mouths shut! If I get the idea you're framing to jump me when I get close, my trigger finger might get sorta nervous!"

There was no more conversation between the two. Longarm was within thirty yards of them when the steer locoed. He hadn't noticed the animal in particular; all along the creek there were cattle running and snorting, disturbed by his shot. The one that panicked hadn't done anything to attract attention; it just reacted in the way half-wild range cattle do at the sight of a moving man on foot. The steer pawed the ground, bellowed, and charged Longarm from a distance of less than fifty feet.

Longarm swiveled and dropped the animal with a single quick shot, but the diversion gave the unknown rustler the chance for which he must've been watching. The instant Longarm swung his rifle to shoot the locoed steer, the rustler dropped his arms and drew.

Longarm caught the move in the corner of his eye and dove for the dirt. He rolled twice before snapshooting. The rustler's slug kicked up dust where Longarm had recently been, but the man dropped before he could get off a second shot. Longarm lay still, his rifle ready. The downed outlaw didn't move. Neither did Lefty. He'd seen Longarm shoot before, and kept his hands safely in the air.

Keeping the deputy covered, Longarm rose to his feet. He walked slowly toward the men, his eyes darting from one to the other. Ten feet from the campfire, he stopped.

"All right, Lefty. Seems like I sorta got in the habit of taking your gun away from you. Lift it out easy, and toss it over here."

Lefty obeyed. When the pistol lay on the ground at Longarm's feet, he said, "I told that damn fool not to try it. He got itchy, soon as he saw you was by yourself. Wanted both of us to throw down on you, but I told him I wanted to live awhile longer."

Longarm nodded. "You was smart, for a change. Who's your friend?"

"Name's Sanchez, and that's all I know. Never heard anybody call him anything else."

"Is he dead?"

Sanchez answered the question with an involuntary twitching. Longarm took two quick steps and kicked the fallen rustler's pistol out of reach. He took his eyes off Lefty long enough to glance at the downed outlaw. Blood was seeping through Sanchez's shirt. The rifle slug had taken him in the side, between his belt and bottom rib. Sanchez was beginning to groan.

"You better see what you can do to help him, Lefty," Longarm ordered. "Probably he ain't worth saving, but maybe he'll live long enough to hang."

Lefty bent over Sanchez, loosened the man's belt, and pulled his clothing aside to uncover the wound. "He's lucky," Lefty said, then added, somewhat doubtfully, "I guess."

Longarm's bullet had plowed through the flesh just above Sanchez's hipbone. It was too shallow to have hit a vital spot. The wound would hurt and perhaps disable the man for a while, but it was a long way from being fatal.

"Put some kind of bandage on him," Longarm told Lefty. "He'll live long enough to tell me a few things I'm curious to know.'"

While Lefty worked over the wounded man, Longarm collected the rifles and pistols belonging to the pair and carried them far enough from the fire so they'd be out of diving distance. There was a coffeepot propped on a stone behind the boulder off which he'd shot the frying pan. He set the pot on the dying fire and rinsed out one of the tin cups that lay by it while he waited for the coffee to heat.

Lefty stood up. "I guess I got him stopped bleeding. He's gonna be sore as hell for a while, though."

"It's his own fault," Longarm said unemotionally. "Only a damn fool tries to draw on a man who's got him covered with a rifle."

"You are wrong, *gringo*." Sanchez's voice was weak, but his tone was positive. "Is better a bullet under the sky with my hands free than a rope in a jailyard."

"Can't say I'd argue that," Longarm replied. "Except that a man's better off not setting hisself up for a rope to start with."

"Look here, Custis," Lefty broke in, "just who in hell are you? You damn sure ain't some drifter that just happened to wind up in Los Perros accidental-like. I'm guessing you're either an enforcer from the cattleman's association, or a lawman of some kind."

Longarm had decided the time had come to begin working on his primary assignment. To get Lefty started talking, he'd have to tell him who he was, and that revelation couldn't be delayed much longer. If he had to keep the word from being passed to Tucker, he'd hustle the deputy past Los Perros on the Mexican side of the river and put him in Roy Bean's jail up to the north, or even haul him to Fort Lancaster.

"That's a good guess," he told Lefty. "You just know the first part of my name, for openers. Custis Long is the full handle, and I'm a deputy U.S. marshal working out of Denver." He took out his wallet and showed his badge.

"You're a hell of a ways from home base."

"Not so's you'd notice, or that it'd make much of a nevermind. Los Perros is like a lot of places, it ain't organized by the state, so that leaves it under federal jurisdiction."

"You checking out the rustling? Or hot on Ed's trail?"

"What I'm really here for is to run down a cavalry captain named Hill, who took off from Fort Lancaster after a couple of his troopers deserted. And there's a Texas Ranger missing, too, name's Nate Webster. That's what got me interested in your rustling ring; Webster was checking to see if the Laredo Loop was working again when he dropped outa sight."

"Jesus! Ed thought him and his partners over here in Mexico was too smart for anybody to catch up with so quick. They figured they'd be able to go five or six years before the law come noseying around, and here it ain't been quite two years."

"Tucker didn't fool anybody. I had him figured for one of the kingpins in the rustling after I'd talked to him for ten minutes."

Lefty sighed. "Yeah. Ed's got sorta careless of late. He ain't the man he was, six, eight years ago."

"That's why you and Spud began scheming to push him out, I'd imagine," Longarm said.

"It was mostly Spud's idea."

Longarm remembered Lefty's efforts to shift the blame for the attempted attack by Luis onto Spud. He recognized Lefty's value as the weak link in Tucker's outfit and pressed on. "This is as good a time as any for you to tell me about the whole setup," he told the deputy. "And I mean all of it, including the Mexican side."

"Sanchez can tell you more about that than I can. He knows it better."

"How about it?" Longarm asked the wounded Mexican. "You ready to talk?"

"*Chinga su madre, federalista!* You don' get nothin' out of me!" Sanchez spat.

Longarm tried reason. "I'll find out soon enough without you helping me, Sanchez. But if you talk, it might save you from hanging."

"*No soy graznido, hombre! No dice nada, nada, nada!*"

"You might as well spill what you know," Lefty advised Sanchez. "I seen this fellow work. He'll find out what he wants, one way or the other."

"*Cago en su boca,* Lefty. *Ahorita, no hablo Inglés.*" Sanchez turned his face away. Longarm knew he'd get nothing more out of the man until he'd had time to apply a lot more persuasion.

"I don't need you to tell me anything," he told the Mexican. "You and your friends left a trail a tenderfoot can follow." He turned back to Lefty. "You going to do like him, or you going to be smart?"

"What'll it get me if I tell you?"

"It might not get you much, except save you a stretched neck."

"Well, shit! I guess I might as well. Ask ahead."

"We can save the rustling part till later," Longarm said. "But you can start by telling me about those four men I'm looking for."

"Spud's the one that'll have to tell you about them nigger bluecoats," Lefty began.

"No. You better tell me, right now!"

"Hell, I don't know where they are!"

"Make a real good guess, then. But do it now. Don't waste my time, or I might run outa patience with you."

"Well." Lefty saw he was cornered. "You know how Spud and Ed is about niggers."

"No, I don't. I might guess, but I'd rather hear you say it."

"They're old Quantrill riders, and anybody who was with *him* ain't exactly what you'd call a nigger lover. Spud's worse'n most, though, I guess. Anyhow, them troopers made two or three real bad mistakes. They come into Los Perros, that's number one.

They strutted into Baskin's saloon, that's number two. Then they sassed Spud, and that's number three. You ain't goin' to find them troopers, not ever, Marshal."

"You still haven't told me what Spud did."

"When they give him hard lip in the saloon, he cut one of 'em down, right then and there. He made the other one tote the body out in the brush somewheres. Don't ask me whereabouts, because Spud never told me, and I had sense enough not to ask him. Anyhow, the live one never come back."

"You're pretty sure Spud killed him, too?"

"Sure as God made little apples. He just as good as told me he did. Spud was havin' one of his mean spells right then, so I didn't wanta rile him by askin' questions."

"All right." Mentally, Longarm wrote off the two deserters. That left two men still missing. "What about Captain Hill? And the Ranger, Nate Webster?"

"They both come through Los Perros all right. The Ranger was the first one to show up, about a month before the army man. Both of 'em visited with Ed, but I don't know what they talked about. He never did tell me. Only thing I'm sure of, the Ranger was in town one day and gone the next, and the captain was, too."

"You're not exactly a gold mine of information, Lefty," Longarm observed. "You'll have to do better than that."

"So help me, Marshal, I'm tellin' you all I know. I can't tell you things I don't know, now can I?"

"You were on the inside, Lefty. Put your mind to it. I'm right sure you'll remember a few things you've forgot."

"Well . . ." the deputy frowned. "I did hear Ed say he'd sent the Ranger kitin' off on a wild-goose chase over the river."

"That's better. Where, over the river?"

"He didn't say where. Just Mexico, something like that."

"What about Hill? Did Tucker give him the same treatment?"

"Just about. Ed knew Spud had killed them troopers, you see. He had to get the captain outa town fast, before he could ask too many questions. So Ed made out the men had hightailed it right on through town and across the river."

"Then the captain followed the trail Tucker gave him?"

"Well, you couldn't call it a trail. He didn't aim the bluecoat in any special direction, the way I got it. And that's all I know, Marshal. It's God's own truth, that's all I can tell you!"

"It all hangs together," Longarm nodded. "And I don't think you're a good enough liar to make up a yarn like that, Lefty."

"If you was to string me up right here and now, I couldn't tell you no more," Lefty said fervently.

"All right. Let's get to this rustling business. Looks to me like you and your friend Sanchez are waiting for a bunch of hands to come and drive this herd on south. Is that right?"

Sanchez spoke for the first time since he'd disclaimed any more knowledge of English. *"Este hijo de puta, Esquivel! Es su tacha!"*

Longarm asked Sanchez, "Who's Esquivel?" When the man didn't answer, he said to Lefty, "I don't need to be told that, I guess. I'd say Esquivel's the fellow that was supposed to be here to meet you, ain't he? To take the herd on south?"

Lefty nodded: "Yeah. Him and his bunch was supposed to be here by sunup. Spud and our boys had to start back by then."

"What about you, Lefty? Were you going to collect Tucker's payoff here, or were you going to the headquarters place for it?"

"Lefty!" Sanchez warned. *"No mandaté esto!"*

"Hell, Sanch, it won't hurt to tell him," Lefty said. "I was goin' along with Esquivel. It's near enough so's I could be back in Los Perros early tomorrow."

Longarm didn't comment on the deputy's remark, though it pinpointed for him the location of the rustlers' headquarters. All he'd have to do was study his map and find a spot where there was plenty of water, within a four- or five-hour ride. Instead, he asked, "How many's coming with this Esquivel hombre?"

"I don't know. Four or five, I guess. Ed didn't say."

"Then, if you—" Longarm began.

A shout from the canyon rim interrupted him. He looked around, and saw four riflemen standing, shielded by boulders, their guns leveled.

"Damn!" he snapped. "Looks like I waited too long to start us heading back to the river! That'd be your pal Esquivel!"

Sanchez started to laugh, though the effort brought a grimace of pain to his face. "You a fool to waste time, *gringo!* Now it is you who will get *el tiro,* not me!"

Longarm looked at the opposite rim of the canyon. Two more men were posted there, rifles covering the camp. His own Winchester was leaning against the rock where he'd put it when he heated the coffee. He estimated his chance of surviving if he tried for it, and gave up the idea. Suicide wasn't in his plans.

A horseman appeared behind the men on the south rim of the canyon. Motioning them to follow him, he walked his horse down the slope. When he'd gotten close enough for Longarm and the others to see him clearly, Sanchez let out a despairing moan.

"Sangre de la Virgen! No es Esquivel! Ahora todos tomen el tiro! Ellos son rurales!"

Chapter 11

When he heard Sanchez's words, Longarm felt better about everything. The *rurales,* the Mexican Federal Rural Police, occupied a position similar to that of the federal marshals in the United States. They operated out of a number of strategically located field headquarters scattered throughout Mexico, and answered only to the national government. He watched the mounted rurales approach with the feeling that after he'd identified himself and explained everything, they'd give him what help was needed to capture the rustler force that was now on its way and long overdue.

Lefty said in a whisper, "God a-mighty, Marshal! If Sanchez is right, we're in trouble up to our assholes now!"

"You and Sanchez, maybe. There ain't no way that bunch your man Esquivel's bringing along can stand up to these fellows."

"Is that how you figure?" Lefty shook his head, and with a sincerity that Longarm knew couldn't be put on, said, "Don't fool yourself for a minute. They won't help you. Shit, they won't like you because you're a gringo and in Mexico. I tell you, the only thing the rurales gives a fuck about is the rurales."

"What're you driving at, Lefty? They're federal police; so am I, only from another country. If you're trying to spook me, get me to help you outa this jackpot by telling them you and me are working together, you're about to be disappointed."

"You ever run up against the rurales before?"

"Sure. About four years ago, when I come down here on another case. They were real helpful. I tagged 'em as a pretty good outfit."

"Four years ago, they was. That's before Diaz got to be boss of Mexico again. The rurales is his boys now, just like me and Spud and the rest of our bunch is Ed Tucker's men. And if you think he's a bad one, you don't know what bad is, yet."

Longarm wasn't convinced that the deputy could be believed, but told himself that he'd find out soon enough. The rider coming down the slope was almost within speaking distance. He carried a pistol in one hand, but a rifle was slung across his back. His men were still only halfway down from the rim; they were moving cautiously, keeping their weapons ready. The horseman reined in and looked at Longarm, Lefty, and Sanchez for a moment before speaking.

"*Qué tenemos aquí?*" he finally asked. "*Quien hace tiros oíagamos un momento pasado?*"

"He wants to know who was doin' the shooting a while back," Lefty translated for Longarm. "What you want me to say, Marshal?"

"I'll do my own talking," Longarm replied curtly. He asked the rurale, "You speak English, mister? *Habla Inglés?*"

"*Sí, un poco.* A little bit, I speak."

"It was me done that shooting." Longarm spoke slowly and distinctly; in a situation like this he didn't trust his slight knowledge of Spanish, even though a lot of it had come back to him since he'd arrived on the border. "I'm a deputy U.S. marshal. Same kinda job you got, understand?" The rurale gave no evidence that he was following the explanation, so Longarm went on, "If you won't get trigger-nerved, I'll reach in my pocket and show you my badge."

His brow knitted, the rurale said, "*Un federalista de los Estados Unidos?* You can prove this thing you say?"

Moving very slowly indeed, Longarm pulled his coat lapel aside and took out his wallet. He flipped it open to show the badge pinned in its fold. "Here. Look at it."

"*Damelό,*" the man commanded. "Give me to it."

Longarm stepped up and handed over the wallet. The rurale

took it, examined the badge carefully, opened the folded wallet, and looked at the money it contained.

"*Muy interesante*," he grunted. A grin began to form on his face. "Anybody can carry a badge, *hombre*." He put the wallet in his pocket. "I keep this for now."

"Wait a minute!" Longarm protested. "That's my badge and my money you got there!"

"*No apasarse, hombre*. I weel take good care of it. And your gun, too." He turned, saw that his men were now just behind him, and ordered one of them, "*Tóme su pistola*." He indicated the rifles that were off to one side, the pistols lying on the ground near them. To another of his men, he said, "*Los fusiles y pistolas ayá, ponerles*."

Both men moved quickly to obey, one starting for Longarm, the other to collect the rest of the guns. When the rurale who was taking Longarm's Colt saw the gold watch chain snaked across his vest, the man reached for it greedily. The commander saw the move.

"*Cuidado, Felipe! Este botin toca al Capitán Ramos! El no le gusta si tome el reloj del gringo!*" he called.

His threat was enough to cause the rurale to pull his hand back as if the watch chain were red-hot. Longarm caught enough of what the commander said to deduce that he wasn't going to be searched thoroughly until he was in the presence of the captain himself. He reminded himself to try to find an opportunity to drop the watch into the pocket that held his derringer, so the chain wouldn't be so highly visible.

There was a moment of inaction while the men who'd taken the guns showed them to their leader. He hefted Longarm's Colt, but didn't find it to his liking, for he waved the weapons away with a disgusted grunt. Longarm used the pause to study the mounted rurale.

He didn't really like what he saw. The commander wore a gold-embroidered charro outfit, short jacket, tight pants, high-crowned felt sombrero, calf-high boots. This seemed to be the uniform of the rurales, though none of the men wore garments as elaborately decorated as that of their leader; what braiding their jackets and hats showed was predominantly silver with an occasional golden accent stitch. It wasn't the commander's clothing that stirred Longarm's concern, but the man's face. He had the cold, slitted eyes that Longarm had seen in the faces of killers who enjoyed their work;

he'd looked into eyes like that too many times to misread their significance. The rurale's face was razor-thin, with a long nose and jutting jaw punctuated by an untrimmed mustache. Longarm bet himself that the man's lips were even thinner than his nose, though he couldn't see them.

"Bueno," the commander said, after his men had bundled the captured weapons for one of their number to carry. He turned his gaze on Longarm. "You say you are *Tejano—"*

"No," Longarm interrupted. "That ain't what I said. My office is in Denver, Colorado, it ain't in Texas at all."

"No significa, hombre. You tell me you are *federalista de los Estados Unidos,* you show me badge, *verdad?* So, now you tell me what you do in my country?"

"I was trailing them stolen steers you're looking at. Them two fellows there, along with some others who've already left, were driving the animals from the U.S. side of the Rio Grande to someplace south of here."

"De verdad? And you make the shootings my men and me we hear while we ride by on our patrol, yes?"

"Yes. That one on the ground cut down on me and I had to wing him. The hole I put in him ain't going to kill him, but if you aim to save him for hanging, you better get him to a doctor to fix it up."

Looking down at Sanchez, the rurale asked, *"Es verdico, el gringo? O es mientrador?"* Sanchez said nothing. The rurale frowned. *"Cabrón! Repuestamé!"*

Lefty spoke for the first time. "Sanchez wouldn't know if the marshal was lyin' or not. He's tellin' you the truth, though."

"Es posible. Es posible tu es mientirador también. Díme verdad, hombre, tu es otro ladron de ganados, no?"

"No, I ain't no rustler! And I ain't lyin' about the marshal. And I'm a law officer, too. Outa Los Perros!"

With a wolfish smile, the leader shook his head slowly. *"Ay,* Los Perros! *El jefe Tucker, no?"*

"Yeah, Sheriff Tucker. I guess you know who he is?" Lefty retorted.

"Sí. Tan mas bueno."

"He's one of Tucker's men, all right," Longarm said. "But he was working with the rustlers."

"He is not with you?" the rurale asked.

"Hell, no! He was with the bunch I was trailing!"

"Pues, es ladron de ganados." Over his shoulder, the commander called, *"Pónese las manillas, esto y el herido."*

Longarm watched Lefty being shackled. He half wished he'd felt able to trust the deputy, but he'd learned by bitter experience that it was a fool's game to depend on a born liar, and a weakling to boot. He felt a little better when the commander didn't order him to be handcuffed. There's a good chance the captain at his headquarters will understand things better, Longarm thought hopefully. Then, to try the leader's temper, he said, "Well, now you got things straight, suppose you give me back my badge and my guns. I'll ride to your headquarters with you, and tell your captain what this is all about."

"Is not so easy like that," the rurale replied. "If you are what you say, you have invade Mexico. This is serious crime, *hombre.* I take you to *mi capitán,* along with these two others."

Longarm snorted. "Like hell, I invaded Mexico! You act like I'm a whole damn army! I was chasing crooks that I guess broke Mexican laws, just like they did ours!"

"Mexico needs no help to enforce our laws from the *gringos.*"

"Well, are you arresting me, or what?" Longarm demanded.

"Quien sabe?" The commander shrugged. "We see what Capitán Ramos want to do with you."

A cry from Sanchez drew the attention of both Longarm and the rurale. The man who was putting the handcuffs on the injured man was lifting Sanchez to his feet. When the rurale let go, Sanchez gave another cry and dropped to the ground.

"Madre de Diós!" he groaned. *"No puedo andar, no puedo cabalagar!"*

"Otra vez!" the leader ordered.

Again Sanchez was helped to his feet, and again he collapsed with a loud moan.

"Creo que es verdad, no puede andar," the rurale said.

"Pues, 'sta bien. Mátale," the commander ordered.

Without changing his expression, the rurale who'd been helping Sanchez picked up the rifle he'd laid aside while putting on the handcuffs and shot Sanchez through the head.

Longarm stared unbelieving. "You didn't have to do that," he told the commander. "Where I come from, we don't execute people until a court finds they're guilty."

"In Mexico, we are not so soft," the rurale replied calmly. "We don' waste the time of a judge on a *pelado* like that one." He turned back to the executioner, who was taking off Sanchez's cartridge belt, and called, "*Ándale, hombre!*" Then, to Longarm, "We go now."

"Ain't you even going to bury him?"

"*Porqué? Los zopilotes*, they got to eat, too."

"What about them other rustlers? The ones that's supposed to come get the steers? Seems to me you'd wait and take them in, too."

"*Hombre*, you say they come. How I know you don' lie? So, we ride now. I take you to *el capitán*."

There was no chance for Longarm to talk to Lefty during the ride to the rurales' headquarters; the leader kept them separated. Nor did Longarm have a chance to talk further with the commander himself. The patrol leader rode ahead of his men, and Longarm was kept between two of the rurales who ignored or did not understand what he said when he made an effort to talk with them.

Longarm used his eyes instead of his mouth. He watched the route they took, which was not a road, but a narrow horse trail that led them southwest, across the low humps of the Burro Mountains foothills. He was pretty sure he could find his way back from the rurales' headquarters, a ride of almost two hours. The headquarters was not an imposing sight. The patrol pulled rein in front of a small cluster of buildings, low-walled adobe structures with vigas protruding little more than head-high. The vigas, beams made of tree trunks, supported roofs that were built up from layers of brush covered with packed layers of dirt. There were three large buildings in the cluster. A corral stood a little distance away, and still farther off, apart from the larger structures, was a straggle of shanties much like those that made up Los Perros.

Neither Longarm nor Lefty were allowed to dismount at once. The patrol's commander disappeared into the building by which they'd stopped while his men stayed on their horses, silently watching the prisoners. After what seemed a long wait, the commander came out. He pointed at Lefty.

"*Tómelo al cárcel,*" he ordered. "*El capitán quiere hablar con el otro gringo.*" To Longarm, he said, "You come talk to *el capitán.*"

Longarm had to duck his head to get through the doorway as he followed the rurale inside. The interior of the building was no more imposing than the outside. Small, narrow windows were set high in the end walls of the big room that stretched across the entire width of the structure. In the wall opposite the entrance, doors led into other rooms, but they were closed, and Longarm could only guess that they might be a kitchen, a bedroom, a private office, perhaps. The inner walls, like the outer, were unpainted, covered with a thin coat of adobe plaster through which the outlines of the adobe bricks showed clearly. The place might have been a fort; indeed, Longarm guessed that it had been at one time, during one of Mexico's wars or revolutions, some kind of minor stronghold or outpost.

When he was shoved by the patrol commander into the front sala, Longarm's eyes were almost useless until they adjusted from the harsh outdoor sunlight to the room's dimness. The man sitting behind the wide, imposing table at one end of the room was a formless blob for a few moments. As Longarm's eyes adjusted, he saw the table first. It was an imposing piece of furniture, eight feet long and half as wide, with massive carved legs at ends and center. Its once glossy mahogany top still bore traces of a fine varnished finish, though now it was scratched and scarred to expose bare wood in places. He wondered how the table had found its way into such surroundings, and decided it must have been looted from some rich family's hacienda.

His voice a deep rumble in the quiet room, the man behind the table said, "*Sergento* Molina have tell me you say you are a *federalista* officer from the United States. Is true, what you tell him?"

"Sure it's true." Longarm blinked to speed the clearing of his vision. For the first time he could now see the captain clearly.

He saw a man who was grossly fat. Ramos's belly pushed out the cloth of the waist-length charro jacket he wore; his was even more ornately embroidered with gold than that of the patrol leader's. Tufts of black hair stuck through the gaps between his shirt buttons, and the shirt itself was grease-stained. His face was moon-round, his eyes encased in pouches of fat that squeezed them thin. Under a wide, scarred nose he sported the narrow, waxed mustache of a dandy. Above a round chin that was almost buried by two other chins beneath it, his mouth was like that of a frog.

Longarm's Colt and Winchester lay on the table in front of the captain. Longarm was tempted to grab for the Colt, but saw Molina watching him closely, and resisted the temptation. He realized that they were probably hoping for him to make just such a move. That, he thought, might be why they put the guns so handy—after they took all the shells out. He looked on the table for the wallet, but it was not there.

He told the captain, "My name's Custis Long, Deputy U.S. Marshal outa Denver, Colorado. Who in hell are you?"

"I am *Capitán* Ernando Ramos, of the *Policia Federal Rural de Mexico*. And you will speak respectfully to me, *gringo!*"

"No disrespect intended, Captain. I just like to know who's talking to me when I'm on official business."

"There is no such thing as a *federalista* of your country having official business in mine, unless he has the permit from my government. Do you have such permission?"

"Can't say I have. Didn't know I'd have to chase a bunch of cattle rustlers into your country, Captain. They started out in mine, and I just followed along. One of them thieves was Mexican, you see, and I don't expect he had official permission to be in my country."

"You can prove you are what you claim to be? You can prove what you say about the rustlers?"

"Well, I showed your sergeant the steers. They all had U.S. brands on 'em. They're still back in the canyon where your men jumped us."

Captain Ramos looked at the sergeant. *"Es verdad, Vicente?"*

Molina shrugged. *"Quien sabe, mi Capitán? Eran ganados, sí. No conozco que será estolada."*

"You didn't let me finish," Longarm said. "This sergeant told one of your men to kill the rustler who could've told you where his gang hangs out. He was the Mexican I was telling you about, if you're interested."

"Un pelado," Molina said with another shrug. *"Herido por este gringo. No puede andar o cabalagar. Tal vez, acerca de muerte."*

"You have hear what *Sergento* Molina say," Ramos told Longarm.

"I heard him, but I didn't understand him. I don't talk your language, Captain, outside of a word or so."

"He say you shoot this man first, and he is about to die."

"Oh, I winged him, sure. He was trying to shoot me, is why."

"To kill a man in my country is murder. Is not so in yours?"

Suddenly, Longarm realized he might be fighting for his life. The shock of learning that the rurales, far from cooperating with a lawman from across the border, were treating him like a criminal, had clouded his thinking. Choosing his words carefully, he said, "I'd call it self-defense. A man's got a right to defend himself in any country I ever heard of."

"We will have to study this question, no? So. You say you are *federalista* from your country. You can prove this?"

"Your sergeant's got my wallet. It's got my badge in it." As he spoke, Longarm hoped the badge was indeed still in its usual place.

Again the captain turned to Molina. *"Tienes el mochila?"*

Stepping up to the table, the sergeant handed over Longarm's wallet. Ramos flipped it open to examine the badge, still in place. He studied the engraved legend carefully. Then he opened the currency compartment and found it empty. Longarm started to protest; he knew there'd been just over $200 in it when he'd surrendered it to Molina. Before he could object, he thought better of the idea. No use in muddying up the water over a little thing like money, when keeping his mouth shut might make Molina feel uneasy. It could work both ways, though, he reminded himself. If he gets nervous, he might want to get rid of you, instead of going easy because you didn't give him away for a thief.

"Does your government not provide you with money?" Ramos asked. He sounded disappointed.

"All I got to do is show my badge at a bank and sign for what cash I need," Longarm lied, gambling that Ramos wouldn't know.

"This badge you say is yours, it looks like it might be real," the captain said thoughtfully. "But how to prove it? Eh?"

"All you got to do is send a telegram to my boss in Denver. Or to Washington, if that's what it takes to satisfy you."

"Ay, quá malo!" Ramos sighed. "Our small outpost, it does not have the telegraph wire."

"Then send one of your men to the closest station. How far'd that be, anyhow?"

"Much too distant," Ramos frowned. Then he brightened. "Now. I will tell you what you must do. You must write the letter to your ambassador in our capital."

"Hell, he never heard of me," Longarm objected. "It'll save time to wire Denver or Washington. A letter'd take too long to get there. It'd be next summer before you'd get an answer."

"We will do it the way I say." Ramos's voice was firm. "I will tell you what to put down."

"I can write it myself," Longarm grumbled.

"Maybe it is that you do not understand. In this letter, the words must be chosen so your government will not make the mistake."

Longarm was suddenly suspicious. "Hold up. Just what kind of letter is it you want me to write?"

"You will see," the captain promised him. "Vicente! Bring a chair for this one." When Longarm was seated at the table across from Ramos, the rurale captain produced paper from a drawer, as well as an old-fashioned quill pen and inkwell. He slid the paper across to Longarm and placed the inkwell in front of him. "Now. You will write as I say you to."

Longarm dipped the quill in the ink and began writing. Ramos reached across the table, grabbed the pen from his hand, and crumpled the paper angrily. His face was livid.

"You will learn to obey my commands! Vicente! *Un gólpe en la cabeza por el gringo!*"

Before Longarm could move, Molina rapped him sharply on the head with his pistol butt. Longarm started to rise, but the sergeant flipped the pistol by its trigger guard and Longarm found himself staring into the muzzle.

"*Sientese!*" Molina growled, motioning with the pistol. Longarm sat down.

Ramos gritted threateningly, "If you need more lessons, you will get them!" He returned the pen to Longarm and shoved over a fresh sheet of paper. "Now. Write this time as I tell you! Not a word more, not a word less!"

"All right. I got the idea. Your man won't need to whop me again," Longarm said. On the fresh sheet, he wrote to Ramos's careful dictation:

"His Excellency, Ambassador of the United States. I am an agent of the federal government. I have murdered—"

Longarm threw down the pen. "To hell with that, Ramos! I ain't murdered anybody! It was one of your men shot Sanchez! All I did was wing him a little bit!"

Ramos studied the vigas in the ceiling. "How you would like it if I write your ambassador, to tell him I regret you have been kill by *los ladrones de ganados?* Do not forget where you are, *gringo!* Think a moment. If I tell Vicente, or any of my men, to take you somewhere from here and to shoot you, do you think they disobey me?"

Longarm remembered the instant obedience of the rurale

who'd been ordered to kill Sanchez. He was beginning to see that he'd underestimated both the power and malevolence of the captain. It gritted on him to knuckle under, but it was better to do that than to die without a chance to fight back.

Still, he decided he'd balk at murder. He said to Ramos, "I'll tell you what, Captain. I'll write down I shot Sanchez, but damned if I'll say I murdered him, because I didn't."

Ramos thought about this for a moment. Then he nodded. "*Esta bién*. But the rest, it must be as I say."

When Longarm finished the letter, brushing up Ramos's wording a bit, it read:

> *I have shot a citizen of Mexico. Because I am an official of our country, the officers of Mexico where I am in prison do not wish to cause sorrow to the United States government by executing me for my crime. They will free me if the United States pays the expenses to which Mexico has been put in conducting my arrest and trial. The expenses are in the amount of 15,000 dollars in gold. You will send this money at once to Capitán Ernando Ramos, at the rurale district headquarters in the state of Coahuila. The money must be paid within one month, or I will be executed. Mr. Ambassador, I appeal to you to save me from this death.*

As he wrote, Longarm's amazement increased. It was clear to him that Ramos hadn't the slightest idea how diplomats worked. Longarm didn't have very much of an idea himself, but once when he'd arrested a Canadian citizen up in Montana the man had appealed to his country's ambassador and the result had been a ruckus that the President himself had had to step in and settle. Longarm kept his grin inward, but he was pretty sure Captain Ramos was in for one damned big shock when this ransom demand was delivered.

"I will read every word before you sign your name," Ramos said, holding out his hand.

Longarm handed him the letter. "It's just what you told me to say."

Ramos read carefully, and finally nodded his satisfaction. He returned the letter. "Now, you will sign your name and put under it your official title. I will send it by a messenger. In three weeks, a month, when the gold is delivered, you will be free."

In a pig's ass, I will, Longarm thought. Once this bastard gets that gold, or gets an answer saying there won't be none coming, I'll get shot accidentally while I'm trying to make a getaway.

Forcing a cheerful smile, he said, "Well, I done what you said, Captain. Now, I guess you'll have a place for me to stay while we're waiting. And a good square meal'd taste mighty good right now."

Ramos smiled without sympathy. "You must have see when you get here, we have little space. But you will have a place to stay." He snapped his fingers in the direction of the sergeant. "Vicente. *Cerrase in el cárcel!*"

Chapter 12

If Captain Ramos's office had been dim, the jail was definitely dark. The squat, square adobe structure had only one window, which was at the end of a corridor onto which the two slat-steel barred cells on each side of the building opened. The cell into which Longarm was thrust stood at the end of the building near the door, so it was farthest from the tiny window. In the dim light that seeped reluctantly from the little opening fifteen feet away, Longarm couldn't see anything during the first moments after Molina clanged the metal door closed behind him and left through the main door.

From the darkness a voice said, "If we're going to be cell-mates, I guess you better tell us who you are and what you're in here for."

"Damned if you don't sound like an American!" Longarm exclaimed, squinting through the gloom. He thought there were two others in the cell with him, but couldn't yet be sure.

"We're both Americans," a second voice spoke up. "I'm John Hill, Captain, 10th Cavalry, U.S. Army."

"And I'm Nate Webster, Texas Rangers," the first voice said. "Now, who're you?"

"Custis Long, Deputy U.S. Marshal, Denver office. And you two men don't know how much trouble you saved me!"

"Listen to him talk about trouble!" Hill said dryly. "Wait'll you've been in here awhile, Long. You'll find out what trouble really is!"

"I didn't mean it that way," Longarm explained. "You're the fellows I was sent down here to locate."

"Well, glory be!" Webster exclaimed. "It's about time somebody tumbled we were missing. Wait a minute, though. How come Bert Matthews went to the federals for help? Why didn't he send one of our own boys after me?"

"Same reason the army didn't send a cavalry troop after the captain, here. You Rangers and the army both fought the Mexicans in wars. I guess they figured if they sent one deputy marshal, it wasn't going to look like an invasion. On top of that, nobody on the other side of the Rio Grande knew where the hell you two had got off to."

"I'll tell you something," Webster said. "I wouldn't mind leading a Ranger company against this bunch Ramos runs here."

"Amen to that," Hill said. "I'd like to have a platoon under me with orders to clean house here."

"It needs a lot of cleaning," Longarm agreed. "I never seen such a mess in my life. Ain't nobody in charge of things in this country got any brains?"

"Old Porfirio Diaz has brains enough," Hill said. "The trouble is, they're the wrong kind." When neither Longarm nor Webster had any comment, the army captain asked, "If you were sent down here to look for me and Webster, Marshal, you must be looking for those two deserters from my outfit, too."

"I was, but I'm not any longer. You don't need to look either, Captain. They're both dead."

"Hell you say." Hill didn't sound too surprised. "The rurales get them?"

"No. They got crossways of an unreconstructed reb in Los Perros. Deputy sheriff named Spud something. He killed 'em and hid their bodies. It's a safe bet you'll never find 'em."

"Well." The captain was taking the news philosophically. "They were pretty good soldiers until they got horny and raped that rancher's wife. I won't say I'm glad they're dead, but if I'd caught them, I'd have had to give evidence against them at a court-martial and watch them executed by a firing squad. I don't think I'd've enjoyed it."

Longarm could now make out details of his surroundings and see his cellmates' faces clearly. Nate Webster was tall, almost as tall as Longarm himself, but a bit thinner and rangier. His face was fading from the deep bronze he'd acquired in his job. Above his eyebrows where his hat brim sat there was a band of white skin between the tan and his sandy hair. Hill was on the short side, with a baby-round face from which the fat was beginning to melt away. Both men were dressed in little more than rags, and neither wore shoes or boots. Their sockless feet were thrust into huaraches of braided leather such as Longarm had seen on the feet of Los Perros dwellers.

Webster saw Longarm eyeing their attire and said, "If you're wondering what happened to our clothes, we ate 'em."

"You did what?"

"I guess you've never been in a Mexican jail before," Hill said. It was a statement, not a question.

"Come to that, I ain't," Longarm replied.

Webster explained, "They don't feed prisoners in Mexico. If you've got food or something to trade, you eat. If not, you starve."

"So you traded your duds for grub," Longarm nodded. "I guess I'd've done the same thing. Guess I got off lucky, then. Don't know how it happened, but them bandits out there missed searching me. I got a little cash in my britches, even if that sergeant did lift $200 outa my wallet."

"I hope you're feeling charitable, Marshal," Hill said. "We've just about run out of anything to trade."

"You know you're both welcome to what I got. Only how do we go about getting grub? My belly's been pushing against my backbone for the last three, four hours."

"Sebastian will be around after a while to see what kind of dicker we can offer," Webster replied. "If you don't mind a bit of advice, don't let him know how much money you've got, and don't pull off your boots when you go to bed."

"Who's Sebastian?"

"He's the jailer," Webster answered. "He looks too old to be worth much, but the son of a bitch is cagey. He'll steal you blind with your eyes open, and trade you outa your socks."

"Thanks. I'll remember. But I might be outa here before too

long." Seeing the questions in his cellmates' eyes, Longarm explained about the letter. "It was a straight-out holdup, a ransom note, but when it hits Mexico City, it ought to bring some kind of action."

"Ramos got you on that, too, did he?" Hill asked.

"You mean he had you write a letter like that?"

"He sure as hell did. He wants $25,000 in gold to let me go back across the river," Hill grinned.

"Well, I'm right took down," Longarm said. "He sure didn't put my price that high."

"You're both going cheap," Webster told them. "The price on me was $30,000. I guess the extra's a sort of revenge for whatever part the Rangers took in whipping them at San Jacinto."

For a moment the three men looked at one another, then burst out laughing. In spite of their serious situation, the idea of a Mexican rurale who'd risen no higher than the command of an isolated, unimportant police outpost demanding ransom from the United States struck them as comical. It wasn't until their laughing spell died down that Longarm remembered Lefty.

"Hold up a minute," he said. "That patrol brought in somebody besides me. A deputy sheriff from Los Perros. How come he's not in here, too?"

"I wouldn't know," Webster said. "They haven't brought anybody else in, though. All the other cells were full until yesterday, but there were Mexicans in the others. The two across from us had a bunch of vaqueros in 'em, and I guess they got turned free. That one back of us had a bandit in it, but they hauled him out and shot him this morning."

Longarm said thoughtfully, "These damn rurales sure don't waste much time. Don't they ever give anybody a real trial in a court?"

"None that I've noticed," Webster replied. "But remember, Long, the rurales today're not like they were in Benito Juarez's time. They used to be a real crack police force then. This bunch now's made up mostly of Diaz's hatchetmen and killers. They don't answer to anybody but him, and the only law they know is what comes out of a rifle or a sixgun."

Captain Hill added, "What they've got in Mexico today is what you saw in Los Perros, Marshal, only on a bigger scale. The army's got a few agents in Mexico, and the reports that trickle down to me in the situation bulletins from staff headquarters keep warning us field commanders to be careful as hell in our moves along the border. The army doesn't want to be responsible for starting another war."

"Too bad Mexico don't feel the same way," Longarm observed.

Their conversation stopped abruptly when the heavy door of the jail building creaked open. An old Mexican with a bent back and a pronounced limp came in. He stopped in front of the cell door and peered at the three prisoners.

"Quien quiere comida hoy?" he asked.

"Todos, los tres de nosotros," Webster answered. He turned to Longarm. "This is Sebastian. Wants to know if we want supper, which is his way of telling us we better have cash or something to swap. You said—"

"I remember," Longarm broke in. "You go ahead and dicker for all of us, you handle his lingo better'n I can. Best I can do is catch a word now and again."

"I'll get us off as light as I can," Webster promised.

He began bargaining in Spanish with the jailer. Longarm caught an occasional word, but most of the haggling went over his head. After about five minutes, Webster turned away from the door and winked at the others as Sebastian watched, trying to hide his eagerness.

"He'll give us meat and frijoles for a dime a head," Webster said. "That's about right, I think, Marshal."

"Sounds cheap enough, considering he's got a tighter monopoly than John D. Rockefeller. Tell you what. See if he'll throw in a cup of coffee apiece at that price."

Webster haggled again briefly, and reported, "He'll add the coffee for a nickel, that's for all three of us. I don't know what it'll taste like, but anything's better'n this horse piss he gives us for water."

"It's not that bad, after you get used to it," Hill explained to Longarm. "It gives you the trots for the first week."

"Them I can do without," Longarm said. "Tell him it's a deal, Nate. At that price, I got enough to feed us for a spell."

Before Sebastian came back with the food, the jailhouse door opened again and two rurales dragged Lefty in. The Los Perros deputy was unconscious, his face covered with blood, his clothes torn and stained. Longarm opened his mouth to protest, but before he could say anything, Webster clamped a restraining hand on his arm.

"Don't!" he whispered. "Just keep quiet. You get them mad, they might come in here and give us the same kind of treatment!"

Longarm subsided. They watched the rurales haul Lefty into the cell across from theirs. The rurales didn't bother to deposit the unconscious man on the low cot that stood in the cell. They dumped him on the floor, clanged the slat-iron door shut, and locked it. Then they left, without a word or glance at Longarm and the others.

"Looks like they gave him a real working over," Longarm said.

"That the deputy from Los Perros you were wondering about?" Webster asked.

"That's Lefty. Or what's left of him."

"What'd he know that was important to them?" Webster wondered aloud.

"Beats me," Longarm answered. "Unless Ramos is figuring to go after that rustler ring Lefty was mixed up with."

"Yes, that could be it," the Ranger frowned. "Or it could be he was trying to get the deputy to give him something more on you."

"That'd be my guess," Hill said. "A deputy sheriff's not quite as big a fish as a U.S. marshal."

"Or an army captain or a Texas Ranger," Longarm added. He got as close to the cell door as he could and called, "Lefty! Can you hear me?" There was no response from the cell across the corridor.

"Wait until Sebastian comes in with our supper," Hill suggested. "Maybe we can get him to swab the man off with some cold water and bring him around."

"Not much else we can do," Longarm pointed out. "I ain't got much use for the worthless son of a bitch, but right now I'd give a hand to anybody Ramos hurts. Besides, I'm curious to know what they were trying to get out of him."

They didn't have to wait for the old jailer to revive Lefty. Before Sebastian returned with their supper, they heard moans coming from the cell across the way and when they crowded up to the door, Lefty was sitting up, holding his head between his hands.

Longarm called, "You all right?"

"No, damn it, I ain't! I hurt like hell, where them greaser bastards kicked me in the balls and poked me in the belly with their rifle butts. But I ain't dead yet."

Longarm asked, "Why'd they whip you? You get crossways of Ramos? Or Molina?"

"Shit, I didn't do nothing. I guess all you need's to be from Texas for them greasers to start walloping you."

"Damn it, they must've asked you something," Webster said.

Lefty squinted through eyes that were swollen closed. "Who in hell are you?"

"Nate Webster. Texas Rangers."

"Now how in God's name did the rurales get hold of you?"

"That ain't important," Longarm told him curtly. "Even if it was any of your business, which it ain't."

"We're all in the same jail," the deputy reminded him. "I can make out somebody else in there with you, too."

"Name's Hill," the captain told him. "Captain, 10th Cavalry."

"Oh, sure. You're the one that come looking for a couple of your troopers that went over the hill. I recall the sheriff sayin' something about you."

"No thanks to him—or you, either—I found out what happened to them," Hill said brusquely.

"Damn it, you two quit butting in!" Longarm was irritated. "I need to find out things from this fellow." He faced the deputy again. Lefty had dragged himself up to the cot now. Longarm went on, "You better tell me what-all Ramos wanted to know."

"He was mainly interested in what you knew, and that's what I couldn't tell him, because I don't know myself. Then he got to askin' me questions about you."

"What kind of questions?"

"Why you come over the border. How long since you got to Los Perros. Who you was really after. If you was honest to God a federal marshal—*federalista,* he called it."

"What else?" Longarm was sure that Ramos's questioning hadn't stopped there.

"He tried to find out how much I know about what you've turned up so far." Lefty moaned, clutching his groin. "Then he wanted to make sure you set out from Los Perros. He had some idea you come from Mexico City, that you was a spy Diaz sent out to check up on him, or try to get somethin' on him."

"What'd you tell him?" Longarm demanded.

"Shit, Custis—Long, whatever your damn name is—what could I tell him? I spilled all I knew after they begun to beat on me, but how in hell do I know who you really are for sure?"

"That ain't what I asked you." Longarm's voice was hard. He'd seen Lefty crawfish more than once, trying to save his own skin at the expense of somebody else. "In my book, you're down as a damned liar and a crook. I don't put it past you to lie to Ramos, just to make it easy on yourself. Now, what'd you really tell him?"

"So help me God, Marshal, I didn't make nothin' up! I can't help whether you believe me or not. I told him what I knew certain-sure, and that was all!"

Longarm saw he'd gotten all there was to get out of Lefty for the moment. He still didn't know what to believe of what the deputy had told him. He said, "All right. If you remember anything else, you pass it along to me. If you do that, I just might help you."

"Help, my ass!" Lefty snorted. "You're in the same fix I am!"

"Maybe. Did the rurales shake you down good? Take all your money and everything else?"

"What'd you think they'd do? They stripped me clean."

"You know about Mexican jails, I guess?"

"Sure." Lefty stopped short, then sighed. "Oh, sweet Jesus! I ain't got a dime to buy a meal with! Not a lousy fuckin' penny!"

"I'm better off than you are," Longarm told him. "They forgot to clean me out. I already promised to help these fellows in here with me; they traded off all their duds for grub."

"Listen, Marshal Long," Lefty pleaded, "I didn't know anything to tell that rurale, and I didn't make nothin' up. You got to give me a hand!"

"I don't figure I owe you one damn thing, Lefty. Now, I might feel different, if you remember anything you forgot so far."

A rattling of the jailhouse lock put an end to their conversation. All four men fell silent when Sebastian appeared. He had a small pot in each hand. The jailer set the pots on the dirt floor outside the cell where Longarm, Webster, and Hill were confined, then went outside and brought in a cloth-wrapped bundle and a steaming coffeepot.

"*Su comida, gringos,*" the jailer announced. "*Dame treinte-cinco centavos, si quieren comer.*"

Being careful not to let Sebastian see that he had other coins in his pocket, Longarm dug out the thirty-five cents and passed the money through the bars. Sebastian unlocked the cell door, opened it just wide enough to slide the food inside, and locked it again. He'd already started to leave when Lefty called to him.

"Hey, *amigo! Donde es mi comida?*"

"*Tienes dinero?*" Sebastian asked.

"No. Esta cosa tu conoces."

"Pues, no dinero, no comida."

"Try trading your boots," Longarm suggested. He felt a small twinge of conscience, but smothered it. If Lefty knew anything more, there was only one way to get it out of him. He went on, "My friends in here swapped their clothes to get fed. You're no better'n they are. Your clothes ain't much more'n rags, but maybe you can get him to swap you a meal or two for your boots."

Pressed up to the bars, the cellmates watched while Lefty dickered with the jailer. Where cash wasn't offered, Sebastian proved to be a very tough bargainer. He and Lefty argued for a good quarter-hour before they came to terms. The deputy passed one of his boots through the bars. Sebastian went out and brought back a battered tin plate on which red beans swam in a redder sea of chili con carne. A small stack of tortillas lay on top of the mixture. Lefty grabbed the plate and started eating. Longarm and his companions ate their own meal, taking turns scooping food from the pots with strips of tortilla.

They all finished at about the same time. Longarm called across the corridor, "Well, you got fed tonight, Lefty."

"Yeah." The deputy's voice was surly. "No thanks to you."

"I said I'd make you a deal. You better think about how long you're going to eat on that one boot you got left. All you got to do is tell me everything you know about the deals your boss is into, and I'll see you keep eating, such as it is."

"What good would it do me? Ain't neither one of us likely to walk outa this trap we're in."

"Maybe. While I'm still alive and kicking, I got a job I'm paid to do, and I aim to go on doing it. The way I see it, a man's good as long as he's alive, but he can't stay that way if he don't eat. What're you going to do when you've ate up your other boot?"

"Damn you! You really know how to squeeze a man when he's down!"

"You just don't know how hard I can squeeze, when I got a mind to. Well, I offered you the deal. If you don't see fit to take it, that's your loss."

"Now, don't be in such a hurry—" Lefty started.

Longarm cut him short. "I got to be in a hurry. I don't aim to stay here, Lefty. Right now, I don't owe you nothing. If that was to change, I might see a way to help you go along when me and my friends go outa here."

"You're bluffing me. You got no more chance of walking outa this place than I do."

"You go on and think that, if you've a mind to. And you think how quick I changed a few things in Los Perros. And you think about that when your belly gets empty again."

There was a long silence from the other cell. Finally, Lefty said grudgingly, "All right. You win. I'll talk."

Chapter 13

Lefty talked for more than an hour. The beating he'd gotten from Ramos's rurales had battered his body and spirit and weakened his will enough for Longarm to break it, but his instinct for survival was still strong. Parts of his rambling confession only repeated what he'd told Longarm earlier, though he did reveal a few new details about the murders of the 10th Cavalry troopers and the operations of the rustling ring that ran the Laredo Loop.

There was a small amount of new information concerning the activities of Sheriff Tucker: frame-ups of enemies, beatings, and other intimidations of Los Perros inhabitants perpetrated for money or for extorting free labor or participation in criminal activities of minor sorts. Little of this was much of a surprise to Longarm, who'd seen towns or counties taken over by crooks of Tucker's stripe in other areas. One of Lefty's admissions was news, though.

"You think you're so damn smart," he said to Longarm. "You got Ed Tucker tagged as the boss of Los Perros. Shit, you ain't even come close to guessin' who the real boss is."

"Well, then, suppose you tell me," Longarm suggested.

"It's Miles Baskin, that's who. He's the real brains behind just about everything that goes on there."

"Baskin? The saloonkeeper?" Longarm was genuinely surprised. Baskin, the one time he'd talked with the man, had left an impression of being a mild, inoffensive type of man, one who'd walk around trouble instead of into it. At the same time, the revelation settled a nagging question that had been in the back of Longarm's mind. From the very beginning of his prodding in Los Perros, he'd been wondering how Tucker could appear so smart at times and so stupid at others. He asked, "You and the other deputies ever get your orders direct from Baskin?"

"No. Not unless it was some little thing, like we was doin' him a favor. He liked to work through Ed."

"Did Baskin lean more toward one of you than the others? Did he like you or Spud or Ralston best?"

"Well . . ." Lefty hesitated. "Spud, maybe. But just a little bit. He was pretty careful not to set one of us up above the others."

"Lefty," Longarm said solemnly, "you better not be lying to me, or trying to save your skin, or Tucker's. Because if you are, I'll sure as hell find it out."

"Honest to God, Marshal, it's the truth," Lefty insisted. "It was Baskin that give Ed most of his ideas about how to make money outa Los Perros after Ed begun to take over the town. And this new Laredo Loop business, it was mostly his idea, too."

"All right. If it's the truth, I'll dig up evidence to back up what you've said."

"I reckon you can at that. Only one hell of a lot of evidence has got buried in them quicksand sinkholes along the river shallows."

"There'll be more," Longarm promised. "And it'll come out. I'd say you've earned your grub, Lefty. You'll eat along with the rest of us. Hell, I might even buy your boot back from Sebastian, if I can get Nate to do the jawbone work for me."

"Be glad to," the Ranger said. "Aside from one thing that's kept bothering me, I've been right interested in hearing what that hombre across the way's been telling you."

"That's bothering you?"

"Well, it appears to me like Lefty was right a minute ago. He said he didn't see it'd do any good if he did tell you everything he knew, long as we're all in this place together."

"Nate's got a point," Captain Hill agreed. "He and I have done a lot of talking about how to break out of here, but it's always looked to us like a case of out of the frying pan, into the fire.

There're twenty-five or thirty rurales outside, with pistols and rifles. All we have is our fists. That's not good odds."

"Let's jaw about that later on," Longarm suggested. "I didn't get a wink of sleep last night, and I rode pretty hard most of today, until the rurales shanghaied me here. I don't know about the rest of you, but I aim to curl up and get some shut-eye. Tomorrow, we'll see what we can work out."

It was still dark in the jail when the sleeping prisoners were awakened by the clinking of the lock on the outside door. It swung open and the flickering light of torches blinded them briefly. Two unshaved rurales came in, their boot soles scraping on the packed dirt floor. Marching to Lefty's cell, the rurales dragged the sleepy deputy into the corridor and through the outer door.

When they left the building, the men did not close the outside door. From their cell, by straining hard against the front bars, Longarm and his companions could see a slice of the torch-lit area outside. Captain Ramos came into view; he carried a pistol in his right hand. The rurales who'd hauled Lefty out of his cell swung the deputy around to face the captain. The distance was too great for those inside to hear what was said, they could only watch and imagine what passed between Lefty and Ramos.

Whatever the rurale captain said or asked brought only vehement headshakes from Lefty. Each time they could see Ramos's lips move, and each time the deputy's head shook in the negative. Even when Ramos slapped Lefty's face, there was no difference in the response he gave. Ramos was obviously growing angry. He brought up the pistol and shoved it hard against Lefty's forehead. Lefty tried to drop to his knees, but the men holding his arms kept him erect.

After a moment, Ramos brought the pistol down. He talked for perhaps a minute. Watching the dumb show, Longarm guessed that Ramos was trying to force Lefty into confessing to something—he couldn't figure out quite what—that would suit the rurale's private purposes, while Lefty kept pleading that it was impossible for him to do what Ramos wanted.

None of those in the cell were prepared for the finale of the pantomime. Ramos pushed the muzzle of his pistol into Lefty's neck, just under the deputy's jaw, and pulled the trigger. The shot sounded thin inside the jail, but Longarm and his cellmates could see Lefty's head shatter in a spray of blood and brains bursting from the top of his head. The deputy slumped and this time the rurales holding him let his lifeless body fall to the ground.

Even men as accustomed to violence as Longarm, Webster, and Hill, they were shaken by the brutality of the killing. They looked at one another in stunned silence, half aware that outside the two rurales who'd held Lefty were dragging away his body, leaving a wide blood trail on the hard-packed ground. The slamming of the outer door and the metal rasping of its lock brought them back to the reality of the moment.

"Jesus!" Longarm muttered. "Them rurales sure don't believe in things like courts and trials, do they?"

"Not this breed, no," Webster said soberly. "That's the Diaz way, though. Like I told you, the rurales aren't a police force anymore. They're Diaz's revenge squad, his executioners. It's one of the ways he keeps Mexico under his thumb."

"You realize that what we saw could happen to any of us," Hill reminded them in a quiet, matter-of-fact voice. "Marshal Long, you said just before we turned in that we'd see what we could work out, and I suppose by that you meant getting out of here. Well"—Hill motioned toward the single window at the end of the corridor, which was gray with the dawn light—"it's today, and I'd say it's time we started working."

"You said just what I was thinking," Longarm agreed. "Let's just squat down and have us a powwow. We'll hear soon enough when that jailer comes to see about breakfast."

"He won't be here for a while," Webster said. "Usually, just a little before noon. This jail doesn't serve but two meals a day."

They sat on the floor, ignoring the hard cot, so they could lean together with their heads close and talk in low voices.

Longarm said, "It didn't occur to me we had to hurry until I watched what they did to Lefty. That changed my mind fast. Now, you men have been here longer'n I have. What've you found out about the way they run things outside?"

"Damned little," Hill replied. Webster nodded agreement, and the army man went on, "You see, Nate and I thought just like you did, Marshal. We talked things over, and decided we had plenty of time before we started to worry."

"How'd you figure that out?" Longarm asked.

"Oh, you know what's happened to those ransom demands Ramos has sent to our ambassador. They're going through channels. Probably our man sent them to Washington for instructions before he said anything to the Mexican government. Those things take time."

"I know my chief's always bellyaching about how long it takes for his bosses in Washington to answer a simple question like what's two and two," Longarm smiled. "But I never was in a situation just like this one before."

"Neither was I," Hill said. "But I did a tour with our embassy in Haiti, right after the war. I was brevetted a colonel during the fighting, but the minute Lee surrendered, I went back to my regular rank, and there were so damned many lieutenants that they shipped a lot of us out as military attachés to get us out from underfoot."

"John tells me that ambassadors don't know their tails from a hot rock most of the time, and the regulars who run our embassies are afraid to pee without asking Washington first," Webster put in.

"Most of those nervous Nellies in the State Department squat to pee, anyhow," Hill said sourly. "But that's beside the point I'm trying to make. I don't think the Mexican government's heard yet about what Ramos is trying to do. Ramos seems to think all he has to do is send a letter to the U.S. ambassador, and wait for the gold to flow. It's not that simple."

"I guess I'm following you," Longarm said. "But go on, spell it out for me."

"Sooner or later, either in Washington or Mexico City, there's going to be a protest made to the Mexican government. When that happens, Ramos is going to find himself up shit creek. And he's likely to panic."

"He sure don't seem bothered now," Longarm pointed out.

"No. I tried to get across to him that he'd have to be patient," Hill explained.

"John and I figured we were safe until the Mexican government got the word we're being held illegally, and that one of their police officers is trying to hold up the U.S.," Webster added.

Hill said, "That's when the real squeeze will come. Diaz isn't stupid. Crooked, mean as hell, unscrupulous, but not stupid. From what I know about him, which isn't much, he'd be likely to send one of his execution squads up here to get rid of us and Ramos both. Then he'd play innocent; he'd say, 'No, we haven't got any American prisoners, and Captain Ramos was killed in a fight with bandits.'"

Longarm took his time analyzing the captain's conclusions. He nodded slowly. "I'd say you've done a pretty good job of figuring things out. And if you're right, then we don't have a hell of a lot of time left for getting outa here."

"Getting out's not going to be a big job," Webster said. "We know how that can be done. It's what we'd do once we were out of this jail, facing that bunch outside without any kind of weapons to give us a chance."

"We don't even know whether they post regular guards, or whether the whole outfit turns in at night," Hill told Longarm. "And until they killed that deputy today, we haven't felt like we needed to tip our plans by showing too much interest in their operational procedures. But as Nate says, the main thing that's held us back is lack of weapons."

Longarm started to tell them about his derringer, but decided that holding the news until just before they finished their plans would give the morale of his cellmates a bigger boost at a time when it'd be needed more.

Hill had been thinking, too. He said, "Weapons or not, I'd say the time's come to do something. And I mean immediately."

"I'm with you there," Longarm assured him. "I guess you've had the same idea I got, looking at the roof up there?"

"We decided it's the weakest point," Webster said. "Breaking through shouldn't be a big job. But then what? Do all of us go, and if we do, where do we go? To the corral and grab horses? Or prowl around looking for some guns?"

"I'd say the first thing we got to decide is whether we all go out at the same time, or if one of us gives it a try by himself."

"One man has a better chance than three of moving around without stirring up an alarm," Hill observed.

"Sure does," Webster agreed. "Well, I'll volunteer. I've done enough scouting so's I can get around quiet in the dark. And I talk the lingo enough so if a guard challenges me I can throw him off long enough to get close to him and shut him up."

"I was about to offer," Hill said. "I'm not what you'd call the world's best scout, but I've done my share of night fighting."

"Now, look," Longarm said, "I don't mean to put myself up to be a hero, or feel like I'm a bit better'n either one of you, but I figure it's my job to get out there and bust us all free."

"I'd like to know how you figure it," Webster said dryly.

"Yes, so would I," Hill chimed in.

"It's real simple," Longarm told them. "First off, you fellows have been in this damn place a lot longer'n I have. Nate, you been here how long? Close to three months?"

"Give or take a week or so," the Ranger agreed.

"And you been here a month or more, John." Hill nodded. Longarm went on, "All the time, you been getting more starved out, cooped up in this little cell without a chance to stretch your muscles or loosen up your joints. I'd say you're both a mite rusty; it stands to reason. My muscles are in better shape than yours are, which'd give me a little bit of an edge."

"There's nothing wrong with my muscles," Webster protested.

"Nor mine," said Hill. "Both of us have tried to keep in shape, you know. Give us credit for that, Marshal."

"Oh, sure. But there's one little thing I been thinking about that might make more difference than anything else."

"What's that?" Hill and Webster spoke almost in unison.

"Your feet. Look at them things you got on. How're you going to run in 'em? Or sneak in 'em? They go shush-shush every step you take. But I still got my boots."

"We could draw straws to see who'd wear them," Webster suggested.

"We could," Longarm nodded. "What size you wear, Nate?"

"Elevens."

"John? How about you?"

"I take size nine,"

"And I wear tens. Now, nobody can move right, whether he's sneaking or running, in boots that don't fit. Am I right?" Reluctantly, both the others nodded. "Well, then, I guess I win the job by a toe. Or maybe a heel. Anybody object?"

"As far as I'm concerned, it's settled," Webster said. "We'll be ready to back you up, Marshal."

"We damned sure will!" Hill nodded. "Now, then, how can we help you form a battle plan?"

"Well, you're getting over my head, John," Longarm replied. "I was just aiming to bull ahead by guess and by God, and hope I do the right thing."

"In the service, we'd call that setting out to look for targets of opportunity," Hill smiled. "In this case, I'd say it's about the only battle plan we can make."

"I got one ace I've been keeping in the hole," Longarm announced. He fished his watch and derringer out of his vest pocket.

"Ramos got so interested in the letter he made me write that he didn't get his men to clean out my pockets. So there's two shots here that might make the difference between us getting out, or going the way Lefty did."

Webster chuckled. "You're like old Captain McNally, who used to run my outfit, Marshal. He always says some men are born lucky, some are born unlucky, but good men make their luck as they go. I don't suppose you made that piece of luck, but it's sure going to help all of us."

"Gentlemen," said Hill, "I'll make a suggestion. If I'm taking troops into an engagement, I try to give them a good rest before the battle starts. We might as well follow the same tactics."

Relaxation came hard during the day's long hours, but they somehow managed to rest and to doze a bit. When Sebastian came in to bargain over their meals, Webster went through the usual routine of dickering. He complained of the price they paid as well as of the quantity and quality of the food they'd had the evening before. The haggling didn't improve their luncheon, but for supper they got a big helping of roast *cabrito*. It was a bit strong, really more goat than kid, but it was a lot more substantial than the soupy chili con carne and frijoles they'd had the previous evening and at noon.

After the jailer had gone out, while they were eating, Longarm told his companions, "I been thinking about this deal off and on all day, whenever I couldn't sleep. Appears to me like I got a choice of two times to make a try. One's right now, while them bastards is eating, maybe swigging a little mescal or pulque. The other's late tonight, after they bed down."

"If you're asking for an opinion," Hill said, "I'd imagine they won't be as alert while they're eating. And we still don't know whether they keep sentries on duty at night."

"Strikes me John's right," Webster said quickly. "I'd bet they do have some kind of night patrol, but when the grub's served, all the pigs rush to the trough."

"I sorta favor now, myself," Longarm agreed. "If we move quick, I can get through that roof and be on the ground outside before they finish their supper."

To keep Longarm as fresh as possible, Hill and Webster took on the job of breaking through the jailhouse roof. The ceiling was low, but still high enough to make it necessary for one man to stand on the other's shoulders while they took turns pulling aside the saplings that had been laid across the vigas to support the layers of brush and dirt that formed the foot-thick roof. The bottom layers gave way easily, but the topmost layer had baked hard, and formed a crust four inches thick. They used the tin plates from their supper as scrapers and prods, bending them into triangles that provided pointed ends for gouging at the crust and wide sides for scraping the dislodged pieces away.

Both roof breakers were grimy from head to foot before the job was completed. Longarm estimated they'd taken less than an hour to finish the job, and the sight through the hole they'd opened, of the clear sky deepened into after-sunset blue, gave encouragement to all three of them.

"Well, let's don't lollygag," Longarm said. "Boost me up as far as you can. Once I get armpit-high through that top layer of 'dobe, I'm home free."

Webster and Hill each took hold of one of his feet and Longarm held his body stiff while they lifted him straight up. The hole wasn't as big as it looked; they'd worked fast and kept their digging to a minimum in cracking through the hard top crust. His shoulders almost stuck, but Longarm managed to raise his arms up straight above his head and scrape through the opening. For a moment, he rested on his elbows, forearms on the roof, head and shoulders protruding through the escape hatch. The adobe wall of the building was only eight or ten inches above the rooftop. Longarm pulled himself out slowly, bending forward, hauling his body ahead with his forearms and elbows, until his booted feet cleared the hole and he lay flat in the scant concealment of the wall.

For a few seconds he lay motionless and listened, trying to locate the rurales who might be on the ground by the sound of their voices. Most of the noises came from a distance. He risked raising his head above the parapet of the wall to check the evidence of his ears and saw that the men were about where he'd placed them mentally. Apparently, the rurales weren't provided with a mess hall. They were clustered around a spit suspended over a bed of coals beside what he guessed was their barracks. The almost-stripped skeleton of a young goat was suspended on the spit.

Several rurales were by the cooking fire, carving strips of meat off the *cabrito* and eating it where they stood. A few had taken plates to sit on the ground, leaning against the wall of the barracks. Most of the rurales had jugs or bottles; Longarm was

reasonably sure these contained either pulque or mescal. He
didn't think the average rurale could afford even the lowest grade
of tequila or aguardiente. There were no rifles to be seen, but all
the men he could see clearly still had on their pistols.

Give 'em a little time, old son, he told himself, long enough
for it to get full dark. By then, they'll be full of meat and pulque
and won't be able to hit the side of a barn if they shoot, let alone
a spry man running.

At one side of the barracks building, thirty or forty paces distant, stood the headquarters. Lights glowing through the high-up
horizontal slit-windows told him that Captain Ramos must be sitting down to enjoy his own supper inside. Through the deepening
dusk he could see other structures, a cluster of jacales beyond the
barracks and some distance away from the larger buildings. The
huts were even more primitive than the jacales of Los Perros.
Fires twinkled in front of most of them, and women as well as
men moved around the shanties. Longarm realized that these
must be the quarters of married rurales, or the dwellings of the lavanderas, the camp followers who were to be found with every
Mexican military force, and who were given with Latin courtesy
their title of "washerwomen."

Whatever men are back at those shanties, or around 'em,
won't be paying much mind to what goes on around the barracks
or jail, Longarm thought. They'll have their women to keep 'em
occupied.

On the opposite side of the barracks from the headquarters, he
saw the corral. Even in the dimness of the rapidly fading light,
Longarm could make out Tordo's gray shape; it stood out among
the roans and chestnuts that plodded aimlessly around inside the
pole enclosure. On the corral rail, saddles were lined up; Longarm tried to count them, but the light was too bad. He guessed
there were about thirty, which was the figure he and Hill and
Webster had estimated as the number of men stationed at the outpost. He didn't really like the location of the corral. To get to the
horses, they'd have to pass by the barracks.

Don't worry about that now, he commanded himself, wait and
see how this damn stunt comes off before you start saddling up to
ride.

By the time Longarm had finished his cautious survey of the
area, darkness was almost complete. From the jacales, a guitar
plinked; if it accompanied a singer, his voice was lost in the dis-

tance. Another sound drew his attention to the barracks. There, a group had gathered around a man playing the concertina. Singly and in twos and threes, voices began rising in the melancholy strains of "La Borrachita."

"Marshal!"

Nate Webster's whisper behind him almost sent Longarm jumping out of his skin. He turned to see the Ranger's head sticking out of the escape hole.

"Damn it, Nate! You like to scared the shit outa me!"

"We didn't hear any ruckus, so we figured you must've made it," Webster whispered.

"Had to get the layout of this place in my head, first." Longarm wiggled backward so they could talk more easily. "Looks like it's all clear. I'm going to see if I can get us some guns and a bunch of shells. These two shots I got won't help much if they take after us."

"You sure it's safe?"

"If I wanted to live safe, I'd be selling calico back of a store counter. I did think of one thing—Sebastian."

"John and I did, too. We're going to grab him through the bars and hold him till you come let us out." He breathed deeply. "God, this fresh air smells good!"

"We'll all enjoy it more, ten miles from here."

"Sure. Well, good luck." Webster's head disappeared.

Longarm belly-crawled to the side of the jail opposite the barracks and lowered himself over the wall. Hanging by his hands, he dropped the few feet between his feet and the ground. He landed running, crouching low, heading for Ramos's office.

Chapter 14

Darkness, sweeping in rapidly, was his friend. Longarm slowed his run almost as soon as he'd started it when he saw there was no sentry posted at the door of the headquarters building. He ambled lazily across the bare area, keeping himself from hurrying, now. Any of the rurales who saw him would, he hoped, think he was just another of their group reporting to the captain.

He reached the deep shade of the building walls. Standing on tiptoe, he could just see inside the big sala. A vigil light flickered in its glass container in a niche near the door. Its flame was so tiny that the circle of light it cast reached barely to the edge of the huge table Ramos used as a desk. There was no one in the room, but another blade of light gleaming along the floor gave him the location of a door; Ramos must be in the room behind that door, he thought.

Hugging the building wall, he made for the door. It was latched with a simple lift-lever. Longarm tested it cautiously. The lever lifted easily; the door was neither locked nor barred. Across the narrow room the knife edge of light became his goal. He lightfooted toward it. As he went, he snaked the derringer from his pocket and freed his watch from it by feel. He'd operated the snap on the chain in the dark so many times that the job was automatic. Dropping the watch back in his pocket, he cocked the derringer before knocking on the door. He tried to make the light tapping sound apologetic.

"*Qué pasa?*" asked Ramos's voice from the adjoining room.

"*Solamente mí, Capitán.*" Longarm had rehearsed the phrase in his mind so often that he had no fear of stumbling over it, in spite of his rusty Spanish. "*Es necessario que habla con usted.*"

"*Mañana, hombre. Vólves temprano, y hablamos.*"

Longarm had expected to be told to come back tomorrow, and had the next phrase ready. "*Anoche, por favor, mí Capitán!*" He tried to make his voice humble and pleading.

A muffled grunt of disgust came through the thick door, then a rustle of movement. Longarm stood aside, hugging the wall, turning his head away so he wouldn't be blinded by the sudden glare of light when the door opened. He counted on Ramos's eyes being used to the bright room beyond; the rurale would be almost blind for the first few seconds when he looked into the dark sala. The door opened and Ramos's bulk filled the lighted opening. He wore only a pair of trousers and was barefoot. Stepping across the threshold, he peered ahead into the darkness.

"*Quien es?*" he grumbled. "*Quien estorbame in mi recamera?*"

In one swift move, Longarm jammed the cold barrel of the derringer into Ramos's temple and with his other hand clamped the man's mouth closed.

Coldly, he hissed, "You make a noise, and you're dead. I'll spatter your brains the way you spattered Lefty's this morning."

He kept his hand over Ramos's mouth until the look in the rurale's eyes told him it was safe to let him talk.

"*El gringo federalista!*" Ramos gasped. "*Como entre por aquí?*"

"Talk English," Longarm commanded.

"How do you get in here?" Ramos asked. "You are in jail!"

"Maybe I'm twins," Longarm suggested, his voice without mirth. "I got tired of your jail. Me and my friends are ready to say good-bye to your place here, but we're taking you along for the ride."

"You think you can take me from my brave men?" Ramos blustered. "Only I call once, and they will come!"

"And they'll find your corpse, if you yell. But maybe you are stupid enough to make some noise, even if it kills you. Back up, into your bedroom." He emphasized the command with a push on the derringer's barrel. Ramos obeyed.

Longarm gave a quick glance around the room. He was so surprised when he saw the woman in the bed that took up most of one wall that he almost pulled the derringer's trigger.

"Who in hell are you?" he asked.

Ramos said, "She is—"

"I didn't ask you!" Longarm snapped. He looked at the woman. "Well? You going to tell me?"

"My name's Flo Firestone. Oh, not really, that's my stage name, but I'm more used to it than my real one. I know who you are, and am I ever glad to see you!"

Longarm shook his head, unbelieving. "You talk like you're an American."

"You're damned right, I am. And it's a real treat to see you standing there with a gun at that bastard's head!"

"Well, whoever you are, we'll save the palaver until later. I guess you're on my side, from what you just said, so why don't you find me some rope or something to tie this hombre up with. Then we'll try to get things straightened out."

She got out of bed, giving Longarm a glimpse of smooth pink thighs as her long legs kicked the covers aside. She stood up; he was surprised that she was almost as tall as he was. She was a blonde, full-lipped, round-chinned, and her sheer nightdress revealed that she was a true blonde. The almost transparent material of the nightgown hid nothing of her figure, which was statuesque, though the erect pink-tipped nipples of her generous breasts pushed the sheer fabric out so that it fell straight to her bare feet. When she moved, the gown clung to her, emphasizing her smoothly rounded stomach, wide hips, and tapered legs. In spite of her size, she was large rather than fat. Longarm had to work at keeping his mind on Ramos while the woman scurried around looking for rope or cord. Finally, she settled for ripping a bedsheet into wide strips.

She handed these to Longarm. "These'll have to do, I guess. If you twist them when you tie him up, they'll hold tight enough."

"Give me a hand," he said. "Put a gag on him first, in case he gets a fool idea about yelling for help." Ramos glowered while she obeyed, pulling the twisted cloth tight through his mouth. Longarm told the rurale, "Now then. You just march over and sit down in that chair. Don't forget, this gun's cocked, and I got a nervous trigger finger."

Ramos could see the derringer at full-cock in the mirror of an ornate dressing table that stood opposite the bed. He obeyed without hesitation. Longarm sat him down in the armless boudoir chair and after the woman had bound his hands, helped her to tie the rurale's feet to the chair legs. He checked the lashing that held Ramos's wrists around the back of the chair, and found them as tight and secure as they'd have been if he'd put them on the man himself. Longarm tucked the little gun back into his vest pocket.

"Now," he said to the woman, "you wanta tell me how you got here, and why?"

"I got here because this two-bit *cholo*—I don't know what that means, except that it's some kind of Mexican insult—decided he wanted to keep me around after his men wiped out the bandits that had kidnapped me off the train that I was taking back to the states."

"How long ago'd this happen?"

"Let's see. I've just about lost track of time, but I guess it was about three weeks ago that Charley"—she pointed to Ramos—"I call him Charley because it makes him mad—ambushed the train robbers. And I don't know where it was, because I rode a day and part of a night with the bandits, and two days with Charley and his crew."

"And how'd you know who I am?" Longarm asked suspiciously.

"Marshal, when you're shut up all the time in a bedroom you don't much care for, you listen at the keyhole and you work out the things you can't see happening. I just about gave up when Charley told them to toss you in the pokey, and you'll never know how glad I am you got out. How did you, anyhow?"

"That'll wait," Longarm replied curtly. He wanted to satisfy himself that the woman was what she seemed to be. "This train you were on, how'd you happen to be riding it?"

"I was trying to get back home. Look, Marshal, I'm an actress. Well, I guess burlesque's acting, in a way. Our troupe got stranded, but we scraped up enough money between us to take the train from Monterrey to Laredo, wherever that is. We thought once we got back across the border, we could work our way back to New York. You know, hitting the tank towns, performing wherever we could pick up a booking."

"What happened to the rest of the people in your outfit?"

"God might know, but I don't. You ever been on a train that ran off the rails because a bunch of robbers dynamited the track? It was a mess—shooting, dark, people all mixed up. I don't know what happened, because I had a sack over my head. I could tell daylight from dark, but that was about all. I could tell you a lot more, but don't you think we'd better save it until later?"

"You're right, Flo. You did say Flo, didn't you?" She nodded, and Longarm went on, "Sounds like a real interesting story, but there's two more fellows waiting for me to get 'em out of jail, and I got to work up some kind of scheme to do it."

"You're going to include me in the getaway party, I hope?" Flo asked.

"Sure, now that I know about you, which I didn't before. But there's something like thirty of Ramos's rurales between us and a clean break. There ain't a way I can see to bull through that many. They'd cut us down fast, we'd be so outgunned if we tried to just bust through."

"If you're looking for guns, there's a whole closetful in a little room off the one Charley uses for his office."

"Ammunition for 'em, too?"

"I wouldn't know what bullets fit which gun. Let's go look. I'll show you where they are."

"Just a minute. Is there anybody in this place except you and him?"

"No. Charley didn't want any interruptions, if you know what I mean. Some woman comes in to cook and clean up, but she won't be here until time to fix breakfast."

"All right. Let's have a look-see. And I'll bolt that front door, so in case anybody does come around they won't just walk in on us."

Flo seemed unconscious of her body gleaming through the filmy nightdress as she led Longarm through the sala to a little storeroom lined with cabinets. She pointed out the one that held the weapons. Longarm opened it and found it crammed with rifles, shotguns, pistols, and boxes and bags of ammunition. There was enough firepower in the cabinet to fit out an army, he thought, and for a moment wished he had one behind him.

Apparently, Ramos kept for himself the best weapons captured by his men from the bandit gangs that were supposed to be the chief targets of the rurales. The guns were all in good condition, most of them relatively late models. Among them, Long-arm found his own Colt and Winchester; he checked to be sure they were loaded before putting the Winchester aside and strapping on the Colt. For the first time since it had been taken from him, he felt fully dressed.

"These'll fix us up real good," he told Flo. Then the relief drained out of his voice as he added, "But they won't be a damn bit of use until I pass 'em on to Nate and John."

"They're your friends who're in jail?"

"An army captain and a Texas Ranger. They was both here before Ramos brought you back, I expect."

"I knew there were prisoners out there, I didn't know who."

Longarm was frowning, concentrating on completing their escape. He thought aloud, "About all I can see to do is wait until all those rurales turn in and get sound asleep. Flo, you know whether they set guards out around this place at night?"

"No. Charley's kept me busy at night, or tried to." She sighed. "Too bad there's not some kind of medicine, like laudanum, in one of these cabinets, something that'd put the men out there to sleep real fast."

"You can say that again," Longarm told her.

"I said—"

"Never mind, I was just talking. Listen, Flo, is Ramos a big drinker?"

"He does pretty well. I guess he grabs liquor whenever he gets a chance to; that cabinet right there's loaded with it. French brandy, Scotch whisky, bourbon, rye, and a lot of Mexican stuff like habanero and tequila. There's enough in there to stock Rector's bar. Look." She crossed the room and opened another of the cabinets, showing shelves crammed with bottles.

"Liquor's as good as laudanum for putting a man to sleep," Longarm said. "It just don't work as fast. I'm beginning to get me an idea. See if you can dig a bottle of Maryland rye outa there, Flo. I need something to stir up my brains while I scheme."

Flo rummaged and came up with the bottle Longarm had requested. A corkscrew hung on a nail inside the cabinet door. She used it expertly and passed him the bottle. He tilted it and let the warm, nippy whiskey slide down his throat. Immediately, he wished for a cheroot to follow, but reminded himself he'd better be grateful just for the bottle.

"Don't you offer ladies a drink in the crowd you travel with?"

she asked. He extended the bottle to her and she took a swallow. Her eyes watered. "God! That's a man's drink!" she exclaimed. "I guess I'd better stick to something mild, brandy or Scotch."

"We better leave it alone for now," he cautioned. "I got the start of a scheme worked out. I'm going to have to ask you to help me some, if you don't object."

"Object! Listen, you tell me what you want me to do. There's not much I'd balk at, if it'll get me out of this place and on a train back to Broadway again."

"Well, what you'd do ain't much. Pay attention now, and I'll tell you what I got figured."

Longarm outlined his plan. Flo listened attentively, nodding now and then, as he explained what she'd have to do. When he'd finished she chuckled throatily.

"My God, you've missed your calling, Marshal! Belasco'd pay you a fortune to write plays for the Lyceum. That's a real fine scene you've worked up, and I'll do my best to ad lib it. Don't worry, I won't blow my lines. Most of the shows I play in are half off the cuff. I'll play it to the hilt!"

"It's both our necks if you mess it up," he warned her. "All right. You go get on a wrap. I'll see if I can rummage out some bags or bottles from the kitchen."

Longarm searched until he found a big, sturdy basket and two burlap bags. He filled them with bottles from the liquor cabinet, choosing the strongest spirits: tequila, habanero, rum, hundred-proof bourbon. Flo came from the bedroom in time to help him. Together they carried the basket and bags to the door of the sala, and put them down just inside the room. Longarm looked at Flo. She'd put on a negligee over her nightdress. The effect, he thought, was just right.

"Glad you like it," she said when he told her this. "I was lucky enough to hold on to my dressing case when I jumped off the train. This night stuff and a suit is all I've got to wear."

"Remember, now, don't overdo things," he cautioned her. "Let Sergeant Molina look, but don't let him get near enough to grab you. Just be sure he'll come back, is all."

"Don't worry. I've had more experience dodging stage-door Johnnies than you know about. They only catch me when I want 'em to. Well, if we're ready, let's ring up the curtain on act one."

"Might as well. Get going."

Flo went out the front door. Longarm followed a step behind

her, and when she continued toward the barracks he stopped in the deep darkness at the corner of the building. He'd brought his Winchester to cover her, if trouble developed. If there's a ruckus, he thought, the damn scheme's ruined before it gets started good.

A dozen paces from the barracks, Flo stopped. She called, "Sergeant Molina! Captain Ramos wants you! Right away!"

Longarm had chosen Molina as his target not only because he was Ramos's second in command, but because the sergeant was the only rurale he was sure understood enough English to make the plan work. He waited while the men still seated around the fire scurried to look for Molina. Just before Longarm was beginning to think he'd come up with a bad idea, the sergeant came around the corner of the barracks building. He peered at Flo, who was still standing where she'd stopped.

"What does *mí capitán* want?" Molina called.

"He has a reward for you and his brave men," Flo called back. "He wants you to come and get it."

She turned at once, without waiting to see whether Molina would follow her. The sergeant hesitated only a moment before doing so. Longarm slipped through the darkness along the wall to the headquarters door and slid inside before Molina got close enough to see him. He crossed the sala and went into the closet, leaving the door ajar and swapping his Winchester for his Colt. Straining his ears, he could hear Flo open the door and come into the sala. There was a moment of silence before Molina spoke.

"Where he is, *mí capitán*?"

"In the bedroom," Flo replied. "He doesn't want to be disturbed. He told me what he wants you to do."

"Qué es?" Molina sounded suspicious. "Why is the *capitán* not here himself?"

"He's resting," Flo replied. She dropped her voice to a low, confidential tone that to the listening Longarm seemed dripping with honey. "I'll tell you the truth, Sergeant. The captain's a little bit, well—a little bit drunk."

"Ah. *Un poco borracho.*" Now, Molina's voice held the verbal equivalent to a shrug. "So. What he is want me to do?"

"Look here." Another silence; this time, Longarm visualized Flo showing Molina the liquor. "Captain Ramos says you and the men have earned a reward, a treat. He wants you to share the bottles with the men."

"*Sangre de mi vida! Que admirable!*" Molina chuckled. "I should go thank *mí capitán* for his gift, no?"

"No. I—he's asleep." She sighed. "And I'm all by myself."

After a long pause, Molina took the bait. "You are lonely, *señorita?*"

"I had expected Captain Ramos—" She sighed again, more deeply. "You know what is said about men who drink too much, Sergeant."

"*Ay, sí!*" Then, philosophically, "It can happen to any man, *señorita*. Tomorrow, the *capitán* will be himself again."

"But that doesn't help me tonight," Flo said seductively. "Now, if there was only some big, fine man—"

Longarm thought she was overdoing her act a bit. He risked peering around the closet door, saw that Flo had let her negligee fall open and that Molina's eyes were fixed on her body.

"You would like me to return, no?" Molina whispered. "After I take the bottles to the men? But what would *mí capitán* say?"

"He's sleeping so deeply, he'd never know."

"*Ay, las rubias!*" Molina chuckled. "*Todavia buscanda un hombre!*" He chuckled again. "What *mí capitán* don' know won't hurt us, you and me? No? *Pues,* I take the bottles quick, and come right back."

"Hurry, then!" Flo urged. "I'll be waiting for you!"

Not only was Flo waiting for Molina when he came back. Longarm was, too. The sergeant rushed eagerly through the door into the sala. Flo had stationed herself a few feet inside, and Molina saw only her. Longarm stepped from behind the door and shoved his Colt hard against Molina's bare neck.

"Stop right where you are, hombre, and keep quiet, or you're dead."

Molina was as startled as Ramos had been. "*El gringo federalista!* Why you not in jail?"

"I reckon because I busted out," Longarm said. "Take his gunbelt off, Flo. Then we'll put him in with Ramos."

While Flo was relieving Molina of his pistol belt, he asked, "*Mí capitán,* he is not *borracho?*"

"No, but I'll just bet he wishes he was," she told him.

"*Rubia perfidia!*" Molina snorted. "You and the *gringo cabrón* have plan this!"

"You finally figured that out, did you?" Longarm grinned. To

Flo, he said, "Come on, we'll put him in where him and his boss can look at each other."

There was plenty of material left in the bedsheet Flo had torn up when Ramos was being bound to provide strips with which to tie Molina to another chair. Longarm kept his gun trained on the sergeant while Flo gagged and tied him. Ramos and Molina sat facing one another, glaring angrily across the few feet that separated them. It was obvious that each would try to blame the other for their plight.

Longarm guffawed. "I'd sure like to be around when they start jawing. I bet a man could pick up a bunch of brand-new Mexican cusswords about that time."

"What I hope is that we'll be a long way from here when they get loose," Flo said. "I've seen all I want to of rurales and Mexican bandits, both."

"It's going to be a while before we can take off," Longarm reminded her. "It sure won't be safe to show our heads outside this place until the whole bunch down by that barracks is blind drunk."

"How long do you think we'd better wait?"

"An hour. Maybe two. I'll look out now and again, to keep an eye on how their party's going. We can tell when the time's right."

"I suppose I can wait that long. But let's go somewhere else, in the big room, where we can have a drink and relax."

"Sounds fine to me. Might as well make the best we can of waiting, since there's no way we can cut it shorter."

"I'll get the only other clothes I've got," Flo said. "This nightgown's comfortable, but if I'm going for a horseback ride, I'll want something more than it between me and the wind."

She groped behind the dressing table, brought up a small portmanteau, and busied herself throwing into it the cosmetics that were on the dresser and the dark dress that hung beside it.

"There. I guess that'll fix me up," she told Longarm. "Now let's get out of this damned room. I don't like the things it makes me remember."

Chapter 15

Longarm stayed in the bedroom long enough to blow out the kerosene lamp on the dressing table. He told the gagged rurales, "It just wouldn't do if one of you was to work your chair over and manage to knock that lamp off. Setting fire to this place'd be a sure way to bring your gang kiting up here, now wouldn't it? So, you'll just have to put up with being in the dark, I guess."

He followed Flo into the sala. She'd dropped her portmanteau and was making a beeline for the liquor cabinet. "I need something to wash the taste of that rye whiskey you favor out of my mouth." She found a bottle of Otard and looked at the label. "This is the best liquor I've seen since a rich stage-door Johnny took me to supper after the show at the Astor House, a week before I left to come down here."

"I'll stick to my own," Longarm told her, tilting the bottle of rye. Flo was using the corkscrew on the brandy bottle; Longarm idly began looking into the other cabinets that lined the room's walls. He found one packed with small valuables of various kinds: rings, watches, bracelets, table silver; his idea that the rurales under Diaz behaved very much like the bandit gangs they were supposed to control was confirmed by the sight of the loot. The next cabinet he opened was packed with clothing, and the garment that lay on top of the heap was the frock coat that had been taken from him the day before. He slid his hand into its pockets. Except for his wallet, their contents were untouched.

Flo said, "Unless you just want to keep on looking around, we might as well go in and sit down at that fancy table in there. It's going to be a long wait, isn't it?"

"Times when a couple of hours seems like a week," Longarm said. "But you're right, we might as well be comfortable."

They moved back into the sala. Flo set the bottle of brandy on the big table and pulled a chair up in front of it. "I'm not a lady drunk," she told Longarm. "But this is a time when a girl needs a little comforting. Don't worry, I won't overdo."

"I ain't worrying." Longarm sipped from the rye. "Talking about drunks gives me an idea, though. I'll just step outside and see how that bunch is doing with the liquor we sent 'em."

He tossed his coat on the table and, more as a precaution than because he thought he'd need it, picked up his Winchester. As he stepped out the door, Longarm heard music coming from the direction of the barracks, and saw the bare ground between the headquarters and jail flooded with firelight. He slid along the headquarters wall until he could get a clear look. The fire at the barracks had been rekindled. Its dancing flames spread over the entire outpost area. Around the fire, an impromptu fiesta was being held. The lavanderas had joined the rurales at the barracks; men and women were dancing around the fire to the music of guitar and concertina. The flames glinted on bottles being passed, lifted, waved.

Longarm watched for several minutes. As his eyes adjusted to the light, he could see that the liquor had already taken a number of the rurales out of action. A half-dozen sprawled forms lay beside the barracks wall, or were propped against it. While he was watching, another man who'd overestimated his capacity, or underestimated the potency of liquor strange to him, staggered and went down. His dancing partner helped another rurale to drag the drunk man to the wall, then she and the man who'd helped her rejoined the dancers around the fire.

Things ought to quiet down soon, Longarm told himself, when there's just enough men left sober to pair off with the women.

He slid back along the wall and into the sala. Flo had given up her chair and was sitting on the edge of the big table. She was sipping from the brandy bottle again. Longarm could see from the smile she turned to him when she took the bottle from her lips that she was feeling good, not from the lift of the liquor, but the euphoria of having her freedom again. It occurred to him that he felt pretty much the same way she did.

"How's the orgy going?" she asked him.

"Oh, they're whooping it up, if that's what an orgy is. Makes me sorta wish I could join 'em, they're having such a good time."

"How long before things will be quiet enough for us to sneak your friends out of the pokey and get away?"

"About another hour, I'd guess. Maybe a little longer. I'd go get Nate and John right now, except that they've built up their fire, and the damn place is just about as bright as noontime outside. Can't risk moving around, they might notice us."

"You might as well have another drink, then," Flo invited.

"I was just going to." Longarm stepped to the table, picked up his bottle of rye and sipped. Flo raised the brandy bottle in salute and sipped, too.

"I don't remember even saying thank you for getting me out of this mess," she said.

"You better save your thanks. We ain't out yet. Most anything could happen after we leave here, and it's still a long ride to Los Perros after we get started."

"Where in hell's Los Perros?"

"About a two-day ride. You never heard of it, Flo. It's a little shantytown on the border. I still got unfinished business there, so has Nate Webster. And John's cavalry post's not too far from it."

"Is there a train I can take out of it for New York?"

"Flo, there's no train tracks inside of two hundred miles of Los Perros. There's a stagecoach that passes by Fort Lancaster, though. I'll see you on a stage that'll get you to San Antonio. You can take a train back East from there."

"How far's San Antonio?"

"About a week on the stage."

Her eyes widened. "You know, God must've had one hell of a lot of spare space on His hands when He created Texas."

Longarm grinned. "There's been some questions asked whether it was God or the devil that's responsible for Texas. Me, I don't take either side. I get along wherever I might happen to be."

Flo looked at him narrowly. "You know, I believe you do. You're quite some man, Marshal."

"Thanks. But I'd feel better if you'd call me by my name,

which I guess we been too busy for me to tell you. It's Custis Long."

"Sure, Custis. Look, before we get off the subject, I was starting out to thank you for getting me away from Ramos and all the rest of this."

"I didn't do it for thanks."

"You've got mine, whether you want them or not. And just to show you I mean it—" She broke off, threw her arms around Longarm's neck, and pulled him to her. Before he knew what was happening, she was pressing her lips on his. He thought it was going to be a friendly thank-you kiss until he felt her tongue pressing his lips apart.

Longarm responded predictably. Flo hadn't yet changed clothes, and the gauze-thin nightgown she wore could hardly be felt when he brought his hands up to cup her generous breasts. His fingertips were hard on her budding nipples as he caressed them. The scent of her body, all aroma of woman not lately soaped or perfumed, filled his nostrils. He broke the kiss and bent to take her nipples in his lips, nipping them gently, pulling them into his mouth and feeling them roughen, swell and grow firm as his tongue's tip flicked them through the thin nightgown.

Flo leaned back, bracing herself with her arms, hands flat on the tabletop, her body upthrust to give Longarm free access to it. His face still buried in the soft flesh of her bosom, he rubbed a hand slowly down over her voluptuously rounded stomach and caressed her blond pubic hair. She gave a dancer's kick to send the skirt of her gown flying upward, baring her legs and thighs. Longarm let his fingers stray deeper; she opened to them and he felt her beginning moisture on the soft lips between her thighs.

Flo was leaning back on only one arm, now. Her free hand was rubbing Longarm's crotch, feeling his erection grow. She worked at the buttons of his fly and tried to slip her hand in, but his britches fitted too closely. With a muttered "Damn it!" she unbuckled his belt and tugged at the waistband until she'd pulled the britches down over his hips and freed him.

"I'm as ready as you are," she said softly when she felt his hard springiness under her fingers.

"No use us waiting, then."

He moved between her legs and went in full and deep. Flo was on the table, Longarm standing in front of it. She lay back and brought her legs up, locked her ankles around the back of his neck.

"Ride me, now!" she commanded. "I want to feel you hit bottom!"

Longarm obliged. He pulled away from her, not leaving her totally empty, but nearly so. Then he thrust deliberately, deeper than he'd been able to go before.

Flo shrieked, a cry in which pain and pleasure mingled. "Oh, God, you did hit bottom! Do it again, faster!"

After a dozen deep, shattering thrusts, Longarm felt Flo's juices begin to ooze. Her cries of excitement, the heat of her body, the dangerous surroundings, were having their effect on Longarm. He was moving fast to orgasm. He pounded harder, bringing animal yelps from deep in Flo's throat. She became rigid for an instant. Her inner muscles tightened around him and he pressed hard for the instant before both of them were seized with a shuddering that ended in a blissful outpouring and a total relaxation. Longarm fell forward, pushing Flo's knees down nearly to the tabletop and penetrating her even more deeply than ever for a shattering instant before he relaxed.

Neither of them moved for several moments. Flo found breath enough to whisper, "I didn't know, a minute ago, just how much man you really are."

"You're a right smart bundle of woman, Flo. But we're a couple of damn fools, you know that?"

"After the past few weeks, it feels so good to be able to let go completely that I don't mind being a damn fool. It didn't last nearly long enough, though."

"We'll have more time, later. After we get away from this damn place."

"I think you're telling me something. We'd better get ready to run the gauntlet, is that it?"

"Something like that."

He pulled away from her reluctantly. Flo sat up and Longarm began to button his britches. His sense of timing told him they'd better be thinking of the men in jail instead of one another.

"Get into your traveling clothes as quick as you can," he told her. "I'll go see what things look like outside."

Longarm looked back across the sala before he went out the door. In the dim light of the vigil candle, he saw Flo in half-silhouette. She was standing beside the table, naked, the light dancing on her tall body, outlining its features. Her upraised arms, stretching luxuriously, pulled her breasts high and taut. Her rounded stomach flowed into flared hips, her pubic fringe matching the hair that fell in glowing gold, long, down her back. Her long legs seemed even longer as she rose on tiptoes in her stretching. For an instant he wanted to turn back, but common sense said no. He went through the door and out into the darkness.

This time, it was true darkness. The fire that had flared a half hour ago was dying down. Only a handful of dancers now moved their feet in time to the thin melody of guitar strings. The concertina was silent. There were more figures lying on the ground and leaning against the barracks wall. A wide belt of deep shadow lay between barracks and jailhouse. Longarm felt a twinge of guilt because he'd made his cellmates wait such a long time. It was, he decided, safe now to risk making an effort to leave.

Flo was wearing a flared skirt of dark material, a man-styled blue silk blouse, and a short jacket. She'd twisted her hair into a bun low on her neck. She saw in Longarm's face that it was time for them to go.

"I'm ready," she told him. "Just tell me what you want me to do."

"Stick close by me. We'll mosey slow across the open space. Most of the rurales and their women are sleeping-drunk, and the ones that're still on their feet are about ready to fall over."

"What if they see us?"

"Don't pay any attention until one of 'em starts to holler, and then let me handle things. Can you use a gun?"

"God, no, Custis! The only gun I ever shot was a toy popgun I used in one of my dance routines."

"Then you'd better carry the ones we're taking for Nate and John. Think you can tote 'em?"

"Dancers have to keep in trim. I'm pretty strong, you ought to know that."

He remembered her arms pulling him down to her, her legs clasping his body. "You are, at that." He picked up the rifles he'd taken from Ramos's collection and helped her balance them in her hands before draping a gunbelt with a holstered revolver over each of her shoulders. He'd looked until he'd found guns of the same caliber as his own Winchester and Colt, and had gathered up all the .44-40 ammunition he could find. This he'd put into bags, which he slung over his own shoulder.

"Just move slow and steady," he cautioned her. "And don't fret. We'll make it, all right."

Their passage through the belt of darkness between the

headquarters building and the jail drew no attention from the dancers still twirling by the waning fire. Longarm hadn't expected it to. The minutes of danger lay ahead, when they'd be working with the horses at the corral. They got to the jail and found the door swinging wide. Longarm slipped inside. It was pitch-black.

"Nate? John?" He kept his voice low.

"We're all right." It was Webster's voice.

"What in hell's name happened that took you so long?" Hill asked.

"Had to wait until the liquor I fed them rurales put most of 'em under. All but a few's passed out now. But we'll still have to tiptoe when we go outa here." His eyes could penetrate the gloom of the jail's interior now. He saw a white form spread-eagled across the door of the cell in which Webster and Hill waited. "What happened in here?"

"We had to throttle old Sebastian." Hill spoke without emotion. "Hated to do it, but he started yelling when he noticed you were gone. Before we could stop him, he threw the keys down the corridor. We couldn't reach them to let ourselves out."

Longarm reached into his coat pocket for a match, thought better of showing a light in the jail, and said, "I'll scrabble for 'em."

While he was groping around on the floor, Webster said, "We heard all the music and laughing, and I shinnied up to look outa that hole in the roof. By then, it was too light from their fire for us to try a sneak."

"We didn't know you'd arranged their party," Hill said. "If we had, we wouldn't have been so nervous, waiting."

Longarm finally located Sebastian's key ring. He said, while he unlocked the cell door, "It was the only way I could figure to put most of 'em to sleep. If we're lucky, we can get away without raising a ruckus."

He led the way outside. When Webster saw Flo standing by the door with the guns, he made a leap for her and would've wrestled her down if Longarm hadn't grabbed him.

"She's with us," he said. "Flo's been a real help. I might not've been able to swing it without her."

"Where the hell did you find her?" Hill asked.

"Ramos grabbed her away from some bandits who'd kidnapped her off a train. She can tell you about it later. She's American, just like us."

"And ready to go home," Flo said.

"She's American, all right," Hill agreed. "Easterner, I'd say."

"New York, New York," Flo told him. "And if I ever get back there, nobody's going to get me west again, not even across the river to Jersey."

"We better be thinking about another river," Webster reminded them. He gestured toward the two or three couples still dancing around the embers of the fire. "If that's all of Ramos's crew that's still able to stand up, we won't have much trouble."

"Let's try to do it without no trouble at all," Longarm suggested. "Here's what I'd like to do: we go down to the corral real quiet, so's not to spook the horses. That gray of mine's the easiest to spot, so I'll pussyfoot in and lead him out while you fellows get us some saddles. We'll load the saddles on the dapple, just any which way, and I'll lead him off. Then you sneak your animals out the same way, one at a time. We'll get far enough so nobody can hear us, then we'll saddle up and be off free."

"Wait a minute," Webster said. "Miss Flo, you know how to sit a horse?"

"I guess Mexican horses are pretty much the same as the ones I ride in Central Park. I had a friend who was—" She broke off. "That's neither here nor there. Yes, I can ride enough to get away from here. I'd ride an elephant, if I had to."

Circling to stay within the increasingly wide zone of darkness, they walked slowly and steadily until they were within a few yards of the corral.

Longarm said, "All right. Everybody knows what we'll do. I'll leave Flo to hold my gray after we're far enough off, and come back to get a nag for her."

Groping along the corral's top pole, Longarm located his saddle by feel. He knew it was taking time, but he hated to part with the old McClellan and have to break in a new one. He tossed three other saddles to the ground and followed them with a heap of saddle blankets, then bridles. He whistled low, and Webster and Hill moved up to untangle the gear. Longarm located the gate pole and ducked under it. One or two of the horses shied and whinnied, but none of them cut up too badly or made a lot of noise. He found Tordo and rubbed the dapple's nose.

"Easy, boy. Come along."

Tordo followed him readily through the gate. With nose pats

and low-voiced words, Longarm kept the gray standing while Webster and Hill piled the saddles loosely on his back.

"I'll head straight north," Longarm told them. That was all he needed to say. He knew both men were trail-wise and would sight on the North Star and stay on a straight course until they reached wherever he'd decided to stop. "Come on, Flo." She joined him and they moved off.

When they were out of earshot of the corral, she said with open amazement, "Those men acted like it was the most normal thing in the world for me to be here, a million miles from nowhere. Why, Custis, they didn't ask more than two or three questions."

"They're both good men. They know when it's time to talk and when it's time to do. Back at the jail, we had to do, not stand palavering all night."

"How far will we have to ride now?"

"Tonight we'll just push far enough on to get a good lead on the rurales. When we come to a good place, we'll stop and rest awhile, and move on at dawn."

"You think Ramos will come after us, then?"

"Damn right he will. He can't afford to let even one of us get away. He likely won't start, though, till it's light enough for his trackers to read trail. We got a little time. Not much, but a little bit."

They walked on in silence for a while. Finally, Longarm said, "I guess this is far enough. I'll saddle Tordo while we're waiting; as soon as I hear John or Nate coming, I'll start back."

"I'm not afraid to wait in the dark, if that's keeping you here." Flo put her arms around Longarm's waist. It wasn't a sexual gesture, but more as though she needed comforting. "But I'll admit, it's a lot nicer to have you to wait with."

"Maybe it's just this wild country bothering you." Longarm was holding her gently. "People that live in places like New York get spooked when they're out away from everything."

"It's not that. I'll tell you, Custis, New York's just a different kind of wild from this place here. And I'm used to looking out for myself."

Longarm had known theatrical women before; he had enjoyed their breeziness and the uninhibited approach to living that characterized those with stage backgrounds. He'd seen them tear through danger, as Flo had earlier, without turning a hair, and then be caught up, just as she was now, in a reaction. Her need for reassurance didn't really surprise him.

"We're going to be fine, Flo. You think about how much better off we are now than we were a few hours ago."

"Like hell we are. A few hours ago, you and I were having one of the best damned fucks I've ever enjoyed. Now, we're out here in the middle of some big black nowhere, don't know where we are, whether those murdering rurales are after us, or what."

"But there's twice as many of us now," he pointed out. "We got guns, and don't you think for a minute we're lost. You settle down, now, keep on kicking for a day or two, and before you know it, you'll be on your way back home."

She leaned back in his arms, and in the starlight he could see that she'd cried a little bit, but was smiling now. "Sorry, Custis. I don't usually act like a baby. I keep telling myself I'm a big girl and don't need anybody to pat my ass and tell me I'm going to be all right. But I guess all of us do, sometimes."

"You'll be fine now, though."

"Sure I will. As long as I can hold on to you for a minute or so, once in a while."

"Whenever you want to. I'll see you're safe."

Hoofbeats told them that either Hill or Webster was approaching. Longarm whistled softly, to help whoever it was in finding them. In a few minutes, Hill came up.

"Nate'll be right along," he said. "Everything was quiet when I left, so it looks like we've pulled it off."

"Now you're here, I'll go cut out a horse for Flo," Longarm said. "It oughtn't to take me long."

He had no trouble at the corral. In front of the barracks building, the fire had died to a few stray red coals and all the dancers had gone. Longarm thought he could see some forms still sprawled against the building's walls, but couldn't be sure. The headquarters was dark; so was the jail. He made quick work of cutting out a horse, wasting a few minutes patting necks and noses, hoping to find one that seemed gentler than most of the Mexican horses he'd seen so far. He wasn't sure whether Flo could really ride, or was just claiming she could for fear of being left behind.

Hill and Webster had the other horses saddled by the time Longarm got back. The fourth was quickly fitted, and Longarm was satisfied when he saw Flo mount easily and with confidence that she'd be able to stay on. He swung onto Tordo's back.

Hill said, "Well, gentlemen—and lady, too, of course—I don't see any reason to stay here. Since we don't have a bugler to sound commands, I'll give them myself. Route pace, ma-arch—ho!"

Chapter 16

A raw September breeze from the low peaks of the Burro Mountains was in their faces as the little group skirted the foothills, riding through the darkness. Without discussion, the men fanned out ahead, calling out when a barrier such as a steep canyon cut across their path, or when the way ahead of one or the other seemed easier. They followed no trail because there was none to follow, but set their way by the stars, bearing consistently northeast. The going was slow and rough on the horses. They circled the deeper canyons, slid down the slopes of shallow arroyos, and pushed through brushy patches that tore at their legs. It was country that called for both chaps and tapaderos, but they had neither.

After four hours of steady but slow progress, Longarm called a halt. "We better let these animals rest," he said. "Far's that goes, I guess we need a breather ourselves. It's still a while before daybreak, and I don't figure the rurales are going to start after us until they can see our sign."

"They'll be moving faster, though," Webster warned. "And some of those cholos are part Indian. They'll know the land better, too."

"We haven't left that much of a trail," Hill protested. "But I'll agree, we do need to rest. I just hate to lose our lead."

"After daybreak, we'll make better time," Longarm pointed out. "I'd say to stop at the first good place we come to, and start out fresh with first light."

"If you're worrying about me," Flo said, "I'm tired, but I'll sure keep on going as long as you men want to. Don't do me any favors just because I'm a woman."

"We ain't," Webster assured her. "It wouldn't be any different if you weren't along, Miss Flo."

They pushed on, moving more slowly now, until they came to a brush-covered slope over which a handful of tall ocote pines towered, their night-black limbs breaking the deep blue sky. Longarm called for the others to stop and urged Tordo into the fringe of the brush that surrounded the trees. The dapple pushed through the shrubs without hesitating. Longarm leaned down to feel the vegetation and found that the stalks of the bushes and their leaves were smooth and free of thorns. He reined Tordo lightly, to turn him, but the animal resisted, wanting to go ahead. Longarm let him. The gray broke into a clearing, and moved faster. Then he stopped. Longarm heard the splash of running water, and then saw the little pool made by a spring reflecting the stars. He let Tordo drink sparingly and went back to tell the others.

"Damn horse had more sense than me, for once. I ought to've known when I felt them huisache leaves that there'd be water, they're thirsty plants. If everybody agrees, this is as good a place to rest as we're likely to find."

There was no dissent. They pushed into the clearing and dismounted. After all of them had drunk and wiped the cool, faintly salt-tasting water over their dusty faces, they let the horses drink, and tethered them with slacked girths at the edge of the clearing.

Hill's military training showed. He asked, "Don't you think we ought to take turns at sentry duty? We don't really know that the rurales aren't on our trail right now."

"Makes sense to me," Webster nodded.

"Me, too," Longarm agreed.

"Since it was my idea, I'll take the first watch," Hill offered. "If we stand an hour each, that ought to take up what's left of the night."

Webster spoke up. "I'll relieve you, then, and the Marshal can stand the wake-up watch."

"What about me?" Flo asked. "I'll do my share, too."

"No need, Miss Flo," the Ranger said. "You've had a real hard day. You get what sleep you can."

"But—" Flo began.

Longarm interrupted her. "Listen to what Nate says. He's got a reason maybe you don't understand. It's not because you're a woman, but because you're a tenderfoot. All three of us'd know if we heard a horse or maybe a deer or goat in the dark. You wouldn't."

"I hadn't thought of it that way," she nodded. "All right, if that's your reason."

There was a brief time of settling down. Hill took his rifle and pushed through the brush, following the trail they'd broken on their way in. Webster, an old hand at impromptu bivouacs, found himself a patch of green weeds far enough from the spring to be on dry ground. He curled up and was snoring in two minutes. Without exchanging a word, Flo and Longarm threaded their way through a patch of brush to the base of one of the ocote pines. They sat down together.

"I wanted to—" she began.

Longarm put a finger across her lips. "No need to talk about it, Flo, honey. I wanted to, too. There's better things in life than just sleeping, ain't there?"

She turned her lips to him. They sank back on the short, curly growth that carpeted the ground where it was shaded by the ocote. Flo shrugged out of her jacket and Longarm began to rub her breasts.

"It was fine, back at the rurales' place, but it was over too quickly," she murmured into his ear.

Instead of answering, Longarm began kissing her. His hands wandered over her body and hers were exploring his. She broke their embrace long enough to slide her short silk knickers off, and he ran his hand along her smooth, tapered thighs. Flo began working at freeing Longarm's erection; feeling it grow in quick pulses set her to breathing faster. She stirred, rolled on her side, and pulled him to her. She took him between her thighs, squeezing him tightly, pushing against him, until the moist heat spreading upward from his groin and the incessant movement of Flo's tongue in his mouth brought Longarm up full and swollen.

"Let me in you now," he told her, and Flo obeyed.

"But slow," she whispered in his ear. "I love the feeling of you going in. I want to enjoy it as long as I can."

Longarm penetrated her as she'd asked him to, slowly and deliberately, and for what seemed a very long time they lay simply enjoying the sensation of their intermingled bodies. Flo began to contract her inner muscles in a gentle rhythm that brought Longarm to an orgasm that was as quick as it was unexpected. There'd been few women he'd known before who'd mastered use of the muscles Flo was employing. She didn't stop her inner contractions while Longarm rested, still hard inside her, and she teased him with gentle nips of her sharp teeth on his neck and ears and lips.

Longarm recovered quickly and rolled on top of Flo. She was as eager now as he was, and opened her thighs to let his slim hips drop between them to sink into her more deeply. He began rocking slowly, feeling her hips roll beneath him. Soft birdlike cries escaped Flo's lips. Longarm read the signal she was giving him and began thrusting faster to meet her growing frenzy. Time stopped for both of them for a while; they were aware of nothing but sensation.

"Faster, now!" she urged him. Her head began rolling, loosening the bun in which she'd caught her hair, and her long blond locks spread over the dark ground.

Longarm began driving, his arms encircling Flo's neck, holding her mouth hard to his while they exchanged tongue caresses. Her hips were bouncing frantically now, but she still controlled her motions, just as Longarm did his. They didn't need to exchange words. Instinct joined experience to guide their movements, hips drawing apart and coming together in unison, in perfect mutual rhythm, to send each of his strokes fully into her depths.

Then the moment came when Longarm felt his control slipping away. He speeded his thrusts, and Flo matched his downward plunges, as they rushed together toward those few final seconds when their desire could no longer be denied and the climactic shuddering began that brought them both pressing together, passing through the little death that left them sprawled inert, helpless and almost senseless.

Panting, they rolled apart. Longarm said, "Damn! You really got it, Flo. If I wasn't a broad-minded man, I'd be jealous of anybody that ever got in you before me."

"Don't be, Custis. The first few didn't get much. Neither did I, for that matter. But I can't remember any man who had more than you've got, or knew how to use it better."

"I guess we've both had about the same amount of practice. I'll give you this, Flo: You know what you want, and don't let anything stop you from taking it."

"I needed somebody like you, after Ramos. He was so little and so damned fat that all he could do was make me want a real man. Besides, I enjoy giving, but I don't like being taken." Flo turned her head suddenly and spat, somehow making the unladylike action a maidenly gesture of utter contempt. "Ramos! *Paugh!*"

"Talking about Ramos, if we don't do more sleeping and less fucking, we're not going to be much good later on."

"I feel like sleeping, now. I didn't before." She stretched like an animal. Longarm could almost see the muscles under her silken skin rippling in the starlight. What he couldn't see, he imagined.

"You move like that another time, I'm going to be all over you again," he warned her.

"Come on. Any time." When he didn't move, she asked, "Sleepy?"

"Some. A mite tuckered, too. And beginning to think about what might happen tomorrow. If I'm feeling drawn-out, you must be, too."

"I'll sleep, if you'll hold me."

"You got a deal. But pull on your drawers, and I'll button up. If we don't, we'll be starting in again."

Cuddled together, they were asleep in a few minutes.

Captain Hill woke them. It was still dark. Hill said, "It's about time for you to relieve Nate, Marshal." He hesitated, and added, "But if the lady feels safer with you here to look after her, I'm still fresh. I'll take another watch."

"No you won't. It's my job, and I aim to do it. You'll be fine as long as you know the captain's here, won't you, Flo?"

Sleepily, Flo replied, "Sure. I'm not a baby anymore." She closed her eyes again at once and was asleep again.

Longarm and Hill walked quietly away from her until they were far enough to be sure their voices wouldn't disturb her. "Looks like she's fallen for you," Hill commented. "Not that it's any affair of mine what you and the lady do, but if it comes to a fight, and she keeps clinging to you, it might get all of us killed."

"I don't think you got anything to fret over. Flo's sensible. I seen that when she was helping me tie up Ramos and Molina. She'll carry her own weight, if it comes to a scrap."

"Good. Well, I'll go back to sleep, then." Hill lay down, using his arm for a pillow, in the manner of a man used to sleeping on the ground. He grinned up at Longarm. "Tell the bugler not to bother to blow reveille. I always wake up before he does, any-how."

Chuckling, Longarm backtracked through the bent-down huisache growth until he found Webster. The Ranger was sitting Indian style on a boulder, his rifle across his knees.

"Nothing so far," he greeted Longarm. "We didn't really ex-pect there'd be, I guess."

"No. Still too soon. If we're lucky, we'll pick up another half-day's lead on 'em before they get to where we are now."

"We better be lucky, then. We're outgunned about eight to one, when they do catch up," Webster said thoughtfully. "Which wouldn't spook me much, if it wasn't for Miss Flo."

"That's occurred to me too, Nate. I got a hunch we can handle Ramos's bunch, though, if we don't make a bunch of tomfool moves."

"Sounds like you been doing some thinking."

"Some. Haven't you?"

"Oh, sure. Trouble is, this deal's a little out of my line. In the old days, you know, us Rangers moved in companies, during the Indian fighting and Mexican wars. The work we do nowadays is mostly single-handed."

Longarm carefully avoided suggesting that the Ranger was old enough to've fought in the War Between the States. If Web-ster'd been in it, then there'd be the risk of stirring up bad mem-ories. And Longarm knew just how bad those memories could be. He'd never rid his mind of the image of the dead rotting under summer rains at Shiloh. Then again, if Webster'd skulked out of the war, he wouldn't be proud of it. Longarm decided it wasn't a good idea to talk in military terms.

"I've got the glimmer of a scheme that might get us across the river without a stand-up fight, Nate," he said. "Tell you what, you go get your shut-eye, and give me a little more time to think. I'll come in at first light and the three of us'll powwow."

Longarm's watch wore itself along uneventfully. He spent his hour sitting on the boulder that Webster had occupied, keeping his ears tuned for sounds that might give warning of pursuit and thinking of ways to keep the rurales at bay when they caught up. He had no doubt that they would catch up, sooner or later.

When the first faint threads of gray showed across the high mesas in the east, Longarm uncoiled, stretched the kinks out of his leg muscles, and walked back to the thicket. He found Webster and Flo still asleep, but Hill, true to his promise, was stirring around.

"I've tightened the girths and put the bridles back on the mounts," the cavalryman announced. "As soon as we mount up, we can move out."

"Let's stay here a minute or two, John," Longarm suggested. "Give Nate and Flo time to duck back of a bush and pee, and wash their faces. Then we'll have a little council of war, if everybody's agreeable."

When they'd assembled, he outlined the plan he'd worked out during his hour of sentry duty.

"We got to figure the rurales will come after us," he began. "We shoved their faces in a hot cow pie when we slipped away from 'em, and Ramos can't let us go free and make trouble for his bosses in Mexico City. Now we know we can't outgun 'em in a showdown fight. Them rurales look sloppy, and sometimes they don't seem right bright, but from what I've heard, they're damn tough fighters."

"They're that," Webster affirmed. "Our only chance would be to hole up in a place where they could only come at us a few at a time. But even if we found a place like that, all they'd have to do is starve us out. Our best chance is to keep ahead of 'em."

"It's our only chance," Hill said. "Not just the best one."

"Sure, all of us know that," Longarm agreed. "We've got to take out of here running and keep running till we get to the border."

"But we can't afford to blow our horses," the cavalry officer cautioned. "They've got remounts, we haven't. Even if it loses time for us, we'll have to breathe them before they drop."

"I figured on that," Longarm said. "My scheme is for us to go like hell when we take off. When the horses need a rest, we'll stop. From there, we'll split up." He saw that Webster was about to object and held up a hand to stop him. "Just a minute, Nate. I'm not done. Far's I know, there's only one place you could call a town on the other side of the river that we'd have a chance to get to. That's Los Perros. Am I right about that, John?"

"Yes. There're a few other shanty settlements along the river, but Los Perros is the biggest one, the only place we'd have a chance to find enough men to help us. The others only have a dozen or so people living in them."

"That's what I'd guessed," Longarm said. "Now, then. When

we split up, we'll do it someplace where two men can hold back Ramos's bunch for a while. It don't have to be for too long, just enough cover to stop the rurales for an hour or two. If the ones that leave ride hell for leather, they oughta get to Los Perros in time to pull some kind of crew together to beat the rurales back."

"What about the two who've fought rear guard?" Hill asked. "Do you think they can outrun the rurales all the way to the river?"

"If they make a sneak and get a start before Ramos's men know they've gone, I figure they can," Longarm replied.

Webster and Hill thought about the idea for a moment, then the Ranger said, "It's about the best we can do, I'd say. We're sorta between a rock and a hard place."

"I'd give a lot to have just one squad of my men at the river," Hill said grimly. He smiled and added, "But I'd give a lot to have a Gatling gun along with us right now. All right, Marshal, it looks like we agree that your plan's our only chance. Nate and I will take the rear guard job, you and the lady ride ahead."

"I didn't figure it that way," Longarm said. "It looks to me like you're the man to get Sheriff Tucker into line and organize whatever kind of bunch he can help you put together in Los Perros."

"I'm not sure you're right about that, Marshal." Hill shook his head. "Tucker and I have had our differences. He propositioned me to be his silent partner a couple of years ago in a plan he'd come up with to turn Los Perros into a honkytonk town. Wanted me to give my troopers extra payday liberty to come in and spend their money at the whorehouses—excuse me, Miss Flo—and the gambling joints he proposed to put in. I read him off and told him I'd do my damnedest to keep my men out of his town in the future. And I have. I don't think he'd forget that."

"No. He ain't that kind," Longarm said. "Damn it! I was sorta counting on you to take care of that part of the scheme."

"I won't say I can't, but I won't say I can. You know army policy. We're not supposed to interfere with civilian government affairs unless we're asked by the authorities for help."

"I don't know you'd call Tucker an authority," Webster put in. "He never was elected to be, except by himself. But John's got a reason to be doubtful, just like I have. I had a run-in with Tucker when I first started looking into the Laredo Loop business. He just the same as told me to go to hell. I've got a hunch that it was Tucker who tipped off his partners in Mexico to get the rurales looking for me after he found out I'd crossed the border."

"That leaves you, Marshal," Hill said. "I think Nate and I both feel you're the man to do it. From what you told us while we were in that cell together, you've handled Tucker before, and you've got the lever on him to handle him again."

"John's right," Webster agreed. "Your scheme might just save all our butts—excuse me, Miss Flo—save our hides, if you can get Tucker to round up a couple of dozen men to cover the two of us when we get close to the river."

"I didn't plan to be the one to split off when I dreamed up this scheme," Longarm said. "But I can see you might be right in figuring the best way to work it out."

"There's only one weak spot I can see," Hill frowned. "Ma'am, can you handle a horse at a gallop over rough country?"

"I never had to, until now," Flo said. "But if I'm betting my life on whether I can or not, I'll do it one way or another."

"Flo's kept up so far," Longarm reminded them. "I ain't too worried about her staying right alongside of me."

"It's settled, then," Hill nodded. "We'll push on, and when the time comes, all of us will know what to do."

"And all we need to make things work," Longarm said, "is some nerve and good shooting and one hell of a lot of luck!"

Chapter 17

"How much farther is it?" Flo asked Longarm. They'd pulled up to give the horses a breather.

"Two hours. Maybe three." He squinted at the sun dipping now to the west, but still well above the humped tops of the Burro range. "You getting tired, Flo?"

"Some. But don't look for me to quit, Custis. I won't do that."

"Didn't figure you would, or you wouldn't be here."

They'd parted from Webster and Hill shortly after noon, at a rock outcrop that all of them agreed was the best defensive position they'd seen so far. The spot was on that single long spur of the Burros that pushes out far past the other rises of the foothills, and runs at an angle to the rest of the range. The spur, instead of lying generally north-south, slants off to the east, in the direction of the Rio Grande.

A fault in the rock had created a fortress in miniature that might have been planned by an engineer. Through the centuries, the crevasse had become filled with broken rock, then topped with rain-washed sand to create a firm, fairly level floor. The rock fissure was triangular, big enough to hold two horses and their riders and still leave room for them to move about. To the south and along the hump of the spur, the rock was unbroken, solid but slick. A horse could not keep its footing on it, and a man would be able to do so only with difficulty. The triangle that constituted the fort was deep enough to protect a horse or a standing man. Behind it, sheer, raw rock rose two hundred feet straight up. Except for the extension of the fissure that gave access to the triangle, there was no way for an attacker to approach it.

Captain Hill had been delighted from the instant they'd seen the place. "That's our spot, Nate! From behind that shelf, we can cover any approach the rurales might want to use."

"Except from behind us," the Ranger pointed out. "If they get a man or two up above us, shooting down, we're wide open."

Hill squinted along the face of the cliff. "I think there's enough of an overhang to shield us. I'll take the chance, if you will."

"Oh, I didn't say I'd back away from it," Webster said quickly. "Time's running out, and this is about the only place we've come to where we'd have a better than even chance."

"You might not have to make a fight at all," Longarm reminded them. "We've kept ahead, so far. You stay here about two or three hours. If they don't show up, ride for the river."

"I wouldn't bet we're going to get off that light," Webster said. "And I wouldn't want Ramos's outfit to get off, either. After what happened to John and me, we're both ready to sting 'em."

"Win, lose, or draw, then," Hill said, "this is where we stay. Three hours, Marshal. We'll guarantee you that much time."

"No," Longarm shook his head. "Don't set a limit, John. Just do your best if they catch up, but don't let 'em get you. If it gets too hot, you and Nate pull leather for Los Perros. We'll try to be ready. Just remember, Ramos ain't Santa Ana, and this place ain't the Alamo."

He and Flo had started off, and had ridden as fast as they dared push their horses without crippling them. Longarm kept a close lookout for familiar country. The trailless foothills were strange to him. The path taken by the rustled herd he'd followed south had avoided the higher country and moved along the narrow strip of flat land between the Burros and the Rio Grande. He'd set a course on a long slant that he'd confidently expected would intersect the rustlers' route. Once on that trail, he'd planned to follow it to the ford above Los Perros. He didn't want to risk a strange crossing; the Rio Grande's reputation for horse-swallowing quicksand beds in its shallows and tumbling, unpredictable currents in its deeper stretches was something he remembered from his earlier trip there. So far, though, there'd been no sign of the rustlers' route.

Now, looking as far ahead as possible from the slight elevation of the ridgeline they'd been following, he still saw nothing that resembled the terrain he'd noted on his way south. He pressed his knees to Tordo's ribs, and found that the gray was breathing easily, no longer panting. Flo's Mexican mount seemed to have eased, too.

"We've given 'em all the time we can spare," he told her. "We better be moving again." He picked up the reins from his saddle horn and was just about to nudge Tordo ahead when he saw the thin column of dust below and behind them. He called to Flo, "Hold up!"

"What's wrong? Did you see something?"

"Dust devil, maybe. It's hard to tell what the wind's doing in country like this." He kept his eyes on the smudge that rose low into the harsh blue sky. The thin cloud wasn't acting the way a dust devil ought to. Those miniature whirlwinds rose fast, moved erratically, and died quickly. This one was moving slowly and kept hanging in the sky. There wasn't enough dust to mark a lot of riders, though, he thought.

Anxiously, Flo asked, "Is that the dust devil, right there?" She pointed.

"That's what I'm looking at. Only I'm damn sure now it ain't a dust devil. It's riders."

"How many?" she asked. Then, as soon as she realized how impossible her question was to answer, she added, "I'm sorry. That was a silly thing to ask."

"For all you know, my eyes might be sharper than yours. But whoever it is or however many, they're still too far off to see."

"You think they're Ramos's men, Custis?"

"Likely as not. Nate and John wouldn't be down on the flat there. They'd be trailing us." Then, as an afterthought, Longarm added, "Unless they're being chased. But if they were, there'd be two dusts instead of just one."

"It's sort of like a Chinese puzzle, isn't it?" Flo asked. "You've got to fit all the pieces together just right, to work it."

"I'm pretty sure I've worked this one. It's just about bound to be some rurales. Not many, only maybe three or four. My guess is that Ramos took up our tracks, figured where we was headed, and sent a few riders to cut us off."

"You think there are more on the trail we left?"

"That's about the only way to figure. Now we got something else to work out."

"What?"

"Whether we want to let them hombres down there go on past us, or try to stop 'em." Longarm saw that Flo didn't understand. He explained, "We let 'em get by, we don't have a fight right here and now, but we'll have one later on. They'll go on to the ford and set up an ambush."

"Which would be the easiest? Now, or later?"

"It's six of one, half a dozen of the other. We've got a little better position now. Later we won't know where they might jump us." Flo didn't reply. She was, Longarm knew, waiting for him to decide. He made up his mind quickly. "Let's keep moving. Maybe we can find a place up ahead before they catch up that'll be better'n where we are now."

They started on down the slope. Longarm kept watching the dust cloud, which grew larger bit by bit as it came closer. He was also scanning the ground ahead, looking for a place that would offer them cover. The land across which they were passing was in the zone where the foothills merged into the narrow plain that almost at once became the river valley. There were no rock outcrops here, only a few shallow barrancas cut by rains cascading downslope during the wet season. The ground was baked hard, too hard for the hooves of their mounts to raise any dust, and while Longarm had no hope of finding a natural fortress like the one Nate and Hill had to shield them, he thought their presence might not be noticed while the approaching riders were still distant. Given time, he and Flo might find concealment.

He checked the dust cloud again. It hadn't changed direction. Their course and the one the unknown riders held to were still converging. He estimated that they'd come together within the next two or three miles. Then, the hump of the ridge down which they rode would no longer hide them from the other group. Somewhere before that distance was closed, he and Flo would have to find cover or risk odds he couldn't yet guess at in a stand-up fight. If he'd been alone, he thought, he'd have taken the odds, sight unseen. Having Flo with him changed things.

Down the slope just ahead, a little below the shoulder of the ridge, Longarm saw a strange angular patch. It was the only feature of an otherwise barren stretch of baked, arid earth. He glanced at the dust cloud again. As nearly as he could tell, their path and that of the unseen riders would intersect only a short distance beyond the strange formation ahead. He still wasn't sure what the patch was, but it was the only unusual feature in an otherwise featureless landscape. It might be an unusual rock formation, or even the foundation of a long-abandoned building. Whatever it was, it was the only thing he could see that promised cover.

Over the drumming of their horses' hooves, he shouted to Flo, pointing, "We'll make for that place there!"

She looked, saw what he was indicating, and nodded. Longarm turned Tordo and tried to get a bit more speed out of the dapple. Flo followed him as he led the way to the strange formation.

As they drew closer, Longarm could see that what had caught his attention wasn't a rock outcrop, but a heap of fallen trees. The water that had once nourished a grove had failed and the trees had died and toppled, crisscrossing one another. It wasn't much protection, only a half-dozen sun-bleached trunks, but it was better than nothing at all. With luck, the windfall would hide them from the oncoming riders. At worst, they'd provide a breastworks he'd have a chance of defending.

They reached the trees only seconds before the other horsemen rounded the foot of the ridge and came into sight. The tree trunks lay too low on the ground to hide the backs of their horses, but Longarm hoped the rurales—he was sure now that the strange riders had been sent by Ramos to cut them off from the river—would pass by without looking too closely in their direction.

He and Flo dismounted with no margin to spare. As they led their horses into the fallen trees, they saw the horsemen galloping across the plain at the bottom of the slope. There were only three of them. Longarm breathed an inward sigh of relief. Three to one were odds he might handle. For a moment, it looked as though the trio of riders would pass on without seeing them, but apparently they'd been pushing their mounts as hard as Longarm and Flo had been driving their own. The three reined in about two or three hundred yards distant from the fallen trees.

Longarm had taken his Winchester out of its saddle scabbard when they dismounted. He studied the three men, in clear sight now that a dust cloud no longer surrounded them. The look removed any doubt as to their identity. All three wore the charro suits that the rurales had adopted as a sort of unofficial uniform.

"Are you going to shoot them?" Flo asked, looking at Longarm's rifle.

"Not now. It might be smart if I did, though. It's either now or later, when we get closer to the river."

"It seems so—well, so cold-blooded. I mean, to shoot them when they're not shooting at us."

"If they see us, they'll be banging away soon enough. And three to one ain't odds exactly in our favor."

At that moment, the question of who'd start shooting first was settled without delay or debate. The rurales, getting ready to move ahead, were scanning the area all around them. Longarm could tell when one of the men spotted him. He gesticulated to his companions. The others swung in their saddles and gazed at the trees. They may have seen the horses' heads and rumps sticking up above the windfall. The three whipped their rifles around to free them from their shoulder slings and lead slugs began to slam into the tree trunks that sheltered Flo and Longarm.

"Guess we were bound to come down to it," Longarm muttered.

He centered the sights of the Winchester on the midsection of the nearest rurale and squeezed off a shot. The slug went high. He saw it kick up dust beyond the riders.

"Damn it!" he swore.

"What's the matter?" Flo was suddenly alarmed.

"Ramos or somebody must've monkeyed with my sights." He spoke while he was aiming again, making allowance for the change. This time his bullet went home. The rurale dropped from his saddle and lay still.

A fresh volley from the other two splatted into the trees, and a stray slug or two whistled overhead. The rurales were firing as fast as they could lever shells into the chambers of their guns. Flo was trembling. Longarm grabbed her and pulled her to the ground. After another shot or two, the firing from below stopped abruptly.

"Do you think they've gone?" Flo asked. The sudden ending of the gunfire had its effect on her voice. Even though their attackers were too far away to hear her, she whispered.

"Not a chance. I stopped shooting. They figure they've put me down. Soon as they can see us, they'll start up again."

Longarm raised his head above the tree trunks for a quick look. The riders below had thrown the body of their companion over his saddle and were disappearing around the shoulder of the ridge.

"Smart sons of bitches!" Longarm growled.

"What're they doing?"

"Just what I'd do, if it was me down below there. Pulling back around the shoulder, where I can't see 'em."

"But they can't see us either, can they?"

"No. But they can cut up the other side of the hump and get above us. Or split up, one come at us from the shoulder, the other one from below. That'd catch us in a cross fire."

Longarm wasted no time making up his mind. While he shoved fresh shells into the Winchester's magazine, he told Flo, "Now you do exactly what I tell you to." She nodded, her eyes wide. "I'm going to take a sneak up that shoulder. Here." He handed her his Colt. "You keep watch down below, there where they were before. If you see one of 'em coming around the shoulder, let go one shot at him. Just one, you understand?"

"Custis, I've never shot a pistol in my life."

"That don't matter. The rurale won't know that. And I don't expect you to hit anything. I couldn't myself, with a pistol at that kind of range. All I want to do is keep him down there."

"What if he doesn't stay there, though?"

"Shoot again. But watch your shots, mind? Only one at a time; you only got five. If he keeps coming, you wait till he's close enough for you to count his whiskers. Then just point the gun at his belly, like you would your finger, and pull the trigger."

"Is that this little lever here? And don't I have to do something called cocking it?"

"No. Just pull." He placed the gun in her hands and showed her how to hold it. "Now. Think you can do it?"

"I can sure as hell try." She shook her head determindly. "No. I'll do better than try. I'll hit him!"

"Good girl! Now duck down and stay down except when you raise up for a quick look."

Longarm started up the ridge. He was pretty sure the two remaining rurales would waste a little time discussing what to do, and he figured he had an edge of two or three minutes on them. He didn't slow himself down by crawling, but ran up the slope and toward the hump, his boot soles slipping now and then on the baked earth.

When he neared the crest of the shoulder, Longarm slowed

down. He dropped flat and began snaking forward. At the top of the rising ground he moved even more cautiously, holding his rifle as ready as he could and edging ahead by inches. The ridge wasn't sharply defined. Its top was rounded, not angular, and when he reached the end of the rise, inches from the slope on the other side, Longarm took time to adjust his rifle in his hands so that he could fire instantly. Then he raised himself to his knees and looked.

He and the rurale saw each other at the same time. The Mexican was crawling up the opposite slope, just as Longarm had climbed up his side. The difference was that the rurale had chosen to sling his rifle across his shoulders and crawl up on hands and knees. The difference cost him his life. Longarm's Winchester was ready. His slug shattered the rurale's face while he was still trying to get his rifle free. The man lurched forward and lay still.

A shot from below kicked up dust inches from Longarm's side. He dropped flat and peered cautiously over the hump. The rurale trio had stopped in the shelter of the shoulder as soon as they'd gotten out of sight of the tree trunks where Flo and Longarm had holed up. Then the man Longarm had just killed had started up the ridge to get above the tree trunk bastion. Longarm's shot had wounded the man he'd hit, but hadn't killed him. The injured man lay on the ground, the third of the rurales bending over him, bandaging him. When they'd heard the shot that finished their companion, the unwounded rurale had started shooting, using his pistol. Now, Longarm saw, he was going after his rifle.

Before Longarm could get off a shot, the wounded rurale clawed his pistol out and began shooting. The range was too great for his slugs to carry, and they fell short. By now, the unwounded rurale had his rifle in his hands. Longarm snapshotted without aiming, and though he missed, both men rolled behind the protection of their horses.

Longarm held his fire when his targets disappeared. The slope rose too abruptly for the rurales to fire from below the bellies of their mounts, but as long as they stayed behind the horses, Longarm couldn't put a slug into them. It was a standoff, but Longarm had been in standoffs before, situations where the first man who moved or exposed himself became an automatic target for his enemy's shot. Keeping his Winchester ready, Longarm studied the layout.

There wasn't much time for decision, he knew that. In just a few seconds the rurales would take advantage of their numbers.

On count, both of them would step around the ends of the horses and present Longarm with two targets, giving him a choice of one, leaving him a target for the other man. The thought of retreating behind the ridge didn't enter Longarm's mind. He saw his only chance, and took it without hesitation.

Allowing for the change somebody'd made in the Winchester's sights, Longarm aimed at the rump of one of the horses and fired. Before the wounded animal had stopped bucking and started running, he'd levered a fresh round into the chamber and pumped lead into the hindquarters of another of the beasts. The third horse saved him the trouble of wounding it. When its companions began rearing and whinnying, it bolted, with the wounded ones close behind.

Longarm used the shell he'd pumped in the chamber to knock down the rurale who was raising his rifle. The wounded man had just bent down to pick his rifle up from the ground when Longarm's next slug knocked him the rest of the way. Neither of the men gave any sign of movement, but Longarm waited with his rifle ready until he was sure they wouldn't. Then he reloaded.

His face grim, Longarm took careful aim at one of the prone men and squeezed off the shot. The body twitched when the slug hit. He stooped carefully, slowly, keeping his eyes on the other rurale, and picked up a cartridge case from the ground. Using it as a screwdriver, he adjusted the Winchester's rear sight. He lined up the buckhorn and the front sight on the form of the rurale who'd been wounded and saw the lead hit true. It wasn't a job he enjoyed doing, but he couldn't risk one of the men playing possum until he'd picked his way down the slope and surprising him with a belly-shot at point-blank range. He watched the two figures for a long moment. When neither of them moved, he started back to the windfall and Flo.

She was waiting, trying to look calm and hide her apprehension. "What happened?" she asked. "I heard the shooting, and then it stopped, and after a while there were some more shots, and I imagined all sorts of terrible things. I was afraid you might be—" She couldn't get the last word out.

"Dead?" Longarm asked her gently. She began trembling in delayed reaction to the strain she'd been under. He took her in his arms and held her for a moment until her shaking stopped. He kissed her before pulling out his soiled and wadded bandanna and wiping away the tears that were welling from her eyes.

"Come on. Let's sit down a minute. Everything's all finished.

Don't fret yourself about it anymore." He led her to one of the tree trunks and they sat side by side, Flo leaning on Longarm, his arms holding her. After a while she sighed and pulled a little away from him. But when she turned her face to him, she'd started to smile.

"I thought I was a pretty hard-boiled dame," she said. "I guess you've figured by now that my life hasn't been a lot of cream puffs and talcum powder. Most of the time I can take a man or leave him alone. If I want something bad enough, I can even put up with a man I don't much like. And even if I like him, I can kiss him good-bye without it bothering me. But damn you, Custis Long! You're different!"

"Now, you're just all upset, in a place that's pretty rough and strange to you. From what you've let on, you must've had a real rough time lately, too. After you get used to me, you'll find I'm just as ornery as any other man that wears britches."

"Like hell you are." Flo kissed him hard. "You're not like any man I've ever met before."

"Look out, now. You're going to make me proud, and if there's one thing I can't put up with it's a man that's vain." Before she could continue the conversation, he went on, "We can't take time to visit, Flo. We've got to get on with what we set out to do. Now, I got one more chore to do down there at the bottom of this hill. You take your time about coming down there to meet me. What I've got to do's something you don't want to see."

He rode Tordo up the hump and down the other side to where the dead rurales lay, stopping at the midpoint of the downslope to pick up the rifle and pistol of the man he'd shot first. The unwounded horse that had bolted wasn't too far away; Longarm hazed him easily back to where the two dead men lay. He loaded their weapons and ammunition belts on the spare horse, tying them with its saddle strings. For all he knew, Ramos's main force might have wiped out Nate and John and be riding fast for the river.

With the captured horse on a lead, Longarm and Flo set off again at a gallop toward the Rio Grande and Los Perros. The clanking of the weapons that had belonged to the dead rurales rang in their ears, a constant reminder that the shooting wasn't over yet.

Chapter 18

"Well," Longarm told Flo, pointing across the slick, green, rolling surface of the Rio Grande, "there it is. That's Los Perros."

She grimaced. "It doesn't look like much."

"No. And when you come right down to it, it ain't much. But it's all we've got to lean on." Longarm nudged Tordo and the tired dapple moved slowly through the chamizal toward the ford that was still a short distance upstream. Flo followed after. Longarm said, "It's better'n nothing at all, I'd say. But we might still have to do a lot of leaning to get Sheriff Tucker to do what we got to make him do."

They'd hit the river at midafternoon, and with the stream as a landmark, Longarm had quickly located the rustlers' trail that led them to the ford. Nothing had happened after the brush with the rurales. They'd ridden across the plain that sloped gently down to the river, and though they'd looked back often, they'd seen no sign of Nate Webster and John Hill. They could only assume that before nightfall the two men would arrive, and that Ramos and his rurales would be there a little later.

Longarm led the way across the ford and turned south on the sandspit. When they reached the shanties and entered the town, the little procession they made drew stares from everyone who saw it. Longarm led on the gray, his chin stubbled with a week's beard, his frock coat ripped in several places and stained with the grime of the trail. The rurale horse was next, festooned with rifles and pistol belts and bandoliers. Flo brought up the rear, her blond hair streaming down her back, her flared skirt draped over her horse, as badly stained as Longarm's coat.

As much as he felt like stopping at Miles Baskin's saloon for a comforting drop of Maryland rye, Longarm rode around the building and reined in at the hitching rail in front of the sheriff's office. Wahonta, the Apache girl, was standing beside the door. She looked at the riders with her opaque obsidian eyes, her face expressionless.

"Is Tucker inside?" Longarm asked.

"Yes. Him there," Wahonta said. She stood aside to let Longarm and Flo enter.

When he saw Longarm and Flo, Sheriff Tucker's eyes goggled. "Custis? Where the billy-blue-hell you been? I've had Spud and Ralston out looking for you the past three-four days, now."

"Had to make a little sashay over the river," Longarm said shortly. "To save you asking, this lady's Miss Florence Firestone. From New York. Flo, this is Sheriff Tucker."

"Pleased to make your acquaintance, miss. You're a friend of Mr. Custis's, I take it?"

Longarm had briefed Flo on the situation they'd be stepping into at Los Perros. She didn't blink an eyelid when she replied, "I am now, Sheriff. He rescued me from a very unpleasant situation."

"Welcome to Los Perros, then, Miss Firestone. Any way I can he'p you, just call on me." Tucker laid the Southern gallantry on a bit thicker than Longarm remembered having seen him show it before. The sheriff returned his attention to Longarm. "You ain't the only one missing, either. You wouldn't happen to know anything about my deputy, Lefty? He dropped outa sight about the same time you did."

"Wish I could say I'd brought him back with me, Sheriff, but I can't. You'll have to find him yourself, I'm afraid."

Tucker's eyes narrowed. "If he don't come back soon, I'm goin' to be a man short. Remember what we talked about the other day? You was goin' to think on it."

"I've been too busy with my regular job to do much thinking."

"That railroad figurin' on building into Mexico, too, is it? You didn't mention that, Custis."

"Let's say I had my reasons." Longarm winked. He didn't know what reasons the sheriff's crooked mind would dream up, but that didn't matter much. He went on, "Right now, we've got a spot of trouble that I'm going to ask you to help out with."

"I don't go back on my word. I told you that since we're going to do business together, I'd he'p you any way I can. What kind of trouble you talkin' about?"

"Well, in about two or three hours, maybe less, there's going to be a bunch of Porfirio Diaz's rurales come galloping up, and they'll be after my hide. Miss Firestone's, too."

Flo said sweetly, "And you said you'd help me, too, Sheriff. Just a minute ago, remember?"

Tucker whistled. "Rurales? You mean you got crossways of 'em while you was over there?"

"Afraid I did. Now, my guess is that the rurales won't pay much attention to that river. They'll be mad and mean, and if you let them get into Los Perros, you're not going to have much of a town left when they get through."

"What d'you expect me to do? I got two men, with Lefty gone."

"You'll have to muster up a bunch of special deputies. If I was in your place, I'd deputize every man I could, and stop 'em cold on their side of the river."

"Hold on, Custis! Damn it, you're askin' me to start a war with Mexico!"

"No, I wouldn't put it that way. If you line enough men up on our side of the river, the rurales won't cross. I don't imagine they'd want it said that Mexico started a war, either. The thing is, you're the duly constituted authority here. It's your duty not to let those rampaging hombres come into your town."

Longarm could see that his cool, matter-of-fact way was baffling Tucker. That was what he'd set out to do. Getting the sheriff off balance, convincing him that his help was in his own interest and not a life-or-death matter to Longarm had been his objective from the beginning.

Tucker said, "Look here, Custis, I better find out what you been doin' over in Mexico before I start a fight with them rurales. For all I know, you might've broke some of their laws, maybe be a fugitive from justice. If that's so, the rurales might have some kind of right to come over here after you."

"Sheriff, your rights stop at the river, don't they?"

"Well, sure, I guess that's so."

"Then, damn it, theirs stop on the Mexican side. And, like I mentioned, if a bunch like that comes storming into town, you're not going to have a town left here. Now, if you don't—"

Longarm's argument was interrupted when the jail door swung open. Spud, Tucker's chief deputy, came swaggering out. He started talking before he saw Longarm.

"Ed, that little greaser bitch don't know a thing about Custis. I had to knock her around a little bit—" He saw Longarm and his words faded out. His eyes stuck out even farther than had Tucker's. "Damn you, Custis! Where you been? And what'd you do with Lefty? I know damn well—"

Tucker cut Spud short. "Shut up! I already asked him about Lefty. He don't know any more'n you and me does."

"I want to know something about who you've been knocking around back in that jail, though," Longarm told Spud coldly. "Far as I know, there's just one woman in Los Perros you might think'd know something about me." Spud didn't answer. Longarm raised his voice and called, "Lita! That you back there?"

"Coos-tees?" It was Lita's voice coming from the cells. "*Ay, que milagro!* I know you come when you find out I am here!"

Longarm turned to face Spud. "If I find you've hurt that girl . . ."

"You'll do what?" Spud challenged. He'd stepped into the office now, and stood facing Longarm across the room. "You know, Custis, I think it's time you found out I'm a better man than you are!"

"Wait a minute!" Tucker shouted. He let the air cool for a few seconds before saying, "You two banty roosters quit shaking your combs. Spud, Custis tells me there's a bunch of rurales on their way here to haul him back to Mexico."

"Let 'em!" the deputy snapped. "We'll be well rid of him!"

"Shut up, Spud!" Tucker ordered for the second time. "Bad feelin's between you and him is one thing. But if them rurales wants Custis bad enough to cross the river to git him, they're goin' to be in a mood to tear this town apart."

Spud obviously hadn't thought of this. He scratched his head. "Well, Ed, what d'you think we better do?"

"We better be ready to stand 'em off. Them rurales don't much listen to reason, unless there's guns backin' it up."

"For this worthless chawbacon? I tell you one thing, I don't aim to stick my neck out to save his!" Spud blustered.

"It ain't Custis worryin' me," Tucker said. "We put a lot of time into settin' ourselves up here. I don't aim to see it busted up. It ain't Custis we'd be helpin', man! It's us!"

"No, by God!" Spud shot back. "We don't have to fight them greasers! All we got to do is grab Custis and hand him over!"

"You figure to do the grabbing, Spud?" Longarm's voice was mild, almost casual. He might have been asking the deputy about the weather.

Lita's voice called again from the jail, "Coos-tees? Why you don' come help me? I don' feel so good."

Longarm took a half-step toward the jail door.

"Custis!" Spud yelled, "I warned you!"

As he spoke, the deputy's hand swooped for his revolver. He almost reached it before Longarm's Colt barked once. Spud crumpled. As he folded to the floor, Flo screamed and Tucker half rose from his chair.

"I'd sit right back down, Tucker, if I was you." Longarm's voice was suddenly as steely as his eyes.

"Jesus God!" Tucker breathed. He sagged back into his chair. "I thought Spud had a fast gun hand!"

Flo hadn't screamed after her first involuntary cry. Her eyes were fixed on the deputy's body. She said, disbelief in her voice, "You—you killed him!"

"He needed it," Longarm told her. To get Flo busy and keep her mind off the shooting, he said, "Do me a favor, Flo. Go back to the jail and see if that girl needs help. Tucker, where's the keys kept?"

"On—on a peg just inside the door."

Longarm continued, "If she's been beat up, get hold of that Apache girl we passed on the way in. Wahonta's her name. She'll get hot water and cloths and whatever else you need."

"You mean that man you shot was beating a helpless girl?" Flo asked.

"You heard him admit it."

"Well! If that's the kind he was, I'm glad you shot him!" Flo bounced across the room with long indignant steps and disappeared into the jail.

Longarm said to Tucker, "Well, make up your mind, man! Damn it, time's getting short!"

While Tucker was still grappling with his indecision, Ralston burst through the door. Miles Baskin was right behind him.

"Fellow run in the saloon," Ralston panted. "Said there was shooting here when he passed by!" He saw Spud's body. "Who done it, Ed?"

"Custis. But it was a square facedown. Spud wasn't fast enough."

Ralston looked at Longarm, who presented a face from which all expression had been carefully removed. After a moment, the deputy said, "Can't say I'm surprised. Spud didn't bother to keep it a secret that he was after you."

"A man's a fool to carry grudges," Longarm said by the way of a reply. "Sometimes they get in the way of his good sense."

Tucker said to Baskin, "Miles, I'm real glad you're here. Custis tells me we're due for some trouble."

Without appearing to be interested, Longarm took careful note of the interchange between Tucker and Baskin. It wasn't yet time to let the saloonkeeper know that Lefty had involved him in the rustling ring as well as tagging him as Tucker's secret boss. Getting the ground cleared for Webster and Hill to get safely across the river and setting up a defense against Ramos's men was the first order of business.

"What kind of trouble?" Baskin asked. "And how do I come into it? You're the sheriff, Ed. You're supposed to handle trouble."

"This is a sorta special kind," Tucker explained. "Custis got crossways of the rurales while he was across the river. There's a bunch of 'em ridin' here to take him back, he says."

"Well? Why tell me?" Baskin asked impatiently. He seemed to be bothered by the sight of Spud's body; he kept looking at it and then glancing away quickly.

"You don't understand, Miles!" Tucker's voice now carried a note of pleading. "If the rurales bust in here, they won't stop till they find Custis, and if they don't find him right off, they'll rip Los Perros from asshole to appetite. And then the army'll be in, and maybe the Rangers, and maybe federal marshals. It'll be one big stinkin' mess!"

"Um. I see what you're driving at," Baskin nodded with a frown. "Well, the answer's pretty damn plain, Ed. Arrest Custis and hand him over to the greasers. Then they'll go home and leave us alone."

"That's what Spud said," Longarm remarked quietly.

Baskin gulped. He looked again at the dead deputy, then at Longarm. He made no reply to Longarm's comment.

As though the saloonkeeper hadn't spoken, the sheriff told

him, "Custis wants us to get some men together and keep the rurales on their side of the river."

"What men?" Baskin demanded.

Without giving Tucker a chance to reply, Longarm said, "You, for one, Baskin. I expect you can handle a gun well enough for a job like this. And we'll want everybody you've got working for you in the saloon: barkeeps, card dealers, swampies, everybody."

"Why should I put my people in danger?" Baskin challenged him.

"Maybe to save their own skins, Baskin. And yours, of course. You see, the sheriff's only got one deputy now, with Lefty gone and Spud dead. He's going to have to deputize a lot of men for this."

"Well, let him," Baskin bridled.

"You understand that if the sheriff deputizes a man who refuses to take on the job, that fellow goes to jail." Longarm was drawling his words out slowly now, and Baskin was beginning to get angry.

"Fine. That's where they belong."

"Glad you think so." Longarm turned to Tucker. "Sheriff, you can start by deputizing me and Baskin, here. Then, if he balks at being sworn in, I'll arrest him for you."

Tucker had already started to rise from his chair when Baskin's angry bellow froze him. "Ed! Why in hell are you letting this man take things over? You know, I've got a good mind—"

Tucker interrupted. "Now, Miles, don't say anything you might be sorry for. Custis ain't running things. I am."

"See that you do, then!" Baskin snorted.

Longarm suggested, "The sheriff might make you a deal, Baskin. If I was in his place, I would. Maybe if you let him have the men that work for you, he'll let you off from being deputized."

"Now that's fair enough, Miles," Tucker said. "How about it?"

Grudgingly, Baskin nodded. "If it'll get this fellow off my back, I'll send my crew over."

"With guns," Longarm stipulated. "I expect you got enough that your bouncer's took off drunks or that you've took in trade for drinks, to fit 'em out."

"All right, damn it! I'll see they've got weapons," Baskin growled. Then he said to Tucker, "Ed, I'll talk to you about all this later on!" He stamped out of the office.

"Well, there's the start of your posse," Longarm said to the sheriff. "Now if you and Ralston can round up a few more—"

Tucker was still too stunned to reply. Ralston answered, "Oh, we can find enough men, Custis. Guns, that's another thing."

"What d'you mean?"

"Well, you see, to cut down on gunplay and general meanness, we grabbed all the guns from the people a few years ago."

"And left your damn town wide open to any crew of gunmen who might ride by? Well, I've got three rifles and pistols and shells for 'em on that horse outside. You can start with those. And I'd guess the sheriff can dig up a few more, somewhere."

"I—I guess I can. We saved a few of the best ones," Tucker volunteered. "You go round up some men, Ralston. I better stay and swear in Miles's people, when they come over."

"Sure," Ralston agreed. But he looked to Longarm instead of to the sheriff when he asked, "How many you think we'll need, Custis?"

"How many will Baskin send over?"

"Well," Ralston said, then frowned. "He's got four barkeeps and three cardsharks and two swampies. Of course, the swampies is Mexicans—"

"That won't matter. That's nine. I'd say another dozen."

Ralston asked Tucker, "That sound right to you, Ed?"

"Yes. And get started, damn it! If Custis is right, we ain't got too much time!" When Ralston had left, the sheriff said to Longarm, "You damned near got us all in trouble, Custis. But I got to say, I admired the way you made Miles tucker down to you. Now, listen, you and me have got to work out a deal. I want you to take Spud's place, be my good right arm, so to speak."

"We'll talk after the rurales leave," Longarm told him. "But I don't mind telling you, what I say's going to depend on what happens when they get here."

"Now don't you worry. I'm goin' to put you in charge of the posse. How's that sound?"

"Good enough. When Baskin's men get here, you send 'em to the sandspit north of town."

"Where the ford is?"

"That's the place. I'm going there just as soon as I check up on Flo and Lita."

He went into the jail. Lita and Flo were sitting side by side on the low bunk in the last cell. There was a bruise on Lita's cheek, but otherwise she seemed unharmed. She jumped up and wrapped her arms around Longarm's neck.

"Coos-tees! I think you maybe don' come back! I am worry," she said, kissing him soundly.

"You take a look, you'll see I'm all here." Longarm smiled over Lita's shoulder at Flo, who was looking amused. "How is she?"

Flo replied, "She's fine, except for that place on her cheek. You know, Custis, I've really got to hand it to you. You beat any damned sailor who ever walked a deck."

"You mad at me?" he asked her.

"Oh, hell, no! Matter of fact, I think you're a pretty good picker. Lita saw you first; you might say I just came along accidentally." She cocked her head thoughtfully and added, "And it's one accident I don't regret. I think we're pretty much alike, you and me. No, I don't mind one bit."

"Good. I was hoping you'd see it that way." Now Longarm grew serious. He took the derringer out of his vest pocket and removed the watch from the chain. "Them rurales ought to be here soon, the way I figure it. I've got to be down at the river to meet 'em. This is about the safest place I know of for the two of you, so you stay right here." He handed the derringer to Flo. "Don't be afraid to use this, if you have to, in case there's trouble." He showed Flo how to use the weapon, kissed her and Lita soundly, and said, "I'll be back to get you after a while."

After he'd mounted Tordo and started for the sandspit, Longarm dropped the insolently calm attitude he'd been careful to maintain with Sheriff Tucker. His jaw was set; a furrow formed between his eyebrows. Somehow, there had to be a way to keep a shooting match from breaking out between Ramos's rurales and the posse that he hoped would be on hand to meet them. Longarm had seen enough of the ponderous mechanism of federal bureaucracy to know what would happen to a deputy U.S. marshal who'd created a serious border clash with a country that was technically friendly.

Old son, he told himself, they say that new federal pen at Leavenworth's a pretty fancy place, but I got no hankering to put in the next twenty years enjoying whatever view I'd get from a cell in it.

Except for a few long-billed herons looking for frogs in the lagoon on the U.S. side of the Rio Grande, the sandspit was deserted when he reined Tordo to a halt at the water's margin. He was getting edgy. The two-hour lead he and Flo had gained when

Webster and Hill remained behind was all but gone. He began worrying about the Ranger and the captain now, and out of habit reached into his pocket for a cheroot before remembering he'd been without for a week. It was, he thought, the only time he'd ever succeeded in quitting the damn weeds.

Even the arrival of Ralston with the score of volunteers he'd assembled didn't ease Longarm's worry about Webster and Hill. He carried it with him while he helped the deputy space out the men in the semblance of a skirmish line, putting those with the best rifles in the center, those with shotguns nearest the river, those with ancient single-shot Martini and Remington rolling-block rifles at the ends. He'd begun to think about crossing into Mexico himself and trying to backtrack in an effort to turn up Hill and Webster when a shout sounded from the men closest to the channel.

"Here they come! Get ready to give 'em hell, boys!"

Weapons were lifted to shoulders along the line. Longarm kept his eyes on the chamizal, which still hid the men on the horses whose hoofbeats were growing louder above the soft murmur of the Rio Grande's opalescent water. The riders burst through the brush and started down the bank. Longarm let go the deep breath he hadn't been aware he was holding.

"Don't anybody shoot!" he called. "These fellows are on our side!"

Webster and Hill urged their stumbling horses across the shallow ford. They saw Longarm and managed to persuade their mounts to make the few final yards necessary to reach him.

Hill surveyed the ragged line of men and said dryly, "You'd never make drillmaster in my outfit, Marshal. But I will say, I'm damned glad to see you've got a greeting squad."

"How far behind are Ramos and his bunch?" Longarm asked.

"Maybe a mile or two," Webster answered. "We been trying every trick in the book to shake 'em, but they've stuck like patent glue."

"How many men's he got?" Longarm tried to keep his voice as casual as Hill's had been, but his anxiety seeped through.

"He's down to about sixteen, now," Hill said. "That's four less than he had when he caught up with us."

"Flo and me took out three that he'd sent to cut off the river crossing," Longarm told him. "I'd say Ramos ain't too happy right about now."

A bit impatiently, the cavalryman asked, "Well, what's your battle plan? Do we shoot on sight, or wait for the rurales to get in the first volley?"

"I been telling these boys not to touch a trigger till I say so," Longarm replied. "I guess that's about the best I've come up with. What's your idea, John?"

"Improve our position," Hill said promptly. "We're too exposed. The rurales can take cover in the chamizal and cut us to pieces. At least we can dig some rifle pits."

Hoofbeats sounding from across the river wrote an end to the captain's suggestion. Longarm said, "Sounds like we're too late for that. I guess it comes down now to who shoots first. What I'm hoping is that Ramos won't have any more of a mind to set off a war than we will."

"Calculated risk," Hill observed. "Worth taking, most times."

"I'd appreciate it if you and Nate would sorta separate and each one of you take charge of part of the men. I got the sheriff's only deputy holding down the middle, but you two've got more savvy about things like this than he has."

Hill and Webster started moving before he'd quite finished speaking. Longarm threw a leg over Tordo and settled into the saddle. The attention of the defenders was concentrated on the chamizal. The hoofbeats from the Mexican side of the river were loud and distinct now. Longarm nudged the dapple's sides and guided him into the ford. In midstream, he pulled up and waited.

His wait was short. Seconds after he'd gotten into position, the chamizal erupted rurales. The strip of shingle at the water's edge was filled with them, it seemed. Longarm saw Molina near the center of the rurale line, but there was no sign of Ramos. He was about to hail the sergeant when Ramos burst through the brush and rode down to the river. He didn't pull rein until his horse's front hooves were in the water.

"*Qué pasa?*" he demanded of Molina. "*Porqué no—*" He stopped when the sergeant pointed to the line of rifles and shotguns aimed at them from the sandspit. Then Ramos saw Longarm.

"*Maldito gringo cabrón! Hijo de puta!*" he shouted. He turned to his men. "*Adelante! Conmigo!*"

Along the rurale line, the men brought up their rifles.

"Ramos!" Longarm shouted. "Hold on! If you don't want to start another war, you better tell your men not to shoot!"

Ramos didn't reply, but he did not give his men orders to fire.

Though the rurales' faces were in the afternoon shadow, Longarm could see the struggle that was going on in Ramos's mind. He waited, not sure what the decision was going to be.

Ramos finally decided. *"Quedarse!"* he ordered his men. *"No tiran!"*

Along the line, the rurales slowly brought their gun muzzles down. On the sandspit, the motley band commanded by Longarm did the same thing. For the moment, at least, Longarm relaxed.

Chapter 19

"Now you're being smart, Ramos," Longarm said. He watched the rurales as, one by one, the men rested their weapons across their saddles. "Sorta surprises me. It's the first thing I seen you do that's halfway bright."

"*Cuidado, gringo!*" Ramos warned. "You keep make to me the insults with your dirty tongue, I come with my knife and cut it out of your head!"

"Now, that ain't your style. You're soft as a pig's turd without a bunch of your men to back you up."

"I don't tell you again, *hombre!* You go on, I tell my brave rurales to shoot!"

"You do that, Ramos! Mexico's never won a war yet. Texas beat you once, the U.S. beat you once; it'll be easy to do it again. So if you want to start the next war, just tell your men to let off one shot!"

"Now you insult my country and my men, too! I do not warn you again, *cabrón!*"

"Oh, you got a right to be proud of them chickens you call men! Shit! They couldn't all of 'em hold on to three of us, even when they had us locked up! How the hell you think they could stand up to my men over there?"

"You play a *gringo* trick on us!" Ramos retorted. He was beginning to tremble with repressed anger. "Why you don't fight like men, not like old wrinkle-up *viejas?*"

"It wouldn't take more'n three old women to send your bunch off yelping," Longarm said. He was beginning to wonder how much longer the rurale captain would hold on to himself. "You had just one woman, but you couldn't keep her from walking away!"

"*Bastardo!* You are steal *mi rubia!* I make you pay for this!"

"I didn't steal her, Ramos. She couldn't wait to get shed of you. She told me you got no *cojones.*"

"That is all!" Ramos shouted. He turned to his men, who'd been growing increasingly restless as their captain talked endlessly and angrily with the *Norteamericano* on the dappled horse. Ramos ordered, *"Tome sus fusiles!"*

Eagerly, the rurales brought up their guns again.

Longarm lifted his rifle and let off a shot in the air. Ramos swiveled quickly in his saddle. His men awaited the order to shoot.

Longarm used the phrase he'd been working on in case he needed to use it. *"Parase! No tiran, o empeza una guerra!"* The rurales hesitated, and some of them began to lower their weapons. In a low voice Longarm said to Ramos, "You better listen to me, hombre. We got a platoon from Captain Hill's cavalry halfway here by now. If just one of your men pulls a trigger, them soldiers will chase your outfit clear to Mexico City. How'd Porfirio Diaz like that, Ramos?"

Ramos's face showed that he had no taste for a fight with the cavalry regulars. At the same time, he couldn't afford to let this gringo shame him in front of the rurales.

Longarm sensed that the time had come to press him. "Act like you have some brains, Ramos! Get them billygoats of yours outa here before we knock the shit outa them!"

"No! My men do not retreat!"

"That's all they know how to do! All you know, too! Like the blonde said, you got no balls!"

"This is too much insult! Now you pay!" Ramos's hand started for his pistol, but stopped when Longarm twitched the Winchester's barrel. Staring into the muzzle, Ramos froze. He said, "You talk big, *gringo federalista.* What kind of *cojones* you got? Enough to fight me, *mano á mano?*"

"Well, now," Longarm tried to put uncertainty in his voice and hoped he was succeeding, "I ain't so sure that'd prove much."

"It will prove I am better man than you! You are afraid, no?"

"No." Longarm drawled out the word. "But there's not much of anything for either one of us in it." He added thoughtfully, "Unless we make a deal that'll settle this thing."

"You want a bargain, no? I will make you one, then. Listen to me, *gringo!* We fight. If I kill you, I get the other two *gringos* and *la rubia*, they come back with me. If I am lose, my rurales don't start the war. They go home. *Es agradable?*"

Hesitantly, Longarm said, "I guess I let you talk me into it. All right. What kind of fight you want? Fists? Knives? Pistols?"

"Fists are for *gringo* pigs! Knives are for *peones!* We fight, you and me, like *caballeros, como soldados!* With pistols, hombre!"

"Suits me." Having gotten what he wanted, Longarm decided to try for some frills. "You tell your men to pile up their guns on the bank and stay away from 'em. I'll tell mine to do the same thing. If you and me're going to settle this by ourselves, there ain't no use in taking a chance some hothead'll turn it into a free-for-all."

Ramos thought for a moment, then nodded. *"De acuerdo."*

"Now, then. Where're we going to do it? On the sand, over there? It's a good clear space." He pointed to the wide expanse of river sand on the spit below the ford.

"Is as good as any place," the rurale agreed.

"Let's get on with it then!"

"No!" Ramos jerked his thumb over his shoulder in the general direction of the setting sun. "It will be too dark by the time we are ready. *Otra cosa*, if we fight now, you have the advantage over me. I have ride hard today, you are fresh and rested. No, *hombre*. Tomorrow, when the sky is bright, before *la salida del sol*, the light will favor us equally. *De verdad?*"

"If that's how you want it," Longarm shrugged. "It don't matter to me whether I kill you today or wait till tomorrow."

"Ay! Qué fanfarron! We will see, mañana!"

Ramos turned his horse in the shallows at the edge of the bank. His men clustered around him, and Longarm could hear them excitedly questioning the captain. He stayed in the middle of the ford until the rurales drew away, into the chamizal, to camp for the night. Then he turned Tordo and walked the gray to the sandspit. Hill and Webster reached him first.

"That was some hell of a long talk you had with Ramos," Webster said. "What was it all about?"

"Couldn't you hear?" Longarm asked.

Hill said, "I was down at the far end on one side. All I could get was a word now and then, when you two were shouting."

"About the same with me," Webster nodded. "I figured you must've had some pretty strong things to say, to get him to pull his men back. They gone for good?"

"Oh, I imagine they'll be around awhile, yet."

"Well, tell us the whole story," Hill said impatiently. "I'm as curious as Nate to find out how you made him withdraw."

"I lied a little bit. Told him a platoon of your troopers was on the way here, to take on him and his bunch. He didn't like that idea very much." Then as as afterthought Longarm added, "Oh, and I agreed him and me'd shoot it out, man to man, just before sunup tomorrow."

"You did what?" Hill exploded.

"Now, we're right close together here, John. You couldn't've missed hearing me."

"You sure you can take him?" Webster asked soberly. "Some of the rurales are pretty good with a sixgun."

"Now, Nate, a man never does really know about a thing like that, does he?" Longarm asked. "But I'll take whatever chance there is."

"I'm not sure I approve of this," Hill frowned. "I'd rather get my troopers here, even if it means a night march. Let them handle things the army way."

"And maybe set off a war?" Longarm asked. "That's what we been trying not to do, John, remember? But I'd take it as a favor if you will back up my bluff, find somebody to ride to the fort with an order for 'em to come on. Then we'd know for sure there wouldn't be any trouble tomorrow."

"You're right. A show of force can stop most trouble before it gets under way," Hill replied. "I'll get that fellow Ralston to pick me out a messenger."

"We'd best set up a guard here at the ford tonight," Nate Webster suggested. "I don't trust rurales. Night raids are their style, you know."

"You do whatever you figure's best, Nate. Right now I'm mainly interested in a square meal and a good night's sleep in a real bed."

When Longarm got back to the sheriff's office, Tucker was nowhere to be seen. Longarm supposed he was back in the ell with Wahonta and decided not to disturb him. He went into the jail to tell the women it was now safe for them to go out. Lita was gone, but Flo was stretched out on the bunk, dozing.

"I thought I'd hear shooting if there was trouble," she said, "and I needed a nap. Lita left right after you did; she said something about having to help her mother serve supper. I tried to keep her, but she just wouldn't stay."

"No harm done, Flo. You must be about as starved as I am. Tell you what. Let's go out to where her mama cooks, and get supper."

"Before I eat, I want to clean up," Flo replied. "I'll enjoy supper a lot more if I get rid of a dozen layers of Mexican dirt first."

"That's easy. Lots of rooms vacant over at the saloon, and the porter'll get you a tub of hot water to bathe in. Rooms there ain't fancy like the hotel you got in New York, but the beds are better'n sleeping on the ground like we did last night."

Flo grinned at him. "I enjoyed it. Not so much the sleeping, but the lullabyes were wonderful."

"We'll have some more of them, for sure," he promised her. "I figure we better get to bed early. I got a busy day tomorrow."

Flo smiled again. "If that's an invitation for me to tuck you in, you already know I'm planning to do just that. I'll enjoy going to bed early, too, under the circumstances."

She didn't ask him why his day was going to be busy, and Longarm didn't elaborate.

While Flo bathed in the room next to his, Longarm asked for a pitcher of boiling water and a bottle of fine oil to be sent up to his room while he waited for the tub. It was a common enough request in any frontier saloon that rented rooms. While he waited for Flo to finish her bath, Longarm stripped his Colt, poured boiling water through barrel and cylinder, swabbed the metal dry, and applied the lightest possible film of oil to the hammer and trigger mechanism. When he reloaded, he chose each cartridge with meticulous care, inspecting it carefully before sliding it into a chamber. He sipped from his bottle of Maryland rye while he worked, and wished again for a cheroot.

He made quick work of bathing. Apologetically, the mozo who served the rooms told Longarm that he'd taken the liberty of taking the dirty shirt and longjohns that Longarm had left in the room "to *la lavandera, señor, si no obedece*," and was surprised at the size of the tip he received for the unsolicited service. When

Flo tapped at the door, Longarm was ready. He'd shaved in the tub, donned fresh underwear, and though he hadn't been able to do anything about the rips his coat had gotten during the past few days, he'd shaken the dust out of it. Flo had brushed off her coat and jacket. As she remarked, "We'd be taken for bums on Fifth Avenue, but we don't look out of place in Los Perros."

Longarm escorted her to the stall where Lita's mother was cooking. Lita served them, her dark eyes flashing with suppressed anger every time she looked at Flo. The food was as tasty as Longarm remembered but the atmosphere was distinctly cool. Lita didn't talk with them beyond the most necessary remarks, and none of Longarm's mild jokes brought laughter to her lips. They hurried through the meal and started back to the hotel.

As they crossed the plaza, Flo said, "I guess I'm not the most popular person in the world with your little friend. Isn't she a bit young for you, Custis?"

"I was a little bit leery of her at first, but when push comes to shove, Lita don't act as young as she looks. Not that she's the woman you are." He looked at Flo curiously. "You ain't a bit jealous, are you?"

"No. I suppose it's not in my nature to be. Maybe because I've learned not to fall in love, I can see jealousy as a waste of energy. Don't worry about your little Mexican girl, Custis. I won't mind her one bit, as long as you give me all I want of you while we're together."

"You know I'm going to do that, honey. Fact is, I'm ready to start just as soon as we get by ourselves again."

"I can't wait, but I will. It'd attract too big a crowd if we let ourselves go right here in the middle of town."

As soon as Longarm locked the door of his room, Flo reached for him. "Now show me you meant what you said."

"We both got too many clothes on for me to prove it real good."

"You help me, I'll help you."

Longarm delayed following her suggestion only long enough to hang his gunbelt in its regular place at the head of the bed on the left-hand side.

They made a frolic of the undressing game, but it became something else when Longarm stood naked. It was the first time Flo had seen him undressed in a lighted room, and the scars he'd earned in scores of brushes with those on the wrong side of the law drew a gasp of dismay from her.

"My God! How can a man take so much punishment and still be healthy?"

"Oh, some of 'em slowed me down awhile. Didn't put me down for good though."

"I can see that." Her hand crept to his groin. "At least, I can see you're not down. Just the opposite." She stroked him gently. "And no scars where they might really have damaged you."

"And you haven't got a scar on you, have you?" Longarm ran his hands down Flo's lush body. He lingered over her breasts awhile, then stroked his hard palms down her waist to the satin skin of her hips and pulled her tightly to him, his erection between them, hard against her belly.

She wrapped her arms around him and began pulling him toward the bed. Just before they reached it she swung around so that Longarm toppled backward, with Flo on top of him. She raised her hips high to get him inside her and fell forward heavily, gasping with unconcealed delight as she felt him going deeper and deeper until their bodies were locked together and there was no more depth that he could seek. Squeezing tightly with the muscles in her buttocks, she began rotating her hips very slowly.

Longarm lay back and let Flo take her pleasure. She prolonged it as much as possible, stopping her hip rotations more and more often for shorter and shorter periods as she fell into the urging of her mounting ecstasy. Then, her blond hair streaming down to enclose Longarm's head and shoulders in a golden tent, she rocked herself up and down until the flood of joy poured hot and wet. Longarm did not let her rest. While she was still limp and trembling, he pulled her higher on the bed and rolled on top of her.

"Not right away!" Flo protested. "I just came more than I ever did in my life before!"

"It ain't too soon. You'll like it better, now your edge is off."

He was already moving, thrusting with full, slow strokes, not hurrying, using only part of his weight and strength. For the first few minutes Flo could only lie quiet and receive him, panting from her own exertions of moments earlier. A little at a time she came to life. Longarm felt her inner muscles responding to his measured churning and began to move faster and drive harder. Flo's eyes were squeezed shut and her lips were opening and closing as little birdlike cries escaped them in rhythm with the movements of his rising and falling hips.

Longarm built to the final moments as fast as Flo did. The

time came for him to let his body set its own rhythm, and he did. He pounded with fast, repeated drives until he could hear Flo's clear, small ululations only dimly as they became a single treble note. He could feel her body's pulsing as it drew him into her with force added to greater force until the gushing he could no longer hold back drained him and he dropped spent upon her.

When their breathing had quieted, Flo said with a sigh, "I didn't think anything could be better than last night. My God, was it only last night that we fucked under the trees?"

"That's when it was."

"Well, last night was good, but tonight's better."

"We didn't feel like taking our time then. Too many worries on our mind."

"Yes." Flo lay quietly for a moment. "You know, Custis," she confessed, "I like to think about fucking almost as much as I like to fuck. Especially when I'm around somebody like you."

"Most folks do, I guess. Only damned few of 'em are honest enough to admit it."

"People are such damned fools. Sometimes I think—"

Whatever it was Flo thought was lost in an insistent rapping on the door. Longarm glanced at his Colt to be sure it was in place before calling, "Who is it?"

"Is me, Coos-tees! Let me in! I got to find out is true, what I am hear!"

"What'd you hear, Lita?"

"I will tell you when you let me in!"

"Damn it, I can't. I'm busy."

"If is *la rubia* in there, I don' care, Coos-tees. Is you I wan' to talk to!" Lita said insistently.

"Oh, let her in," Flo told him. "I don't care if she sees what I've got; I've shown damn near as much on the stage. Might do her good to have something to compare herself to. And unless I'm a bad guesser, she's seen what you've got more than once."

Reluctantly and somewhat suspiciously, Longarm got off the bed, slipped his Colt from the holster, and opened the door just wide enough to let Lita enter. Her eyes widened when she saw Flo's pink and gold nakedness lying relaxed on the rumpled bed, but she ran to Longarm and grabbed him in a tight embrace.

"Is true, Coos-tees? Is true, this thing I hear?"

"You tell me what you heard and I'll tell you if it's true."

For the first time, Lita saw that he was holding his pistol. She

cried out, "Is true, or else you don' got to be so careful not to let
me in until you get *la pistola!* You think I bring somebody to
shoot you, yes? Ay, Coos-tees! You don' trust me!"

"Sure I trust you, Lita. Now settle down. I let you in, didn't I?
What did you hear that's got you so wrought up?"

"Down in the plaza, they talk about how you make the fight
with *el capitán rurale* tomorrow, the fight with *pistolas.* Is true?
You do this, Coos-tees?"

"Sure it's true. But that's not much to get worked up over."

"Maybe she's worked up because I'm here," Flo suggested.

"Is not so!" Lita objected. "I don' care if Coos-tees make
chinga with you, *rubia.* But I rather he do it with me!"

"Come on to bed with us, then," Flo laughed. "He's man
enough to handle both of us. And I want to find out more about this
gunfight you've got set for tomorrow, Custis. You didn't say anything to me about it, any more than you did to Lita. Honey," she
said to the girl, "it looks to me like we're in about the same boat.
You might as well get off your clothes and enjoy the voyage."

"You mean this thing?" Lita asked. A corner of her mouth
twitched in the beginning of a smile.

"Sure I do. We both want the same thing from the same man.
No reason for us to fight, is there, when we can share?"

"Coos-tees?" Lita appealed to Longarm. "Is all right if I stay?"

"If you feel like you want to," he told her. He was thinking of
the last time he'd shared a bed with two passionate women. That
was in Cripple Creek, with the Stowers sisters. "If Flo says you're
welcome, I sure do, too."

"Good! Then I stay!"

Lita's fingers flashed nimbly at the waistband of her skirt and
it dropped to the floor at her feet. Longarm remembered that, like
tonight, she'd worn nothing under it the night on the sandspit.
She pulled at the neck-string of her low-cut blouse, shrugged it
off her shoulders, and let it slip down her body to fall atop the
skirt. She went to the bed and lay down beside Flo. Longarm felt
himself getting hard just looking at them: Flo's soft white skin,
pink breast rosettes and blond hair and bush; Lita's perfect con-
trast of smooth brown skin, her dark nipples budding in anticipation, her groin a mystery of midnight.

Flo looked at Longarm and started chuckling. "You see, Lita?
I told you it'd be all right. He's thinking about you right now."

Lita was smiling, too. "Then come here, Coos-tees. *Dame su grifo magnifico! Dame todo!* Maybe I show you *las trigueñas tienen mas deluce como las rubias!*"

Longarm didn't wait for her to ask a second time.

Darkness still filled the room when Longarm snapped awake. At once, his mind jumped ahead to the appointment that was waiting for him at daybreak. Then memories of the night came back, a confusion of warm, seeking mouths and hard-tipped breasts, of legs and thighs brown and white upraised and clamped around him, of clutching hands and wet inner recesses flowing hot while he strained to fill them. At some time, quite early, Lita had shed her anger and jealousy. She and Flo had become friends of a sort, joining together to please Longarm, lying side by side while he moved from one to the other, from brown to pink to brown and back to pink, sustaining their frenzy while increasing his, and never knowing who'd be partners during the instants of the final spasm.

While all three had lain exhausted for brief interludes of recovery, he'd told them of the duel that was to take place at dawn, and both had kissed him tenderly, their eyes shaded with a fear that all his calm assurances couldn't drive away. It had been Flo who'd ended the night, persuading Lita to leave when she did, so that Longarm could sleep. And when they'd left, he'd slept the deep, sound sleep of exhaustion after pleasure.

A light gray tinge was marking the window of Longarm's room. He held his hands up and studied them in silhouette against the faint light, watching for a twitch or tremor. They were both rock-steady. He stretched. He didn't feel tired, just pleasantly relaxed. He rolled out of bed and dressed quickly, wishing he had a fresh Prince Albert coat to put on. He took one wake-up sip out of the rye bottle, and savored its warmth and bite. Then he collected his possibles, distributing them in their accustomed pockets, and gave his Colt a final quick inspection after he'd adjusted his holster to the exact position where he wanted it to rest.

There was already a crowd waiting at the sandspit when Longarm pulled Tordo to a halt. Apparently, all of Los Perros had come to watch. Across the river, he saw the glow of dying fires where the rurales had made camp. He tilted his head to look at the sky. It was cloudless and brightening rapidly to pink in the east. The chamizal on the Mexican side of the river stirred and Ramos and his men pushed through.

As though their appearance was a signal, hooves thudded from the direction of Los Perros and a detachment of the 10th Cavalry rode up in squad column. Captain Hill rode at the column's flank. The troopers' faces, ebony black to mulatto, were set and serious, their eyes trained straight ahead. Longarm knew they'd been in the saddle all night, but anyone who didn't know it would have thought the group was fresh from the parade ground. The crowd parted to let the troopers through. At the edge of the sandspit the riders turned alternately right and left, to form a fence of horseflesh across the sand and keep the spectators back.

Hill rode up to Longarm. "You feel all right?"

"Fine. Be indecent if I felt any better."

"We'll be keeping an eye on Ramos's men." Longarm nodded, his eyes on the rurales, who were beginning to string across the ford. A bit diffidently, the cavalryman said, "Well, good luck, Marshal."

"Thanks." Longarm nudged Tordo through the line of troopers and stopped just beyond them. A hand touched his knee. He looked down and saw Nate Webster.

"That sergeant from the rurales, Molina, was over here a while ago," Webster said. "Maybe I butted in, but I took it on myself to work out some rules with him."

"Like what?"

"Everybody'll stay back outa your way. I'll walk up with you, and Molina'll come out with Ramos. Molina swore they wasn't fixing up any monkeyshines, but I still don't trust 'em."

"All right, so far. What then?"

"Me and Molina will draw a middle line. Then we'll step off fifteen paces in both directions from it, and draw deadlines. You and Ramos start out back to back from the middle. You can walk or run or belly-crawl, however you want to do it, long as you don't draw before you get to the deadline. Then you turn around and face it out."

"Sounds fair enough to me," Longarm told the Ranger. "Captain Hill says his troopers'll be watching the rurales to see they don't cut no didoes."

"I'd say everything's covered." Webster studied the sky. The pink was fading in the east, a harbinger of sunrise. Above them, the air was bright and the sky clear. "Guess me and Molina better get on with it. I'll wave you out, when it's time."

Longarm lounged in the saddle and watched the Ranger and the rurale pace off the deadlines and mark them with furrows scraped by boot heels. Behind him, the babble of the crowd grew louder as the onlookers observed the preliminaries. Webster and Molina walked back to the center line after marking the deadlines. Webster waved to Longarm, who dismounted and walked leisurely to the furrow from which the duellers would start. From the cluster of rurales at the river end of the spit, Ramos was walking toward them.

An argument developed between Webster and Molina. It was brief, and not especially heated. When they left the line and went over to the crowd together, Ramos and Longarm both stopped to watch what they did. The Ranger and the sergeant were searching the faces that stared from behind the line of cavalrymen. Finally, both nodded and simultaneously signaled one of the spectators forward. There was a brief three-sided discussion and the trio returned to the center line. Longarm and Ramos resumed their approach.

"This hombre's going to start you off." Webster put his hand on the shoulder of the man he and Molina had picked from the spectators. "He'll count, then he'll run like hell to get outa the line of fire. You can see he's Mexican. He lives in Los Perros and he swears he don't hold sides for either one of you. That all right?"

"How many numbers will he count?" Ramos asked.

"Three," Webster replied.

"Uno, dos, tres," Molina supplemented.

Ramos nodded. So did Longarm.

"Might as well go ahead then," Webster said.

Longarm and Ramos did not shake hands as they walked to opposite sides of the center line and turned to stand back to back. Webster and Molina moved away. The tension that had slowly been building now began to make itself felt; the air was charged with unseen currents. The only sound was the bubbling of the Rio Grande's opaque water.

His voice high-pitched and strained, the man chosen from the crowd began to count, *"Uno—dos—tres!"* His heels scuffed softly in the sand as he ran from the line.

Behind him, as he started walking, Longarm heard the muffled crunching of Ramos's footsteps. He tuned his ears to the rhythm of the sound and tried to match his own pace to that of the rurale. Ahead of him, the deadline grew more sharply defined with each step.

Longarm divided his mind. Half of it counted the paces he must take to reach the furrow, the other half concentrated on translating the almost inaudible scratching of sand on boot soles into the length and speed of Ramos's steps.

A jarring note in the rhythm of Ramos's paces warned Longarm. The rurale had begun to run. Longarm leaped forward over the furrow of the deadline. In midair, he curled his body. He landed prone and rolled, drawing as he landed. He saw Ramos over his sights and fired. Ramos dropped before he could trigger the revolver he was raising.

While the echo of Longarm's shot was dying, two more reports that sounded almost as one broke the disturbed morning air. Longarm, still lying on the ground, saw the spurt of sand raised by a pistol slug rise like a tiny geyser, a foot from his shoulder. He looked around. Molina was crumpling. Webster was standing with his revolver still extended.

"Bastard drew when he seen Ramos drop," the Ranger called to Longarm.

There was a murmur of agreement from those in the crowd who'd seen Molina's move, of surprise and doubt from others. The rurales started forward as if on order. The cavalrymen advanced, closing into platoon front, their carbines resting on their thighs. The rurales stopped, clustered around the bodies of Ramos and Molina. When the Mexican force stopped, the troopers halted as well. In sullen silence the rurales picked up the dead men and draped them across horses. They turned and rode off the sandspit into the water, splashed across the ford, and disappeared into the chamizal.

Only after the conical tops of the rurales' sombreros could no longer be seen above the brush did the crowd let go its breath in a great collective sigh. The onlookers began to trickle back toward town. The cavalrymen held their position, watching for movement on the Mexican side of the river.

Longarm walked over to Webster. Both men were still holding their pistols, so brief had the interval been after the first shot.

"Thanks, Nate," Longarm said. He fished a cartridge out of his pocket and looked it over carefully before putting it into the Colt's cylinder. Then he told Webster, "I got to go back to the sheriff's office now and finish up the job I came here to do. I'd be proud to have your company, if you want to come along."

Webster nodded. Both men mounted and rode side by side back toward the shanties of Los Perros.

Chapter 20

As he and Webster rode into the plaza, Longarm said, "We'll need to stop by the saloon before we go to the sheriff's office. Both of us could stand a drink about now."

"Looking for Baskin?" Webster asked casually.

"Yep. You heard what Lefty said there in the jail before they killed him."

"It's not something I'd be likely to forget. But it's been your play, mostly. I'll let you call it."

Longarm tilted his glass of rye quickly and left Webster at the bar while he went upstairs and tapped at the door of Flo's room.

"Who is it?" she called. Her voice wasn't cheerful.

"Who'd you think it'd be?"

He heard her footsteps running to the door. It swung open. Flo said, "I didn't stay after the gunfight. I didn't know whether you'd feel like talking."

Longarm kissed her. "Don't fret over what's past. I just got a minute, but I'll be back when I'm done."

"You mean you're almost ready to leave here?"

"Pretty quick now. If you got any getting ready to do—"

"I'm ready any time." She sighed with relief. "I wasn't sure you were going to ask me to go with you."

"I'm asking, but only if that's what you feel like doing."

"You know I do. Where?"

"We'll talk about that later, after I get back."

He rejoined Webster at the bar. The Ranger asked, "Want to tell me what you've got in mind?"

Longarm poured another glass of rye and sipped it before he answered. "Well, we got what my boss would call overlapping jurisdiction. Only I figure you got a better claim than I have, not that I want any at all, Nate."

Webster frowned. "Trouble is, I don't know how much of a case I could make against the sheriff. Now Baskin, he's sure to go up a long time for rustling. But even if he turns evidence against Tucker, I don't know that a jury'd go hard on him, since Baskin's been his boss."

"Tell you what. You take Baskin. Let me worry about Tucker."

"Fair enough," the Ranger agreed. "But it's still you who'll call the turns."

"If that suits you, it's good enough for me. Come on."

Longarm led the way back to Baskin's office. They entered without knocking. Baskin was kneeling in front of the big office safe, pulling out papers, ledgers, and money bags and stuffing them in a disorderly jumble into saddlebags that were already bulging. He leaped up when Webster and Longarm entered.

"Sorta thought you might've waited till you seen whether me or Ramos come out winner before you got ready to hightail," Longarm said mildly.

"Now, don't shoot me, Custis! If it's money you're after—"

"What the hell's he talking about?" Webster asked.

"Baskin's clock's running a little late," Longarm explained. "He's still got me tagged as a hard case on the dodge." He pulled out his wallet and flipped it open to show his marshal's badge. The saloonkeeper's jaw dropped. Longarm said, "I guess your friend the sheriff didn't introduce you to this gent here, when he passed through town before. He's Texas Ranger Nate Webster. I don't know how many federal laws you broke, Baskin, but Nate can damn sure make a good state case against you, so I'm letting him have you."

"Let's see now," Webster began. "There's rustling, which is about all I need. It'll get you a good long sentence when your part in the new Laredo Loop comes out. You don't look like you got guts enough for murder; I'd say you had your killing done by the sheriff and his boys, but you'll wind up as an accessory. And there'll be more before it's over, when Tucker starts talking."

"You don't have to wait for him to talk," Baskin said eagerly. "Just tell me what you want to know. Maybe you'll take it light on me if I—"

Webster interrupted. "I don't need you to make my case. No deal, Baskin. You'll take your chances with the rest of your bunch."

"As a favor, Nate, you might haul him with us when we go see the sheriff. Tucker still ain't caught on that this crook's kingdom he's set up has been busted to hell."

"Sure. If you're ready, we'll get on with the rat catching," Webster grinned.

With Baskin in tow, they went out the back door of the saloon and walked the few steps to the sheriff's office. Ralston was sitting behind the desk. He leaped up and ran forward when he saw Longarm, stretching out his hand.

"That was the neatest piece of gun handling I ever saw, this morning—" Something in Longarm's eyes stopped him and his grin faded away. "What's the matter?"

"That's what we come to find out," Longarm told him. "Where's the sheriff?"

"He's still back in his rooms, him and Wahonta."

"Guess you better get him out here. We got a little business that needs to be settled."

Ralston hurried through the door into the ell. Tucker hadn't been in bed, for he returned with the deputy almost immediately, fully dressed even to his ivory-handled revolver in its tooled holster.

"What the hell's so important that I get roused out before I finish my breakfast?" he demanded. He saw Baskin then, and Webster standing beside the saloonkeeper. His florid face paled, but he tried to bluff things through. "Glad to see you got back from that trip to Mexico, Ranger. I hope them tips I give you panned out."

"You might say they panned out better than I thought they would." Webster's tone was carefully neutral.

Baskin's anger had been growing faster than his fear and caution. He blurted, "Damn it, Ed! Where'd you hide out last night and this morning?"

"I felt sick, Miles," Tucker answered. "Real sick, all night. Still don't feel too spry."

"You're a fool!" Baskin snorted. "You were blind drunk last

night, if I know you, which I sure as hell ought to by now! Drunk, and wallowing in bed with your Apache whore! Do you know what happened in Los Perros last night and today at daybreak?"

"Well, I guess if it'd been somethin' important, I'd've heard about it," the sheriff said defensively.

"You've got shit where your brains used to be," Baskin said contemptuously. "I guess it's partly my fault. I knew you were getting past your time, but I didn't realize you'd gone so far."

"Now, you got no right—"

"I'd say he's got every right," Longarm broke in, "seeing as he's been your boss all these years. What Baskin's trying to tell you is that you're finished, Tucker."

His pig-eyes narrowed and Tucker said, "What're you doing, Custis? Trying to take Los Perros away from me?"

"You still ain't thinking straight. First off, Custis is only the first half of my name. The rest of it's Long. I'm a deputy U.S. marshal."

"He's dealing it to you straight," Webster said, when Tucker looked to him for confirmation. "Marshal Long was sent down here to find me and Captain Hill, after you hared us off into Mexico, and for all I know, tipped off the rurales to be on the lookout for us. And I don't think the marshal would want Los Perros, even if you could hand it over to him."

"Damn you, Custis, or Long, or whatever your name is! You been trickin' me all along! You sneaky son of a bitch—"

Longarm's voice was steely as he cut Tucker short. "Mind what you say! Up to now I ain't held no personal grudge, so don't give me a reason to!"

Ralston volunteered, "The marshal outdrawed that rurale captain up on the sandspit at dawn today, Sheriff. Best gunplay I ever seen. If it was me, I'd apologize right quick."

"Well," Tucker grunted, "I guess I oughtn't've said that."

"No. You oughtn't," Longarm agreed. "I was aiming to turn you over to the Rangers with your boss—"

This time it was Tucker who interrupted. He looked at Baskin. "Is he tellin' me the truth, Miles? You standing so close by that Ranger because you're his prisoner?"

"If you hadn't been such a constipated jackass, you'd've seen that first thing!" Baskin shot back. "And it's mostly your fault. I'm going to see that you spend just as many years in jail as I do!"

"You didn't let me finish what I started to say," Longarm went on, his voice almost casual. "Now, the Rangers could stand you up alongside of Baskin in a Texas court, but you might just get off too light. When you flapjawed at me, I decided you need a good, long sentence, so I'm taking you in on federal charges."

"You got no federal charges against me!" Tucker blustered. "I was real careful not to get crossways of that damn Reconstruction gov'mint we got now! Once it come out I rode with Quantrill—"

"They'd put you away for life, wouldn't they?" Longarm asked.

"They damn sure would, and you know it! That's why I was so careful—"

Again Longarm interrupted. "You wasn't careful enough. That Apache girl, now. She's a federal ward, like any other reservation Indian. She can't consent to lay up with no man, white or Indian, till she's legally married to him."

"You can't—"

Longarm went on as though he hadn't been interrupted. "But that's not the worst I'll charge you with, Tucker. You confessed to me that you bought that girl. Now, there's an amendment to the U.S. Constitution that makes buying a human being a federal crime. That's the big charge they'll keep you in jail for." He turned to Webster. "Sorry to take him away from you, Nate, but—"

Something in the Ranger's eyes alerted Longarm. He whirled as he drew and faced Tucker just as the sheriff's hand closed over the ivory grips of his pistol. Longarm's slug went to Tucker's heart.

In the silence that followed the shot and the thud when Tucker hit the floor, Webster said, low, in Longarm's ear, "You really think he'd've gotten life for monkeying with that Indian girl, Marshal?"

"No. He'd have been tried in Texas, and I ain't betting a jury here'd stick him a long term on both them charges."

"If you didn't have that badge in your pocket, I might be taking you in for inciting to murder," Webster said, unsmiling. Then he added, "But I can't say I blame you. I get mad when a man calls me a son of a bitch."

"Who don't?" Longarm asked as he slid his Colt back into its holster.

Late the next morning, Longarm helped Flo aboard the Butterfield stage that he'd flagged down at the river crossing just outside Fort Lancaster.

"Wish I could ride with you," he told her. "I got a few loose ends that still have to be tied up in Los Perros, and then I got to take my horse back to the remount depot in San Antonio."

"I've got a feeling one of those loose ends is named Lita," Flo smiled. "I halfway wish I'd decided to ride with you instead of taking the stage to San Antonio."

"You'll be more comfortable on the stage," he assured her. "And I'll beat the stage there. You take a hack to the Menger Hotel. It ain't grand like New York, but it beats Baskin's saloon. We'll have a few days there before you go on East."

"I've changed my mind about taking the train from San Antonio," Flo said. "Captain Hill told me I can get an express train from Denver that'll get me to New York quicker than the one I'd take from San Antonio. We'll have a few days, and then a few more."

Longarm watched the dust of the stage settle as it lurched down the rutted road. He'd have a day or two in San Antonio before the stage pulled in. He wondered if Cynthia Stanley—whose best friends called her Cyn—would get along with Flo as well as Lita had.

That's going to be something interesting to find out, old son, he told himself as he nudged Tordo with his knee. The dapple moved off.

GIANT-SIZED ADVENTURE FROM
AVENGING ANGEL LONGARM.

BY TABOR EVANS

2006 Giant Edition:
LONGARM AND THE
OUTLAW EMPRESS

2007 Giant Edition:
LONGARM AND THE
GOLDEN EAGLE SHOOT-OUT

2008 Giant Edition:
LONGARM AND THE
VALLEY OF SKULLS

penguin.com

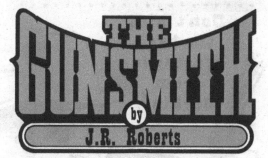

M10G0907

P.O. 0005172337 202